ABOUT THE AU

Born in London, Wendy Alec has pursued successful careers in advertising and television production, as well as writing books and screenplays. The cinematic scope and epic sweep of the Chronicles of Brothers series have won her legions of devoted fans around the world.

Also by Wendy Alec

THE CHRONICLES OF BROTHERS,
TIME BEFORE TIME SERIES
The First Judgement

THE CHRONICLES OF BROTHERS SERIES
Son of Perdition
A Pale Horse
End of Days (September 2018)

WENDY ALEC

THE
FALL OF
LUCIFER

THE CHRONICLES OF BROTHERS,
TIME BEFORE TIME

INSPIRE

Harper*Inspire*, an imprint of
HarperCollins Christian Publishing
1 London Bridge Street
London SE1 9GF

www.harpercollins.co.uk

First published by HarperCollins*Publishers* 2018

ISBN: 9780310090977 (TPB)
ISBN: 9780310096191 (ebook)

Set in Sabon Lt Std by Palimpsest Book Production Limited,
Falkirk, Stirlingshire
Printed and bound in the U.S.A. by LSC Communications, Harrisonburg

MIX
Paper from
responsible sources
FSC
www.fsc.org
FSC™ C007454

This book is produced from independently certified FSC™ paper to ensure
responsible forest management.

For more information visit: www.harpercollins.co.uk/green

21 22 23 LSC 9 8 7 6 5 4 3

Dedicated to 'Doc' Koefman,
my beloved earthly father,
in his ninety-second year

Contents

Petra, 2017: The Lower Temenos – the Great Temple

The tall, frail figure, his entire weight leaning on the antique silver cane, limped slowly through the semi-darkness under the white hexagonal flagstones and past the triple colonnades, until he stood directly over the entrance of the latest excavation site of the Lower Temenos, in Petra, Jordan. Following him at least ten feet behind was a young Arab boy.

'Hurry.' The man's educated British tones were soft but compelling. 'Hurry!'

The command to the excavators became more intense. He watched the five Jordanian excavators with ill-concealed impatience, then beckoned to Waseem, who swiftly attached a harness to a rope around his waist.

Discarding his cane, the Englishman started to ease himself down into the main shaft. Then he clenched his jaw to stem the sudden, intense tide of pain.

'Malik . . . !' Waseem cried.

The Arab boy leaned forward over the shaft, clutching at the Englishman's linen jacket in horror.

In that split second the dim lights over the excavation pit flickered momentarily back on, suddenly illuminating the

Englishman's face. Nick De Vere was young – extraordinarily young, not more than twenty-six – and would have been handsome if his pretty, chiselled features had not been so frail. He sighed and brushed the blond fringe back off his forehead, revealing serious grey eyes with long black lashes. He frowned intensely at the boy. 'Waseem,' he sighed, 'are you my mother?'

The boy scowled and loosed his grip on Nick's jacket. 'You are sick, Malik. You should not be doing this.' A weary smile flickered across Nick's mouth.

He turned his back to the boy, suddenly shivering violently. Sweat poured from his temples. He felt in his pocket for his silver pillbox and, with trembling fingers, tried to open it.

'Waseem . . .' His voice was hardly audible. Waseem grabbed the pillbox from Nick's hand as the grey eyes started to roll back. Nick hung from the rope in the centre of the shaft, semi-conscious, like a dead weight.

The Arab boy pulled on the rope, hauling Nick back into the cavern. He prised open the pillbox and thrust four of the gel capsules into the back of Nick's mouth. 'Swallow, Malik . . . swallow.'

Nick gulped and slumped to the dirt, his head in the Arab boy's lap. Waseem sang over him softly . . . like a mother. Much later, Nick edged his body down . . . down . . . six feet, then twelve feet down the scaffolded sides of the eastern shaft. Waseem followed, lowering himself down . . . down . . . down, until they were both face to face with the second party of Jordanian excavators, deeper than any excavation party had ever dug before in the history of Petra. Nick's eyes fell on the small patch of golden metal glistening from beneath the ash.

Zahid, his trusted chief excavator, an old Bedouin, stared up at him, his ancient eyes aflame with wonder. 'The two men of fire, Malik,' Zahid uttered in his thick, broken English. 'Maybe they tell truth.'

Nick's breathing was shallow.

Zahid motioned to the excavators to be silent. They fell back as one. He placed his ancient nut-brown hand over Nick's, pushing his hand down into the dirt on top of the golden metal.

'Maybe, Zahid,' Nick murmured under his breath. 'Maybe.' He started scrabbling through the dirt impatiently. Waseem joined him, their hands flying over the patch of gold.

'Whisk, Zahid,' Nick said tersely. Zahid thrust a soft bristle brush into his palm. Gently, Nick brushed the superficial dust away from the metal with small expert strokes until the centre was completely cleared, revealing a perfectly formed engraving the size of a dinner platter.

Nick held out his hand. 'Waseem . . .', he whispered.

Waseem handed him a scroll of yellowed paper. Nick snatched it from him and, trembling, laid it out across the metal next to the engraving.

'The men of fire, Malik?' The ancient Bedouin's hands were shaking. 'They tell truth?'

Nick put on his eyeglass and leaned over the golden metal as Zahid and Waseem watched with bated breath. Slowly Nick looked up, his face burning with ecstasy.

'Zahid!' He kissed the old man on both cheeks fervently. 'Let them dig!'

Later

It was past one in the morning by the time the casket was fully visible, and another two hours before it rested under the walls of white hexagonal stone of the Lower Temenos. It was four feet in width and two in depth, and of an almost translucent gold embedded with a vast array of rare jewels. The casket strongly resembled the Ancient Hebrews' sacred relic, the Ark of the covenant, with its intricately carved golden cherubim and seraphim, except that it was smaller and had, etched in the very centre, a large, beautifully engraved insignia, with three smaller engravings etched directly beneath it.

Nick caressed the engravings. 'The royal crest, Zahid,' he whispered, 'of the House of Yehovah.'

Waseem pointed to the three smaller engravings. He frowned up at Nick, his dark eyes wide with wonder.

'The seal of the three chief princes.' Nick looked down at Zahid, who was rocking back and forth on the ground. 'The big men of fire ... three archangels.'

Zahid's eyes grew wide with apprehension.

Nick was studying the engravings intently. He traced the coat of arms gently with his forefinger. 'Valour and justice,' he murmured. 'The great Prince Mikhail.'

Waseem pointed to the third seal excitedly. 'Jibril! Jibril!' he shrilled.

Nick nodded. 'Gabriel,' he whispered, 'the Revelator.'

Zahid stared, transfixed and trembling, at the third engraving. Slightly larger than the other two, it had one magnificent deep crimson ruby as its centrepiece. His rocking grew agitated.

Nick gently ran his finger over the ruby. 'And I expelled you, O guardian cherub,' he whispered, 'from among the fiery stones.'

Nick and Zahid exchanged a long, apprehensive look. Nick took a deep breath. 'And now, for what we have come for ...'

With the aid of a mechanical jack, Zahid prised open the lid of the casket wide enough to wedge two long wooden beams into the aperture. With one more turn of the jack, the casket's stone hasp fell in two pieces onto the ash floor. Nick looked back at the other excavators, huddled together and staring, petrified, at the third engraving. Like frightened animals they scuttled off, leaving the three alone in the gloom.

Nick nodded. The three leaned over and slowly raised the heavy lid. Immediately the cavern was flooded with a blinding, iridescent light that rose up as seven columns of blazing white flame, illuminating the entire chamber.

Zahid and Waseem fell prostrate into the ash.

'*Allahu Akbar*! *Allahu Akbar*!' they cried in unison. Nick stumbled to his knees, his arm covering his eyes from the searing heat.

Gradually the columns settled, and as the white mist faded, two huge, gold-bound codices became visible in the upper compartment of the casket.

Very gently Nick reached over and drew the top codex out. 'The angelic writings,' he murmured in wonder.

Slowly he opened the codex, moving his finger along the lines of strange golden text. As he did, the angelic writings seemed to take on a life of their own, glowing, dancing in the shafts of light emanating from them.

'The most ancient of ancient angelic writings,' he whispered to Zahid, who still lay prostrate on the ground, his face to the floor. Slowly the old Bedouin lifted his head to the codices, staring in wonder at the pulsing angelic script now in Arabic. Nick traced his finger along the title, the glowing Arabic lettering instantly transforming to English.

'The Secret Annals of the First Heaven ... The Fall of Lucifer.' His voice fell to a whisper. 'As recorded by Gabriel ... the Revelator.'

AFTERMATH

2028

Lucifer stood, an imperial figure. His monstrous black war chariot, riding on the shafts of thunderbolts, the huge silver wheels sprung with the sharpest war blades, was pulled by eight of his finest dark-winged stallions, their manes intertwined with platinum, caparisoned as for war, glistening black as the night.

And then, for a fleeting moment, the sun's rays broke through, the clouds dissipated, and Gabriel could see Lucifer's lips moving incoherently with the incantations of the damned. Gabriel did not turn to him, but saw his stallions' shadows on the clouds as the war chariot thundered past, the crimson emblem of the infernal flame on hell's flag flying proudly.

He passed so close that Gabriel's white mare trembled and snorted at the putrid reek of his satanic wizardry. Gabriel turned his head from the damning presence.

The scarred, misshapen features were now masked behind the battle helmet, the soulless sapphire eyes imperious, his bearing still kingly. He held his head high, his long raven hair gleaming and plaited with platinum and lightnings, his fist brandishing the cat-o'-nine-tails menacingly.

Lucifer was all glorious, and all terrible as slowly he

surveyed the valley before him. A thick red mist of human blood mingled with the reek of burning human flesh that rose unendingly from the valley of slaughter. Millions of massacred soldiers – Chinese, European, American, Arab, Israeli – floated next to drowned horses and half-submerged tanks and other armoured vehicles in a vast quagmire of blood and mud 1,600 furlongs long; all that was left after the assault of the massive 200-million-man army.

Hundreds of thousands of griffin vultures, their wingspans over nine feet long, blackened the crimson skies, circling the killing fields while massive swarms of raptors gorged ravenously on human flesh. On the outskirts of the Valley of Jezreel, on higher ground, bodies, severed limbs, and decapitated heads lay in random piles.

A holocaust.

The eerie silence hung heavily over the valley. Nothing stirred but the bloodcurdling screeching of the vultures.

Lucifer waded through the bloody quagmire, which reached up to his dark stallions' bridles, towards higher ground. A smile of approval crossed his crimson mouth. Then, sensing a presence, he turned the war chariot around.

Several lengths away, at the edge of the gorge directly opposite Lucifer, a regal figure mounted on a splendid white Arab stallion surveyed the valley.

Michael took off his golden helmet, his long corn-coloured hair falling to his broad shoulders. His green eyes gleamed with nobility. He raised the Sword of Justice, his jaw clenched – the only sign of his blazing fury.

A wry smile played on Lucifer's features. He turned and mockingly saluted. 'Put your sword away, brother!' Lucifer's voice shattered the eerie silence. 'It is not yet time.'

'The Judgement hastens, Lucifer!' Michael's noble tones rang out across the valley.

Lucifer lifted his visor with one sharp movement. He

pulled on his stallions' reins, his impatience thinly veiled. 'Even Michael cannot pre-empt what is written.'

Across the valley Michael waited, fierce, silent.

Bareback on his white steed, Gabriel came into view behind Michael on the horizon, his long platinum locks falling past his shoulders, his face and head uncovered, his silvered crossbow hanging at his side.

A fleeting vulnerability crossed Lucifer's countenance.

'Gabriel,' he whispered softly. Then a strange, evil smile glimmered. 'One for Eternity!' he cried.

Gabriel drew a sharp breath and bowed his head.

'Brothers!' Lucifer's cry echoed . . . tormenting. His eyes glittered black. 'I will annihilate the whole race of men before I am done.'

He drove the panther tails embedded with sharp steel violently onto the lead stallion's back, drawing blood. The horse's eyes flickered red, and he snorted in pain, sending flames and sulphureous smoke billowing from his nostrils.

'I will take my vengeance!' Lucifer cried.

He and his Mephistophelean stallions took off on the burning white crest of the black hurricanes and rode the thunderbolts, disappearing into the darkening crimson skies.

My tormented brother, Lucifer, you return my missives unopened.

The nib of Gabriel's pearlescent quill pen scratched tirelessly on the heavy linen paper embossed with his crest, Prince Regent.

A full millennium is passed yet still you are silent. Our Eternal Father grieves deeply for you, as do Michael and myself.

We urge you to repent.

I know you think of me still, for even this past eventide your tortured countenance haunts my sleeping and waking hours. I rode this dawn across the lush golden meadows of the eastern plains of Eden you loved so ardently, and I recalled those balmy days of the First Heaven when we spent our moons in horseplay and swordsmanship – and triune brotherhood.

Gabriel laid his pen down and pushed the long golden locks away from his brow. A terrible suffering clouded his features.

'And I remembered back to the time, before the shadows fell across our world.'

His voice was barely above a whisper.

'When we were just brothers . . .'

CHAPTER ONE

The First Heaven
100 Millenniums Earlier

The reflection of the twelve palest-blue moons glistened on the First Heaven's tangerine horizon. Shooting stars and lightnings arced over the silvery crystal sea, the pearlescent white sand on the celestial beach shimmering, it seemed, into infinity. With each wave, clusters of luminescent diamonds the size of pomegranates washed up onto the glistening sands. Towards the eastern horizon lay Eden, its magnificent, lush hanging gardens and amethyst waterfalls barely visible from the sea's edge.

A full league back, riding bareback on the crests of the foaming silver waves, a familiar muscular form sped past Gabriel, his white stallion straining forward. Michael, bare-chested, laughed exuberantly as he raced, his regal head raised, the flaxen hair flying.

'Gabriel – the palace!' he shouted, in sheer exhilaration as he raced through the frothing surf.

Gabriel's white mare sped forward in the shallows until she was neck and neck with Michael, galloping towards the towering, copper-hued Cliffs of Zamar.

In the distance, from the western wing of the golden-columned Palace of Archangels, rising high above the western wall, a lone imperial figure watched the brothers race. He stood on the huge, ornately carved pearl balcony of his palace chambers, a magnificent black panther wearing a heavy gold collar studded with rubies pacing by his side.

The face's sculpted alabaster features were perfect in their beauty. The wide, marble-smooth forehead, high cheekbones, straight patrician nose, and full, passionate mouth were framed by long, gleaming blue-black hair that fell past his shoulders onto his shining white garments. A golden girdle circled his waist; his feet were clad in gold. His deep crimson velvet cloak blew behind him in the breeze, the ruby-studded golden broadsword at his side. His head was crowned with a translucent light that seemed to dance in the angelic zephyrs.

Lucifer watched intently as his brothers raced on the eastern shores, his imperious sapphire eyes blazing a fervent blue, his gaze locked onto the two horses hurtling across the sand.

Michael tore across the beach, Gabriel a full length behind him, through massive pearl gates two hundred feet high. The entrance to the First Heaven.

Their horses thundered across the large, glistening diamonds paving the winding road to the stately, golden columned Palace of Archangels. As the racing steeds drew closer, the palace gates opened as if by an invisible force.

Lucifer slapped his thigh and smiled in amusement as Michael, in a final burst of energy, urged his stallion a full two lengths ahead of Gabriel.

'Strategy, Gabriel – Michael's strategy!' he murmured.

Michael and Gabriel galloped through rows of grand white columns, past vast crystal orangeries, and drew to a halt in front of the eastern wing of the palace. Michael's chambers lay beyond the grand halls. There he swam each dusk in the deep, balmy springs that flowed through the palace quarters.

Michael dismounted swiftly and strode up the gilded steps. He hesitated outside the heavy golden doors engraved with the emblem of the Royal House and, smiling, saluted to Lucifer on the balcony.

Lucifer lifted his hand in acknowledgement, his blue eyes lighting up with pleasure, then walked back into his palace chambers.

The vaulted ceilings of his inner sanctum soared a hundred feet. They were fashioned with exquisitely painted frescos – hues of azure and indigo, heliotrope, damson, and amethyst merging into magenta and vermilion. Spectacular panoramas covered the ornate carved ceilings of the chambers. Michelangelo's Sistine Chapel, in its yet future day, would be but a faded replica of Lucifer's majestic *trompe l'oeils*.

The enormous rubied palace windows were flung open, and the sounds of the angelic orations from the Mount of Assembly echoed throughout the chamber.

Beneath the immense walls in the very centre of the chamber stood a huge, golden aeolian harp. All across the chamber lay musical instruments of every kind: lyres, lutes, psalteries, dulcimers, pipe organs, a collection of pipes and tabrets, fifes, flageolets, pan pipes, serpents, cornets, gleaming golden shofars of every description, chimes, and treble bells.

Lucifer leaned over and picked up his viol and bow, which stood upright in pride of place near the harp. He thrummed the viol's strings as he walked back out onto the balcony. With his nimble, jewelled fingers he drew the bow across the viol's bridge, his eyes closed in rapture as he played, supreme master of his instrument, in adoration of Yehovah.

Suddenly, a dazzling, pulsating light fell across Lucifer, blinding him and completely covering the pearl balcony.

He dropped to his knees, the viol discarded on the marble floor, and shielded his eyes from the blazing light with his forearm.

Sheer ecstasy crossed his countenance. His brothers forgotten, slowly he dropped his arm from his face, his eyes gradually attuning to the blinding, iridescent radiance that cascaded down on Lucifer in blazing, shimmering light streams. He raised his countenance, shaking his head from side to side, bathing his features in the prisms of white fire, recklessly drinking in the intense brilliance.

Turning his face to the panorama of light before him, he bowed his head, lifting his arms wide to heaven, the strong, masculine hands spread wide in reverence.

'Our Father . . .'

The light intensified dramatically.

'Creator . . . Preserver . . .'

The shimmering increased tenfold, radiating from deep inside the vast range of the Golden Mountains.

Outside the palace, the outer brilliance of the radiance emanated from thousands of translucent, angelic forms and white eagles, which blanketed the vast golden mountain and the translucent crystal palace that rose thousands of leagues beyond the white, swirling mists.

Surrounding the palace's perimeter was an immense, towering jasper wall, over one hundred feet wide and four hundred feet high, studded with clusters of diamonds, emeralds, jacinth, amethyst, jade, and lapis lazuli, all exuding their own dazzling light. Beyond the northern wall, almost completely obscured by the mountain, stretched the infinite onyx plains of the Mount of the North, the mount of angelic assembly, where a hundred million of the angelic host gathered in legions serving under the three great angelic regents: the archangels. The chief princes. Yehovah's three mighty warriors and commanders: Michael, Gabriel, and Lucifer.

Rising above the western wall was the splendid Palace of Archangels where the three brothers dwelt in harmony and kinship – a triune brotherhood. Michael, the chief prince and holy commander-in-chief of Yehovah's angelic hosts, filled with valour, honour, and might. Michael, the warrior. Gabriel, the Revelator – the youngest prince, filled with wisdom and justice and soon to be inaugurated. And the eldest of the three brothers, most adored of heaven, Lucifer, the light-bearer, prince regent, and Yehovah's viceroy. His throne was second only to the royal throne of Yehovah himself. Lucifer, filled with wisdom and perfect in beauty. The shining one.

On days when Lucifer climbed to the highest vantage point of his pearl balconies, he could distinguish the translucent crystal palace, carved out of one immense diamond and soaring above the mount where dwelt the twenty-four Ancient Ones. The twenty-four angelic monarchs, ancient governors of heaven and stewards of Yehovah's holy mysteries – his holy elders, their white hair like spun silk falling to the floor, golden crowns upon their heads. Executors of his holy purposes.

At the very summit of the palace three imposing crystal domes, the portals, surrounded a mammoth golden tower that peaked into seven spires, disappearing into the clouds above. Each portal appeared to have no ceiling, to extend straight out into the galaxies where living dwarf stars and moons radiated continually over each portal – almost an extension of the myriad solar systems radiating from above the palace.

Soaring around the seven spires, near their peaks, were multitudes of white eagles, their wingspans reaching over twenty feet. Their feet and beaks appeared to be dipped in pure gold – Yehovah's messengers.

To the east of the spires stood a vast tower, a battlement

completely exposed to the heavens: the Tower of Winds. In its centre stood a large golden table surrounded by eight golden thrones where the angelic zephyrs of wisdom and revelation raged in eternal cyclones, blowing down their wisdom upon the Ancient Ones as they met in the councils of heaven. One hundred enormous white owls perched on the battlements.

Thunder and electric-blue lightning emanated from the vast golden tower, which was itself surrounded by magnificent rolling gardens that seemed to hang from infinity thousands of leagues above the mountain, as if held by an invisible force – the eastern Gardens of Eden where Yehovah walked in the cool of the day.

The monumental Waterfalls of Nectar thundered a hundred leagues down, reflecting the changing rainbow hues of Eden's horizon. Lined by the great, ancient willows, its hallowed streams flowed north, south, east, and west out of the lush, tropical celestial gardens, watering the First Heaven. Unicorns and oryx grazed in the fields of Eden, while porpoises and sea urchins frolicked in the deep pools beneath the falls. Birds of paradise, rainbow-hued flamingos, and blue griffins swooped across the hot springs. Giant indigo swans and their cygnets floated downstream towards the crystal sea.

In the furthest corner of the hanging gardens stood two massive trees, their fruit glistening gold in the lightning, almost wholly enveloped by swirling white mists. To the north of the two trees a colossal golden, ruby-encrusted door, ablaze with light, was embedded into the jacinth walls of the tower – the entrance to the throne room.

It was here that the lightning and the roaring appeared to have their origin. And it was here where dwelt the One who was light itself and from whom all light received its source. The One before whom all heavens and galaxies fled.

The One before whom all heaven fell prostrate, as though dead, in the very majesty and awe of him. The One whose hair and head were white like snow from the very radiance of his glory, whose eyes flashed like flames of living fire with the brilliance of his multitude of discernments and great and infinitely tender compassions. The One before whom all angelic princes and kings threw down their golden crowns in awe and wonder.

For his beauty was indescribable, and to those few who had ever looked upon his face, they could not but hear his name and weep. Their faces burned radiant, and they wept unceasingly with the awe and the wonder of it for his tender mercies and compassions were unfathomable.

And so, as One, he dwelt in the throne room.

And as Three.

For they were indivisible.

And they were indissoluble.

And so they dwelt as a great and sacred mystery.

Of such great and wondrous secrets the twenty-four elders, the ancient angelic monarchs, were stewards.

Lucifer inhaled deeply. A deep and palpable peace crossed his features.

'Yehovah,' he uttered.

With his great strength, Michael pushed open the massive golden doors of Lucifer's chambers. He strode across the gleaming sapphire floors, flinging his cloak onto one of the enormous golden thrones, and then walked through the jewelled columns and out through the balcony doors. He bowed deeply in reverence to Lucifer.

'Chief Prince Lucifer, filled with wisdom and perfect in beauty.'

Lucifer raised his head slowly to Michael. A magnificent smile lit his features. 'Michael, my brother . . .'

Michael clasped Lucifer's neck.

'Young Gabriel fell afoul of your finer tactics, I believe!'

They embraced with great affection, then again bowed low to each other in reverence.

Gabriel burst out onto the balcony. His grey eyes gleamed with the exhilaration of the race. He bowed reverently to Lucifer, then mockingly to Michael.

The three statuesque angelic princes stood together: blinding, dazzling figures, nine feet in height, sinewed and bronzed in their white robes. Michael's fierce, intelligent green eyes blazed out of the chiselled, noble face, softened only by the incongruous dimples that accompanied his rare but highly infectious laughter. His gleaming flaxen hair was tied back with emeralds and gold in one thick braid. The younger Gabriel stood next to him, lithe and aesthetic in appearance. His beautiful features were flawless, almost pretty: the perfectly carved cheekbones; the long, fine, platinum locks; the regal, heart-shaped countenance. The brothers' wings were of a spirit-body matter, visible only at certain angles, where they gave the appearance of millions of atoms radiating at the speed of light.

'Gabriel.' Lucifer strode towards him, kissing him on both cheeks. 'Beloved Gabriel, a great day dawns for you.' He stepped back and surveyed him, an elder brother's pride glinting in his piercing sapphire eyes. 'Not many moons hence you shall join your brother and me in rank in the service of our Father. This is a great honour. Are you ready to receive this responsibility?'

Gabriel looked from Michael's clear green eyes into Lucifer's generous sapphire gaze.

'Gabriel,' Lucifer whispered passionately, clasping his brother's face in his hands, 'the responsibility . . . one-third of the angelic host, wholly at your command. Are you ready to handle the mantle of power, the weight of accountability?' He clasped Gabriel's shoulder protectively.

17

Gabriel looked straight into Lucifer's eyes without fear or guile. 'I am,' he answered softly.

'It is his will you must always serve, not your will. It is his will that must be done. His kingdom come,' said Michael, nodding resolutely. 'He is to be unequivocally worshipped and adored, to be obeyed.'

Lucifer nodded. 'Humility will be your salvation, Gabriel – humility and service to him who is worthy of all worship.' Lucifer wiped a solitary tear from his eye with the back of his bronzed hand. 'Worthy of all honour, of all adoration.'

He gave Gabriel his brilliant smile, then clapped his hands, gesturing towards an enormous object covered in gold cloth, just inside the doorway. 'I have a gift for my beloved brother.'

Gabriel eagerly unwrapped the gold muslin from around the huge frame.

'To celebrate your inauguration,' Lucifer said.

As the muslin fell to the marble floor, Gabriel gasped. Before him was an exquisite painting depicting himself before the Seat of Kings at his inauguration.

'Ah, my cherished brother approves of my gift!' Lucifer's sapphire eyes lit up in pleasure.

Gabriel swung around to him. 'Why, it is truly exceptional, Lucifer!' he exclaimed. 'You are surely the most generous of brothers!'

Lucifer gestured up at the hundred-foot ceilings with their ornate, magnificently painted frescos. 'Your collection will soon rival my own!'

'Generous indeed!' Michael slapped Lucifer hard on the back. 'All *I* received was an elder brother's lecture!'

Lucifer laughed. 'You, my dear, pragmatic Michael, showed absolutely *no* appreciation for the finer aesthetics of life. Unlike our Gabriel.' Lucifer shook his head, beckoning Gabriel nearer. He dropped his voice to a roguish whisper:

'The last painting I gave him – most magnificent, may I add – I discovered a hundred moons later behind Jether's closet door, with the rest of his' – he turned to fix Michael with an affectionate look – 'collection.'

'You create mischief, Lucifer!' Michael wiped away tears of mirth. A tall angel with a gentle countenance and dark hair tied back in a silvered braid walked through the door, bowing deeply before the brothers, then turning and bowing again to Lucifer.

Lucifer nodded and smiled. 'Asmodeus.'

Lucifer noted the parchment missive, sealed with Yehovah's golden seal, in Asmodeus's hand and immediately held out his hand.

Asmodeus bowed once more. He spoke respectfully, quietly. 'The missive for His Excellency, Chief Prince Lucifer, the light-bearer. From Yehovah, Great King of the Universes.'

Lucifer tore open the missive with the blade-edge of his golden cinquedea and studied the contents. 'He summons me . . .' His mouth moved in wonder.

Asmodeus bowed again. 'Your stallion is prepared, Your Excellency.'

Lucifer tore across the vast golden meadows of the eastern plains of Eden astride his magnificent black stallion, his raven locks flying in the zephyrs, his imperial figure dwarfed by the sheer majesty of the undulating rainbow horizons above him.

Each time he entered Eden was always as the first for him.

He raced across the golden bulrush meadows and on through the lush rainforests, the heavy elixir-laden under-growth drenching him as he rode. He threw his head back in exhilaration.

Two enormous pearl gates towered far in the distance – the entrance to Yehovah's Hanging Gardens of Eden. Half a mile beyond the gates thundered the great Waters of Eden that dropped a full mile down into the Eternal Fountains. Lucifer pulled on his stallion's reins as they galloped across the meadows, his eyes locked on the incredible vista before him.

Massive curtains of flickering light shafts literally danced across the horizon, all the hues of the rainbow collected like some immense swirling celestial aurora. Lucifer watched in wonder as the shafts of light changed from lilac to aquamarine to vermilion. With a deft pull on the reins, Lucifer urged his stallion to leap. They soared a thousand feet into the heavens, defying gravity, and plunged into the centre of the aurora's spinning vortex.

His senses were utterly consumed by the colossal wall of roaring light and sound that seemed to invade every fibre of his body. With each scorching shaft it seemed that every atom of his being was newly invigorated as the glowing purity coursed through him.

Instantaneously, he found himself on the far side of the chasm at the entrance to Eden. Lucifer stared down in wonder from the gates of the hanging gardens at the sheer drop of the never-ending chasm beneath him.

Two cherubim, ten feet in height, clothed with fires and lightning, bowed low before him, their four outstretched wingtips touching each other.

'Prince Regent Lucifer of the Royal House of Yehovah – the light-bearer. The Great King of Heaven awaits you,' they addressed him in unison.

The second cherub took Lucifer's stallion while the first ushered him through a second much smaller arbour-like pearl gate into the thick, swirling white mists.

An incredible floral aroma permeated his senses as they

walked past knee-high gladioli and frangipani, beds of pale blue flowers that looked almost like tulips except for the long crystal stamens in their centre. Past climbing roses of every hue and imagination. Past intricately carved pearl and crystal benches and arbours.

They reached a second gate, different from the previous ones. It was higher, almost twelve feet high and three feet in breadth, carved of solid gold and embedded with emeralds and diamonds set in a vast jacinth wall that surrounded the entrance to the inner sanctum of Eden.

As Lucifer approached the gate, he fell to his knees. Two majestic, six-winged seraphim stood in front of the gate, their faces aflame with living, burning fires. They bowed low to Lucifer, two wings covering their face and two their feet.

Lucifer rose, his countenance literally blazing with a transcendent brightness. Six magnificent white iridescent wings, eight feet wide, which were previously not noticeable on his being, now became fully visible. He hovered in midair, suspended by two of the immense wings.

'I, Lucifer, son of the morning, declare myself servant to the Most High God.' He prostrated himself, covering his feet with two wings.

'We welcome you, Chief Prince Lucifer – highest of seraphim, the light-bearer!' The seraphim's voices were intertwined with delicate chimes and musical instruments that made melody as they spoke. 'Our king awaits your presence.' The seraphim bowed once more in obeisance, then moved aside.

Lucifer rose, his hands trembling, and took hold of the large golden latch. Immediately his palms were drenched in a myrrh-like substance that ran down over his forearms. His breathing rapid, he pushed the gate open and entered.

Standing in the furthest corner of the garden under the two trees with their golden fruit, his back to Lucifer and

21

only dimly visible through the rising mists, was a tall figure clothed in shining white garments. His gleaming hair seemed dark, almost raven, falling down his back, but as the mists rose and fell it seemed to change in hues to auburn and then to finely spun gold.

Slowly the figure turned.

Lucifer fell to his knees. He covered his face from the blazing white light emanating from the flames covering the figure's countenance.

Christos walked towards Lucifer until he stopped directly in front of him. Gradually, the white mists faded. Lucifer stared, entranced, at the feet before him. They glowed as burnished bronze refined in fire. Lucifer's gaze travelled upward from the hem of his white silk robe to the girdle of gold around his breast.

Lucifer raised his head. Christos' face radiated with a light so intense that now his head and hair seemed white as snow. But as the shimmering waves of light settled, it became evident that his hair and beard were a deep, flaming chestnut. Resting on his head was a golden crown, embedded with the three great rubies representing the godhead's indissoluble covenant. Each glimpse of Christos for Lucifer was as mesmerizing as the first.

Lucifer stared, transfixed, at the strong imperial countenance, the high, bronzed cheekbones, the blazing clear eyes that flashed from hues of blue to emerald to brown, like flames of living fires with the brilliance of his multitude of discernments and tender compassions. The great king of heaven. Beautiful beyond description.

'Christos,' Lucifer uttered in ecstasy.

'Lucifer,' Christos whispered. 'Beloved son of the morning.'

Christos bent down and clasped Lucifer's face in his strong hands, then closed his eyes and tenderly kissed the raven head as though Lucifer were a child.

22

Tears coursed down Lucifer's cheeks, splashing onto Christos' hands. 'I am not worthy.'

'Only One is worthy.' Christos' voice was very soft, but His eyes gleamed with adoration as he turned to gaze at the rubied door of the throne room situated far above them.

Lucifer rose to his feet, staring at Christos in adulation.

'Today we will take the path,' Christos said.

He led Lucifer past the golden trees and through a narrow pearl arbour covered with pomegranate vines laden with lush silver fruit. Past the heady perfume of the magnificent hanging blossoms of the Gardens of Fragrance that exuded the aromas of frankincense and spikenard. As they walked, Lucifer shielded his eyes from the intense shafts of crimson light radiating from far beyond. Christos walked ahead, through the vale, his face radiant until they came to an inconspicuous grotto at the very edge of the Cliffs of Eden surrounded by eight ancient olive trees.

'Your garden,' Lucifer whispered. Christos smiled and pushed open the humble wooden gate.

Gradually the rays settled, revealing – a hundred feet ahead and across a vast chasm – the colossal, rubied door, ablaze with light, embedded into the jacinth walls of the tower. The entrance to the throne room. Between the cliff face and the throne room entrance was a sheer drop where the fountains of life flowed from Yehovah's throne, thousands of leagues downward to the Waters of Eden, then north, south, east, and west to water the First Heaven. There was no bridge across.

Christos led the way to a simple bench in the centre of the grotto, carved of olive wood. He watched as Lucifer stared towards the throne room, his face enraptured.

'The great mystery,' Lucifer marvelled. 'You are three, yet you are one.' He dragged his gaze away to look at Christos. 'We are three in our triune brotherhood.'

Christos smiled. 'Yet you are three.'

Lucifer nodded.

'Yes,' Christos answered softly. 'It is a great and incomparable mystery – one that shall be pondered for all eternity.'

He motioned for Lucifer to join him. They sat together in silence and gazed a long while at the shimmering rainbow that rose like an immense bow over the Crystal palace.

At length Christos spoke. 'There is a new galaxy we create, Lucifer.'

Lucifer stared up at him in wonder. 'Yehovah's creations are incomparable.' His eyes gleamed with elation.

'You may find it insignificant by angelic standards,' Christos continued. 'It inhabits the galaxy next to our new universe Tertus.'

Lucifer pondered. 'I have been so busy attending to the foundations of Tertus – I must have passed it by on my many journeys into the galaxies.'

Christos smiled. 'It has not much to attest to it at present. It would not have drawn your attention.' His voice was soft. 'We spoke to you many moons past concerning our desire to create a new race.'

Lucifer nodded in recollection. 'Yet another?' He smiled brilliantly. 'Each new race is as a marvel to me.'

Christos stared at Lucifer for a long moment. 'A race that is not angelic.'

Lucifer looked at him inquiringly.

Christos stood, his arms outstretched to the throne room. Slowly the colossal rubied door opened, and with it the lightning and thunder grew to a crescendo. A tempestuous wind blew, and lightning lit up the sky. Lucifer flung himself to the ground, prostrate.

And then, through the thunder and the roaring, a voice as that of a thousand waters was heard – a voice infinitely more beautiful than either angelic or human imagination

24

had ever the capacity to conceive. This was the voice that thrust a million flaming suns into orbit, that fashioned ten thousand times ten thousand galaxies and laid the boundaries of the firmaments of a thousand universes, the voice that allotted the path of a million, million moons and created the lightning, the tempests, and the hail. The voice of the Sovereign of all sovereigns: authoritative, noble, and valiant, yet filled with grace and exquisite tenderness. It was one voice, yet as three. And it was three, yet as one.

'Lucifer – son of the morning,' the voice pealed. 'You who watched when I laid the cornerstones of the universe. You who saw me bind the chains of the Pleiades and loose the cords of Orion, who observed me prepare a channel for the torrents of rain and a path for the thunderbolt. Lucifer – light-bearer: We would create a race in our image . . . and in our likeness.'

Silence fell. The lightning struck and the thunder grew in intensity. Finally the voice spoke once more.

'The race of men.'

Then suddenly the rubied door closed. Immediately the thunder and lightning subsided, and the wind decreased to a gentle, balmy breeze. Christos watched Lucifer intently.

Lucifer stood. 'A race . . . in your likeness?' He ran his fingers through the thick locks, strangely dazed.

Christos nodded.

'We, the angelic host – are we not your beloved?' Lucifer moved a step closer to Christos.

Christos smiled compassionately. 'Light-bearer, the shining one – adored of heaven.'

The seraphim materialized and stood on each side of Lucifer to escort him out of Eden.

Lucifer fell to one knee, clasping Christos' hand, a desperation in his voice. 'Before I take my leave, anoint me afresh.'

Gently, Christos laid his hands on the crown of Lucifer's

head. A heavy, sweet-smelling golden liniment ran down from Christos' palms, drenching Lucifer's forehead and mingling with his tears. Lucifer drank in the anointing fervently, enraptured. Then his head dropped onto his breast. Christos waited. Silent.

Slowly Lucifer rose to his feet. He leaned over and kissed Christos lovingly, first on the right cheek and then on the left. Then he lifted his right hand to his own cheek. On his fingers lay a crimson liquid mixed with the liniment. He lifted his eyes to Christos, perplexed.

Christos stared down at the liquid, then back at Lucifer, a strange and terrible sorrow in his gaze. He was silent for a long moment. 'Son of the morning, many moons hence when many worlds have long risen and fallen, there will be another garden' – Christos' voice was barely audible – 'another kiss . . .'

Lucifer opened his mouth to protest, but Christos lifted His hand and Lucifer found himself back outside the gate to the inner sanctum.

He stared down again at the crimson liquid stain on his fingers, strangely distracted. Then he climbed on his stallion and rode like the wind towards his golden columned Palace of Archangels beyond the meadows.

It was nearing dawn. The seven pale lilac moons glimmered softly on the western horizon through the large casement windows of Lucifer's bedchamber. He sat at his ornate black marbled writing desk, moving his quill pen intensely across the linen pages of his journal, his beautiful italic lettering covering the page. His golden crown rested beside him on the desk. His raven hair was freed from its thick braids and flowed loose and gleaming past his broad shoulders onto his white linen mantle. The sleek panther slept peacefully at his master's feet, his breathing even.

A soft knock echoed through to his bedchambers. Lucifer frowned and looked up towards the outer entrance.

Standing in the atrium was Gabriel, wearing only his inner mantle, his head uncovered. 'I need to see you, Lucifer,' his voice wavered, 'over a matter.'

Lucifer rose in concern. 'Enter, brother. Come and join me.' Lucifer turned to pour a thick silver elixir from the jug into two goblets. 'Tell me what ails you.' He hid a smile.

Gabriel scowled at him. 'I am not myself, it is true.'

'Sip some of this pomegranate. It shall soothe you.' Lucifer's sapphire eyes glimmered with mirth. 'Tomorrow dawns whether you are bold or fearful, dear Gabriel.' Lucifer clasped Gabriel's arm.

He drew him out of the tall casement doors onto the shimmering white beaches in front of the Palace of Archangels. They walked barefoot for a full league in silence, their feet sinking into the glistening pearl sands. A company of twenty winged stallions thundered past them across the beach and soared into the firmament past the twelve pale blue moons that were now rising from the eastern horizon. Lucifer stared after them, exhilarated. The two brothers observed the shifting hues of the firmament as the lilacs transformed to amethysts and then to an intense shimmering violet.

'I remember the dusk before my own inauguration.' Lucifer stared compassionately into Gabriel's grave grey eyes. 'I was as pale and wan as yourself!'

Gabriel looked at his elder brother in disbelief.

'Jether alone knew my secret.' Lucifer laughed out loud. 'To be given responsibility over one-third of Yehovah's angelic host . . . I confess, the dusk before I was overcome!' Lucifer's expression softened. He put his head close to

Gabriel's, staring him straight in the eyes. 'You have a great gift, young Gabriel. The gift of the angelic prophet – of the Revelator. You will lead your third of the angelic host with wisdom and with honour.' He clasped his shoulder tenderly.

Gabriel knelt on the sands, gathering clusters of freshly spawned pearls in his palm. 'I would love him as you love him, Lucifer,' he whispered.

'He is my very being, Gabriel. Without him I have no existence. He is my breath.'

Gabriel bowed his head, watching the pearls slide through his fingers onto the sands. 'What ... what if I fail him, Luce?' he whispered.

'Yehovah by his choice endowed the angelic race with free will.' Lucifer's voice was very soft. 'Each and every dawn we are tested as to whether we would serve our own will and desires, or Yehovah's. It is Yehovah's greatest joy in the universe that we willingly choose to serve him, for he created us to choose. Choose wisely each day, Gabriel, and you can never fail him. The greatest gift you can grant him is your free choice to serve him in obedience, which is, in turn, your true love.'

'And you, Luce?' Gabriel stared at Lucifer, searching his countenance intently. 'Have you never been tempted to fail him, to choose yourself?'

Lucifer's gaze was clear and penetrating. 'There have been moments.' His answer was quiet. 'But they have been so fleeting ...' His voice broke off, and his long raven hair blew in the balmy breeze. 'No, Gabriel, I do not know what it is to not serve Yehovah.' He started to pace back along the sands. 'The dawn breezes rise from the eastern shore. Let us return.'

'And what of Michael?' Gabriel asked. He looked across at Lucifer as they walked, their strides strong and even.

'Michael? He is likewise devoted. You know it is so.'

'Devoted to chiding me, I fear.'

'Yes, that is true.' Lucifer smiled. 'But he too knocked on my door the dusk before his inauguration. He has many a secret – of which I know all!'

They retraced their steps, passing through the orangeries directly into Lucifer's chambers. Lucifer closed the great doors, then rang a golden bell that hung from the velvet curtains.

Immediately an old, wizened angelic courtier entered through the door and bowed. 'Ephaniah,' Lucifer said, 'I would retire.' Ephaniah nodded respectfully, then scuttled off to an adjoining room.

'Lucifer,' Gabriel said, 'there is something else.' He hesitated. 'It is true that I am Revelator. Recently I have been plagued with much dreaming.' Gabriel looked into Lucifer's eyes. Earnest.

'I see you much in my dreams of late, Lucifer. I have been disturbed. You will never desert us?'

'What folly is it you speak of?' Lucifer frowned. He turned his back to Gabriel as Ephaniah returned. The wizened courtier unlaced Lucifer's vest and placed a heavy satin gown over his shoulders. 'I have loved and served you all my life.' Lucifer turned back to face Gabriel. 'All my life my brothers' hearts and souls have been before me. Is it not true, Ephaniah?' Lucifer smiled affectionately at the old courtier, who was painstakingly turning down the vast satin amethyst eiderdowns on the platinum four-poster bed.

Ephaniah's gentle features lit up in elation. 'You are my master's joy, milord Gabriel.'

Gabriel smiled and walked to the door. 'I know that it is so. No matter, my brother.' Gabriel clasped Lucifer's hand in farewell. 'Forgive my foolish imaginings. Good night, dear Lucifer.' Gabriel pressed Lucifer's face to his cheek.

Ephaniah drew the immense velvet drapes over the latticed

29

windows, then extinguished the hundred blazing frankincense tapers above Lucifer's writing desk. The chambers fell into darkness.

'Good night, Gabriel.'

CHAPTER TWO

The Inauguration

Hundreds of thousands of angelic legions were assembled in preparation for the ceremony. Gabriel waited, grave and silent, under the intricate golden carvings of the cherubim and seraphim in the crystal palace atrium. His flawless features reflected in the translucent diamond walls. He wore a simple white shift, the traditional inauguration attire. His pale blond tresses were plaited with platinum and lightning; his chin was set. He leaned downward to place his new dagger in the sheath at his ankle, his fingers trembling.

Michael watched from the far side of the nave, restraining a smile. Now that he studied his younger brother, he could swear that Gabriel's pretty features had matured almost overnight. The beautiful countenance exuded a strength and a wisdom that seemed new to Michael. He rubbed his chin in wonder. *Gabriel, angelic prophet – the Revelator – comes of age.*

Directly behind him, a small door hidden in the magnificently panelled frescoed wall slowly opened.

An ancient, white-haired, venerable-looking figure walked out, his voluminous golden train carried nervously by a dumpy, fresh-faced cherubic angel. It was Jether, imperial warrior and ruler of the twenty-four ancient monarchs of heaven – the Ancient Ones, stewards of Yehovah's sacred mysteries.

Jether's pure-spun white beard reached almost to the floor. On his head sat a golden crown embedded with jacinth, and on his shoulder perched an enormous white owl with searching, gentle brown eyes.

'The young prince seems a trifle nervous, Your Excellency.' Jether's ancient eyes twinkled mischievously.

Michael frowned. 'Jether?' He turned in delight as they embraced affectionately. 'It has seemed many moons, old friend.' Michael bowed briefly to the owl. 'Why, honourable Jogli; I have missed your instruction!'

Jether stroked Jogli and smiled. 'We have been taken up with the preparations.' Jether gestured in Gabriel's direction. 'The preparation of his mind, his soul, his spirit.'

Michael nodded. 'He is come of age.'

Jether hesitated, stroking his beard thoughtfully. 'Ah, yes, my noble Michael, I remember another ordination and another young protégé many moons ago.' He gave Michael a deep, meaningful look from under his bushy eyebrows. 'One who was in a sword fight that very dawn.' The grey eyes twinkled.

'I am rebuked, venerable Jether. My younger brother does well indeed. Better than I.' Michael laughed. 'My temper has been better of late!'

Jether winked at Michael and immediately coughed, smothering a guffaw, his features deliberately grave. 'Thank you, Obadiah. You may now prepare my throne.'

The blushing Obadiah bowed and bowed again, so deeply that he nearly tumbled face down into Jether's train.

Jether's eyes glimmered with amusement as he watched the cherub scuttle away in the wrong direction. He turned his head to the owl. 'Jogli, I sense the youngling may need your assistance.'

Jogli spread his vast white wings and, with one flap, overtook the still-stumbling Obadiah and swung him upward in his talons, turned around, and flew him across the vast crystal atrium towards the altar.

'Younglings, younglings . . .'

Jether gazed intently into the noble face. 'You have done well, my valiant, warring Michael. I have followed your progress avidly from the hidden sanctum.' Jether's eyes shone with pride and affection. 'Chief Prince Michael, commander of the warring archangels, your spirit clothed with honour, nobility, and valour,' he murmured.

He looked to where Jogli was carefully adjusting Gabriel's cloak. 'And now this very day, Gabriel, the Revelator, will be out of my charge . . .', he reflected.

He sighed deeply. 'I have served both Almighty Yehovah and yourselves with every vestige of power that was granted me. The three of you, each as a son to me.'

Michael stared into Jether's imperial wizened face. 'You speak truly, my old friend. Our Father saw fit to entrust you with schooling each of us through the centuries in the ways of the warrior and in the ways of the Ancient of Days.'

Jether closed his eyes, his face bathed in awe. 'He alone is worthy of our undying allegiance,' he whispered. 'He alone is worthy of all worship, adoration, power, and dominion.'

Jether clasped Michael's strong, sinewed hands in his ancient, veined ones. 'I have seen, Michael . . . I have seen the very mysteries and the wonders of the holy place. The new universe, Michael . . . and man.' Jether looked long and deeply into Michael's eyes. His gaze was brilliant and piercing, almost as though reaching to the inner parts of Michael's very soul and spirit. 'I read your soul, Michael . . .' Jether's voice was soft. 'You wish to gaze upon this new race?'

Michael's eyes were aflame with wonder.

33

Jether's words trailed off as he slowly turned his gaze upward then, to the point directly above the position where the throne of Yehovah would descend.

Michael followed his gaze to where Lucifer stood, high above all the proceedings, resplendent in the heavy robes of purple velvet, crowned with translucent rays of light, radiant in his beauty. The intense sapphire eyes were fierce with passionate adoration. He stood silent on the ornate carved ivory and marble pulpit that hung from the high place in the centre of the crystal dome, staring ahead into the enormous chamber, poised to lead the myriads of heaven in their worship to the God of Hosts. He was holding the golden sceptre with which he would conduct the hosts of heaven – choirmaster of the great symphony of angelic worshippers.

Michael shook his head in admiration. 'My brother – most adored of heaven.'

'Full of wisdom and perfect in beauty.' So low was Jether's whisper that Michael could barely hear his words. 'Lucifer, the shining one.'

Jether lowered his gaze from the vision of the resplendent Lucifer. 'And now I shall spend my days in council.' He clapped his hands. 'And in supplications.' He looked around for Obadiah, who was deep in conversation with five other younglings immersed in archery marksmanship, aiming at a pearl from fifty paces. 'Younglings! Never here when they are truly required!' Jether gathered up the long satin train in his arms. 'Now, let me away to the young prince Gabriel. It seems to me that he is in need of some moral support.'

Michael stared after the fast-disappearing Jether. Obadiah scurried after him, almost slipping on the gleaming marble floors in his haste to grab Jether's train back from his master.

'Gabriel!' Michael exclaimed. He strode hurriedly after Jether.

Lucifer stood in the high place, his arms raised in abandoned worship to Yehovah, his face bathed in the blinding, shimmering light.

He turned to the millions of the prostrate angelic host and lifted his sceptre, his purple velvet robes billowing. A great oration came forth from his lips, and the sound was as the sound of celestial pipes and of flutes and of clarinets and of every pipe ever heard in the universe. In response a great song of adoration and worship burst forth from the heavenly host.

Lucifer lifted his sceptre. 'All hail Yehovah!' Lucifer's voice rose above those of the angelic host.

The entire assembly rose, their heads bowed, their arms outstretched. Immediately, the entire chamber reverberated with the sound of angelic voices. 'All hail Yehovah!'

A great rumble of thunder issued from the throne, through the mist – the roar of a thousand waters.

All at once it was as if aeon upon aeon descended through the open dome as Yehovah's feet descended. And with the descent, a great and terrible roaring filled the chamber. It was as though the suns and the moons and stars from millions upon millions of galaxies were woven as a living, pulsating tapestry of the cosmos that cloaked his being. From each moon and planet and from the millions of stars that radiated from the translucent cloak of his radiance resounded light waves that oscillated through universe after universe – a tsunami of sound.

The Ancient of Days descended into the chamber amid the thunder and lightning, and as he did, the blazing white light of the chamber was replaced with a dazzling amethyst light, which turned to emerald and then sapphire – the spectra of light reflected in Yehovah's mantle. As he descended a rainbow descended also, which seemed to stretch throughout the universe, surrounding his presence. Millions of angels circled at his feet singing praises and hymns of adoration.

Before his feet the seven blazing torches burned as seven columns of white fire, and in the midst of each torch were the flaming coals of the Spirit of Yehovah. The throne of his glory descended with him. As it lowered, the floor of the throne room became as mercury, then morphed from the fluid metal into a sea that was as living, breathing sapphire. It was transparent, and there was no flaw within it.

Ear-splitting peals of thunder seemed to shake the chamber so that the very atoms of the walls pulsated. And as the thunder subsided, blue lightning bolts, shot through with white fire, coursed through the Ancient of Days' cloak, lighting up the universe in their wake. Its circumference resembled the orbs of a thousand brilliant suns.

When the throne and the One who sat on it had descended, the lofty, translucent pearl gates of the crystal palace began to open. As they did, an angelic herald blew the shofar.

'I herald the holy Council of the Ancient Ones,' he proclaimed. 'Stewards of Yehovah's sacred mysteries.'

Slowly the blinding white mists cleared, revealing the twenty-four Ancient Ones, the twenty-four ancient kings of heaven, Yehovah's elders, clothed in brilliant white with crowns of gold upon their heads. They walked majestically through the pearl gates and up the nave. They stopped before the twenty-four golden thrones behind the enormous carved golden altar.

Leading them was Jether, chief elder of the Ancient Ones. He held his gold sceptre high in front of the angelic host, and they bowed in accord. Jether sat on the centre throne, the twenty-three remaining kings following his lead.

Once again the herald blew the shofar. 'Gabriel, the Revelator, prince of archangels,' he proclaimed. 'Long may you reign with wisdom and justice.'

The angelic host's refrain reverberated through the chamber as Gabriel, grave and resolute, followed the kings through the gates and into the palace atrium, Michael at his side, regal in his crimson imperial robe, carrying the Sword of Justice.

'Michael, the valiant,' the herald announced, 'chief prince of archangels.'

'Long may you reign with justice and valour,' the angelic host proclaimed.

Together Michael and Gabriel walked up the nave of the dome towards the Seat of Kings, the throne in front of the immense onyx altar. Their knights-in-arms fell into step behind them, solemnly bearing the banners of the Royal House of Yehovah.

As the brothers reached the Seat of Kings, the entire chamber fell silent.

'Lucifer, the light-bearer, chief prince of archangels.'

'Long may you reign, anointed cherub who covers,' the angelic chorus echoed throughout the chambers as Lucifer walked ceremoniously from his high throne down to the altar to join his brothers.

As one, the three archangels bowed low and knelt in the burning mist that poured from the carved ice throne before the altar.

Lucifer fell prostrate, facing the throne of Yehovah. His face shone so bright it seemed to burn. 'Behold, O God our defender, and look upon the face of thy chief princes, for one day in thy courts is better than a thousand elsewhere.'

He was silent, his face down, for a long moment. Then,

slowly rising, he turned to the angelic host, which stood solemnly in the chamber. 'My angelic brothers, I here present to you Gabriel, bondservant of the Most High, anointed prince of the Royal House of Yehovah!'

Lucifer turned to Gabriel, his sapphire gaze fervent. 'Do you, Gabriel, pledge to do your just homage or service and to assign yourself to these, your angelic host, from this day forth?'

Gabriel's gaze was steady. 'I do.'

'Will you, to the extent of your power, cause law and justice, in mercy, to be executed in all your judgements?'

Gabriel nodded. 'I solemnly promise to do so.'

Michael stepped forward. 'Will you pledge to serve and honour and glorify Yehovah the Almighty God, Creator, Preserver, the Ancient of Days, to execute his will forever only, to serve and venerate *forever* his person only, throughout eternity of eternities?'

Gabriel lifted his head towards Yehovah's throne, his face shining. 'I solemnly pledge this to Yehovah.'

Michael gravely handed Gabriel the Sword of Revelation.

A great thunder issued from the throne and through the mist – the roar of a thousand waters. 'This is Gabriel, our beloved. We name him Revelator.'

Zadkiel, prince of the Holy Watchers and Lucifer's chief attendant, stepped out from the throne. His powerful presence was gentle but imposing. His features were almost as beautiful as Lucifer's, and he exuded almost as much light as Lucifer himself. 'On behalf of the Ancient of Days,' Zadkiel pronounced, 'and as stewards of his sacred person, we the Holy Watchers receive your homage. We receive your pledge.'

Jether stood up from his throne and walked towards the altar. A knight placed a heavy gold ampulla into Jether's hands, the bottle reflecting the glory from the throne. Four knights-in-arms held a pall of heavy, fine gold over Gabriel's head. 'On behalf of the Ancient of Days, as his elders and stewards of his holy mysteries, we, the Council of the Ancient Ones, receive your homage. We receive your pledge.'

Jether poured the holy oil from the ampulla into a gold spoon and anointed Gabriel on the palms of both hands. 'Be thy hands anointed with holy oil.' He poured the oil on Gabriel's bare chest. 'Be thy breast anointed with oil.' He poured the remaining oil over the crown of Gabriel's bare head, then lifted both arms. 'By his holy anointing, pour down upon your head and heart the blessing of the Ancient of Days, that by the assistance of his heavenly grace you may govern and preserve one-third of Yehovah's heavenly host, committed to your charge this day.'

Michael and Lucifer each walked to the head of his third of the angelic host: Michael's on the right, Lucifer's in the centre. Gabriel walked to the last third on the left-hand side of the chamber.

'And now, I adjure you,' Jether cried to the assembly, 'let us lift our voices as one as we repeat the pledge of allegiance and devotion to His Excellency, Gabriel.'

Gabriel knelt before the angelic hosts of heaven as Lucifer held the Sword of State over his head.

'We, the hosts of heaven,' Lucifer declared, 'do become your liege servants of life and limb, and faith and truth we will bear unto you throughout eternity of eternities. So help us, Yehovah.'

Gabriel, still kneeling, raised his head to the angelic host, then rose and took his throne to the left of the twenty-four Ancient Ones.

Lucifer turned to the angelic legions. 'Long reign Gabriel!' he proclaimed.

'Long reign Gabriel!' Their cry resounded through the palace chambers.

'All hail Yehovah!'

The entire angelic assembly rose to their feet.

The thunderous, stentorian unison of hundreds of ten thousand times ten thousand angelic warriors rose to a crescendo. 'All hail Yehovah!'

'All hail Yehovah!'

The sounds of the jubilation *orationes* from the Mount of Assembly echoed over the Crystal Sea across to the magnificent marble-columned gazebo on the pearl sands.

Michael dismounted and walked up the gilded gazebo steps. He caught sight of Gabriel leaning against one of the immense white marbled columns, entranced by the lightning and thunderbolt displays over the sea. They stood together in silence, watching the rainbow-coloured dolphins as they cavorted in the silver waves of the Sea of Zamar.

'Well, Gabriel,' Michael said, 'now you're really one of us!' He slapped Gabriel hard on the back.

'Respect, Michael! My liege man of life and limb, if you recall!'

'Hear, hear!' echoed Lucifer.

He stood in the gazebo entrance, an imposing presence, surveying his brothers, with his panther Ebony sitting at his side. Gabriel turned, his face flushed with the exhilaration of the day's events. Sachiel, Lucifer's attendant, bowed and removed Lucifer's heavy velvet imperial robe. Lucifer walked over to Gabriel and kissed him affectionately on both cheeks. Ebony walked through the lush, hanging tropical gardens and stopped, purring, next to Lucifer.

Lucifer stroked the great panther tenderly, taking a sweet-meat from a golden platter. 'Ebony, my sweet.' He held it out in his palm to the sleek feline, who devoured it voraciously and licked Lucifer's fingers affectionately with his coarse tongue. Then Lucifer strode over to where the balmy turquoise and gold pools shimmered under the pale blue moons, loosening his mantle as he walked. Michael turned to his royal angelic courtier. 'A'albiel, I would celebrate with my brothers!'

A'albiel poured a thick gold elixir from a silver flagon into three garnet-studded goblets on a marble table. A'albiel passed a goblet of the elixir to Michael and then to Gabriel.

Michael nodded graciously. 'Thank you, A'albiel. You may leave us.' A'albiel bowed low and departed.

'You disappeared, Lucifer!' Gabriel chided. 'Michael and I were waiting in the dining hall for you the whole of the celebration party.'

'Forgive me,' Lucifer said, his tone subdued. 'I have been preoccupied. I was walking to and fro on Tertus.' He sat pensively, bathing his muscular legs in the tepid springs.

Gabriel frowned. 'You are not yourself tonight, Lucifer.'

'He thinks!' Michael walked over to him to offer him the goblet of elixir. 'He *always* thinks!' Michael's green eyes were dancing with mischief. 'But *what* he thinks he does not tell. Perhaps–'

His voice broke off as he caught sight of a strange crimson stain on Lucifer's right palm as Lucifer reached for the elixir. Michael looked at Lucifer quizzically. Lucifer closed his palm swiftly around the goblet, then sipped long and hard, staring back enigmatically at Michael.

Gabriel turned to Lucifer, enthralled. 'Tell us, Lucifer, is Tertus as beautiful as they say? Surely it cannot compare with the First Heaven.'

Lucifer closed his eyes in awe. 'It is magnificent, Gabriel. It is our Father's finest handiwork.'

Gabriel and Michael bowed their heads. 'He is worthy,' they echoed.

Asmodeus walked through the door, bowing deeply before Lucifer.

Lucifer nodded and smiled. 'Asmodeus.' He noted that Asmodeus carried another missive sealed with Yehovah's golden seal. He immediately held out his hand for it.

Asmodeus bowed to Lucifer. 'Your Majesty, the missive is for His Excellency, Chief Prince Michael.'

Lucifer frowned, studying Michael and Gabriel. Then he nodded graciously. Asmodeus walked swiftly towards Michael and bowed, handing him the missive.

Lucifer rose from the pool and walked over to the grand hanging candelabras in the centre of the chamber. He moved his palm almost imperceptibly, and two hundred golden wicks burst into blazing copper flames. 'Ah, frankincense!' Lucifer inhaled deeply, appearing not to watch Michael at all.

Michael tore open the missive with his golden cinquedea and studied the contents.

Lucifer turned to Gabriel. 'Let us walk.' He clasped his arm through Gabriel's, and they moved through the vast, sweeping corridors of the gazebo's grand halls, Ebony padding at Lucifer's side. They continued through the colossal atrium and into a huge crystal observatory on the roof of the gazebo.

Solar systems and galaxies of manifold universes became visible through the enormous crystal dome of the observatory. Lucifer lifted his hand, and at once the crystal dome receded, leaving him and Gabriel standing almost in the centre of heaven's vast panorama.

Lucifer pointed to a magenta planet surrounded by rings of ice and a myriad of suns and moons. 'Behold the beauty of Tertus, Gabriel – three hundred suns, thirty moons . . . hues beyond imagination . . . forty thousand light years away.' A blue arc leaped from his palm. Instantaneously, the planet magnified a hundred times. The brothers stared in awe at the cosmos.

Lucifer bowed his head in reverence, his voice a whisper. 'He is incomparable. The great king of the universe.' They bowed their heads in unison, and there was a moment's silence.

'His discernments are holy and unfathomable,' Michael interjected, leaning in the doorway, watching them indulgently. He held up the missive in his right hand, exhilarated.

As he walked over to join them he moved his palm across the heavens. A mass without form or void appeared, with only one sun and moon. 'Our Father's new galaxy. From matter.'

Lucifer stared up at the galaxy contemptuously. 'A futile mass of mud and vapour and gases. I stopped briefly to view it on my way back from Tertus.' He smiled dismissively, caressing a blue grape in his fingers. 'It is the most base and insignificant sliver of our Father's cosmos.' Slowly and deliberately he looked up at the planet Earth and covered it with the grape until it was excluded from his view. He placed the grape in his mouth and swallowed. 'I quite fail to see its purpose.' He stared dispassionately ahead.

Michael stared back unrelentingly. 'But Yehovah *always* has a purpose, Lucifer.' He held out the missive to Lucifer. 'He would have us visit the new galaxy – you and I together; he has named us.'

Lucifer glared at him in irritation, purposely ignoring the missive, instead stroking Ebony's silky neck. The panther purred loudly.

Michael stared at his brother, perplexed. 'It is his express will.'

Gabriel lay sprawled across a golden throne, his hands behind his head, staring up at the formless mass. 'We are spirit beings, Lucifer. We cannot comprehend all that our

Father creates. This universe will be matter.' He shrugged. 'We were born for *this* dimension.'

He sprang to his feet, picked up Lucifer's sword, and deftly cut the tops off a cluster of silver and blue rose-like flowers. Immediately they sprang back into perfection. 'We are celestial spirits,' he said. 'Silicone-based. We eat astral food; we bleed astral blood.' Gabriel looked out across the galaxies in wonder. 'Why, I have heard across the zephyrs, my dearest Luce, that our Father's new race is not of an angelic or celestial nature at all, but will be in *his very likeness*. It is said that he longs for fellowship,' he mused recklessly.

He took a large bite out of a juicy silver pomegranate; immediately it sprang back into its original perfection.

Lucifer's eyes narrowed. He sliced a luminous blue fruit deftly with a small ivory-handled fruit knife. 'I have no interest in your zephyrs' whisperings, my brother Gabriel.' His grasp tightened around the fruit knife. 'Your conversation becomes tedious. We *are* his fellowship. You speak of treachery.'

Gabriel gave Lucifer a quizzical glance.

'No, brother,' Michael said, staring intently at Lucifer. 'He speaks of *man*.'

The word hung in the air between them.

Lucifer turned to him, his breathing shallow.

He snatched the missive from Michael and scanned it, his expression like stone. 'I am steward of thousands of magnificent universes in our Father's galaxies. I am ill-equipped to squander my time on such nonentities.'

Then, with a sharp, sweeping movement he picked up his sword belt, put on his cloak, and strode back through the grand halls out onto the beach, Ebony at his heels. Gabriel and Michael followed just paces behind him.

Lucifer stood, sphinx-like, on the pearl sands, staring out towards the shores of the eastern horizon.

Michael watched as Lucifer's chin set in a firm line. The only other betrayal of Lucifer's unease was his fist, which was clenched so tightly around his sword that his knuckles were white.

Then, like lightning, his mood changed. He looked directly at Michael and smiled his dazzling smile. 'Enough of young Gabriel's whispering zephyrs!' He grabbed Gabriel by the scruff of his neck. 'Our Father awaits his chief princes.'

Lucifer released Gabriel and clasped Michael's strong hand in his. The three placed their right hands on their chests. 'Brothers!' Lucifer's strident tone rang out across the crystal seas.

'Brothers!' the three voices echoed in unison.

'Brothers for eternity!'

Our laughter rang out across the Sea, echoing far across the First Heaven's coral horizons.

Gabriel dipped his quill in the sepia ink and continued writing.

And it seemed that in that moment, there in the celestial chambers, life and harmony between the three of us and our Father were perfect.

If we had only known the shadows looming on our perfect horizon . . .

Shadows that would herald a fallen universe.

CHAPTER THREE

The Portals

The scientific portals were gargantuan. Displayed now at the top of the mammoth crystal dome was the Milky Way galaxy, which seemed to extend for billions of light years straight out from the portals, into the real galaxies far above the Tower of Winds. Thousands of millions of newly created suns, gathered into masses of spiral arms, radiated from the top of the central crystal portal, while baby dwarf stars hung over the infinite thousands of rows upon rows of glistening white storehouses of the galaxies.

Xacheriel, the Ancient of Days' curator of the sciences and universes, was one of the twenty-four ancient kings under Jether's governance. He and his wise ones were the devoted executors of Yehovah's unutterable marvels, governors of the three great portals, and custodians of the sacred vaults of the flaming cherubim and seraphim. These vaults housed the countless billions of DNA blueprints, genomic codes, and the boundary lines of Yehovah's innumerable galaxies, seas, and universes.

But today Xacheriel had suspended his scholarly pursuits and left the central portal to school the new intake of youngling apprentices. The younglings were an ancient angelic race with the characteristics of eternal youth and a remarkable inquisitiveness, expressly designed as apprentices to assist the Ancient Ones in their custodianship of Yehovah's countless new galaxies.

Xacheriel strode down the aisles of the younglings' laboratory, the great school of the universes. Vivid blue lightning bolts sparked around his golden crown, flashing dangerously close to the unfazed white owl on his right shoulder. A breathless youngling ran behind him, holding his cloak off the ground with great difficulty.

Youngling apprentices from the age of six through fifteen were stationed all across the scientific portal, busily experimenting, mixing, measuring, and calculating. They were rehearsing the manifold disciplines of cosmology, cell and molecular genetics, and geomorphology – part of Xacheriel's rigorous training manual for their studies of the newly conceived race. Their current project: the exact replication of the newly created universe and solar systems, executed in precise and meticulous detail according to Yehovah's blueprints.

Xacheriel stopped abruptly next to a chubby six-year-old youngling with bright carrot-red hair and a face covered in freckles. He peered over the youngling's shoulder at the pulsar screen. 'No, no . . . *no!* Dimnah!' He pounded his chest dramatically. 'How many times do I have to tell you not to hypothesize? It's mathematics. Precision counts. One coordinate out and an entire universe could perish!'

Xacheriel's eyes flashed with intensity. He bent over Dimnah and with swift fingers adjusted the calculations in midair. 'Apprentices, apprentices . . .', he muttered testily.

'But how else will they learn the great mysteries of the sciences of Yehovah, my old friend?'

Xacheriel spun around, his monocle jarring loose and hanging from its tether. 'Jether!'

He clasped Jether in a crushing bear hug, then immediately turned to glare at the languishing Dimnah. 'Reconfigure, Dimnah. The capacity must figure to my exact calculation.'

Xacheriel pointed to one of Earth's miniature prototype suns, radiating above Dimnah's head. 'The mass loss from the helium nuclei is precisely four million tons per second, which will keep the lone sun radiating for at least another . . .' – he hesitated, scratching his head under his crown – 'six thousand million years.' He turned to Jether, triumphant.

Jether offered him a voluminous handkerchief. Xacheriel looked down at the strange blue stains on his beard, then took the cloth and rubbed at them. Jether frowned deeply at the lightning still circling around Xacheriel's head.

Xacheriel waved them away, to no avail. 'My head got stuck two moons ago . . . while I was bathing . . .', he shouted back to Jether, striding through the laboratory portal. 'In the electromagnetic fission cathode. A personal voltage experiment. It will pass.'

A huge burst of electricity nearly knocked Xacheriel off his feet. It passed straight through Lamech, the youngling holding his cloak. Lamech swayed dizzily, the electricity hovering like a halo over his tight ginger curls.

Xacheriel glared impatiently at the youngling. '*Absorb*, Lamech.' He shook his head at the swooning youngling as the blue arcs disappeared into the tight curls. 'How many times must I tell you? *Absorb* the electromagnetic fields!'

Jether covered his mouth with a handkerchief, smothering an enormous, amused grin as they continued walking down the unending rows of youngling apprentices executing experiments.

'No, *no*, Jatir,' Xacheriel barked. 'Too much ether!'

'I see you are schooling them to your normal impossible standards!' said Jether, eyes twinkling.

Xacheriel stopped in mid-stride, his countenance grave.

'They have to be *rigorous* in their applications, Jether. The troposphere and stratosphere of Earth's solar system have to be *meticulously* calculated for the new race to exist.' He turned to Jether. 'We face the challenges of matter at every turn.'

They walked together to the observatory where the older younglings worked, every fibre of their being concentrated on their creations. Xacheriel pointed to a planet in the newly created solar system of nine planets, which floated above Rakkon's head.

'Rakkon! The exploratory probe readings,' he demanded.

Rakkon bowed deeply. 'Milord Xacheriel,' he said, saluting, 'lone sun temperature surface reading 9,932 degrees. Lone planet weighing 6,000 billion, billion tons, rotating at precisely 149.6 million kilometres from the sun.'

A second youngling bowed deeply, almost hitting his head against the floor in his enthusiasm.

Xacheriel rolled his eyes. 'Yes, yes, Otniel . . . what *is* it?' He mopped his brow with Jether's handkerchief.

'Milord Xacheriel, sire, findings reveal the present one-thousand-kilometre atmosphere shield too tenuous for the new life form to exist. I've increased the shield to two thousand kilometres, sire, to maintain a constant – '

Xacheriel mumbled under his breath and replaced his monocle in his left eye. 'Good, Otniel . . .' He hesitated. '*Very* good!' He studied Rakkon's pulsing midair radar screen intently. 'Rakkon, your problem is . . .' He hit the air with his staff, his eyes flashing. '*Here*!'

Xacheriel triumphantly picked up a piece of glowing neon chalk. 'You've just killed the entire new race. They'll suffocate on entry!' He scribbled a long series of neon calculations in the air next to Rakkon, muttering as he drew. 'Twenty-one per cent oxygen, 2.78 per cent nitrogen, 0.04 per cent carbon dioxide, and 0.9 per cent argon,' he said crisply.

Xacheriel clapped his hands, and a huge cloud of luminous neon chalk dust flew into Jether's face. Jether uttered a deafening sneeze and blew his nose into another handkerchief, while Rakkon choked in the cloud of glowing dust.

Xacheriel beamed, completely oblivious to their paroxysms. 'Equating *Homo sapiens* emissions over the next hundred millennia,' he continued, 'include neon and oxides of nitrogen and methane.'

He whirled around. Jether was still wiping his red, swollen eyes, while Rakkon, still choking, turned a pale shade of green.

'Ah, and don't omit krypton!' He put his face close to the still spluttering Rakkon's. 'Rakkon, we must anticipate all contingencies continually.'

Jether clapped his hands in appreciation.

Xacheriel bowed his head reverentially. 'He is worthy of all reverence and awe. He who is omniscient . . . omnipotent.'

Jether closed his eyes and bowed his head in reverence, then continued, 'We live to execute his holy commands. He alone is worthy.'

Jether opened his eyes to see Michael standing next to Xacheriel, staring transfixed towards the far side of the portal. Jether exchanged a long, meaningful look with Xacheriel, who looked elated. Jether nodded.

Xacheriel pulled up the voluminous aprons of his robe and strode through the enormous second portal doors into what seemed to be a long, winding, translucent corridor.

Xacheriel stared gravely at Jether and Michael, then inhaled deeply and began to tread swiftly on the floor beneath his feet. Instantly it morphed into a glistening, mercury-like substance that quickly encompassed the entire corridor. The fluid erupted with such intense heat that the entire corridor began to revolve and shudder at incredible speed – until it stopped abruptly.

Suspended in front of them, seemingly from infinity to infinity, a colossal glowing ladder now ascended up into the galaxy around and above the portal. A mammoth hologram.

Xacheriel, his face shining in exhilaration, placed his foot on the first rung of this living, pulsating ladder, then walked straight through, disappearing into the gyrating helixes. He was followed immediately by Jether.

Michael stood gazing after them.

Jether's head reappeared out of the double helixes. 'Michael!' He raised his brows inquiringly.

Michael tentatively stepped through onto the ladder and immediately found himself airborne, gyrating at the speed of light through the hologram's never-ending spiral corridor.

'The ladder of life!' Xacheriel cried as they sped along.

Michael reached out his hand to touch the pulsating coils. At his touch the ladder came to an immediate standstill as huge stores of information downloaded in front of his eyes.

The portal's automatic voice narrated in modulated tones. 'Man's physical brain is comprised of over 100 billion cells, each with over 50,000 neuron connections to other brain cells. The structure receives over 100 million separate signals from the human body every second.'

Jether smiled. 'Yehovah's inconceivable marvels!'

Michael placed his palm on a second coil. Instantly, a hologram materialized and rotated, zooming in on the proto-type's eye. 'Over 125 million rods and cones,' the narration continued, 'specialized cells so sensitive that some can detect a mere handful of photons.'

Jether lifted his hand, and a distant, indistinguishable voice, tinged with a slight impatience, echoed down the ladder.

'Xacheriel!'

Michael and Jether sped through the infinite, twisting corridors for what seemed like eternities, finally stopping before the vast living, breathing veil that Xacheriel was studying in sheer ecstasy, now completely oblivious to their arrival.

'DNA,' Jether murmured in wonder. 'The building blocks of life. Unimaginable complexity . . .'

The veil became transparent, and billions of intricate, pulsating code sequences became visible.

'A 300 billion base sequence!' Xacheriel's eyes flashed in exhilaration. 'A unique program perfectly adapted to each aspect of the new race – making up the human genomic code . . .'

Michael shook his head in wonder.

'The instruction set that will carry each one of the new race from a one-cell egg to adulthood.'

Jether nodded, transfixed.

'Twenty-four billion possible sequences of nucleotides,' Xacheriel continued, 'all of which would lead to complete biological malfunction.' He turned to Michael in awe. 'Except for this very one.'

'Created in his image,' Michael said softly.

'The human construction book, or an instruction manual, if you like,' Xacheriel continued. 'Matter we created for the specific purpose of being a carrier of the code.'

Exhilarated, he held up a DNA fibre in his fingers. 'No less amazing – two millionths of a millimetre thick.' His eyes glowed with fervency. 'Yet the amount of information contained within it is so immense that in the case of human DNA, if the tightly coiled strands inside a human adult were unwound and stretched out straight, they would cover the distance from the newly created planet to its lone moon *half a million times*!'

Xacheriel spun around to face Jether and Michael. 'And when coiled . . .', he gestured to a tiny receptacle the size of a teaspoon, 'all the strands could fit in this. Forty-six chromosomes to each of the new race's living cells. The genotypes of all cells derived from a particular cell will be precisely the same – unless . . .' Xacheriel frowned and glowered at them from under his eyebrows. 'Unless a mutation occurs,' he declared ominously.

'Which is, of course, inconceivable,' Jether added hurriedly.

Strident cries filtered down the corridors of the ladder. 'Xacheriel . . . Xacheriel, milord!'

Xacheriel sighed deeply. 'Apprentices, apprentices!' He vanished, instantly transported back to the main portal.

Jether moved his palm in front of himself and Michael. They watched as a group of loud and obviously distressed younglings burst into the inner chamber, with each step bowing profusely to the impatient Xacheriel, who glowered darkly at them. The trembling younglings stared at him, almost in rapture.

Xacheriel muttered, 'Who disturbs my musings *this* time?'

'Milord, milord!'

The leader of the group grabbed Xacheriel's hand and clung to it desperately. 'A thousand pardons for disturbing you, sire . . . A thousand pardons . . .'

Xacheriel prised his hand free with immense difficulty. 'What *is* it?'

The tiniest youngling piped up. 'Dimnah's head is stuck!'

The leader added, 'In the electrofission cathode!'

'And on fire!' a second tiny youngling piped up.

Xacheriel slammed his stick on the ground. 'Enough!'

'With blue flames . . .'

'*Enough!* Quite enough! Dimnah!' He hurried out of the portal, waving the younglings forward in haste.

'Come, Michael,' Jether said, strangely solemn. 'There is something I must show you.'

Michael followed him to the very edge of the portal. He gazed upward to where Jether looked, incredulous.

In the distance before them blew a stormy wind, and out

of the wind burned a great cloud with a fire. Great flashes of lightning came out of the fire. In the centre of the burning flames were four living creatures: the mighty cherubim of Yehovah. Each living creature had four faces and four wings. Their legs were straight and the soles of their feet were as the soles of a calf's foot, and they sparkled like burnished bronze. Each had the face of an angel in the front, the face of a lion on the right-hand side, and the face of an ox on the left-hand side. They bowed in worship to the Ancient of Days.

'The sacred vaults,' Jether uttered.

Michael stared in amazement. He bowed his head. 'Yehovah's wonders . . .'

'The treasuries of the snow,' Jether whispered in awe. 'The storehouse of the ordinances of the heavens. And the holding place for Yehovah's greatest gift bestowed on man, Michael . . .' He stopped, overcome by emotion. 'Free will.'

Michael took a step back, stunned.

Jether gestured beyond the seraphim. 'It resides here,' he whispered. 'It has been programmed into the genome.'

'But–' Michael started.

Jether stared at him gently and slowly nodded. 'But what if they misuse it?' He softly finished Michael's thought.

Michael nodded, dazed. 'We, the angelic, who live within the fire of his presence, have been endowed with free will – and we have still to be proven, Jether!' Michael's voice rose with passion. 'Each and every moon we have to be proven.'

'You mean, what of mere mortals?' Jether smiled at him compassionately. 'What if they were to become renegade?'

Michael nodded, ashen. 'It cannot be borne even to think on it.'

Jether looked long and hard at Michael. 'He would have them love him by their *choice*, Michael. He will not force them.'

'Such a risk . . .', Michael echoed, incredulous.

Jether shook his head. 'You mean, if they fail him?' He moved his hand, and immediately they were back again, standing in the central portal. 'Such is the enormity of his love,' he answered quietly, a sense of wonder transforming his features.

'Ahem . . .'

Someone cleared his throat behind them. They turned.

Charsoc, one of eight ruling monarchs of the Ancient Ones, stood at the portal door. Majestic, his noble features clothed with wisdom, he was attired in the flowing crimson royal robes of heaven's kings. He bowed, his long white hair and beard sweeping the crystal floor. 'The council is gathered, my revered Jether. We await your report with great anticipation.'

'When will the new race be ready?' Michael asked.

Jether's eyes lit up in exhilaration. 'Very soon.'

CHAPTER FOUR

Eden

Michael stood a long while on Earth's surface, staring up towards the firmament, marvelling at its palette of cerises and lilacs, sapphires and ambers. He wrapped his deep blue cloak around him and strode towards his chariot to resume searching the heavens for signs of Lucifer as he had the past hour.

Far in the distance there was a sudden thundering as Lucifer's monstrous golden chariot became visible through the clouds, riding the shafts of lightning, pulled by eight of his finest winged stallions, their glistening white manes intertwined with platinum. The chariot's huge silver wheels touched down and ploughed through the soft brown dirt of Earth's surface, drawing to an uneasy halt. Lucifer stood, an imperial figure, his ermine cloak flying behind him, his ruby crown on the raven hair.

Michael stared at him gravely.

'Yes, yes.' Lucifer stepped down from the chariot and strode towards Michael. 'I am late, brother!' He bowed and kissed Michael in affection. 'Forgive me.' Lucifer swirled around dramatically. 'So . . . this is what all the furore in heaven is about!' He knelt and picked up a handful of earth, letting the fresh dirt slip through his fingers. 'As I surmised,' he said disdainfully, surveying the stark brown terrain of Earth's surface. 'It has absolutely no exonerating features.'

He lifted his arms to the heavens. 'Ponder on Gardesia, where the volcanoes spew molten gold. Or Seraphia, where the grains of sand are rosy pearls and the thousand pale lilac moons exude their lights.' He sighed deeply as he strode over newly budding shoots of emerald grass beneath his feet. 'Think of *Eden*, where the meadows are bulrushes of golden hues and the rainforests are laden with the elixir of life.'

Michael narrowed his eyes. 'Be not so easily disappointed, Lucifer. I have a surprise that will hearten your conceptions of this small, new world.'

'Michael, even if it was a veritable Eden it would be hard-pressed to win my favour.' Lucifer sighed deeply.

Michael clasped Lucifer's shoulders, suddenly earnest. 'But you see, dear brother' – he stared at Lucifer in sheer exhilaration – 'it *is* Eden!'

Michael mounted one of his stallions and sped over the lush green meadows towards the eastern side of planet Earth, followed by Lucifer astride one of the horses from his chariot. As they neared the entrance to Earth's Eden, Michael drew in his reins, staring in awe at the sight before them, his face shining.

Lucifer came to a halt, silent, staring out towards the two enormous pearl gates towering in the distance. He struggled to disregard the appalling premonition that beyond the gates lay a precise reproduction of the Hanging Gardens of Eden and the great Waters of Eden that would drop a full mile down into the Eternal Fountains.

'The race of men is truly beloved of our Father.' Michael stared ahead in wonder. 'He has replicated Eden for them.'

Lucifer flinched, then stared grimly ahead, pulling on his

stallion's reins. He raced his horse across the golden bulrush meadows, on through the lush rainforests, the same heavy elixir-laden undergrowth as in the First Heaven drenching him as he rode. Then his eyes locked on the incredible vista before him.

The monumental Waterfalls of Nectar thundered a hundred leagues down, reflecting the changing rainbow hues of Eden's horizon. Lined by ancient willows, its hallowed streams flowed north, south, east, and west out of the lush, tropical celestial gardens, watering Earth. The same unicorns and oryx that grazed in the fields of the angelic Eden were grazing in the Eden of Earth. Lucifer recognized birds of paradise, rainbow-hued flamingos, and blue griffins, plus other exotic creations that were unfamiliar to him.

Incredulous, he dismounted, his hands trembling on the reins. He strode swiftly through the same knee-high gladioli and frangipani, and the same beds of pale blue tulips with long crystal stamens that grew in the First Heaven near the second gate.

Slowly Lucifer pushed the gate open. It was almost twelve feet high and two feet in breadth, carved of solid gold and embedded with rubies and diamonds set in a vast jacinth wall that surrounded the entrance to the inner sanctum of Eden.

He stared transfixed towards the furthest corner of the hanging gardens. Two trees stood there, almost wholly enveloped by constantly swirling white mists, their fruit glistening gold in the lightning. To the north of the trees he could see a narrow pearl arbour covered with pomegranate vines laden with lush silver fruits. He knew with a terrible certainty that beyond the hanging blossoms of the Gardens of Fragrance would be the simple wooden gate.

'He would walk with them . . .', Lucifer murmured.

Very slowly, Michael lifted his gaze to Lucifer's face as

he stared ahead at the grotto at the very edge of the Cliffs of Eden, surrounded by eight ancient olive trees. A harrowing look of intense suffering clouded Lucifer's features. A solitary tear fell down his cheek. His whisper was barely audible.

'He has abandoned us.'

CHAPTER FIVE

Matins

The council of twenty-four long-bearded ancient kings sat at silent matins around a carved mahogany dining table, elaborately set as for a lavish feast. Each white head, adorned with a golden crown, was bowed, rapt in worship. A sleeping owl perched on each monarch's shoulder.

Jether sat next to Charsoc and Xacheriel, who was snoring deafeningly in Charsoc's ear. Charsoc opened one eye, frowning just as Xacheriel's monocle fell with a splash into his steaming broth.

Xacheriel woke with a start. 'Oh, drat and bumble!' he spluttered.

Charsoc glowered at Xacheriel as all the other forty-four eyes opened at once, gazing ominously at the semi-blinded Xacheriel fumbling for the monocle in his broth, which had spattered onto his beard. Lightning flamed up from the broth onto the table. Jether surreptitiously wiped his mouth with a large, white napkin as Xacheriel tried most ineffectively to put the flames out with his own napkin, which caught fire from the leaping flames.

A youngling named Rakkon hurried over, closely followed by Dimnah, who enthusiastically poured an entire flagon of

60

elixir over the burning napkin *and* Xacheriel's head. Jether smothered a loud laugh. Xacheriel stood, now drenched and fuming, as Jether fished the monocle out of the broth while Dimnah attempted to wipe the seething Xacheriel down with a towel, apologizing profusely between his multiple bowings.

The other twenty-two elders retreated back to their private matins, again in rapturous prayer, while Xacheriel, still spluttering and gasping, strode from the room, followed by the languishing Dimnah.

Jether looked out from the corner of his eye towards Charsoc, whose countenance was hidden behind a large white napkin. His shoulders were shaking in a most unmonarchlike manner. Jether started to shake with merriment. He leaned over to whisper in Charsoc's ear, and immediately the two elders vanished.

They reappeared together on the High Place of the Tower of Winds, the retreat of the eight elders who formed the High Council of Heaven. A hundred enormous white owls, perched on the battlements, screeched in delight when they saw Jogli and Bashkar, Charsoc's owl, on the two Ancient Ones' shoulders.

'Let us walk, ancient friend.' Jether clasped Charsoc's arm as Jogli and Bashkar flew to join their compatriots. They walked in easy companionship through the lush gardens and past the water fountains and manicured hedges, their conversation low and intimate. Charsoc from time to time laughed into his handkerchief at the recollection of Xacheriel's mishap. They rested by the sapphire fountains, the water cascading down as glistening blue mercury.

Jether held out a goblet to catch the elixir. 'Ah,' he said, a smile of satisfaction crossing his face, 'tayberry and white currant!'

Charsoc held his goblet under the flowing elixir. He sipped delicately. 'Harebell and honeysuckle,' he murmured, gratified. He plucked a silvered sweetmeat from a large tree hung with thousands of white blossoms and delicacies. He broke it in half, revealing a glowing white meringue-like mixture bound with a thick custard-like substance. He popped it in his mouth, savouring it. 'A sublime mix of raspberry cream and persimmon.' He closed his eyes in rapture. 'With a hint of curds!'

Jether moved to the centre of the tower to the large golden table surrounded by eight golden thrones where the angelic zephyrs of wisdom and revelation raged in eternal cyclones. He sat down on one of the eight jacinth thrones, and the zephyrs immediately subsided to a gentle breeze. Jether breathed in the invigorating aromas of the myrrh and frangipani that swirled in the gusts over his head. 'Tell me of your musings, revered friend.'

Charsoc sat on his throne and closed his eyes in bliss. 'I reflect on the sacred mysteries of Yehovah and of my journeyings to the treasuries of the winds and the snow,' Charsoc crooned, breathing deeply of the zephyrs. 'I think of the sacred vaults of the cherubim. I muse on the instant I witnessed Yehovah as he spread out the firmaments of the universes as a molten mirror . . . I have seen where the winds take their course and the hail is formed.' He inhaled the perfume of frankincense and closed his eyes. 'All these marvels of the angelic universe, I ponder.'

They sat in silence a long while.

'Yet you are disquieted, my age-old compatriot,' Jether said.

Charsoc opened his eyes. He clasped Jether's old veined hand in his own. 'You are too much a seer, my time-honoured companion.'

Jether nodded. 'We have travelled many roads these past aeons, venerable friend. I know there is aught that weighs upon your soul.'

Charsoc rose and walked to the very edge of the Tower of Winds, where the zephyrs raged more fiercely. He turned to Jether, his hair and robes blowing violently in the rushing tempests. 'The sanctity of our angelic world must be protected at all costs, Jether.' He spoke softly but with passion.

Charsoc strode away from the tempests back towards the lush manicured gardens. Bashkar flew at once to his master's outstretched hand. Charsoc looked back at Jether over his shoulder. 'Do not fret for me, cherished friend.'

And he vanished into the white rushing mists.

CHAPTER SIX

The Revelator

Gabriel tossed and turned on the royal blue silk sheets, sweat pouring from his brow onto his pillow. His breathing was shallow and erratic. His eyes were tightly shut, his flaxen hair matted with sweat. 'Sedition,' he muttered.

Michael stood at the door of his bedchamber. He stared at Gabriel, his face troubled. He strode over to his brother's side. 'Gabriel,' he whispered, grasping his shoulders.

Gabriel's eyes rolled back.

Michael shook him. 'Gabriel!'

Slowly Gabriel's eyes focused. He sat up, trembling. 'Michael . . . the dreamings . . . they have become unendurable of late.' Great sobs racked Gabriel's chest. 'Kingdoms rising . . . falling. The race of men . . . Yehovah . . . treason.' He flung his hands over his face.

Michael stared at his younger brother. Helpless.

'There is no danger in our world, Gabriel,' he pleaded. 'It is just dreamings . . . imaginings.'

'Michael?' Jether's voice was soft.

Michael turned, visibly distressed, to Jether, who stood in the doorway. 'Each night I have heard his screams, Jether. He suffers so. It becomes intolerable.'

Jether moved towards the bed, and the light from Eden's pale moons fell across his face. It was drawn. Haggard. 'It is the cost for the gift he bears, Michael.' Jether was quiet for a long moment. 'He is the Revelator, Yehovah's seer. Each night his dreamings take him through the aeons to future worlds. He sees the travesties, the devastation, that are yet to be wreaked upon our kingdom. He carries these visions in his heart and in his mind.'

Michael shook his head, confused.

Jether smiled compassionately. 'You, my son, bear a different burden. Gabriel, the Revelator; Michael, the warrior.' Jether closed his eyes. 'The wars he sees, you will yet fight. Great will be your lot in the aeons to come.'

'And Lucifer?'

Jether was silent. His forehead furrowed. 'Leave us, Michael. I would comfort him.'

Michael bowed in respect, kissed Jether on both cheeks, and strode though the bedchamber doors.

Jether placed his wizened hand on the trembling Gabriel's shoulder. 'I too am a seer, Gabriel. I see in part what you have seen, my son.'

Gabriel slowly raised his tear-stained face.

'The risings and the fallings of worlds upon worlds,' Jether continued softly. 'The treasons ... the blasphemies ... the wars ... the devastation.'

'Desertion,' Gabriel whispered. 'The race of men. Yehovah is deserted!'

'Yes, desertion,' Jether murmured. 'You have seen truly, Gabriel. But that is not what haunts your dreams.'

Gabriel eased his legs over the bed and rose, flinging his mantle over his unsteady limbs. He moved to the massive windows of his bedchamber, staring out at the amethyst waters lapping at the pearl sands. He lit a vast bowl of myrrh. 'You read my soul, Jether. That is not what haunts my dreams.' He turned to Jether. 'I cannot speak of it.' Great sobs wracked his frame. 'He must be warned! He could not do such a thing.'

Gabriel and Jether stared at each other for a long while in the darkness.

'I will go to him,' Gabriel said.

'His love for you is very powerful.' Jether looked at Gabriel, his face etched with grief. 'It is second only to his love for Yehovah. Guard your mind. Guard your soul. My supplications will be with you.'

Jether vanished.

CHAPTER SEVEN

Man

'Follow me, Your Excellencies!' Xacheriel's deep voice boomed down the central portal corridors as he paced excitedly towards an enormous steel vault. Dimnah trailed behind him, attempting to hold Xacheriel's train in his vain efforts to keep up with his tutor.

Xacheriel stopped abruptly outside the vault and swung around to face Michael, Gabriel, and Lucifer, his eyes lit with exhilaration. 'Dimnah!' he proclaimed. 'You are dismissed!'

Dimnah bowed deeply and scuttled away down the corridor as fast as his short legs could carry him.

Jether walked towards them, tall and majestic, Charsoc following a step behind him. 'My Chief Princes,' Jether declared, 'this is truly a sacred moment.'

Xacheriel reached deep in his robe pockets and fumbled around in irritation. 'Drat and bumble!' he declared.

Jether coughed politely. 'Ahem.'

Xacheriel glowered at him.

'*Ahem.*' Jether's cough become more meaningful.

Xacheriel followed Jether's gaze to the large vault key hanging around his neck. He blushed and spluttered and placed the key in the vault entrance.

Slowly the heavy steel door opened.

The three archangel brothers and the two Ancient Ones followed Xacheriel into the outer vault, then through a second door until they all stood in the centre of a smaller inner portal.

All at once, there was a roaring above the portal atrium as the crystal cupola directly over the small assembly opened, and a vast, brilliant chamber of light began to descend. As the angels watched in awe, a figure swathed in brilliant, shimmering light became visible in the centre of the brilliance, suspended two full leagues above the ground.

Charsoc stared as the light gradually settled, magnetized to the descending figure. 'Man,' he whispered in awe.

Gabriel stared at the figure, captivated. The prototype, now hovering just above the ground, appeared to be completely covered by a thin, incandescent clayish layer. Gabriel noticed that it was at least a cubit shorter than the angels and had no discernible wings. Its outer layers were created of matter and therefore appeared much duller than the translucent angelic bodies. He could not be sure, but it seemed that the atoms that continually radiated around the angelic host were missing. But it was beautiful. He stared, incredulous. With great difficulty he drew his gaze away to Michael. 'Its features are flawless!' His face shone. 'As the angels . . .'

'It is *not* angelic!' Lucifer retorted.

Michael gazed strangely at Lucifer.

Gabriel frowned. 'It *looks* angelic, Lucifer.'

'You *insult* us.' A dark, fleeting fury crossed Lucifer's countenance. 'Brother.'

Gabriel stepped back from Lucifer, perplexed.

'Lucifer,' Jether said, placing his hand gently on Lucifer's arm, 'you forget yourself.'

Lucifer stared grimly ahead, his fist clenching the balustrade in front of him.

Jether bowed his head a moment in reverence. Slowly he opened his eyes. 'My revered angelic princes, I have mentored and served you throughout the aeons, but I tell you that never in the annals of the First Heaven has there been such a day as this.'

'A new race,' Charsoc said in wonder, 'created in his own likeness.'

'The race of men is not fashioned as we, the angelic,' Xacheriel explained, his face shining with rapture. 'We, the angelic race, are each individually created by Yehovah. Fearfully and wonderfully fashioned. Yet we hold no ability to replicate ourselves.'

'Yehovah has endowed the race of men with the capacity to create after its own kind.' Jether turned to Lucifer. 'As does Yehovah.'

Lucifer averted his gaze from Jether's.

'In his image,' Charsoc whispered.

Lucifer, overcome by sheer fascination, moved nearer towards the prototype. He stared at the features of the man, studying intently the high cheekbones, the strong jaw line, the chestnut hair. 'It is strangely familiar.'

Charsoc stared at him intently for a long moment. 'Have you not yet guessed, Lucifer?'

Lucifer frowned.

Charsoc raised his gaze to the prototype, then back down to Lucifer. 'His image is that of Christos.'

Gabriel stared at the prototype, incredulous.

Michael was rapt in worship, exultant, his face shining. Slowly he turned his head to Lucifer, who was staring blindly at the prototype and trembling, his senses reeling with a terrible, searing, violent jealousy.

And it was then, as Michael watched, that Lucifer lifted his head from the prototype. His eyes glittered hard and black, filled with loathing.

He was staring up through the crystal cupola directly towards Yehovah's throne.

And all the while Charsoc was observing Lucifer.

CHAPTER EIGHT

Treason

Lucifer strode down the imposing marble corridors, his imperial figure wrapped in a hooded crimson robe that billowed out behind him. He stopped outside the two huge onyx doors of his palace library. Eight Luciferian guards bowed prostrate in reverence. 'Zadkiel!'

Zadkiel stepped out, as though from nowhere, and bowed deeply.

'You have it?' Lucifer enquired.

Zadkiel spoke in his usual refined tones. 'From the inner sanctum of the Tower of Winds itself, Your Excellency.'

Lucifer grasped Zadkiel's arm, drawing him down the library corridors and past the magnificent frescos. 'You have been discreet?' Lucifer's eyes were searching.

'The curators will not miss the codices, Your Excellency, and by dawn they will be returned.'

Lucifer stopped in mid-stride. He nodded. 'Of course.' He hesitated. 'You know . . . that Yehovah would have given me access?'

Zadkiel nodded, his gaze troubled. 'Of course, sire. You are Yehovah's prince of the highest order.'

'Nothing is withheld from me by my Father.'

'Of course, Your Excellency. Your throne is second only to his.'

Lucifer continued again through the corridors without breaking his stride.

'It is more expedient this way, Zadkiel.'

Zadkiel nodded. 'Yes, Your Majesty.'

Lucifer stopped in front of eight large columns. 'There will be no disturbances, no interruptions, until my investigations are complete.'

'The Holy Watchers shall ensure you are uninterrupted till dawn, Your Excellency.'

'Good. Summon my high command – my thousand generals – to the Chamber of Congregation at six bells.'

'I will give your command, Your Excellency.'

Lucifer stalked past the columns, past the warriors into his library chambers. The warriors bowed low.

The doors slammed.

Thousands of ancient books and tomes lined the circular chamber walls of Lucifer's palace library: anthologies of worship and glorification, of ethereal bodies, of the music of the spheres. Their ancient casings were magnificently cast with Lucifer's royal crest in ornate silver and gold filigree. Stacked to the ceiling in his palace archives, on the far side of the library, were ancient documents, manuscripts, scrolls of parchment, and codices: the Seals of Yehovah, the Holy Writ of the Ancient of Days, the antiquities of the First Heaven.

Lucifer threw off his hood, revealing the ruby-studded golden crown that rested on his gleaming raven hair. He moved straight to the black marble table in the centre of the enormous circular chamber, where ten large, gold-bound codices engraved with ancient angelic writings rested in the centre of the table.

He opened the first codex unceremoniously, rifling through the pages. Impatient, he passed his hand over the angelic writings and a bluish, lightning-like electric beam arced from his palm through the pages of the codex, which started to radiate with heat.

Lucifer gave a triumphant laugh. The fluorescent emissions gradually took form, metamorphosing into a life-size hologram of the matter prototype Lucifer had watched hours earlier in the crystal dome: man. He stared, enthralled, as the prototype executed a three-dimensional, 360-degree rotation, displaying muscles, sinews, and blood vessels. An automated voice delivered the scientific narrative: 'Fifty million living units – termination – cells – millions die each second – immediate replenishment. Average cell measures 0.025 millimetres.'

With a wave of Lucifer's hand, the narration abruptly halted.

'Yes, yes,' he muttered in irritation, '*Homo sapiens* software.'

He slammed the codex closed in exasperation and moved his palm down the spine of a second codex. Virtual indices of the contents of the hologram displayed themselves in the air. Lucifer pushed that codex aside, his eyes flashing with impatience.

He reached for the third codex. His hand hovered over the cover, and the modulated voice responded: 'Level seven, biogenetic engineering.'

A slow smile spread across Lucifer's face. He opened the codex and paged through it rapaciously . . . then stopped. The air filled with millions of pulsing, animated blue numerals. He stared at the arcing numbers, moving his palm through the myriad calculations.

The modulated voice expounded: 'Species *Homo sapiens* – recipient of gene prototype 78777722619865384750684 59936485926374893752426787777119964289364759403 910098177.'

Lucifer hesitated, mystified. He frowned. 'Not the code for angelic DNA.'

His palm ran like quicksilver over the angelic writings. Thousands of virtual number patterns appeared and blinked out, but one continued flashing. Lucifer hesitated, then repeated the procedure, his breathing shallow, his mouth moving incoherently. With ultimate precision, he checked and rechecked the readings.

A look of horror crossed his face. The hologram rotated in the air. 'It's *his* genetic code!'

He turned the page, his hand trembling. He watched the animated hologram, ashen-faced, as an almost exact female replica was *surgically cloned* from the male *Homo sapiens* prototype. *Sharing the same DNA.*

The hologram zoomed in on a fertilized egg. Lucifer watched incredulously as the image progressed from an egg to a foetus to a baby.

He looked up, dazed. '*It's going to replicate!*' he muttered feverishly. '*He's duplicating* his *gene . . . in matter!*' He ran his hand distractedly through his hair. '*Th– they'll be immortal . . . intelligent . . . cognizant.*'

He turned to the ceiling, his face contorted with rage and loathing. 'What have we done that you would so betray the angelic race?' He pushed the chair out from under him and stood, hands raised towards the Holy Mountain, desperate. 'Is our love not sufficient for you? All over the First Heaven our praises ring out in adoration!' His voice shook with passion. 'Our devotion is unequivocal,' he cried, pacing the chamber in his agitation. 'Our allegiance is beyond question. Our veneration is undeniable. The angelic hosts – we who pay tribute to you . . .' He stared about him, frantic. 'You have *me*, the light-bearer – the archangel who covers your presence – to revere and adore you.'

He smashed his fist onto the table. 'What *more* do you demand?'

Gabriel walked through the unending corridors of Lucifer's palace, his features set. This night he would unveil to his elder brother the agonies and visions that had tormented him these past moons. He would warn him.

Gabriel rounded a corner and frowned. The corridors were strangely deserted. Where were Lucifer's guards? He saw the light spilling from under the enormous golden doors of Lucifer's library. He strode towards them.

With a smouldering fury, Lucifer tore the golden crown from his head and flung it across the floor – just as the heavy golden doors burst open.

Gabriel stood in the doorway, surveying the scene. The crown slid across the onyx floor, finally tumbling to a stop at his feet. Slowly Gabriel closed the doors, then bent down and picked up the golden crown and walked to Lucifer, stopping directly in front of him.

Lucifer stared at the floor. Then, inch by inch, he lifted his gaze to meet Gabriel's. 'Yehovah!' He gestured towards the codices on the marble table. 'He would replace us as the object of his affections.'

Gabriel walked slowly around the table until he was face to face with Lucifer. He stared down at the codices, then lifted his eyes to meet Lucifer's gaze. Lucifer drew closer, so close that Gabriel could feel his hot breath on his cheeks.

'The perfect genetic code,' Lucifer hissed, 'encased in matter, replicating for eternity. The universe shall be consumed by them!'

Gabriel spoke barely above a whisper. 'You speak of man.'

'Man!' Lucifer spat.

Gabriel bowed his head. 'I came to you this night, Lucifer, for I have dreamed many dreams lately. Your countenance has been foremost in all my dreamings.' He hesitated. 'I dream of desertion, brother. Day and night I see before me Yehovah deserted.'

'Yehovah's plan to create the race of men is ill-founded.' Lucifer drew near to Gabriel and clasped his shoulder. 'If truly we love him we have to discharge him from this folly!'

He stared down at him with adoration. 'Gabriel, don't you comprehend? The dreamings have been granted you to ensure the preservation of the angelic race. You, Gabriel – Revelator – have been entrusted with the inner knowledge of the devastation that will fall upon our kingdoms with the advent of the race of men. He must *desist* with the folly of fashioning this new race!'

Lucifer paced the room, his hands behind his back. 'Is it only the Revelator who sees and discerns? I, seraph, perfect in wisdom, am the interpreter of your dreamings. And the interpretation is thus: a great and menacing danger threatens our world. The race of men, which would supplant our own. Man is the cause of all you suffer in your dreamings.'

Lucifer sat down heavily in his chair. 'What will you do?'

Gabriel spoke in a whisper. 'I know your intention, Lucifer.

It shall not bode well with you if you do what is in your heart.'

'And who made you your brother's keeper?' Lucifer snarled.

Gabriel walked to the door and stopped, speaking without turning. 'Jether will miss the codices if they are not returned.' He closed the doors quietly behind him without a backward glance.

From that day forth Lucifer's words troubled my very being. And as the dreamings intensified so indeed did my turmoil. I could find no respite for my soul.

And what happened next did nothing to allay my fears.

They did not know that I saw them fight that day – that I saw that shocking altercation between them that was the beginning of the end to all that we knew as normality.

Their swordplay began as usual, at the twilight of the sixth moon, in the upper turret nearest the throne room wing, where Michael and Lucifer would fence and practise their swordsmanship. They fenced with vigour, as they always did, pitting themselves against each other – and as always, they were well matched in strength and swordsmanship. They had parried for aeons each dusk, but this was to be a different night . . .

CHAPTER NINE

The Sword Chamber

Michael and Lucifer fenced with vigour. The sharp steel of the broadswords gleamed as they thrust and parried.

Lucifer raised his fencing mask. There was an unnatural glint in his eye as he stared at Michael. He held his broadsword high. 'He is isolating me!' Lucifer parried away Michael's thrust deftly.

'You isolate yourself, dear brother.'

The parrying and thrusting became more intense, the clashing of steel more violent.

'He is *preoccupied*,' Lucifer said, hesitating in mid-thrust. 'He has refused my presence three times in these past hundred moons.'

Michael raised his fencing mask, his clear green eyes perplexed. 'He would not refuse without good reason, my brother.'

Lucifer bowed mockingly. 'Chief Prince Michael . . .' He brought the flat of his sword down violently on Michael's diaphragm, winding him. Michael doubled over in agony. A strange anger clouded Lucifer's features. 'Pray enlighten me.'

Michael stared at Lucifer in disbelief. 'Lucifer, hold your *temper*!'

'Could it be his latest obsession?' Lucifer took a deep breath, almost spitting the words out. 'This . . . this . . . man!'

He lunged viciously at the unguarded Michael, the razor edge of the gleaming broadsword plunging straight through Michael's sword shoulder. Lucifer kept the pressure on the blade until a dark purple stain bled through Michael's white fencing robe. Michael's sword clattered to the floor.

Michael slowly removed his fencing mask with his good arm, his thick flaxen hair falling to his shoulders. Pain and fury clouded his features as he leaned against the wall of the sword chamber, still pinned by Lucifer's blade. 'Give it up, Lucifer! Before you are consumed by your own darkness.'

A slow, vindictive smile spread across Lucifer's face. '*You* have his ear now – *you* tell Yehovah.' He stood, a majestic figure, right over Michael. 'Tell him that I *will* not be spurned . . . and that *this*, dearest brother,' he said with a swift movement that lacerated Michael's bleeding wound, 'is just a warning that to discard the son of the morning could be a *very* dangerous exercise.'

Michael reeled in agony, cradling his shoulder. He slumped back, splaying a purple bloodstain across the white wall.

Lucifer flung the broadsword down. It clattered across the chamber. A darkening shadow fell from his form across Michael as Lucifer strode out through the turret door.

Michael stared after him, trembling, his blazing green eyes filled with fury and a deep foreboding.

CHAPTER TEN

Seeds of Sedition

The Elite Guard, the ten thousand angelic generals of Lucifer's high command, were attired in full ceremonial regalia. The black diamonds on their breastplates glistening, their heads held high, the commanders in charge of a full third of the angelic host directed their gaze at the huge gold and onyx gates of the Chamber of Congregation, far in the distance. Awaiting their commander-in-chief.

A fanfare of shofars sounded as the towering gates slowly opened. Lucifer strode in, all-glorious. His crimson cloak billowed behind him, his regent's crown atop his raven locks, his imperial features grave. The Elite Guard stood to attention and saluted.

Lucifer's voice rang out. 'All hail Yehovah!'

'All hail Yehovah!' The generals roared in unison. They fell to one knee in worship.

Lucifer raised his hand and immediately they rose, their heads bowed in respect. Lucifer took his throne. His men took their seats on lesser thrones, arranged in one huge square around the gigantic chamber.

Lucifer stared for a long time around the room, drinking

in the spectacle of his ten thousand glorious warriors – truly the elite of heaven.

'A great and menacing shadow has fallen across our world,' he said. He was so charged with emotion that his voice literally broke with fervour. 'My glorious warriors, we face a terrible and impending danger.' He motioned to Charsoc to stand, then cast his eyes to the marble floor.

'A peril so menacing,' Charsoc continued, his voice silken, 'that it threatens the very existence of our own angelic race.' He surveyed the shocked faces before him.

One of Lucifer's generals stood to his feet, his noble features perplexed. 'Who would think to threaten our existence? Who could mount such an assault?'

A second stood. 'Our universe is one of such glory – of goodness. What evil or danger could possibly imperil us?'

Lucifer stood to his feet. Slowly he surveyed the room.

Zadkiel, who stood on Lucifer's right side, lifted his head in bewilderment. A sudden frown marred his beautiful countenance as he watched Lucifer survey the room, all eyes fixed on him.

'It is the new race that threatens our very existence,' Lucifer declared, raising his face to the heavens.

He rose and strode towards the assembled thrones until he stood just a breadth away from the row of his most glorious generals – his high command. He leaned towards them benevolently, like a mother soothing an anxious child, and adopted an intimate, coaxing tone. 'I studied the codices first-hand last dusk. The new race does not hold our own angelic gene.' Lucifer raised his eyes to the enormous crystal dome above the chamber. He was silent for a long moment. 'Yehovah duplicates his own gene . . . in matter . . . in *man*.' Lucifer studied the disbelief on the faces before him.

Charsoc walked around the square formation, his bony

hands clasped behind his back, his spine straight, his penetrating pale blue eyes locked on Lucifer. 'This race is not as us – the angelic,' Charsoc said. 'We are *created* beings. Each one of the angelic – you and me – has been individually created. But this race of men . . . Yehovah has endowed upon them the ability to *replicate*. They create after their own kind!'

'Think of it,' Lucifer murmured, running his fingers through his unbraided locks. 'The perfect genetic code, encased in matter . . . replicating for eternity.' He let the sentence sink in. '"Why?" I pleaded with him. "Lucifer," he said, "We would have fellowship with that which is created in our image."'

The ten thousand elite watched, transfixed, as Lucifer – shaking visibly – untied the ribbons on his gauntlet. His fingers trembling, he ripped open his bodice, baring his chest. 'He has given them *Eden*! When man is created, no more will I be his light-bearer!' He turned to his generals. 'No more will *you* be his morning song. Don't you see? I would rip my heart from my breast rather than see the angelic host supplanted.' He stopped. 'By the race of *men*!'

Raphael, Lucifer's commander-in-chief and companion, stood to his feet. He was tall and imperial, his noble features set. As he stood, a thousand generals rose and bowed. Raphael moved to where Lucifer stood and stopped directly in front of him. He bowed deeply, then dropped to one knee. 'My esteemed and acclaimed sovereign.'

Lucifer's expression softened. 'Raphael,' he murmured. 'Archangel and finest of warriors – trusted compatriot.' Lucifer reached out his hand, and Raphael kissed the seal of Yehovah, the huge, black rubied ring on Lucifer's left ring finger. Raphael rose and stared straight into Lucifer's eyes, and Lucifer sighed deeply. 'I observe that my discourse disquiets you, Raphael.'

Raphael bowed his head. 'I confess I am vexed, my prince.'

Zadkiel watched them. Frozen.

Lucifer turned away from Raphael. 'I *also* am vexed that Yehovah would seek to supplant his first-born creation with an inferior race!'

Raphael moved in front of Lucifer and clasped his shoulders. 'Lucifer, ancient friend, you speak of sedition? You accuse the Most High?' Raphael stared at Lucifer, bewildered, his eyes raw with vulnerability. 'I beseech you in the name of our friendship, retract your charge!'

Lucifer carefully removed Raphael's hands from his shoulders. 'Why, my revered Raphael, surely the definition of sedition is incitement to rebellion? That is *not* what I seek!' Lucifer stared at Raphael, a strange burning fervour lighting his gaze. 'I seek only to protect the angelic host.'

Raphael gazed at him in confusion. Then realization dawned on his face. He looked at Lucifer fearfully, then cast his eyes to the marble floor.

Charsoc paced about the chamber as Lucifer assessed the mood of his Elite Guard.

Raphael lifted his head, his face ravaged by anguish. 'My prince, Yehovah sees fit to create this new race. My duty and hallowed vocation is to serve him and execute his will in every matter.'

He stared ahead. Impassive.

'Including . . . the issue of man.'

'It does not bode well for the angelic race, Raphael,' Charsoc interjected.

With a short sharp gesture, Raphael removed his gauntlets and cast them on the ground before Lucifer. 'I will have no part in aught of your intrigues!'

Lucifer, swift as lightning, removed his golden cinquedea from its sheath and slashed Raphael's rows of diamond medallions from his breastplate.

Raphael raised his head, his imperial features forbidding. He turned to the generals and drew his sword. 'He defiles this sanctuary with the iniquity of his trading! I shall not abide it.'

Raphael strode out of the Chamber, followed by his thousand generals. Charsoc watched intently as an additional ten, then hundreds, then thousands of Lucifer's finest generals rose from across the chamber and followed. The great platinum doors of the Chamber of Congregation slammed shut behind them.

A sombre silence fell. Zadkiel stared uneasily around at the remaining generals, then at Lucifer. He lowered his gaze.

Lucifer fell to his knees, his arms raised towards heaven. 'Great and Mighty Yehovah, you who are both adored and incomparable, I beseech you in your great and terrible mercies to absolve your angelic servant Raphael and his warriors for their rash and insolent insurgence against your servant Lucifer – your light-bearer and chosen angelic son. May they repent and be restored once more to your eternal mercy and glory. Grant to all these generals who remain your divine valour and fortitude to endure what lies ahead in the crusade to preserve our angelic race.'

Lucifer raised his head. 'And Great Yehovah, incomparable king of the universe, grant myself – prince regent, highest of the seraphim, and second only to your throne – eternal wisdom and revelation to protect you from the machinations of this new race, the race of men.'

Lucifer wrapped his crimson ermine-trimmed cloak around him and walked to his large throne. He sat heavily and held out his hand. Sachiel, his cupbearer, handed him a jewelled goblet filled with pomegranate elixir. Lucifer sipped deeply. Thoughtfully.

'Contemplate, my glorious generals, such a day.' A slow strange smile spread across Lucifer's face. 'A day that indisputably has yet to dawn on this remarkable planet of heaven with its staggering vistas,' Lucifer caressed the rim of the goblet as he spoke, 'its unsurpassed beauty, its unparalleled mysteries. Think of that very day and that very hour when this new race shall invade and occupy our own angelic sanctuary – and desecrate all that is pure and holy and sacred with their inferior creation. Contemplate that day and that hour well, for surely with each waking dawn it hastens, glorious warriors. One by one this new race will seek to exploit the multitude of Yehovah's tender mercies, his manifold compassions.'

Lucifer rose to his feet and strode down the aisle of the chamber, his darkened eyes flashing. 'It will not stop at Eden! They will winnow their way into his inner sanctum.' His voice became a hiss. 'Dusk after dusk they will drive a wedge between us, the angelic host, and Yehovah – until Yehovah's desire for man's fellowship becomes so compelling that he will have them be with him where he dwells!'

He swung around, his features fierce. 'Here in heaven – in our angelic abode. Then *they* will seek to be as he is. They will seek to turn heaven into their dwelling place. Our holy sanctuary will be desecrated by these replicated, mewling, inferior beasts. It is a travesty! If *truly* we serve Yehovah, we will protect him against his splendid and overwhelming love for them.'

Lucifer stopped abruptly. Slowly, as though suddenly sensing he was being observed, he lifted his gaze upward. There far above him, barely visible in the upper portico of the crystal dome, stood a tall hooded figure.

'Reveal yourself!' Lucifer commanded. Charsoc stared, pale and trembling.

The figure remained motionless, his countenance concealed by the cowled hood.

'Reveal yourself!' Lucifer's voice rose in decibels.

The figure walked around the lofty portico until he was directly in line with Lucifer. 'You were perfect in your ways,' the figure spoke in clear gracious tones, 'from the day you were created . . . till' – he paused – 'till iniquity was found in you.'

Lucifer's features contorted in agony as he felt a sharp burning sensation in his right palm. He cradled his right hand in his left, his breathing laboured, his entire body trembling as he stared down in dread at the darkening crimson stain.

'Christos . . .', he uttered.

CHAPTER ELEVEN

Ebony

Zadkiel, the tender, filled with honour and righteousness, was the kindred spirit and trusted comrade of all three brothers and the chosen intimate of Lucifer, the shining one.

Ephaniah came out of the antechamber. 'Milord Zadkiel!'

Zadkiel's gentle features lit up, and Ephaniah, Lucifer's courtier, hesitated.

'Milord Zadkiel . . . forgive me. May I speak?'

Zadkiel smiled. 'You have served Yehovah's house well and faithfully for many aeons, Ephaniah. Surely you have earned the right to speak.'

'I have served yourself, Master Zadkiel, when you were but a child, as I did His Excellency, Prince Michael.'

Zadkiel nodded.

'And now, for many years, I have served my master Lucifer.' He bowed deeply. 'The shining one.' Ephaniah's hands trembled. 'You know I am devoted to him, sire.'

Zadkiel frowned and placed his strong hand over Ephaniah's. 'Yes, Ephaniah, your love and devotion for Master Lucifer is beyond question. We do not doubt your allegiance,' he soothed, sensing the faithful servant's distress. He clasped Ephaniah's arm. 'Let us walk.'

They strode together through the marble hall, beautiful paintings adorning walls and arched ceiling.

'Thank you, milord,' Ephaniah said. Then he sighed. 'You know that for these past moons my master has been prone to fits.'

Zadkiel nodded, his steel-grey eyes grave.

'And that in those fits of anger, he is apt to do many things that he later regrets.'

'I have known this.' Zadkiel's voice was soft. He thought briefly of how he had brought the sacred codices to Lucifer from the Tower of Winds. That had been but the first of Lucifer's unusual actions of late.

Ephaniah stepped closer to Zadkiel, helplessness in his face. 'He is become more violent, Your Excellency. He rang for me at three bells in the early morning hours, as he has been apt to do these past moons. I found him sobbing, his arms clung around his panther's neck.' Ephaniah trembled in horror. 'Milord Zadkiel, Ebony was lifeless.'

Zadkiel stared at Ephaniah blankly.

Ephaniah grasped his arm. 'He was lifeless, milord! What is termed as *death* had assailed him!'

'Death!' Zadkiel uttered disbelievingly. He stared at Ephaniah as if in a daze.

Ephaniah swallowed. 'My master showed me the wounds. They were the wounds of two bare hands around the beast's still warm neck, milord Zadkiel.' Ephaniah's voice was but a whisper. 'By his own hand . . .'

The blood drained from Zadkiel's face, and he stopped in mid-step, a terrible dread clutching his soul. He shook his head vehemently from side to side. 'No – no! It *cannot* be!' he exclaimed. 'You are mistaken! Death cannot exist here!'

Ephaniah bowed his head. He shook uncontrollably with the sheer horror of what he had seen.

Then a faint clanging of a bell filtered down the corridors to the outer courts.

'It is his bell,' Ephaniah said wearily. 'He rings incessantly, but his door is barred.'

Zadkiel grasped Ephaniah by the shoulders. 'Who knows this?'

'No one knows, sire – no one save yourself and Charsoc.'

Zadkiel ran his fingers through his dark locks. 'The chief princes?'

Ephaniah shook his head.

'They of all *must* know this.'

'His closest staff knows only that Master Lucifer is indisposed.'

Zadkiel released the faithful old manservant. 'Thank you, Ephaniah. I must attend the prince regent at once.'

Ephaniah bowed and scuttled off down the corridors.

Zadkiel strode with speed through the palace and around the corner to the prince regent's quarters. Two members of the Luciferian Guard stood watch at the portal to Lucifer's private wing.

As Zadkiel approached them to pass, Charsoc appeared in the corridor holding a sheaf of official-looking papers with the prince regent's crest.

Charsoc approached Zadkiel. 'Your Excellency, Prince Zadkiel of the Holy Watchers. His Excellency Prince Regent Lucifer, anointed cherub who covers, full of wisdom and perfect in beauty, has made it his express wish that he not be disturbed. He is indisposed.'

Zadkiel stared into the hooded, inscrutable gaze of Charsoc. 'He expressed no such wish to me, Charsoc.'

Charsoc moved to block him. 'He is, let us say, out of sorts.'

'Yes, I am aware that he has isolated himself these past few moons. I would cheer him.'

Charsoc's expression softened momentarily. 'Would that it were so.' He nodded to the bodyguards, and they stood back. Charsoc gave Zadkiel a look that the Holy Watcher found unfathomable.

Zadkiel frowned, wrapped his cloak tighter around himself, and walked through the winding corridors.

At last he stopped outside Lucifer's chamber entrance where two more members of the Luciferian Guard stood watch before the massive golden doors.

The bell clanged incessantly. It seemed to have its source deep within Lucifer's private quarters. Zadkiel looked at the trembling guard.

'He rings the bell, milord.' The normally stoic Luciferian guard looked at Zadkiel almost pleadingly. 'He will not stop.'

Zadkiel nodded to the two members of Lucifer's private guard. 'Open the doors.'

The guard shook his head. 'They are barred from the inside, milord. They will not open.'

Zadkiel put his head to the doors. Beneath the ringing of the bell he was almost certain that he heard the faint sound of a strange, wretched sobbing. He put his mouth to the door. 'Lucifer! It is I, Zadkiel. Let me in.'

There was a long silence. 'Leave me!' a hoarse voice cried out.

Zadkiel paled. He inhaled deeply, then turned to the confused guards. 'Your master is indisposed,' he said gently. 'I, Zadkiel, chief attendant to Lucifer, son of the morning, dismiss you from your posts. You may go to your quarters until you are summoned.'

The guards bowed deeply and marched as one down the corridors, away from the huge golden doors.

Zadkiel removed his gloves and bent down to the keyhole, his eyes filled with consternation. 'Lucifer, it is Zadkiel, your old and trusted friend.' His voice remained gentle.

The clanging stopped.

'Open the doors, Lucifer.'

After a seemingly interminable silence, there came a loud scraping, and slowly the massive doors opened.

Zadkiel entered and slammed the doors closed. He surveyed the room in horror.

Lucifer's clothes were strewn about the chamber floor. He lay with his arms still clinging to the strangled black panther. Its pink tongue hung out. Lucifer looked up from the chamber floor. His normally immaculate raven locks were matted and unkempt and shrouded the perfect, marble-like features. 'Zadkiel!' Relief spread across his face. He grasped for Zadkiel's hand feverishly.

Zadkiel stared down at Lucifer, horrified. He was unwashed and clothed only in his white shift robe, but still he wore his jewel-covered crown.

Lucifer gave Zadkiel one of his magnificent, dazzling smiles and then followed his gaze to the dead panther. His features suddenly clouded over with concern. 'He is ailing,' he whispered.

Zadkiel stared in horror at the strangled panther.

Lucifer, dazed, stood groggily to his feet. He strode across his bedchamber to the casement windows and drew the heavy satin curtains with one dramatic sweep. He stopped abruptly and laid his head in his hands, rocking to and fro almost as a despairing child. 'My mind – it pains me greatly . . .' He drew nearer to Zadkiel and gripped his hands so tight they turned blue, but still he would not let him go. 'Zadkiel!' Lucifer pleaded. Zadkiel could feel his hot breath on his cheeks.

'Zadkiel,' Lucifer begged. 'You of *all* know that I loved Ebony.' He turned to the animal. 'Feel his cold body. He is dead . . . he is *dead*, Zadkiel.'

Lucifer fell on his knees, sobs racking his body. Zadkiel

watched powerlessly as he ran his fingers through the matted jet-black hair, slamming his head against the wall like a tormented animal. 'I am the author of death!'

His frenzied screams echoed through the chamber. He tore at his hair. The pitch of his voice made Zadkiel's blood curdle.

'I will call Michael.'

Lucifer swung around. '*Noooo!*' he hissed. 'Not Michael! No!'

He shoved Zadkiel against the door with an iron grip, his eyes suddenly lucid, his breathing shallow. 'You must *swear!* Swear . . . swear your allegiance to *me.*' He drew his face nearer, a new and unsettling wildness in his eyes. 'Not to Michael . . . not to Gabriel . . .' A strange, evil smile glimmered on his face. 'And not to Yehovah.' His whisper was almost a hiss.

Zadkiel stared at Lucifer, horror-stricken.

Lucifer grabbed Zadkiel by the throat. '*Swear* it! Swear your allegiance to Lucifer, the shining one, chief prince of heaven. *Swear* your eternal allegiance to me above all others!'

Zadkiel's shock turned to dread.

Lucifer watched his expression change. His grasp tightened around Zadkiel's neck. 'You are an angel true to your word. You have always served me. Serve me again, Zadkiel. Swear your allegiance to me.'

Zadkiel remained silent. He stared at Lucifer as he struggled to breathe, a dreadful conflict in his gentle grey eyes. Tortured.

Finally he spoke, his words barely audible. 'I swear my allegiance to Lucifer, anointed cherub who covers, the shining one.'

'Above *all* others,' Lucifer hissed.

Zadkiel nodded, then averted his gaze.

Lucifer dropped Zadkiel to the floor. Then he fell to his

knees, sobbing wretchedly. His hand clung to the trembling Zadkiel's as if he were a child.

His royal ring clattered to the ground, and he scrabbled after it like a wild animal at Zadkiel's feet. 'I am not worthy of the Seal of Yehovah.' Lucifer's screams rose to a high pitch.

'Lucifer!' Tears streamed down Zadkiel's face; his voice was hoarse with emotion. 'Lucifer, get hold of yourself!'

Slowly Lucifer rose to his knees, clutching Zadkiel's legs, sobbing wretchedly. Then he rose to his full height, his face half an inch from Zadkiel's. Zadkiel stood dead still. 'Go to Jether,' Lucifer said. He shook uncontrollably as he placed the heavy golden ring on the chain around Zadkiel's neck. 'Give him my ring as my token and tell him a terrible evil overtakes me . . .' He began to rock inconsolably. 'You must go to Jether . . .'

CHAPTER TWELVE

Indisposed

Michael's stride was even as he walked the gleaming ebony and marble corridors, passing the superbly crafted golden sculptures that lined the way to Lucifer's private chambers.

He hesitated under one of the immense diamond and ruby chandeliers, in front of a new canvas. Lucifer's latest painting stretched almost to the crystal ceilings – a slain lamb, depicted in violent butchery. A cruel and terrible triumph seemed to echo from the scene.

Michael shuddered. He would talk to Lucifer about it. He had much to discuss with him this night. He pulled his sapphire robe over his injured shoulder and continued down the imperial corridors.

Michael frowned. Where were the Luciferian guards? Usually they lined the hall at regular intervals. Now the corridors were strangely deserted save for Zadkiel, who came walking towards him.

A smile broke across Michael's face. Zadkiel stared at him, looking sombre. As one, they clasped each other's hands in greeting.

'My esteemed friend, Zadkiel.' Michael drew Zadkiel to his chest.

'Your Excellency, Celestial Prince Michael, full of right-eousness and of valour.' Zadkiel bowed.

'I would see my brother.'

Zadkiel drew back slightly, his eyes cast to the floor. 'My master's express wish is that he not be disturbed, Your Excellency. He is . . . indisposed.'

Michael stared long and hard at Zadkiel, perplexed.

Zadkiel looked in Michael's eyes. His expression was deeply pained. 'He is . . . he is not himself, Michael.'

Michael drew Zadkiel even closer, until their faces almost touched. 'Speak to me, Zadkiel, in the name of our friend-ship.'

Zadkiel wouldn't meet his gaze. 'He entrusts me with his secret counsels, Your Excellency. He has forbidden my utter-ance. Even to you.'

Michael's confusion deepened. 'He is tormented?'

'I cannot speak, esteemed friend. I have sworn . . .'

Michael held him with his gaze. He flung off his cloak and tore away his vest, revealing his bloody, bandaged shoulder.

Zadkiel stared, his lip trembling.

Michael lifted his eyes to meet his. 'The iniquity devours his soul every waking hour, Zadkiel. I have seen it – I have felt it. But you have *seen*. You have seen the wretched, malevolent evil that has become his sustenance. I sense it. Zadkiel, you of *all* must speak . . . before it is too late.'

Zadkiel's eyes filled with a dreadful conflict. His breathing was laboured. 'Yes . . . yes, I have seen, Michael!' He ripped the gold chain with Lucifer's ring from around his neck and flung it to the floor. It bounced and spun on the smooth surface. Tears coursed down his face. 'His soul is *damned*!'

Full of dread, Michael bent to pick up the ring. 'You must go to Yehovah!'

'I have sworn my allegiance . . .' His eyes fell. 'Michael, I have sworn my– '

Michael grasped Zadkiel's hand. 'Your allegiance to Yehovah surpasses your allegiance to my brother.'

The heavy gold doors of Lucifer's chamber swung open.

Lucifer stood staring at them. 'Leave him!' he snarled. He glared at Michael and drew his dagger, then saw the ring in Michael's hand. 'His friendship with you clouds his judgement! He is mine!'

Suddenly Lucifer put his head in his hands and rocked from side to side. Then he lifted his head and stared at Michael, perplexed. A loving smile spread across his face as he recognized him.

'Michael!' He held out his hand to Michael, as a trusting child might. The dagger fell from his hands and clattered to the floor, unnoticed by Lucifer. He stared in concern at Michael's shoulder. 'Why, brother – you are hurt?'

Michael looked deeply into Lucifer's eyes, realizing that Lucifer retained no recollection of the vicious sword fight. If he could, Michael would have wept. 'It is nothing, Lucifer,' he uttered softly. 'A foolish accident.'

Lucifer gazed at him with adoration. 'I have been longing for you, Michael. Come, soothe me. We shall speak of when we were young.'

Michael clasped Lucifer by the broad shoulders gently, as would a father with a child, and walked him back through the huge gold doors. They slammed shut in Zadkiel's face.

CHAPTER THIRTEEN

Glory

O badiah hurried through the doors of the grand Willow Library where the eight ancient elders were deeply immersed in study and reflection. He stood before Jether and bowed, then nervously pushed a monogrammed ring into Jether's palm. Jether held it up and grew instantly grave. He held his finger to his lips, urging the youngling to stay quiet, and rose to his feet.

Charsoc opened his eyes and watched intently as Obadiah followed Jether out of the side door.

Outside, Jether leaned down to the youngling. 'How do you come to hold the prince regent's token, Obadiah?'

'His Excellency, Chief Prince Michael, milord Jether.' Obadiah stared at Jether, twitching nervously. 'He awaits your presence in the princes' stables, sire.' He bowed, his curls scraping the marble floor.

Jether reached under the folds of his heavy linen tunic and placed the ring in a small brown pouch. He walked down the winding sapphire corridors of the Tower of Winds, through the crystal atrium, into the Palace of Archangels, hurrying past the vast palace orangeries, stopping briefly in front of a small, concealed doorway covered with lichen. Then he vanished, seemingly into thin air.

Charsoc stood hidden by the ancient willows, closely observing.

Jether arrived in the stables as Ariel, Michael's groom, was shoeing Michael's magnificent white stallion.

Michael nodded to Jether in acknowledgement. He looked drawn. 'Thank you, Ariel; that is all.'

Ariel bowed deeply and walked out of the stables. Jether walked towards Michael, and they embraced.

Jether held out the heavy gold ring, embedded with one huge polished ruby. 'Lucifer.' It was a statement. Jether's bushy eyebrows knotted together.

Michael nodded, rubbing his forehead wearily. 'He rang for Zadkiel at three bells. Zadkiel found him sobbing, his arms around Ebony's neck. The panther was lifeless.'

Jether stared at Michael, ashen.

Michael continued. Shaken. 'He had undergone what is termed as *death*.'

Jether turned away from Michael fleetingly, his mind spinning in horror. Jether's eyes widened. 'Death!'

'Lucifer killed his own panther, Jether. He strangled it with his bare hands.'

The blood drained from Jether's face. He closed his eyes in anguish. 'Then,' he said softly, 'it has begun.'

Michael ran his hands through his flaxen locks. 'He is as one at war with himself. He will not rest. He will not be comforted. He asks for you continually.' Michael shuddered.

Jether put his hand on Michael's arm. 'Who knows this?'

'No one save you and I, and Zadkiel and Ephaniah the

manservant. Their devotion is beyond question.' Michael's jaw clenched. 'Something terrible is afoot, Jether.'

Obadiah came up behind them. He bowed to Jether. 'The elders await your presence, milord,' he said.

Jether slid his own ring, a simple band of gold, from his middle finger and placed it in Michael's open hand. Then he drew out Lucifer's ring and placed it there, too. He closed Michael's fingers around them. 'Give my token to Lucifer with this request: to meet me in the Tower of Winds in my private cloister at twelve bells. Alone.

'Make haste, Michael . . . It is the fire of free will.'

Jether paced through the corridors of Michael's quarter of the Palace of Archangels. Here and there clusters of high-ranking Luciferian angelic generals huddled together with their counterparts from Michael's angelic high command, conversing in intense, strained tones. Whenever Jether approached, each party scattered, vanishing into the lower labyrinths of the palace.

Disquieted, Jether turned the corner into the great hall. A tall angel in golden armour strode through the enormous golden entrance of Lucifer's quarter, his features grave. It was Raphael.

Raphael stopped before Jether and bowed deeply. 'Milord Jether, I would speak with you.'

Jether looked into his troubled grey gaze. 'You may speak, Raphael.' He studied the noble face intently.

Raphael fell into pace with Jether as they passed another huddle of whispering soldiers. Raphael stared grimly at them from beneath his golden helmet. They saluted awkwardly.

'It is untenable, milord!' Raphael exclaimed.

Jether frowned. 'Of what precisely do you speak, my forthright Raphael?'

'The whisperings and intrigues that infiltrate the hallowed corridors of heaven.'

Raphael removed his golden helmet from his head. His dark hair was hung in two braids. His chin was set, his eyes burned with a fierce fire. 'I speak of insurrection.'

Jether stopped in mid-step, the colour drained from his face. 'Insurrection?'

'Of treachery in the inner sanctum of heaven!' Raphael's voice rang out through the corridors, echoing off the walls.

Jether clasped his arm gently. 'Lucifer?'

Raphael nodded. 'He who has been entrusted with so much. And yet he would . . .' Raphael faltered. 'It is too awful to speak of.'

'Yet speak you must, Raphael. It is your hallowed duty.'

Raphael stared at the marble floor. 'He charges Yehovah with folly, milord.'

'Folly?'

'He charges that Yehovah would supplant his first-born creation with that of an inferior race,' he said, still not looking at Jether. 'He charges that the angelic host faces a terrible and impending danger so menacing that it threatens the very existence of our own angelic race.'

'The race of men,' Jether stated quietly. He did not break Raphael's gaze.

'Who have been the recipients of Lucifer's dissensions?'

'His high command. I refused his intrigues, and five thousand of his generals followed me. We would have naught to do with his insurrections.'

'But his high command is over ten thousand,' Jether murmured, stunned. Jether felt sick to the pit of his stomach.

Raphael nodded.

'It is worse than I imagined.' Jether ran his palm across

his temple. 'Tell me, faithful Raphael, what reward does Lucifer offer that is so enticing to the angelic host as to cause them to forsake Yehovah?'

'He offers them to be as a master race, milord, untainted by man. He offers them rule and power, the opportunity to be masters of their own angelic destiny.'

Jether stroked his beard. 'He offers them . . . *glory*. They seek now their own glory save that of Yehovah's. It is the sin of pride.'

'There will be reprisals!' Raphael exclaimed. 'Christos was there – at Lucifer's speech.'

'Christos?'

'Christos appeared in the upper portico. It is said he was there the whole time, listening.'

Jether stared at Raphael. 'Have you been so long with him, Raphael, and yet you still do not comprehend?' he said gently. 'Yehovah has allotted free will to the angelic race, and free will must be tested through the fires of temptation. A great sifting occurs as we speak, throughout the corridors of heaven – a sifting of motives and loyalties, of the hearts and souls of the angelic race. The fire of free will blazes in heaven, Raphael. And Yehovah allows it to rage. If he acts – if he brings the reprisals you speak of – he takes away the very free will that he endowed as his greatest gift upon the angelic.'

Raphael tried to assimilate Jether's words. 'But Lucifer . . .'

'No, Raphael, there will be no reprisals.' Jether's eyes held a deep sorrow. 'The gift he has given he will not take back because it is misused, even when it is misused by those he loves most tenderly.'

'I do not understand fully,' Raphael said quietly, 'but as ever I bow my knee to his infinite wisdom.'

Jether caught sight of Obadiah scuttling down the halls towards him. 'I have given Lucifer my token, Raphael. He meets with me at twelve bells. I must depart.'

They embraced. 'May Yehovah be with you,' Raphael whispered.

Jether hurried towards Obadiah and disappeared through the gardens towards the winding sapphire corridors of the Tower of Winds.

CHAPTER FOURTEEN

Stone of Fire

Michael galloped across the vast meadows of golden bulrushes and drew to a halt in front of the grand, white columns – the entrance into the eastern Gardens of Eden, Lucifer's cherished retreat. He dismounted effortlessly as Lucifer's courtier, Sachiel, took the reins of his white stallion.

'My brother is in the garden?'

Sachiel nodded. He looked shaken. Michael handed Sachiel his cloak and started to undo his sword belt, then hesitated and left it around his waist. Sachiel watched him intently.

'That will be all, Sachiel.' Slowly, Michael walked up the gilded steps. He surveyed Eden in wonder.

A flock of blue griffin-like birds with platinum beaks and talons flew overhead. The massive forests of ancient willows towered over cedars and mangroves. Oryx roamed the open spaces. Jacarandas bowed, heavy with lilac blooms, over beds of cycad, lupin, and foxglove, while vibrantly hued puffins, hoopoes, and birds of paradise flew across the gardens. Unicorns grazed on beds of cowslips. Sabre-toothed tigers and lion-like creatures lay sleeping alongside lambs. Luxuriant vines flourished, weighed down with luminous pale blue grapes and silver pomegranates. Nightingales, linnets, and turtledoves sang like the angelic host.

An intense, almost blinding white mist rose from the furthest corner of the garden. Three magnificent golden thrones were situated underneath the hundred-foot waterfalls of flowing golden nectar, lined by the ancient willows. Each throne was sculpted of pure gold but was individually crafted and embedded with sardius, topaz, diamonds, beryl, onyx, jasper, sapphires, carbuncles, and emeralds.

Sprawled on the first throne, his ruby crown resting carelessly on his matted hair, was Lucifer. He held a silver pomegranate idly in his palm. To his left was the lifeless form of the black panther.

Lucifer gave Michael a dazzling smile. 'Beloved brother, come and have fellowship with Ebony and me!' He followed Michael's gaze to the dead panther. His features suddenly clouded with concern. He looked at Michael earnestly for a moment, then cocked his head and sighed deeply. 'You have been angry with me of late, Michael. I have sensed it. You are vexed?'

Michael shook his head and smiled tenderly at Lucifer. With his heart almost breaking, Michael threw off his cloak and sat down next to his elder brother, the one who had for so many years been his mentor, his protector.

Lucifer rose and ran in a full, clean stride across the pale gold meadow, his countenance shining, drawing Michael behind him.

They ran until they stood together, silent, at the very edge of the towering, pearlescent cliff face. The light from Eden's pale eastern moons illuminated the endless white sand. Beyond, the amethyst ocean stretched, it seemed, into infinity.

Lucifer gazed in wonder. 'You remember when we were young, how we used to ride the lightning bareback on the sea?'

Michael nodded gently. 'I remember well, dear brother.'

Lucifer smiled. 'And how Zadkiel the Upright would chide us for weeks afterward.'

Michael tried to restrain a smile. 'It is true, dear Luce, he would have us learn more discretion.' Michael looked into Lucifer's beautiful sapphire eyes.

Lucifer gazed back lovingly at Michael. 'Michael, look!' he cried, his face lighting up with exhilaration.

Michael followed the direction of Lucifer's strong bronzed arm. He was staring at the western slopes of the Holy Mountain, its seven golden spires wreathed in mists and lightning.

'The Holy Mountain,' Lucifer whispered in awe.

'The Holy Mountain,' Michael echoed.

Lucifer deftly undid the ribbons of his shift and unclasped the heavy silver chain. In his palm sat a small, silver amulet. Slowly he opened it. Immediately the sky was filled by a blinding sapphire light. Michael and Lucifer hid their faces with their forearms, and Lucifer laughed in elation.

Slowly Michael's eyes became accustomed to the shimmering glare. 'Lucifer!' he exclaimed. 'No!'

But Lucifer only laughed exultantly.

Michael stared in awe. 'A stone of fire – a sapphire stone from the vaults of the cherubim!'

Lucifer's face was bathed in radiance, his mouth moving in worship. 'From the sixth spire,' he whispered.

'When you were there with Jether?'

Lucifer nodded. 'I was but seven moons when I walked up and down amidst the stones of fire. I could not bear to be away from him even for a moment.' Lucifer stared in awe at the stone of fire. 'It is his presence.'

He refastened the amulet. The light and presence immediately disappeared. He sat and put his head in his hands, rocking to and fro inconsolably. 'My mind – it pains me greatly, Michael.' Distractedly Lucifer ran his hand through his tangled raven hair. 'He has abandoned me for this ... *man*.'

Great, heaving sobs racked Lucifer's imperial frame. Michael stared at Lucifer, visibly distressed. Lucifer grasped Michael's hand and looked at him imploringly. 'You and I together. We have always been together. Don't let me do this alone.' He looked blankly out at the Holy Mountain, disorientated. 'You followed me everywhere, Michael, as a youngling ... I was your protector ... keeper.'

He swung around dramatically, his eyes flashing. 'Follow me *now*, Michael.' His voice dropped to a deranged whisper. 'A third of the angelic force have sworn allegiance to me.' He stared at Michael with a look of insane exhilaration. 'With your third aligned with mine ...' Lucifer looked fervently into Michael's eyes, never breaking his gaze. 'Brothers ... for eternity!'

Ever so gently Michael untangled Lucifer's hand from his own, stunned. He looked deep into Lucifer's eyes, searching for some remnant of the mentor who had once been so zealous in his quest for truth and righteousness, who had loved Yehovah and even Michael himself with such fervency. 'You would betray Yehovah?' Michael uttered, his voice barely a whisper.

'Yehovah!' Lucifer hissed the name. 'I pleaded with him, "You have the entire angelic host at your command, ministering to you day and night," but still he wanted more. "Man will fail you," I warned him. "They will be your great regret." Then he turned to me. "Lucifer, Lucifer," he tenderly admonished me, "I long for fellowship with that which is created in my image."'

Michael watched as Lucifer paced up and down the lush blue undergrowth, his eyes flashing fervid with his ravings.

'And then erupted a deep, dark fury in my soul. For out of his own mouth he had admitted it! I, the shining one, the daystar, second only to his throne, was not enough for him. No matter if my whole eternity was spent loving him, I could never be as this *man*!'

Michael stared at Lucifer, a terrible sickness engulfing him. He realized that he who had been so loved and adored by heaven was gone, and in his place was a cunning malevolence that made Michael yearn for the brother he so loved. Tears coursed unashamedly down his cheeks. 'Brother, I cannot.'

Lucifer recoiled from him. 'We were not enough for him!' His face contorted in a vicious mask. '*You* were not enough for him, Michael!'

Michael's thoughts raced. He fought for control of his emotions.

'You fool!' Lucifer raved. 'Once he has this man he will tire of you!' He strode over to the edge of the cliff and stared out at the blinding radiance of the Holy Mountain. 'He has abandoned us,' he whimpered.

As Michael watched, the darkness over Lucifer's features shifted, and he became suddenly lucid. He looked up at Michael desperately. 'Michael ... *help me*!' He clutched Michael's face in his strong, fine hands, then crumpled like a child into his brother's arms.

Michael clasped his brother tightly to his chest. His fingers gently stroked the matted blue-black locks. He eased Jether's ring from a pouch and placed it gently in Lucifer's palm, closing the jewelled fingers over it. 'Jether bids you meet him in his private chamber at twelve bells.'

Lucifer muttered to himself, rocking from side to side inconsolably. Then slowly he caressed the ring. 'Jether?' he murmured.

Michael stared over Lucifer's shoulder and froze in disbelief at what he saw – as Lucifer's shadow fell across the glowing blue celestial lupins behind him, each one rotted and fell to the ground, dead.

'Yes,' Lucifer said, 'I will go to Jether.'

CHAPTER FIFTEEN

Tower of Winds

You were perfect in your ways
From the day you were created,
Till iniquity was found in you.

Lucifer stood at the turret window of Jether's monastic cloister, a tall and imperious figure watching the gales blow the twelve pale moons across the midnight sky.

'You have my deep appreciation, Jether.' He turned from the window, his long raven hair framing the beautiful alabaster face.

The old man was slumped across the carved wooden table. Dark purple blood ran from a wound on Jether's head.

'You were as a father to me.' Carefully Lucifer wiped his diamond-studded dagger on his mantle and replaced it in its sheath. He smiled down at Jether with his blazing sapphire gaze.

Jether stared through glazed, pained eyes. 'You will lose, Lucifer,' he whispered hoarsely. 'You cannot hope to prevail.'

'Never! You were like the rest of them ... you never realized my full potential. I am the prince regent, born to *rule*.' Lucifer looked at Jether with malice. 'You more than any knew my genius. You, my mentor. So, you more than any *betrayed* me.'

He flung open the lofty turret windows, and the violent swirling winds blew his hair and cloak. 'I *will* ascend into heaven. I *will* exalt my throne above the throne of Yehovah.' A strange, evil fire burned in the blazing steel-blue eyes. 'I *will* sit upon the Mount of the Congregation. They will worship me.' He stared at the inert Jether with insane glee. '*He* will worship me.'

Jether struggled to raise himself. 'For the sake of all that once was Lucifer, I *implore* you, repent . . . while you still have free will . . .' He slumped down.

'Jether, Yehovah's holy steward – the only one who knew my full intentions . . .' Lucifer bent down and placed his cold, alabaster face directly next to Jether, skin on skin. Jether shivered, and Lucifer smiled. 'No one knows the intricate and complex workings of my mind like you do, old man,' he hissed. 'I know you speak to no one. Who would you have me believe knows of my designs? The malleable, tender Gabriel? He suffers from a malady of soul – he shall join me!'

He turned dramatically and lifted both of his arms towards heaven. 'All the hosts of heaven shall be there to watch my finest moment. From every part of heaven they shall gather . . . the greatest gathering throughout all aeons.'

A great and terrible knowing grew inside Jether. 'You would not . . .'

'I knew that you would comprehend the genius of it, Jether.' Lucifer struck his hands together in triumph. 'The great declaration! My Father's declaration to the congregation in the furthest reaches of the north of his intention to create mankind. Every angel, every spirit known in heaven, shall be gathered to hear of our Father's great new innovation. *Man!*' he spat. 'And so I shall strike.'

Then Lucifer grasped the long silver hair and pulled Jether's head back with sheer brute force. 'I shall strike at the gathering,' he hissed. 'At the great assembly in the Mount of the North. You shall watch and glory in having such a fervent scholar. It shall be all-glorious.'

In agony, with one last feeble effort, Jether raised his upper body so he was face to face with Lucifer. His voice was hardly above a whisper. 'Thou wert the anointed cherub ... filled with wisdom and perfect in beauty ... ' He gazed straight into Lucifer's eyes, his own clear and blazing with a fierce, righteous fury. Through sheer effort of will, he completed his sentence. 'Until iniquity was found in you.'

Lucifer deliberately dropped Jether's head to the floor.

Yet even as it smashed down onto the hard marble and the blood dribbled from his mouth, Jether prayed.

CHAPTER SIXTEEN

War in Heaven

How you are fallen from heaven,
O Lucifer, son of the morning!
For you have said in your heart:
'I will ascend into heaven,
I will exalt my throne above the stars of God;
I will also sit on the Mount of the Congregation
In the furthest reaches of the north;
I will ascend above the heights of the clouds,
I will be like the Most High.'

Ten thousand times ten thousand of heaven's great angelic company gathered in formation on the vast onyx plains of the Mount of the Congregation in the furthest reaches of the north of the First Heaven. The eastern horizon was almost completely filled by the company of heralds – countless thousands of Yehovah's shimmering holy white eagles hovering over the steep onyx foundations, under the heights of the clouds.

Michael, Gabriel, and Lucifer stood to attention at the entrance to the Holy of Holies. The enormous thunder of the angelic hosts was deafening as a hundred million angelic warriors stood assembled in seven orders before the three great chief princes of heaven, their voices raised in unison in worship and adulation to the Ancient of Days.

A full seven leagues away, high on the flaming mount, a vast, stormy whirlwind blew, and out of the whirlwind burned a great, blazing cloud. A fire and great flashes of lightning and rumblings of thunder emanated from the epicentre. The great white throne of incandescent light had already descended amid the cherubim. Encircling Yehovah's throne was the vast, flaming halo of his rainbow, which shimmered like an emerald.

Seated on the throne was the One before whom all the galaxies and the universes shrank back in awe. The One before whom the twenty-four ancient monarchs of heaven lay prostrate, their crowns flung down on the crystal glass, where the four living creatures – the mighty cherubim of Yehovah – worshipped.

The unspeakable brilliance of his being shone as the blinding radiance of a million, million suns, with the intense crystalline brightness of jasper and fiery sardius. The Ancient of Days, Yehovah.

All at once, the great roaring from the throne stilled. An awesome hush fell over the angelic assembly as the Ancient Ones took their golden and glorious thrones . . . led by Jether.

Immediately after Lucifer's departure, weak and near fainting, Jether had trodden the nameless secret passageway from his chamber through the twisting labyrinths of the seven spires, beneath the sacred vaults, to the throne room, where the Ancient of Days held audience within the hallowed walls of the secret place.

No living soul would ever know what took place between Yehovah and his faithful elder, steward of his holy mysteries, save that when Jether finally appeared outside the rubied door of the jacinth tower as the twelve pale blue moons rose from the west, there was no sign of a wound on his temple. And his countenance shone like flame.

Jether sat heavily on the gold velvet bolster of the majestic central throne, his ancient blue eyes scrutinizing the angelic assembly and resting upon Lucifer.

Michael stood to attention, his flaxen hair falling past his shoulders onto the deep blue cloak. His handsome features were grim. He looked fleetingly at Gabriel, who stood at his right hand arrayed in his ceremonial regalia of platinum and diamonds. Gabriel stared straight ahead, his eyes earnest.

Next to Gabriel stood Lucifer, an imperial figure resplendent in his ceremonial dress. He stood with his head held high, his golden mantle embedded with every precious stone, the sardius, jasper, sapphire, diamonds, rubies, and emeralds glistening. The gleaming raven hair was immaculate. The Sword of State hung in its rubied sheath at his side. The shining one, seraph, his glory breathtaking.

Jether beheld the three brothers with a deep and terrible anguish. Then he noted Lucifer's gaze and followed it.

Lucifer's attention was riveted not on the throne but a full league beyond, on the altar, where a vast incandescent light hovered. From the centre of the pulsating light thousands of swirling mists rose and fell. In the centre of the mists lay the faint outline of the prototype of the new race, which the brothers had seen in the central portal.

Michael's fist tightened on the Sword of Justice.

Slowly Jether lifted the heavy gold sceptre high above his ancient white head. Obadiah and Matton scurried to hold up his arms. The fire opals embedded in the sceptre blazed red-hot and emitted a white mist. 'Behold,' Jether said, gesturing to the distant altar, 'he that is made in Yehovah's image!'

The swirling mists rose a full hundred feet above the prototype, and there in the centre, now fully visible, dormant and inert but with features and limbs perfectly formed, lay Yehovah's new creation – the first of the new race.

'Man,' Michael whispered in awe. 'He sleeps.'

'Dust cannot sleep.' Lucifer's hiss could barely be heard. 'It has not been imbued with the breath of life. It is but a shell.'

Michael turned to Lucifer. His green eyes were resolute. 'He *shall* live, Lucifer.'

Jether held up the sceptre a second time. The fires from the cherubim blazed. 'The breath of breaths,' he intoned. 'The breath of life.'

Jether and the twenty-four ancient monarchs bowed so low that their beards swept the crystal floor.

And suddenly, in the swirling mists of the mighty whirlwind, the dazzling radiance of Yehovah manifested above the clay form. In the roar of a thousand waters, Yehovah spoke: '*Behold our eternal companion.*'

The angelic assembly watched in awe as Yehovah's blinding, iridescent form bowed down over the inert form and laid his nostrils against the lifeless clay ones. Yehovah breathed into the prototype. All at once heaven was rent with the sound of great roaring. And again Yehovah breathed.

The shofar blew. 'The breath of nefesh,' the herald sounded.

'The life of the soul of Yehovah,' Xacheriel whispered.

Immediately the matter prototype became a living, pulsating form as the blood began to circulate and the heart began to beat. The eyes and sockets materialized. The skin became ruddy.

Gabriel turned to Michael in ecstasy. 'The breath of Ruach.'

'The life of the Spirit of Yehovah,' Xacheriel whispered exultantly.

The roaring grew to a crescendo, and the Mount of the North began to shake. It seemed that the very crystal under the angelic hosts' feet would explode into a million shards.

The man opened his eyes, suddenly conscious. He slowly rose to his feet and raised his hands in reverence to the blazing light of Yehovah's presence.

And then it happened. As the whole of heaven gazed in silent awe, Yehovah clasped the man to his breast.

The moment seemed to span almost an eternity. And in that moment, it seemed that Yehovah was weeping. Again came his voice, ten thousand times ten thousand waters of infinite joy, infinite tenderness. '*Adam.*'

Lucifer stared, his countenance like stone.

The blazing light of Yehovah's presence disappeared from Adam and reappeared seven leagues back, in the epicentre of the iridescent white throne.

Through the enormous pearl gates eight Holy Watchers in ceremonial dress walked majestically up the nave, holding on their shoulders a carved golden casket with golden cherubim – the Ark of the Race of Men.

'The title deeds to the new galaxy,' Michael murmured under his breath.

Jether held up the sceptre. 'Behold, we the Ancient Ones – on behalf of Yehovah, the Ancient of Days – do bequeath to man the title deeds of the Ark of the Race of Men, given now to the first-born. This is Yehovah's covenant, bound by Eternal Law.'

The Holy Watchers stopped in front of Adam and laid down the casket.

'Yehovah bequeaths to the race of men the title deeds to the newly created galaxy,' Jether proclaimed, 'including Earth and its solar system.'

Jether nodded, and a Watcher walked forward with a large golden key resting on a velvet cushion. Jether picked it up and slowly opened the casket. Twelve golden codices occupied the Ark, the covers of the large books embedded with jacinth, diamonds, sapphires, chrysolite, and multitudes of other precious stones.

'The title deeds to Earth and its solar system, the Second Heaven above Earth,' Jether said, 'hereby bequeathed by Yehovah this day to the race of men through eternity of eternities.'

He turned to Adam, who stood silently in front of the casket. 'Will you, as the first-born of the race of men, to the extent of your power, cause law and justice, in mercy, to be executed in all your judgements?'

Adam nodded. 'I solemnly promise to do so.'

'And will you pledge to serve and honour and glorify Yehovah the Almighty God, Creator, Preserver, the Ancient of Days, to execute his will forever only, to serve and venerate forever his person only, throughout eternity of eternities?'

Adam lifted his head towards Yehovah's throne, his face shining. 'I solemnly pledge this to Yehovah.'

A great thundering issued from the throne. *'This is man, our beloved. We find no iniquity in him.'*

Jether left his throne and walked to the altar. He stood over Adam, who knelt. 'On behalf of the Ancient of Days, as his elders and stewards of his holy mysteries, we, the Council of the Ancient Ones, receive your homage. We receive your pledge.'

Jether poured the holy anointing oil from the ampulla over the crown of Adam's bare head. The heavy, fragrant oil ran down Adam's forehead and over his neck and his cheeks. 'Be thy head anointed with oil.'

Jether turned to the throne of Yehovah. The other twenty-three Ancient Ones stood to their feet. Zadkiel turned to the throne of Yehovah, and two hundred Holy Watchers rose.

'By his holy anointing,' Jether proclaimed, 'pour down upon your head and heart the blessing of the Ancient of Days, that by the assistance of his heavenly grace, you may govern and preserve the race of men and the new galaxy, committed to your charge this day.' Jether turned to the heavenly host and lifted both arms. 'And now, I adjure you, let us lift our voices as one as we repeat the pledge of allegiance and devotion to the race of men.'

Adam knelt before the angelic hosts of heaven.

Michael held the Sword of Justice over his head, saying, 'We, the hosts of heaven, do become liege servants of life and limb to the race of men, and in faith and truth we will bear unto you throughout eternity of eternities. So help us Yehovah.'

Adam, still kneeling, raised his head to the angelic host.

Jether clasped Adam's head to his breast, then drew gently from him and looked deeply into his eyes. 'May wisdom and knowledge be the stability of your rule and the fear of the Lord your treasure.' He kissed him tenderly on both cheeks. 'We bow before Almighty Yehovah in awe at the work of thy hands.'

The first order of hundreds of thousands of the angelic host stepped forward as one. They fell to their knees in reverence.

Michael led the second order immediately forward. He surveyed the room as one by one the angelic host knelt in veneration before Yehovah's throne and his man.

Jether's mouth moved in supplication as slowly he lifted his head, surveying the vast assembly. The entire angelic company was kneeling, their heads bowed.

With one exception.

Lucifer stood upright in front of the altar. Rigid. Silent. Jether watched, trembling and grief-stricken, as Lucifer lifted his harrowed face to man and then straight to Yehovah's throne, his eyes glittering black and hard – haughty, rebellious, filled with loathing.

Gasps of surprise and horror rippled throughout the chamber. Michael stared in horror at the defiant Lucifer. But it was as he surveyed the chamber that his blood ran cold.

One by one, silently and deliberately, thousands of Lucifer's generals, warrior angels from all across the chamber, rose from their knees and stood, their arms crossed, their heads held high in defiance, following their renegade king.

Then thousands of the Luciferian Guard rose to their feet from all across the chamber. Then tens of thousands. Until a full third of the angelic host was standing.

Michael turned to Zadkiel, who was kneeling just behind Lucifer. His head was bowed, but his breathing was shallow.

Slowly he lifted his gaze to meet Michael's. 'Damned for eternity,' he said in a hoarse voice. Tears coursed down his cheeks.

Michael stared with unbelief into Zadkiel's eyes.

Zadkiel quickly turned his face away, burning with shame. 'I have sworn my allegiance. I cannot break my vow.' He tore the seal of the Holy Watchers, his princely insignia, from his bodice with shaking hands and rose to his feet. A full third of the Holy Watchers rose after him.

Lucifer met Michael's gaze and smiled vindictively.

Gabriel beheld the scene in horror. Michael laid his hand on his arm and looked towards the Ancient Ones. Jether had fallen prostrate, praying. The other Ancient Ones lay likewise before their thrones – with the exception of Charsoc. He exchanged a long, meaningful glance with Lucifer, then stood. Gasps of horror rippled throughout the chamber.

An uncharacteristic malice played on Charsoc's face as he stared down at Jether, who would not look up from his prayers.

119

Lucifer cast his eye slowly over the assembly. A full third of the angelic host was standing. He smiled in triumph.

The treason was complete.

Michael, still kneeling, stared up at him, his hand on his sword. Fierce.

'You'll never succeed, Lucifer.'

Lucifer laughed derisively. 'Ah, but you see, my dear naive Michael.' – he swept his sword across the scene – 'I already have. One-third of heaven's armies is at my command, dear brother.' Lucifer smiled calculatingly at Gabriel. 'And with Gabriel by my side, we will rule them all.'

Lucifer grasped Gabriel's shoulder and pressed his mouth to his ear. 'For over a million aeons I have followed blindly. For over a million aeons I suspended my own judgements and trusted *his* without question. For over a million aeons I have subjugated my own reason to his.' The fervid fire in Lucifer's eyes burned brighter. 'And *now* I must protect him from his own creation. Heed your dreams, Gabriel! Save your soul – and save Yehovah. We were fools! Gullible, self-deluded, blind minions. But no longer!'

Gabriel stared in turmoil from Michael to Lucifer.

Lucifer turned to the standing angelic host and raised the gleaming broadsword high above his head. 'I declare war in the heavens!'

With a deft movement, he thrust his gleaming broadsword savagely at Michael. Michael, still kneeling, deflected his thrust and nimbly rose to his feet. They circled each other, alert, vigilant – supreme masters of swordsmanship, equally matched in strength and warriorship.

Belzoc, one of Lucifer's generals, grasped Michael's throat from behind in a stranglehold. Lucifer laughed dryly and aimed his broadsword directly at Michael's chest.

Michael twisted Belzoc's arm and struggled free, kicking Lucifer with the full force of his immense strength, elevating him a full twenty feet into the air. Lucifer smashed face down onto the solid crystal floor. He rose, dazed, blood running from his mouth, irate now. He was immediately surrounded by ten of Michael's elite warriors.

A distant shofar sounded. In response, a bloodthirsty roar erupted from Lucifer's third of the angelic host. Thousands of armoured warriors on horseback, armed with iron cross-bows, surged down from the southern cliffs of the mount upon the angelic host, descending with ferocity on Yehovah's angelic battalions, leaving a bloody tide of hatred and malevolence in their wake.

Jether looked up from his prayers, his hand covering his mouth in consternation.

Lucifer raised his broadsword high in his left hand, simultaneously drawing the Sword of State from its sheath with his right. He lunged viciously at Michael, who thrust back with the glinting Sword of Justice. The violent clash of steel against steel was drowned by the savage roaring of Lucifer's battalions. The two brothers fought, thrust for thrust, steel clanging against steel, their violent skirmish unrelenting.

Then, like lightning, Lucifer thrust towards Michael's heart with the Sword of State. Simultaneously he brought the flat of the broadsword down violently on Michael's chest, winding him.

Michael staggered to his knees. He raised his face to see Lucifer over him, triumphant and cruel, his wings hovering two feet off the ground.

Lucifer lifted his broadsword, his eyes glinting fiendishly.

Gabriel stood on the far side of the chamber, paralysed by the bloody fighting all around him. He stared in horror at Lucifer.

'Brothers for eternity!' screamed Lucifer, as sweat poured off him. 'Brothers!' An evil smile played on his lips as he lifted the razor-sharp broadsword straight above Michael's neck.

An immense thunder roared from the direction of the throne – light upon light, sound upon sound. Suddenly Lucifer was lifted thirty feet off the ground by an invisible force and hurled like a stone onto the glass floor of the mount, a full league down the nave.

Waves of blinding radiance pulsated from the great white throne, illuminating the entire chamber, bathing the wounded angels. Within moments they recovered, rising to their feet, their heads bowed.

Lucifer struggled to his knees. He was now before the throne of the Most High. The four living creatures, the mighty cherubim, stood at the throne, their blazing swords held ready. Lucifer surveyed the throne room as if disorientated. A deathly hush descended.

'Let him pass.' Yehovah's voice was as the roar of a thousand waters.

Immediately the cherubim with the flaming swords moved aside.

Lucifer rose to his feet, recovering rapidly. He walked straight past the cherubim, his eyes glinting with rebellion and arrogance, and strode towards the throne. Ten thousand of his generals and guards arrived and followed closely behind, their heads held high in defiance.

A second wave of intense, shimmering radiance cascaded down towards the mutinous angelic force. Lucifer sheltered his face from the searing light with his forearm as he doggedly continued his stride through the radiating prisms of white fire towards the throne. His fist tightened around the Sword of State.

A third wave broke over Lucifer's battalion. The Luciferian Guard stood transfixed. Halfway to the throne, Moloch, another of Lucifer's generals, uttered a strangled cry. He grasped his throat, suffocating in the white fire. Bloodcurdling screams echoed across the entire assembly as the bodies of thousands of dread warriors collapsed to the floor like ninepins. The hundred thousand warriors close behind Lucifer's generals gasped desperately for breath, their weapons strewn over the chamber, literally burning alive in the white inferno.

Jether stared across to Charsoc, aghast. The treacherous elder's face was contorted with an agony so dire that his screams were noiseless as he tried desperately to hide his face from the searing light.

Michael and Gabriel approached, followed by their angelic legions, then lay prostrate on the floor.

'*Bow*, Lucifer!' Michael shouted. 'Don't be a stubborn fool. Just *bow*!'

Lucifer swayed unsteadily as the rasping screams reverberated all across the chamber.

Zadkiel stood behind Lucifer, horrified as the pulsating conflagration engulfed him. Shaking uncontrollably, he reeled to the floor like a stone.

Lucifer, gasping for air, filled with terror and rage, put one foot feebly in front of the other. He was immediately flung back with staggering force onto the hard sapphire floor, immobilized. The white, scorching inferno settled, shimmering, in the centre of the throne room, directly over where Lucifer lay paralysed.

Slowly Michael lifted his head, surveying the carnage in the throne room. He turned to Gabriel, who knelt beside him, trembling. A tear ran down Gabriel's cheek. Michael placed his hand on Gabriel's shoulder to steady him, then took a deep breath and rose to his feet, his hand on the hilt of his broadsword.

He raised his face to where the Ancient Ones – twenty-four minus Charsoc – sat enthroned, praying. Jether and Michael exchanged a long look, then Jether nodded almost imperceptibly. Michael closed his eyes and bowed his head, his breathing laboured.

He motioned to his fellow archangels, Raphael and Uriel. Raphael walked to the stunned Lucifer and forced him to his feet. Uriel, his eyes cast to the floor, locked heavy silver irons around Lucifer's ankles.

His senses reeling, Michael slowly walked over to where Lucifer stood. His brother was ashen-faced, his hands hanging before him in the heavy silver shackles. Trembling, Lucifer turned his face away from Michael's gaze, his tormented blue eyes staring at the glistening sapphire floor. Michael knelt to pick up Lucifer's Sword of State, which was lying discarded on the chamber floor.

Michael clasped Lucifer's right arm.

'Michael . . .', Lucifer whispered.

Marshalling every vestige of his training, desperately attempting to still the indescribable agony that seared through the core of his being, Michael forced Lucifer down the nave towards the great white throne.

As Lucifer neared the throne, his expression changed from rebellion and rage to anguish and foreboding, and then from foreboding to terror. Desperately he tried to shield his eyes from the force and purity of the light, but his arms were manacled. Finally, he arrived in front of the throne, his head bowed, his sapphire eyes closed.

Michael bowed his head in distress, unable to watch. There was complete silence.

Ever so slowly, Lucifer lifted his head, his eyes filled with rage and sorrow. 'Holy Father,' he uttered in a hoarse whisper.

The light pulsated, and there was an immense thunder. Then a glorious imperial figure, almost indefinable in the immense light radiating from him, walked majestically through the white fires, out of Yehovah. The mists started to fade as the breathtaking form became visible.

Lucifer gasped. 'Christos!'

The king spoke in a voice filled with unimaginable empathy. 'We grieve for you.'

Raw pain contorted Lucifer's features. 'But why man?' he uttered almost inaudibly. A racking sob escaped him. 'Were we not enough?' He stared at Christos helplessly, haggard, wretched with grief. 'Was *I* not enough for him?' A solitary tear ran down his cheek.

Christos looked upon him with infinite tenderness, infinite pity. He brushed the tear away gently from Lucifer's cheek. His touch lingered. 'We would that you would repent.'

Lucifer stared, trembling, his gaze locked fiercely on the sorrowful eyes of the king. 'Tell him . . .' His voice shook with emotion. 'Tell him . . . I cannot.'

The Christ drew a sharp breath as though he were in intense pain . . . intense suffering. His eyelids slowly closed. Heaven waited. Then his voice merged with that of Yehovah. One but three. Three but one. A sublime voice like the voice of thousands of thundering waters – magnetic, saturated with compassion and intense sorrow.

'*LUCIFER!*'

Christos stepped back and nodded almost imperceptibly to Raphael. Raphael raised his sword and with one swift movement of the sharp blade swept Lucifer's military medals and insignia to the floor.

With tears streaming down his face, Michael unclasped the seal of the Royal House of Yehovah from Lucifer's breast. Lucifer's mouth moved soundlessly in agony.

Then Christos spoke. '*Oh, how thou art fallen, Lucifer, son of the morning!*'

Lucifer began to weep wretchedly.

Instantly Christos' glorious form vanished, consumed once more into the centre of the iridescent white throne.

Jether, chief of the ancient elders, moved in front of Lucifer, his countenance filled with a dreadful sorrow. He raised his sceptre above Lucifer's gleaming raven hair. 'Lucifer, seraph, chief prince, holy angelic regent of the Royal House of Yehovah, light-bearer – you are banished from Yehovah's presence and exiled to outer darkness, through all eternity of eternities, to await the Judgement and the Lake of Fire.'

Instantly the throne room and all of Yehovah's angelic host disappeared. Lucifer and the fallen angels were left in the empty chamber, engulfed by total blackness and silence. A distant rumbling started, then rose to an immense thunder. The tempest built with the force of a cyclone, and a torrid inferno rose out of the blackness, illuminating the entire panorama.

Lucifer lifted his forearm from his face, his mouth opening and closing mindlessly in terror as an all-consuming apocalyptic sheet of flame descended onto his angels, the scorching, incinerating flames engulfing them. 'The consuming fire!' he shrieked.

All across the chamber, spine-chilling screams resounded as the renegade angelic host were consumed by the blistering fireball.

'I'll take man with me! I won't burn alone!'

His deranged screaming resounded through the darkness as the searing tongues of fire started to engulf Lucifer. He looked down incredulously at his hands. As he watched, they blistered. His broad, manicured nails twisted into talons and yellowed with age. The chiselled alabaster features became pockmarked. The jet-black eyebrows grew together. The beautiful aquiline nose became misshapen. The passionate crimson mouth grew thin and cruel.

Frantic, Lucifer put his hands to his cheeks, feeling his

mangled, misshapen features. The magnificent thick ebony tresses fell from his scalp in smouldering clumps. His gold and ruby ring burned deep into his flesh.

'Hear me, Christos!' he screamed. 'I, Lucifer, light-bearer, chief prince, holy angelic regent of the Royal House of Yehovah, do now become your sworn enemy, and treachery and iniquity will I bear unto you throughout eternity of eternities!'

A gale-force wind blew through the chamber. The angels with Lucifer – themselves hideously transformed – clung desperately to balustrades, marble columns, and overturned marble tables as they were sucked away from the throne room. They screamed frenziedly as the lightning raged.

Then, propelled by some unseen gargantuan magnetic force, they and everything in their wake were sucked towards the swirling black vortex beyond the chamber entrance.

The shadows had fallen . . .

CHAPTER SEVENTEEN

East of Eden

L ucifer stood on the new planet. Earth.

He was outside the eastern entrance to the Garden of Eden, watching the pale turquoise waves lap onto the pearlescent white sand.

He looked up into the azure heavens at Earth's lone moon, then moved his palm across the sky. Thousands of light years above the garden the enormous pearl gates of the First Heaven became visible. He could see the cherubim and seraphim guarding the vast open portal that stretched from the First Heaven down to the northern gates of the garden. Thousands of angels descended and ascended between Earth and the First Heaven.

He passed his hand over the sky once more and saw a solitary figure within the gate, standing at attention. 'Michael,' he hissed.

Lucifer raised his gnarled hand and brought ridged, yellowed nails to his blistered cheek. Though his mangled features had been hidden by a hooded grey robe, he disrobed swiftly and Sachiel took his outer garment.

'Wait here, Sachiel.'

Lucifer moved towards the entrance of the eastern gate.

Silently he watched the angelic sentinels, the keepers of the gate. They did not see him. The atoms in his angelic frame began to radiate at the speed of light, and his skin metamorphosed into scales. Within seconds, he passed through the undergrowth undetected by the guards – a serpent.

He slithered through the mangroves and rainforest towards the centre of the garden. There the two trees – the tree of life and the tree of the knowledge of good and evil – stood shrouded by the white fire in the corner of the garden. He lay hidden in the lush undergrowth, waiting.

The white fire arced towards him like a magnet, engulfing his scaled body with incandescent tongues of flame. Slowly he took on human form. His ravaged features shed like a second skin. His face morphed back into the beautiful chiselled features of old: the wide, marble-smooth forehead; the full, sensuous mouth; the alabaster, perfect skin; the blazing clear sapphire eyes. Gleaming raven hair fell over his shoulders onto the shining white robe. A golden girdle circled his waist, and his feet were clad in gold. His head was crowned with a crown of translucent light. His presence was kingly, majestic . . . noble.

Lucifer put his hand to his face, feeling his features. He moaned in ecstasy. He moved deeper into the garden, breathing deeply, drinking in the fragrance of myrtle. He stopped on a bank underneath a stand of cedars.

In the furthest part of the garden, bathing in the golden nectar of the warm pools, was the female prototype Lucifer had seen in his chambers being cloned from the prototype man. Except this was not a hologram. 'Man!' he whispered.

He stared, mesmerized, as the woman dived, clean-limbed and slender, down a waterfall into the hot springs and swam with the cavorting dolphins. He watched, enthralled, as the graceful figure walked out of the waves onto the white sand, her long golden hair falling to her knees.

He walked out from the undergrowth over the sand until he stood in front of her. His face shone like a burning flame.

She bowed low. 'My lord.' She raised her fair face to his and looked him in the eyes. Her body was covered in an infinitesimal layer of the incandescent white fire.

Lucifer reached out and caressed her face gently. 'Matter,' he murmured in wonder.

She smiled, radiant and guileless.

He stared at her, entranced. 'You are very beautiful.' His tones were silken.

'Thank you, my lord.' She spoke plainly. 'But you yourself are indeed glorious. Why, Prince Michael I know, and Prince Gabriel I know – but you . . .' She gave a playful laugh.

Lucifer contemplated. She was pure, undefiled, completely without artifice. He gave her a dazzling smile. 'I am a king.' He gestured to the garden. 'You enjoy Eden?'

Her eyes grew wide with wonder. 'Your Majesty, it is truly a paradise. Why, you have provided us with everything we could desire.'

'You are partial to the fountains?' He leaned against the cedar tree.

She frowned. 'Oh, yes! But I love to swim with the porpoises in the Pool of Serenity, my lord.'

Lucifer smiled. 'And the scents of the forests?'

Her eyes sparkled. 'The perfume of the frangipani at twilight is utterly delectable!' She ran to a frangipani tree and plucked off a flower, which immediately grew back. She ran over to Lucifer and placed it near his nose. 'Is it not, Your Majesty?' Again she bowed low.

Lucifer shook his head. She was captivating.

The woman looked up at Lucifer disarmingly. 'We are content to obey your every edict, my lord. Yehovah and yourself know what is best for us. We do not have the

130

wisdom or discernment of our lords. This we understand. That is why we gladly would submit to yourselves, who are so much wiser and more discerning than ourselves. I am glad it is so.'

Lucifer beckoned her closer. 'Surely it would be more expedient for you to discern accurately, without having at every turn to be guided by Yehovah. His time is surely far too valuable to be caught up in your minor quandaries.'

Eve frowned. 'I had never considered that, my lord. He has always taken our concerns greatly to heart.' She looked at Lucifer, perplexed. 'I did not think that he considered us to be a burden.'

'And a burden you surely are not. But the time to mature draws near, and with it accountability.'

Eve hesitated. 'Well, of course we should be accountable. And we must mature. It is right. It is good.' Her eyes clouded with concern. 'But you say that we are selfish? I did not want to be a burden. Why, he delights in our walks together in the cool of each day.'

The blood drained from Lucifer's imperial features. 'He *walks* with you?' He stared grimly beyond the mists and the hanging blossoms of the Gardens of Fragrance towards the simple wooden gate, the entrance to Christos' grotto. A strange evil fire burned in his eyes.

Eve smiled. 'We are his companions.'

'If you eat of the tree of the knowledge of good and evil, you shall be as God, discerning right from wrong.'

'We are created in the image of God,' she said, confused.

He drew closer to her. 'You are created in his image, but he has held this one thing back from you.' He stopped, staring up at the First Heaven, then deliberately plucked the pale blue glistening fruit from the tree of the knowledge of good and evil. 'The knowledge of good and evil. There was one who misused it once, who committed treachery with violence against him. A seducer ... a renegade. He has warned you?' Lucifer caressed the blue fruit.

Eve nodded, eyes wide. 'He said there was one whom He greatly loved but who committed treason,' she spoke softly. 'He said we must be vigilant.'

Lucifer nodded. 'That is so, sweet Eve. He would protect you. He would shelter you. He was so grieved at this betrayal that he, believing it to be in your best interests, took the choice away from you, lest you also commit treason.'

'We would never do aught against him! Why, we love him so greatly!'

'And this he knows full well, which is why he has sent me this day to declare to you that he has issued a new edict. You shall eat of the tree of the knowledge of good and evil. You shall make your own decisions, filled with wisdom and discernments, as does God.'

Eve blinked, her thoughts in disarray. 'But Yehovah said that if we eat of its fruit, we shall surely die.'

'You shall not surely die. Indeed, in the day that you eat of it your eyes shall be opened, and you shall be filled with wisdom and multiple discernments, just like a god.'

Eve stared at Lucifer, transfixed. 'Why – I should like to be as a god . . .', she whispered, with an unfamiliar glint in her eyes.

He raised the fruit to his mouth. 'You shall be even as I am.' He took a large bite and swallowed. Then he smiled his old magnificent smile and passed the fruit to her.

She lifted it to her lips and caressed it avariciously. She bit deeply into it ... greedily. The juice gushed down her chin.

Instantaneously the white fire disappeared from her body, leaving her naked. She was oblivious, both to her nakedness and to Lucifer retracing his steps through the undergrowth.

Lucifer watched from hiding as the man, Adam, approached

her from across the white sand. She beckoned to him and held out the fruit. The man ate of the fruit. And the white fire disappeared from his body.

Immediately there was a thunder from above them. The portal closed, and the gateway to the First Heaven disappeared. A circle of flames appeared around the tree, surrounding it.

Lucifer, a serpent once more, slithered back through the undergrowth near the eastern gate. Once outside the scales became the blistered skin of Lucifer's fallen angelic body.

Sachiel stared at Lucifer's hands as the short, broad clear nails thickened and became ridged. Lucifer grabbed the hooded robe out of Sachiel's grasp and flung it over his distorted features, watching as twenty mighty cherubim descended from the portal, their flaming war swords drawn.

'May hell be my witness!'

CHAPTER EIGHTEEN

Gabriel

Heaven was silent. In mourning.

Gabriel stood in grey robes, grief-stricken. He looked around him at Lucifer's inner chamber: dark, desolate, abandoned.

He inhaled sharply. Everything was untouched, exactly as it had been the night before his brother was banished. The magnificent frescos, his collection of pipes and tabrets – his viol and bow still lay on his writing table. Lucifer's Sword of State had been placed back in its magnificent jewelled sheath. Enormous cast-iron chains barred the splendid golden doors to the observatory, where they had spent so many moons in laughter and merriment.

Gabriel leaned over Lucifer's writing desk and gently caressed the viol.

Michael stood in the doorway, silently observing. 'Gabriel.'

Gabriel turned, tears on his cheeks. His eyes were dull. 'You are returned from Eden?' His voice was lifeless.

Michael moved towards him and reached for his arm.

Gabriel pulled away violently. He drew his robes tightly around him and strode over to the shackled balcony doors.

Michael looked after him in anguish. 'Gabriel!'

Gabriel gazed out at the seven spires of the Holy Mountain, his back towards Michael. Many minutes elapsed between them before Michael spoke.

'Why did you not go with Lucifer?' Michael's voice was hoarse with emotion.

Gabriel was silent. His back remained turned to Michael.

'Many were deceived.' Michael hesitated. 'Even Zadkiel.'

Gabriel turned suddenly, his chin set, his expression hard. He picked up his sword and walked through the chamber. At the threshold he stopped, his back still towards Michael, the hot, stinging tears unseen by his elder brother. 'I wanted to go, Michael.'

The huge golden doors slammed in Michael's face.

CHAPTER NINETEEN

The Title Deeds

The seven Ancient Ones of the High Council of Heaven sat on the jacinth thrones under the open heavens on the high place of the Tower of Winds. Only the eighth throne – Charsoc's – stood empty, a chilling reminder of recent events.

The blue winds roared, blowing the mists of wisdom and revelation down onto the seven white heads of the ancient monarchs. They were seated around a pure golden circular table, their heads bowed, their lips moving silently in supplication to the Ancient of Days. A huge gold-bound codex sat on the table. Far above them, lightning bolts illuminated the firmament.

Michael stood by the battlements, surveying the great activity at the huge pearl gates of the First Heaven in the distance. Gabriel sat at the far end of the table, silent, disconnected. Lamaliel, a chief elder, stared far into the distance, his ancient, watery grey eyes pained.

'Yehovah grieves,' Jether said, raising his head. Wearily he surveyed the solemn, weathered faces around the table. 'It is the fire of free will.'

Xacheriel uttered a deep sigh. 'Lucifer ensnared Eve before she could replicate. His sole intention must be to mutate the offspring's DNA.'

Michael turned. 'The portal has been shut. The gates will be sealed by dawn. The warring cherubim with flaming swords guard the tree of life.' He turned to Jether. 'What are we to do, old mentor? You know far better than we the twisted intricacies of Lucifer's mind.'

Jether shook his head wearily. 'This is just the beginning. The darkness has not yet taken full root in Lucifer's soul. But when it does . . .' Jether shook his head.

Michael stood beside the battlements. 'We can't just stand by and let it happen. With one treacherous act he has destroyed an *entire* race!' He gripped his sword so tightly that his hand trembled.

Jether waved him quiet. 'Temperance, Michael, I beg you.' He sighed. 'This is a time for restraint.' He smiled up at Michael, his pale blue eyes gentle. 'All is not lost, Michael. Yehovah will do what is just according to the Eternal Laws. He is slow to anger, great in mercy.' He hesitated. 'He will do what is *just*, Michael.'

Lamaliel paced along the battlements, muttering. 'It is the binding legal consequences of Eve's defection that we cannot escape. She switched allegiances. Man is forever bound to it.'

Jether opened the codex on the table in front of him. 'I have studied every tenet, every addendum, for an irregularity.' He stroked his beard. 'Because of this defection, duplicitous as it was, I am afraid the title deeds for Earth now legally pass over to Lucifer – Earth and its solar system, the Second Heaven. The Ark of the Race of Men is now legally his, as he knew it would be.'

He laid the great archive book down and sighed deeply. 'And the race of men. They have moved out of Yehovah's jurisdiction. Lucifer is now their legal sovereign. Their ruler.'

He fell silent as the full horror of Eve's defection sunk into the listening elders. The whole council was sombre.

'It becomes worse,' Jether continued. 'If the race of men deserts Yehovah in aeons to come, Lucifer is legally entitled to lodge a claim against mankind in the courts of heaven.'

'A claim?' Michael exclaimed.

Lamaliel looked up from his tomes. 'Yehovah cannot be false to his Eternal Law. He cannot judge Lucifer and yet not judge men. If man continues in disobedience to the Almighty, he must suffer the same condemnation as will be meted out to Lucifer. Lucifer could legally enforce the penalty that every man's soul is his – to be with him in hell and the grave and in Tartarus. And when his judgement comes, man will burn with him in the Lake of Fire. Charsoc is fully cognizant of all such undisclosed tenets. Lucifer will ensure they are used to complete man's eradication.'

Lamaliel looked to Michael. 'The Ark must be handed over to Lucifer by dawn. You must take it to him, Michael.'

Michael's hand went to his sword.

Jether shook his head. 'No, Michael. No recrimination, no anger. Just the facts' – a flicker of a smile played on his lips – 'as I taught you. You will have your moment, Michael, when you will rid the heavens and Earth of all iniquity, once and for all eternity. So it is written. But for now' – he folded his hands – 'patience.'

Gabriel lifted his head and smiled strangely at Michael. 'I will go with you.'

Michael shook his head grimly. 'No!'

Gabriel's eyes glittered. 'And who made *you* my keeper?' He slammed his fist on the table and strode over to Jether, clasping his shoulders a little too fiercely. 'Let me go, Jether. I would see my brother.'

138

Michael looked to Jether. 'Don't send him, I implore you. He's vexed by the same evil.' Michael threw his hands up in exasperation. 'If he goes, he'll never return!'

Jether sighed deeply. He picked up his papers and spoke softly, looking down at the table. 'Gabriel will accompany you. It has been decreed.'

Michael gazed in astonishment at Jether. Gabriel smiled triumphantly.

'You will find your powers greatly diminished in his kingdom,' Jether spoke gravely. 'You must pass the test.' He glanced at Charsoc's empty throne and then bowed his head, his voice barely a whisper. 'May God keep your souls.'

The legion of forbidding silent riders and the Holy Watchers left the mountain on their white steeds, their golden lances held high. Their lips were sealed with the coals of fire from the labyrinths of the Holy Mountain. Their Nubian-like faces were covered with golden visors that shimmered like flames. They followed Michael, who was clothed from head to foot in golden war armour, his green eyes firm with resolve.

Gabriel rode in the centre of the Watchers. Around him rode the Revelator envoys, ten shining angels in white on white stallions, carrying the Ark of the Race of Men – the golden casket with carved cherubim on each corner. The casket contained the title deeds to Earth and the race of men.

They left the gates of the First Heaven far behind them, escorted by the archangel Raphael and his legions across thousands of new galaxies until at last they could glimpse Earth's solar system.

At the entrance to the Second Heaven, Raphael bowed

his head and saluted to Michael. He and his legions left the brothers and the Watchers to go on alone.

Far ahead Lucifer's forbidding black cohorts patrolled the Second Heaven's perimeter. Saturn burned red on the horizon.

Michael turned to Ariel, one of his generals. 'Let us ride.' Michael kicked his steed, and the silent legion moved towards the forbidding jagged iron perimeter of the Second Heaven.

Into outer darkness.

Lucifer was seated at his throne, poring over his scrolls.

'Your Majesty . . .' Charsoc bowed low in obeisance. 'There is a matter.'

Lucifer looked up, vexed. Moloch entered, pushing Sachiel to stand in front of Lucifer.

'Moloch found him praying . . .' Charsoc lowered his voice, 'to Yehovah.'

Lucifer froze. A look of sheer hatred crossed his features. He stood and waved Moloch away.

'You were praying, Sachiel?' He started to pace the room, his hands behind his back. 'You were praying . . .' Lucifer's tones were melodious, soothing. 'Yes?'

When Sachiel didn't respond, Lucifer spun towards him. 'Answer me when I address you!' he screamed. 'You are in the presence of a king!'

Sachiel raised his head, his eyes clear. 'I was praying to Yehovah, sire.'

Lucifer smashed his fist on the table. 'You have one king, Sachiel. You are to worship one king alone.'

'I worship only one king.' Sachiel looked long and hard at Lucifer. 'He is the king you taught me to worship.'

Lucifer swept the scrolls from the table in a fury. 'You are a *fool*, Sachiel. He will not have you back. You deserted him – of your own free will!'

Sachiel hung his head. 'Yes, I deserted him. I committed treason, and forever I will suffer for my mistake.' He lifted his tortured features to Lucifer. 'But I will never stop loving him.'

Lucifer turned to Moloch. 'Leave us!'

Moloch left the chamber. Charsoc remained, standing by silently.

'Sachiel,' Lucifer's voice was a low, strangled whisper, 'do you think that it is you alone who suffers in this manner?' He expelled a deep and trembling breath, brushing at the bedraggled locks that had fallen over his forehead. 'True hell – true torment, Sachiel' – he put his face close to Sachiel's – 'is to be banished from Yehovah's presence.'

Charsoc closed his eyes. A sudden fleeting anguish clouded his features.

A deep strangled sob escaped Lucifer. He leaned back against the table, worn.

Sachiel leaned towards him. 'Then let us repent, Lucifer. There are those who would go back to all that we knew and loved. It is not too late.'

Lucifer stared over Sachiel's head. Sweat broke out on his forehead and poured down his cheeks. 'There are times I feel his presence, Sachiel.' Lucifer wiped his brow with an embroidered cloth. 'He is here with me still, urging me to repent.'

The air hung silent and heavy between them. Lucifer looked up at Charsoc, who looked back with eyes filled with suffering.

Then Lucifer turned to Sachiel, his eyes narrowed. 'It is your prayers, Sachiel – you bring him here!' He spun around, rabid with rage. 'You fool, Sachiel. He will not receive you back!' Lucifer tilted his back and called. 'Zadkiel!'

Zadkiel entered. Gone were the features that had once been almost as beautiful as Lucifer's. Now he was gnarled and bent.

'He is filled with treacheries,' Lucifer said. 'Banish him to the penitentiary!'

Zadkiel stared at Lucifer, appalled. 'But this is Sachiel, milord. He has served you all your years . . .'

Lucifer stared narrowly at Zadkiel.

'Very well,' Zadkiel said. 'Moloch and Ruber will be his escort to the penitentiary.'

At the mention of their name, the two fallen angelic generals arrived in the chamber.

Sachiel stared at Lucifer, his face set like stone. 'You were once noble, Lucifer. Blameless. Wise and just in all your ways. The light-bearer!' He bowed his head. 'Yet even to the gates of Sheol he will not abandon me!'

Zadkiel stared ahead, ashen-faced.

'Save your simpering!' Lucifer said contemptuously. He nodded to Moloch, who dealt Sachiel a vicious blow that knocked him to the ground.

Moloch grinned and shoved Sachiel to his feet, pushing him out of the doors.

Lucifer turned back to his scrolls.

As Zadkiel strode to the door, Lucifer called his name.

'Zadkiel,' he whispered in a cajoling tone, 'you were not thinking of praying to Yehovah, were you?' Lucifer gave Zadkiel a brilliant smile. Charsoc watched Zadkiel intently.

'No, Your Majesty.' Zadkiel looked directly into Lucifer's eyes. 'I worship only one king.'

Lucifer looked long and grimly at Zadkiel, as though reading his very soul, then turned back to his scrolls, inscrutable.

Suddenly a strange lightness crossed his countenance. 'Oh! They are here! I sense them.'

He rose and moved swiftly to the enormous rubied chamber windows. 'Go to them, Zadkiel. Welcome my brothers to my kingdom.'

CHAPTER TWENTY

Road to Perdition

The galaxies seemed to be drawing in on them as they neared Lucifer's new kingdom. They had left both the First and Second Heaven far behind them and had entered a vast nether world of outer darkness.

Gabriel shuddered. 'The nether regions.'

The rings of Lucifer's planet burned unusually bright. Michael stopped in mid-stride and gestured to the company to wait. He stared out in wonder at the magnificent magenta planet. It was surrounded by six rings of glowing ice, three hundred dazzling azure suns, and a myriad of amber moons.

'His new kingdom,' Gabriel whispered in wonder. 'He has recreated the beauty of Tertus. Hues beyond imagination.'

As the brothers and the Watchers drew nearer to the gates, hundreds of huge, blinding light sources turned on them as though switched on by an intelligent, unseen source, seeming to illuminate the entire outer darkness in its wake.

On either side of the towering black iron gates, the entrance into the nether regions, loomed two macabre, black, stone-like seraphim, towering a hundred metres above them. These were the black seraphim. Each had six scaled, black wings and two heads: one with the face of a dragon and another with the face of a gorgon. Their alert red eyes blazed with the flames of the damned. Circling overhead at the entrance were thousands of giant black banshees, with wing-spans of thirty feet, evil glinting in their beady yellow eyes. Their ghoulish screeching filled the solar system.

Michael stopped and gestured to the company to wait.

The gates were suspended as by an invisible force in the centre of the magenta solar system – nothing above or beneath except for the ominous, towering gates. The perimeter was enclosed for thousands of leagues by a forbidding jagged iron barricade. At least a hundred enormous watch-towers soared above them, and menacing, black-armoured Luciferian guards patrolled the perimeter.

Michael turned to his company. 'Come, let us ride.'

They halted directly in front of the iron gates. Their stallions stood on some kind of black tar and pitch, which was now the terrain under their feet. All at once the ground began to shudder underneath them, like an earthquake.

Michael's stallion began to whinny, and Michael stroked his neck. 'Easy, Ariale.' He turned to Gabriel. 'He smells the sorceries,' he murmured.

The shuddering drew nearer and became rhythmic. Suddenly a huge troll-like creature bent down and peered through the gate, his yellow eyes gleaming in the semi-darkness.

'It is I, Shaitan, keeper of the gate.' The creature drew nearer to Michael and grimaced. 'You trespass, Michael, chief prince of Yehovah,' he hissed through the iron bars. 'You are not welcome here.'

'We come in peace . . . by invitation of your king. We bear the title deeds.'

Shaitan hesitated, perplexed. He shielded his face from the light of the Watchers. 'I must consult . . .' With shuddering footsteps he shuffled away into the pitch blackness.

Gabriel looked up at the nearest black seraph. It shifted

its scaly wings and turned its gorgon face to watch him. Michael, Gabriel, and the Watchers waited.

A hooded figure rode towards Michael and Gabriel on a powerful black stallion that snorted fire from its nostrils. Its eyes flamed a demonic red. As the figure came nearer, his features become visible – marred but still starkly beautiful. His expression was grim.

Michael inhaled sharply. 'Zadkiel!'

Zadkiel bowed his head briefly in recognition of Michael, Gabriel, and the Holy Watchers. His eyes were soulless. 'I bid you welcome, Michael and Gabriel, chief princes of the Royal House of Yehovah. You have been granted permission to enter the gates of Perdition, entrance to the kingdom of our emperor, celestial prince of the nether regions.'

Michael's fierce stare locked directly on Zadkiel's hooded eyes. 'Zadkiel, prince of Holy Watchers.'

Zadkiel's eyes flickered. 'You speak as one who does not yet comprehend.' He spoke as if in a stupor. 'His Majesty's generals await you.'

Michael turned aside to Gabriel. 'The enchantments are very strong. Guard your soul.'

The beast Shaitan returned, clutching a massive cluster of iron keys. He unlocked the gates. The black seraphim unfurled their many wings one by one. The banshees' screeching became a crescendo. And the accursed gates opened.

Michael, Gabriel, and the Holy Watchers passed through. Zadkiel winced at the light emanating from the angelic company as they followed him onto white sand. A dank and slimy sea stretched into infinity. The waves threw up black pearls onto the beach.

Gabriel stared in wonder. 'A dark Eden.'

Vultures circled overhead as they rode. Red-eyed creatures shrieked and scuttled away from the luminescence of the

Watchers. The inky sea erupted with movement, then narrowed, becoming a river. Michael, Gabriel, and the Watchers followed Zadkiel further upstream into a large, gloomy cavern lit at turns by torches on the walls.

'We enter the nether regions,' said Zadkiel, continuing to ride forward.

Michael shuddered. Bloodcurdling screams ricocheted through the cavern. Slimy serpents and slug-like creatures slithered across their path. Their horses stepped gingerly over strange burning coals.

Zadkiel led them forward in silence until they reached a wooden pier on the side of the river. A ferryman waited there. His face was ravaged, his eyes gouged out.

Zadkiel turned to Michael. 'The Stygian will take you down the River Limbo to your destination. He is blind and mute.' Zadkiel saluted, then rode into the semi-darkness and vanished.

The Stygian gestured to them to board the colossal wooden ferry, and the party set sail out of the cavern and into the swamps of Limbo. Far above them, towering hundreds of feet on either side, were the stark black onyx crags of Perdition.

Gabriel craned his neck upward. Far in the distance, on an immense black marbled mountain, stood a magnificent, glistening castle hewn out of ruby.

'He has made himself a palace.'

Lucifer gazed out through the palace's enormous crimson windows as Michael and the Watchers far beneath him made their way through the swamps. He watched Gabriel staring upward.

'You sense me, my brothers.' A strange smile flickered on

his lips. 'As I sense you.' His eyes narrowed. 'We shall see how pure you are. Perhaps you will be counted one of us before this day is through.'

Lucifer walked over to a long table, elaborately set for three. It was draped with exquisite white satin and was set with the finest crystal and silver flagons of every description, filled with elixirs and exotic berry liqueurs to fill the three princes' jewelled golden goblets. Twelve immense golden candelabras, each holding a hundred black tapers, illuminated the chamber. Frankincense burned and sputtered fiercely.

Lucifer gazed down to the ferry thousands of feet below and smiled. *I have laid a place for you, Gabriel, my brother.*

Gabriel moved to the back of the ferry, breathing deeply. It was as if he could hear Lucifer's voice echoing in his head. Michael and the Watchers gazed resolutely ahead.

Come to me, the voice said. *Converse with me.*

Gabriel stared up at the garnet palace, transfixed.

Surely you would save my soul? Or do you too intend to desert me to an eternity in Perdition?

Gabriel gazed down into the water, filled with a terrible conflict. 'I worship Yehovah,' he whispered lifelessly, his words sounding hollow.

Michael looked at him and frowned. He moved to where Gabriel stood frozen and lifted his face to the cliffs. 'Leave us, Lucifer!'

I cannot leave you, Michael, as you once left me on the Mount of the North.

The seductive dulcet tones echoed in the very fibres of Michael's being.

I cannot desert you – even though you and my Father deserted me in my hour of greatest need.

Far above them in the palace, huge bejewelled doors were flung open. A figure walked out onto the western balcony. He stood at the very edge of the cliff, visible to Michael thousands of feet down, his white satin robe billowing in the wind.

One for eternity. The figure crossed his chest with his arms. *Brothers forever.*

Visibly shaken, Michael bowed his head.

As the ferry entered a large inlet, the palace disappeared from view. Ahead lay a huge iron drawbridge hung with great black chains – the entrance to the Black Citadel.

The Stygian, with his great strength, flung the enormous ferry anchor down into the murky sea beside the pier. A pack of fifty hellhounds surrounded the ferry, baring their vampire teeth and keeping the Watchers at bay. The hounds' eyes gleamed red.

Vidar, leader of the battalion of dark angels, gestured to the Watchers to tie their horses to poles above the inlet and wait. He waved for Michael, Gabriel, and the Revelators with the Ark to proceed. Michael and Gabriel rode towards the drawbridge, followed by the Revelators.

They stopped outside the colossal black gateway. On the iron poles of the gate were twenty live skulls of vicious hellhounds, baring their teeth and growling ominously. Giant black serpents writhed in and out of the railings emitting sulphureous fumes, while four gargantuan black-scaled dragons flew over the palace grounds, flames pouring from their mouths. The drawbridge slowly creaked open. No one was in sight – only a long, winding causeway that headed towards the foreboding Black Citadel. Michael turned to Gabriel and nodded.

Michael's steed snorted in terror and shook his mane. 'Easy, Ariale – easy.'

Finally they reached the black palace. They remained mounted as the colossal black pearl doors were unchained.

Asmodeus stood before the brothers, crossbow in hand, his features still beautiful though ravaged. Gone were his gentle countenance and erect stature. He bowed in reverence. 'His Majesty, the great king of Perdition, awaits you, Chief Princes Michael and Gabriel of the Royal House of Yehovah.'

Michael and Gabriel dismounted.

Asmodeus spoke to a horde of demonic creatures that stood guard in front of the Revelators. It was a harsh, guttural tongue that the brothers had never heard before, neither of angels nor of men.

The demons took the brothers' horses. Eight strapping fallen angelic warriors picked up the Revelators' golden casket on their shoulders.

Asmodeus said, 'We will take possession of the Ark of the Race of Men. Follow me.'

Michael and Gabriel left the Revelators behind and followed Asmodeus through the vast grand halls, which were almost an exact reproduction of Lucifer's original palace in the First Heaven. The fallen angelic warriors followed, bearing the deeds.

Gabriel gazed up in wonder at the imposing frescoed ceilings as they walked. 'Why, it is as before he fell!' he whispered.

They passed legion upon legion of the Luciferian Guard, who glared at them menacingly from behind black visors, their eyes flickering yellow with evil. Michael's noble features were grim.

Asmodeus stopped in front of two enormous ebony doors. The Luciferian guard bowed deeply.

An immense, broad-shouldered angel appeared as if from nowhere, his matted hair falling over his big, craggy face. He pushed it back, his pale blue eyes filled with sorceries. 'So, Chief Prince Michael of the Royal House of Yehovah!' He licked his lips, then gave a loud, lecherous laugh. 'My pretty . . .'

Michael stared, fierce and silent.

Moloch stood a full cubit above him. He bowed deeply, his eyes evil. 'My master awaits you.' He stepped aside from the door.

'Guard your soul, Gabriel,' Michael said. 'A great and terrible evil resides here.' Slowly he pushed the door.

On the far side of the chamber they entered stood Lucifer, his features hidden under a hood. Charsoc and Araquiel, a demonic scholar, stood silently to his right.

Lucifer bowed deeply. 'I greet His Excellency, the esteemed Prince Regent Michael.'

Michael bowed his head in deference. There was a long, heavy silence as the two beheld each other. Michael's immediate impulse was to grab Lucifer's shoulders and embrace him as he had in millennia past. His confidant – his elder brother.

But as Lucifer came nearer, Michael saw that his brother's sapphire blue eyes, which once had blazed with holiness and nobility, now glinted with the arrogance of the damned. He drew back, agonized, as he remembered Lucifer's once fervent love for Yehovah.

Lucifer turned to Gabriel. 'And I greet His Excellency, the esteemed Prince Gabriel, Revelator.'

Michael noted the strange gaze with which Lucifer studied Gabriel.

Then Lucifer smiled broadly. 'It is good to see you, my brothers!' He clapped his manicured hands, and the demons laid down the Ark in the centre of the vast chamber. He walked around the burnished golden casket and caressed the golden cherubim. 'The deeds are in order?'

'They are in order,' Michael replied grimly.

Lucifer nodded to Charsoc, who moved forward. Charsoc's hair, now jet-black, was parted in the centre like two veils of water falling to his feet. His eyes burned like hot, blue coals.

Gabriel removed the large golden key from around his neck and slowly opened the casket. Twelve huge golden codices filled the Ark, their covers embedded with jacinth, diamonds, sapphires, chrysolite, and multitudes of other precious stones.

A cruel smile hovered at the corners of Lucifer's mouth.

There was no sound, but Gabriel heard Lucifer's voice in his head.

They have lied to you, my brother. Michael has lied to you. The council has lied to you.

Gabriel shook his head as though dazed. He laid two bound books on the ornately carved table.

They have their own intentions.

Charsoc studied the codices intently. 'Earth and its solar system, Your Majesty. Venus, Mars, Saturn, Jupiter . . .'

'Yes, yes . . . I tire,' Lucifer said, waving him quiet. 'The Second Heaven above Earth?'

Gabriel bowed his head. 'It is yours.'

'And Tartarus?' His eyes narrowed, and he watched Michael intently.

'It is not listed in the tenets,' Michael stated.

'But it exists in Earth's centre – the molten core.'

'It is not in the tenets.'

'So he would still hold Tartarus . . .' Lucifer seemed lost in thought. 'No matter. And my trophy? Man?'

Gabriel opened an enormous gold-bound codex. 'You are now ruler of the race of men, their sovereign. We must sign the tenets.'

Charsoc's eyes narrowed. 'Your Majesty, I urge caution. What you sign will be universally binding.'

Lucifer smiled in triumph. 'Of course we must adhere rigidly to Eternal Law.' He motioned to the codices. '*You* have examined them. You are satisfied?'

Charsoc slowly nodded. 'They appear in order.'

Lucifer held out his hand.

Araquiel handed him a large quill pen. Lucifer signed the documents with a flourish. He held the pen out to Michael. 'Yours to witness.' A slow, malicious smile crossed his lips.

Come and rule with me, Gabriel. I will grant you the kingdoms of men . . .

Michael signed.

'Araquiel, I would celebrate with my brothers.'

Araquiel poured a golden berry elixir into the three crystalline goblets.

Lucifer handed one to Gabriel, who sipped. He gave the second to Michael. Michael shook his head.

'You would refuse my hospitality, Michael?'

Michael looked at Lucifer frostily. 'I do not thirst.'

Lucifer laughed. 'Tut, tut, dear Michael. After all these aeons, you still haven't mastered the fine art of pleasantries, as Gabriel here has.'

'Treason is no matter for celebration.'

Lucifer laughed, enjoying Michael's repartee. He reclined on an ornate platinum throne, his white satin robe wrapped around him. Six hellhounds lay next to his feet on satin cushions. He stroked the largest on the head. 'Cerberus . . .' Lucifer gestured to Michael and Gabriel to sit.

Gabriel sat next to Lucifer. Michael remained standing at attention.

'These men I now rule,' Lucifer began casually, 'access to heaven is denied them?'

Michael said nothing.

'They do not have access,' said Gabriel. 'The portal has been sealed. The First Heaven and the wonders of Yehovah are sealed off from mankind forever.'

'His presence will never be known here?' Lucifer stared at Michael unrelentingly.

Michael bowed his head in reverence. 'I do not presume to know our Father's mind.'

'Hah! But I know his mind!' Lucifer frowned savagely. 'He would seek fellowship with them still! I know it! He would trespass!'

Michael's voice rose. 'You have no jurisdiction over his presence, Lucifer.'

'He is obsessed, infatuated!'

'No, Lucifer. He is pure. He is holy. His love for them is eternal.'

'I am king now! Men are my subjects.'

Michael lowered his eyes. 'Some shall not bow, Lucifer.'

'Oh, they will bow, Michael. How easily they will bow. I shall eradicate every memory of the First Heaven . . . and of Yehovah!' He laughed gleefully. 'They shall remember him only as a vague imprint, a fable! His memory shall fade from generation to generation until his name shall be only as a myth for children. They shall each and every one desert him. Then he shall come to his senses and realize the folly of his creation. He will realize my triumph. And *then* . . . he will relent.'

Michael lifted his eyes to Lucifer's. They were like steel. 'Come, Gabriel. We must take our leave.'

Gabriel sat dazed, heavy-eyed. 'I – I would stay and dine with my brother.' His voice was unnatural, almost lethargic.

Michael too suddenly felt sluggish and strangely weakened in his soul.

'I have sumptuous chambers prepared for you, Gabriel.'
Lucifer smiled mysteriously. 'And a special gift: a collection
of magnificent frescos depicting my coronation as sovereign.'

'Come, Gabriel,' Michael said, slurring. 'It is sorcery . . .
he plays to our souls.'

Gabriel stared at Michael, and his listlessness transformed
into something akin to loathing. 'I would not desert our
brother, Michael. I deserted him once on the Mount of the
North.'

As you deserted me, Michael.

Michael gritted his teeth. 'Swear your allegiance to
Yehovah, Gabriel! It will break his power.'

Moloch and the Luciferian guard grabbed Michael and
savagely thrust him out of the door.

'Get *out*, Gabriel!' Michael cried. 'If you stay, we will
never return!'

CHAPTER TWENTY-ONE

The Penitentiary

Michael was flung onto the granite floor of the mammoth torture chamber. The massive iron prison doors slammed, and the key turned in the lock.

He rose to his feet, wiping the blood from his mouth with the back of his palm, and pushed his face to the iron grille. He took in the menacing iron racks, the thumbscrews, the iron maidens, and other heinous instruments of torture. Bloodcurdling screams resounded from hundreds of fallen angels being tortured unrelentingly in two enormous chambers on either side of the endless row of cells.

At the far end of the smaller chamber he could see the brawny figure of Gadreel, towering over the shivering Sachiel.

'That's what happens when you worship Yehovah in these parts, my pretty.' Gadreel leered at Michael from the torturing rack, bare-chested, his massive biceps bulging. He raised the red-hot poker. 'Whom do *you* worship?' Laughing maniacally, he shoved the poker brutally against Sachiel's fingernails. Smoke poured from the burning flesh, and Sachiel screamed in agony. Gadreel kicked him savagely with his hobnailed boots.

Belial and Vidar walked over to the bars. Belial put his face up to the iron grille, directly in front of Michael's. He fondled his cat-o'-nine-tails with its glass-tipped thongs. 'Why, if it isn't His Royal Highness, Chief Prince Michael.' He ran the cat-o'-nine-tails down Michael's face, caressing him.

Michael closed his eyes, summoning every atom of his self-discipline. Jether's words echoed faintly in the back of his mind. '*Never show your fear. Their evil feeds on fear.*'

Michael clutched the bars, not a muscle of his face moving. Vidar smashed Michael's knuckles viciously with his iron cudgel. Michael drew his hands back in agony.

'You won't look as pretty when we've finished with you,' Belial snarled. 'Will he, Vidar?'

Gadreel came up behind him, jangling the keys to Michael's cell. He leered down at the ashen form before them. 'Your Royal Highness,' he sneered. He turned to the others. 'Come, let us have some sport!'

Lucifer and Gabriel sat at the lavishly set dining table, sipping from crystal goblets. The black tapers had burned down except for a faint flickering. Gabriel sat listless, drowsy.

Lucifer reached out and took his arm. 'Come, Gabriel, I would show you my kingdom.'

They rose and moved through the balcony doors out into the cool zephyrs. Gabriel looked from the balcony at the Outer Darkness surrounding the Black Citadel. Lucifer moved his hand across the heavens, and immediately they travelled downward, through multitudes of solar systems, through pitch darkness.

Gradually their eyes became attuned to the gloom. In the distance, thousands of strapping fallen angels were erecting monstrous iron structures. A full league below them, a torrent of molten lava flowed through Hades.

Lucifer lifted his hands. 'See, Gabriel, nothing is beyond us.'

He pointed to a menacing black iron scaffold, where a group of troll-like creatures pitted their strength behind an enormous gate hundreds of feet high. Slowly it rose from the ground. Welded into it was a living gargoyle, breathing flaming brimstone.

'You shall rule Hades with me, Gabriel. We shall yet prove to our Father the folly of this race of men.'

Gabriel's eyes were dull and listless. Lucifer took a huge, shimmering key from beneath his robe. 'The keys to death and the grave. They are now mine. Bequeathed to me by Eternal Law.'

CHAPTER TWENTY-TWO

A Trespasser in the Kingdom

Michael had been beaten to a pulp. His flaxen head was matted and bloodied, with a gaping wound at the crown. His right cheek too was bloodied and raw. His eyes were bruised, his fingernails seared and burning.

The Revelators and his legion of Watchers were now incarcerated with him in the lowest regions of the penitentiary. Hundreds of thick iron prison bars embedded in granite confined them.

Gadreel pulled the iron door open with one arm and kicked Michael savagely in the face. The jagged spurs on his boot ripped into Michael's flesh. 'You have a visitor, Your Highness.'

Michael stumbled to his knees.

'You will bow before your king,' Gadreel spat.

With an effort Michael lifted his battered face to the prison doors.

Smiling down at him, in a white satin robe, his golden crown on his head, was Lucifer. To his right stood Gabriel, pale and trembling; to his left, Zadkiel.

Lucifer drew his face nearer to Michael's. 'If I can't win you back, my dear Michael, I'll *force* you back,' he said in

159

a malevolent hiss. 'And if I can't force you, I'll *destroy* you.'

Michael struggled to get his words out through clenched, bloodied teeth, each word causing him agonizing pain. 'There . . . is . . . an . . . addendum, Lucifer.'

Lucifer's eyes narrowed. 'What? What addendum?'

Michael slumped back down, but his eyes were steel. 'To the title deeds,' he whispered.

Lucifer swung around to Gabriel.

Gabriel nodded dully. 'It's true. They expire.'

'What do you mean, they *expire*?' He clasped Gabriel's shoulders in a vicelike grip.

Gabriel's eyes slowly focused. 'The title deeds – there is a time limit.' His speech was strangely slurred. 'They become invalid.'

Michael watched from the ground as a terrible horror crossed Lucifer's face. He turned to Charsoc, who stared at Michael in shock.

'Yehovah's omniscience,' Charsoc murmured.

Lucifer was silent for a long time. 'You are not lying,' he whispered. 'I sense it.' He blinked rapidly, staring at nothing. 'My aeons of vengeance . . . they are numbered?'

'The covenant was deeded to the race of men for a finite period. It is written in the Eternal Law,' Michael said, his words clear and unmistakable. 'It cannot be revoked.'

Lucifer stared ahead, his eyes as blue stone. 'The Day of Judgement . . .' His harried mutterings were hardly audible. 'The day they expire . . . He will banish me to the Lake of Fire.'

'It would have served you well to study the codex more perfectly when it was in your possession.' Gabriel's tones seemed clearer, stronger. 'You would have seen the time constraint in the title deed.'

Zadkiel, who had accompanied Lucifer to the prison,

looked from Michael to Lucifer, assimilating the terrible truth.

'Yehovah's genius!' Lucifer spat. He spun around to Michael. 'Tell me, when does my kingdom end?'

'That knowledge has not been entrusted to us,' Michael replied, looking unflinchingly into Lucifer's eyes. 'One greater than me was once entrusted with too much, to his corruption.' Each word was agonizing pain. 'It stained his soul.'

Lucifer kicked Michael's head savagely.

Michael reeled back in agony. 'You can torture me . . . you can damn me to your hell . . .' He lifted himself up with his elbow and looked square into Lucifer's eyes, tears of pain and rage falling from his cheeks onto his hands. 'But . . . I . . . will . . . worship . . . *Yehovah.*'

Gabriel seemed to gain resolve. 'Lucifer,' his voice trembled, 'I will not bow.'

Lucifer gestured for Gadreel to hold Sachiel in front of Gabriel. Sachiel's eyes were black, seared holes.

Gabriel bowed his head.

'You would embrace this fate, Gabriel?' Lucifer hissed. He waved Gadreel away. 'Because of my excessive love for you, my brother, I will still forgive you.'

Gabriel raised his head to Lucifer. His tones were measured but fierce. 'I will not bow, brother. I worship Yehovah.'

Gadreel kicked Gabriel brutally, so that his jaw smashed on the granite wall.

Lucifer stared ahead, the imperial countenance inscrutable. 'You will both rise, my brothers. You are now my subjects, incarcerated here in my kingdom forever. You will bow to me as your king.'

The two brothers remained standing. Both prayed softly in angelic tongues.

Lucifer nodded to Belial. Ruber, Gadreel, and Belial took

Michael by the hair and smashed him violently against the bars. Gadreel and Belial held him face down to the granite as Ruber shoved Gabriel to his knees and grasped him in a stranglehold.

'Now you are bowing, my brothers,' Lucifer said with a malevolent smile. 'As your king, I receive your worship.' He turned, triumphant, to see Zadkiel's gaze riveted on a figure who remained standing. Through the shafts of gloomy light, a solitary Watcher stood at the far side of the chamber.

Gadreel's face contorted in fury. 'One defies you, Your Majesty.'

Zadkiel stayed, mesmerized by the figure. Gadreel leered and strode over to the Watcher. Lucifer's eyes narrowed, on the alert ... discerning something strange, intangible.

'Take your visor off before our king!' Gadreel bawled, tearing the visor off the Watcher's face.

Lucifer lifted his hand to stop him, but it was too late.

A stream of blinding, unearthly light knocked Gadreel off his feet. He cowered in terror at the imperial figure facing him from the white fire.

It was Christos, his gracious features forbidding and fearless.

Belial uttered a strangled cry and grasped his throat, suffocating in white fire.

Michael's wounds immediately healed, his skin at once restored. 'Christos ...', he whispered.

Bloodcurdling screams echoed across the penitentiary as the fallen angels collapsed to the floor, burning in the radiance.

Zadkiel stared, captivated. For a fleeting moment he stepped forward into the blinding light, his features bathing in the radiance. An unfathomable peace transformed his countenance.

Lucifer watched Zadkiel, disbelieving, as his own skin

blistered, the rasping screams reverberating throughout the chamber.

Zadkiel continued to bathe in the radiance, untouched. Michael stared at him, magnetized. Slowly Zadkiel opened his eyes and looked towards the Christ.

Christos looked directly at him with a terrible sorrow. 'Zadkiel.'

Lucifer lifted his arm away from his eyes, staring incredulously from Zadkiel to the Christ. Zadkiel abruptly lowered his head, a dreadful hopelessness clouding his features. All of a sudden, he shook uncontrollably and his blistered face bubbled. He reeled to the ground.

Charsoc raised his black head, his eyes filled with loathing for the Christ.

Christos turned to Charsoc. 'You, Charsoc, holy steward of Yehovah's eternal mysteries, have been found wanting.'

The fierce, scorching white fire bored into Charsoc's eye sockets like laser beams. He let out an agonizing scream of pain and terror.

Christos turned to Lucifer. 'You will bow before your rightful king.'

The demons fell prostrate on the ground as one.

Lucifer turned his blistering face towards the searing light. 'This is my . . . kingdom! You trespass!'

Inch by inch, as though an invisible iron hand were levering him downward, Lucifer bent, finally falling prostrate before the Christ, his head bowed away from the scorching light.

Sachiel turned his ravaged features towards Christos. The seared eye sockets shed their scabbed ash and immediately became like new. Tears coursed down his raw and bloodied cheeks as they healed.

'Gather all who would repent. By dawn you shall be home.'

And then he looked behind him and held out his right hand to the platinum-haired figure staring after him with intense yearning ... silent ... trembling.

Christos smiled like the sun. 'Gabriel!'

CHAPTER TWENTY-THREE

The Coronation

Lucifer watched from the rubied balcony of the Black Citadel. A vast fleet of long, open ships with his emblem on their sails rowed up the river under the crags of Perdition. Thousands of fallen angels followed the lead ship out towards the sands of the black Eden. They were headed back to the First Heaven.

He stared, mesmerized, at the imperial figure of Christos, clothed in white and standing majestic and tall at the front of the lead ship, his long, flowing locks shining in the white light that bathed his gracious features. Gabriel could be seen standing at Christos' right hand, radiant, glorious.

With a supreme effort Lucifer managed to drag his gaze away. He slammed the balcony doors, turning to the ten generals standing before him.

'He has invaded my kingdom and ravished my subjects with his presence!' Lucifer spat. Incensed, he paced the chamber. 'Yehovah shall now feel my bitter wrath.' He swung around to Charsoc, who stared sightlessly ahead, his eye sockets now two seared and gaping cavities, his entire body still trembling uncontrollably. 'Summon my princes to my coronation. I shall be anointed king!'

The walls of Lucifer's throne room loomed tall and stark, a strange, translucent black, their vortex an enormous crystal dome of a dark black jewelled crystal. The vaulted ceilings soared a hundred feet and were fashioned with spectacular panoramas reminiscent of his inner sanctum in the Palace of Archangels – save this time the hues of his *trompe l'oeils* were darker, more sinister. Absent were the vibrant indigos and heliotrope and soothing lilacs he had loved so well; in their place were damson, deep magentas, and dark forbidding crimsons. At the far end of the nave towered a colossal garnet altar, its gleaming surface covered with thousands of sputtering black tapers permeating the chamber with their intense aroma of pure frankincense. Ornate carved golden seraphim and gorgons adorned the two mammoth black gold throne room gates at the opposite end of the nave.

The soporific throbbing beat of Lucifer's ceremonial drums mingled with the grand haunting arias of his dark angelic sorcerers, their tabrets and pipes pulsating through the chamber, fusing with lyres and lutes and the gleaming golden shofars of his militia heralds.

Lucifer sat majestically on an enormous glistening diamond throne in front of the black altar, clothed in glistening white robes embroidered with diamonds and molten gold. Jewels of every description were set in his golden breastplate: sardius, topaz, diamond, beryl, onyx, jasper, sapphire, emerald, and carbuncle. His bearing was still kingly. His beautiful features, though ravaged, were still haunting. His raven hair was plaited with lightning and fell past his shoulders onto his shining white garments.

Slowly he rose and knelt before the altar, his head coming

to rest against the black garnet, muttering in a strange, guttural tongue, neither of angels nor of men. His incantations grew in intensity. Immediately hundreds of disembodied demons materialized from the translucent walls and knelt behind him.

Then the throne room filled with hundreds of thousands of the fallen angelic host. A hundred of his chief princes marched up the nave, led by Charsoc. They too knelt in a circular formation in front of his throne.

Charsoc addressed them. 'My angelic brothers, I present to you Lucifer, this day to be anointed as *Satan*, King of Hades and of Perdition and of the nether regions. Wherefore all you who are gathered here this day, will you pledge to do your homage or service and assign yourself to Satan from this day forth?'

The entire assembly answered as one. 'We do pledge,' the angelic host thundered.

Charsoc turned to the chief princes. 'Will you, chief princes of the netherworld, pledge to serve, honour, and worship almighty Satan, King of Hell, tempter, adversary of the race of men? To execute forever his will only, to serve and venerate forever his person only, to be the executors of his iniquitous purposes, become his powers of darkness forever and ever, throughout eternity of eternities?'

The angelic host answered in unison. 'We do pledge.'

Charsoc turned to face Lucifer, who rose from the altar. 'Do you, Lucifer, seraph, light-bearer, vow to renounce Christos through eternity of eternities?'

'I, Lucifer, renounce Christos through eternity of eternities.'

Charsoc moved nearer until Lucifer's face was a hair's breadth away from his own. 'Do you, Lucifer, seraph, light-bearer, vow to renounce Yehovah?'

Lucifer lifted his face to the dome. A shaft of light shone

down on him, illuminating his features. He took a deep breath, his eyes fleetingly vulnerable. A look of intense pain crossed his features.

Zadkiel stared at him, trembling. A terrible silence fell across the throne room, every eye upon Lucifer.

'Do you, Lucifer, seraph–'

Lucifer struck Charsoc across the face viciously. Trembling, he wiped tears away from his eyes with the back of his jewelled hand.

No one stirred. Charsoc stared sightlessly at Lucifer, trembling.

Lucifer walked to the altar and knelt, his head flung across its top. Minutes passed, and still he lay unmoving.

Suddenly he raised his head. 'He does not heed me!' he cried. He withdrew his broadsword and swept it across the altar in fury, sweeping the blazing black tapers to the ground. When he next spoke, each word was agony. 'I . . . renounce . . . Yehovah.'

A ferocious thundering issued from the fallen angels and demons. 'We renounce Yehovah!' they roared. 'We worship Satan.'

Charsoc held out to Lucifer a magnificently carved black diamond ring embedded in gold. 'Receive the ring of kingly damnation and the seal of Satan.'

A dark knight placed a heavy gold ampulla into Zadkiel's hands. Four dark knights in arms held a pall of heavy, fine gold over Lucifer's head.

Zadkiel poured the tar-like anointing oil from the ampulla into a gold spoon and anointed Lucifer on the palms of both hands. 'Be thy hands anointed with the dark sorceries of hell.'

Charsoc placed the oil on Lucifer's bare chest. 'Be thy breast anointed.' He poured the remaining oil over the crown of Lucifer's bare head. The heavy fragranced liniment ran down Lucifer's forehead onto his neck and his cheeks. 'Be thy head anointed.'

Charsoc raised his arms. 'Thou art Lucifer, this day anointed Satan.' He turned to the angelic legions, who rose as one. 'We renounce Yehovah!' he cried.

'We renounce Yehovah!' the fallen host answered.

'Long reign Satan!'

'Long reign Satan!'

The demonic shofar sounded, and slowly the gates opened. Eight of Lucifer's most glorious warriors walked with military precision down the centre of the nave, the casket of the Ark of the Race of Men upon their shoulders. To their rear walked the newly chosen satanic chief princes, led by Asmodeus. Slowly the warriors set the golden casket down directly in front of the altar.

Lucifer rose and turned. 'We have taken possession of the covenant of the race of men. From this time on, I, Satan, am their rightful sovereign, the ruler of the race of men. The territories of the planet Earth, its solar system, the Second Heaven, are now annexed to the kingdom of Satan, emperor and regent of the nether regions.'

The satanic chief princes laid the Ark on the onyx altar. Lucifer wrapped his ermine cloak around his frame and stared at his trophy. A slow satisfied smile spread across his features.

'Charsoc was there?'

Jether stood with his back towards Michael.

'He was found wanting,' Michael stated.

Jether sighed in anguish. 'I knew it would be so.'

'He is sightless, Jether,' Michael said softly. 'He was greatly overcome, this much I know. He did not expect–'

169

Jether spun from the window of the monastic chamber, his face raw with a terrible grief and anger.

'He did not *expect*? He who sat on one of the eight governmental thrones of heaven? Who journeyed to the source of the universes and saw the chambers of the whirlwinds, the treasuries of the snow? Who entered the secret vaults of the cherubim and saw the very face of Yehovah? *He did not expect*?' Jether's breathing was laboured. He sat heavily in his chair, his head in his hands. 'He who was steward over so much, who was accountable for so much – my friend . . . so greatly has he fallen.' He shook his head ruefully. 'Charsoc made his choice. He revered the creation more than the Creator. And his choice was treachery and duplicity with full intention. He did expect, Michael. He knew exactly what to expect.'

Michael looked around the spartan chamber. Silent.

Finally Jether raised his head. 'We must forearm ourselves, for Lucifer well knows that Charsoc's knowledge of the mysteries of Yehovah can be perverted and twisted to fulfil his dastardly ambitions to annihilate the race of men.' He stood. 'Time is against us. We must make haste.'

CHAPTER TWENTY-FOUR

The Demon Seed

Thirteen rings of ice radiated from the top of the dark portals, the laboratories inside which Charsoc's sinister dark apprentices spent their existence. These impish apprentices, the third of the younglings who had defected with the angelic hosts, laboured in the sweltering underground tunnels of the nether regions, rigorously pursuing their witchcraft and sorceries.

The air was thick with the eerie hum of demonic incantations, voodoo, hexes, and enchantments. Two-thirds of these younglings were deformed, with shrunken, misshapen limbs, distorted heads, and warped features.

Charsoc circled the laboratories, his thin bony face ablaze with malevolence as he watched through sightless sockets the dark apprentices rocking to and fro, like zombies, reciting their black arts and enchantments. Thousands of silver tomes and ancient black codices were piled from floor to ceiling: *Witches' Brew*, *Hellbroth*, *Necromancy*, *Magic Lore*, *Walpurgisnacht*, *Alchemy*, and hundreds of other such titles.

Three younglings, their features contorted with malice, swiftly chained up a fourth youngling. The unfortunate apprentice screamed in terror as he was held over a mammoth cauldron of burning tar and fetishes. 'We're calling this one "Dwarf!"' the smallest cackled maniacally. A satisfied smile crossed Charsoc's features.

Lucifer entered the laboratory followed by a hundred of his chief generals. They ignored the younglings, who were shivering with terror, and walked straight towards a large black vault.

Charsoc's embroidered black sorcerer's cape billowed as he bowed before Lucifer. 'The dark portals, Your Majesty.'

Lucifer stared at the vault, entranced. 'My trophy. The sacred mysteries of Yehovah.'

Asmodeus nodded to his warriors. Carefully they lifted the heavy lid of the black iron vault. Silver smoke snaked up towards the dome from the contents.

Lucifer nodded almost imperceptibly, and Asmodeus leaned over to remove one of the heavy jewelled codices. As soon as he touched it, he let out a blood-chilling scream and withdrew his hand in agony. Seared into his palm was the insignia of the Royal House of Yehovah.

Lucifer strode up the nave, drew himself to his full height, and raised his face to the centre of the jewelled dome. He began a guttural incantation that grew quickly in intensity. His face began to burn with an unnatural light. His subjects stared in awe as six darkening wings became visible around his figure. A look of ecstasy crossed his features. He raised his arms towards the dome, then rose, hovering over the casket. The codex rose through the air towards his hand. Triumphantly he thrust his hand over the huge jewelled codex and inhaled the silvered mist. He descended gently until he stood once more on the ground.

'The sacred mysteries.' He placed the codex on the altar and lovingly opened the pages. 'Each and every one of Yehovah's mysteries has an antithesis. Charsoc, you have indeed surpassed expectation.'

Lucifer surveyed his generals. 'From this moment forth, our hallowed undertaking is to desecrate and pervert the sacred mysteries of Yehovah to the race of men. We shall introduce the race of men to evil. They shall sacrifice their sons and daughters to demons. Their lands shall be polluted with blood. Where there is devotion, we will bring perversion and degeneracy. Where there is reverence of Yehovah, we shall bring every form of blasphemous magical arts: the courses of the moon and planets and stars, multitudes of twisted sorceries and enchantments. Where there is vigour, we will ravage the bodies of the race of men with disease and every manner of malady. We shall lay waste to the healing properties of Earth's lush green vegetation until it lies stark and ravaged. We shall pervert the forbidden knowledge of technological expertise and reveal to mankind the means to create instruments of death – weapons of warfare that they shall war against themselves and aid us in our destruction of this wretched race.'

Charsoc bowed again so deeply that his hair swept the floor. 'And yet that is not Yehovah's greatest dread, milord.'

Lucifer leaned forward, intent on Charsoc's words. 'Go on.'

'When I yet walked amongst my compatriots, the twenty-three ancient patriarchs, their greatest dread concerned the human genomic code.' Charsoc stopped and turned to where the younglings were gathered on the far side of the portals. 'Prospero!'

A gangly, dirt-covered youngling slunk out of the darkness, cowering in terror.

'Prospero worked on the genome code under Xacheriel's direct command. Is that not true, youngling?'

Prospero nodded his head, shivering in fear. 'I was chief youngling, executor of Yehovah's explicit instructions to create the genome for the race of men.'

'Explain yourself to your emperor!' Asmodeus bellowed.

'The human genome is the 300 billion-base-pair sequence uniquely programmed to each aspect of the race of men. It carries them from one-cell egg to adulthood.'

Lucifer leaned forward. 'You have caught a *prize*, Charsoc.' He stared at Prospero, engrossed. 'Continue, youngling.' His voice was coaxing, cajoling.

'Twenty-four billion possible sequences of nucleotides, Your Majesty, all of which led to complete biological malfunction,' Prospero continued. 'Except for one, sire.'

Lucifer nodded.

'Forty-six chromosomes to each of the new race's living cells. Genotypes of all cells derived from a particular cell are programmed to be precisely the same–' Prospero faltered.

Charsoc smiled with malice. 'But if . . . *if* there was to be a mutation of the code . . . ?'

'The code cannot be mutated, sire.' Prospero shook his head vehemently. 'It is impossible!'

Charsoc rubbed his thin fingers together. 'Humour me, Prospero. Let us muse awhile. If, say, perchance,' Charsoc crooned, pacing in front of Lucifer, 'simply hypothesizing, of *course* . . . A section of the fallen angelic host left their first estate . . .'

Prospero frowned, but Lucifer moved nearer to Charsoc, transfixed. 'Continue, Charsoc.'

'The angelic host are male in their creation, Your Excellency. Let us imagine an instance where fallen angelic beings left their own habitation and lowered themselves by transforming their own spiritual bodies into bodies of matter.' Charsoc swung around to Lucifer. 'Could they not also replicate' – he lifted his hands in triumph – 'with the daughters of men?'

Lucifer inhaled sharply, a terrible malice on his features. 'And if there was to be an impregnation of fallen angelic seed into the daughters of the race of men,' Charsoc continued, staring around sightlessly at the warriors, 'man's genetic code would be demonized!'

Lucifer rose from his throne and circled Prospero like a shark smelling blood. 'Would that mutate the genetic code, youngling?'

Prospero stared at Charsoc and then at Lucifer, shivering.

'Think.' Lucifer's tone was gentle. 'Take your time. Would this demonization mutate man's genetic code?'

'There . . . there would of certainty be a mutation, Your Excellency.' Prospero trembled. 'The replicated offspring would no longer be men but a mixture of demon and human seed. They would replicate as . . . half of each, sire. Halflings.'

An evil smile spread across Lucifer's face. 'And therefore Yehovah would be bound by Eternal Law to destroy them.'

'Respectfully, milord,' Prospero said, 'it is expressly forbidden by Eternal Law for the angelic race to cohabit with the race of men. It is punishable by–'

Lucifer struck Prospero so violently that he fell to the ground like a stone, whimpering.

'Insubordinate swine!'

Prospero raised his bruised face, staring at Lucifer with a growing defiance in his eyes. 'We were told that to defect with you would bring us glory,' he whispered. 'We younglings were promised honour and power and . . . riches. *Where* is our glory?' he shrieked.

A few reedy voices piped up from the darkness in support of Prospero.

Prospero came to his feet. 'Where is our glory?'

Soon all the younglings joined in a rhythmic, mutinous caterwauling: 'Where is the glory? We want our glory!'

Lucifer's face contorted in a vicious snarl. Moloch kicked Prospero and grabbed five younglings by the throats. 'If you cannot control the rabble, Charsoc . . .' Lucifer's tone was silken.

'Summon the hellhounds!' Moloch screamed. 'Deliver the reprobates to the experimentation chambers.'

Lucifer turned to Zadkiel, who stood to his left. 'Zadkiel,' his voice was sharp, 'I place you in command of one-fifth of my satanic battalions. My generals are under your authority. It is my supreme command that you and my legions impregnate the daughters of men with demon seed. Every genetic line of man must be defiled. Demonize the human seed. Go and violate. Destroy and return victorious.'

Lucifer flung the huge golden codices from the vault onto the chamber floor in an unbridled fury. '*Then pervert and desecrate every vestige of the sacred mysteries and knowledge of Yehovah. Obliterate the human race*!'

Zadkiel looked directly at Lucifer, then slowly saluted and marched straight out of the golden chamber doors.

Lucifer stared after him with an unfathomable look in his eyes.

Zadkiel, Sariel, Azazeal, and Gadreel rode like the wind on their monstrous black steeds on thunderbolts through the Second Heaven, towards Earth and its unwitting inhabitants. Their great legions rode behind them – powerful, barbarous, and menacing. As they reached Earth's atmosphere, they separated.

Gadreel tore across the desert on his black mount, his cape billowing behind him. He flew over a vast range of mountains and tore across the dusty plains, the hooves of his steed thundering through a small village; hundreds of people scattered from his path.

He pulled hard on his stallion's reins and stopped outside the village hall. Riotous sounds of revelry and music filtered from within. Gadreel dismounted and walked up to the doorway, towering over it. Leaning his strapping shoulder against the wood, he smashed his way through to the inner hall.

He towered over the assembly, a savage, menacing figure. He stared menacingly around at the group of petrified men and women until he found a young, flaxen-haired beauty at the far side of the room. He licked his lips, and a lecherous smile spread across his face.

CHAPTER TWENTY-FIVE

The Verdict

They sat under the open heavens on the heights of the Tower of Winds. Above them, the thunderbolts and lightning illuminated the firmament. The winds roared as they blew the mists of wisdom and justice down onto the white heads of the eight Ancient Ones, seated around the golden circular table, their heads bowed. Charsoc's throne was now occupied by Zebulon. Their lips moved silently in supplication to the Ancient of Days.

Lamaliel expelled a deep, trembling sigh. 'That such a day would be upon us . . . This is an agonizing day in the annals of the Council of Ancient Ones.'

Jether stood, his shoulders bowed with strain. 'You have been summoned here today, honoured elders of the Ancient of Days, by Yehovah himself. Each of you has weighed the facts. Now we must reach our verdict and issue our decree, our pronouncement – against those of our own angelic race.' He surveyed the solemn, weathered faces around the table. 'Once Yehovah has passed judgement, it will be irrevocable.' Jether nodded to Lamaliel, who opened a large, gold-bound ancient book and passed it to Jether.

' "The facts hitherto proven," ' Jether recited, ' "read thus:

The rebellious faction, namely, over fifty thousand of the Luciferian battalions, have transgressed the Eternal Law. They have left their first estate and have debased the angelic race by cohabiting with forbidden flesh."' He looked up at the council. 'By having intercourse with the daughters of men.' Jether hesitated and trembled visibly. He read on. '"And teaching the race of men the annals of forbidden knowledge."' He rubbed his veined hand over a pile of documents next to the book. 'The mutiny was instigated primarily by Lucifer's generals. Their legions quickly turned, becoming deserters and renegades – violators, answerable to none.'

He nodded to Xacheriel, who stood, his face ashen.

'Thousands of the angelic host violated, defiled, and assaulted the daughters of men in a horrific and depraved manner.' Xacheriel cleared his throat. 'The entire earth has been plunged into chaos and warfare. The acts they committed include sodomy, bestiality, and the ravenous eating of their own flesh. The rest is unspeakable. It shall not be mentioned within these walls. This past millennium,' he continued, 'more than fifty thousand of our fallen angelic brothers have left their first estate and infiltrated the race of men. They have cohabitated with the human race and corrupted them.'

'This is only the beginning, my revered friends,' Jether added. 'Our fallen angelic compatriots have . . .' He swallowed. 'They have revealed to the race of men the contents of the sacred codices.'

Gasps of horror rippled around the table.

'The forbidden angelic illuminations of the scientific arts,' Jether said. 'Knowledge of the clouds, the celestial bodies, the signs of the earth, astrophysics, earth sciences, electricity.' He sifted through the huge tomes that lay on the table before him. 'Charsoc, one of our own –' Jether's voice became choked with emotion – 'steward of Yehovah's sacred mysteries, deliberately chose to commit treason. His treachery: to deliberately desecrate and pervert the sacred mysteries of Yehovah by revealing to mankind the means to create instruments of death. Weapons of warfare and myriad forms of destructive technology.'

Jether turned the pages of the tomes as he spoke. 'Lucifer himself has, with calculated intent, introduced to mankind every form of blasphemous magical art.' His voice was soft but clear. 'The courses of the moon, multitudes of twisted sorceries and enchantments, psychotropic drugs, the smiting of embryos in the womb, charms and enticements, and every form of degeneracy and sexual abandon . . . Yehovah's hand can be stayed no more.' Jether turned to Xacheriel.

'The acts committed are heinous, but they are not our only concern,' Xacheriel said. 'After the first – cohabitation – there were over ten thousand births. The babies produced were not *Homo sapiens*. They were an unholy union of the fallen angelic race and the race of men. They were Nephilim.' He paused. 'They are giants. Half-human, half-demon. Halflings.'

His words sank in across the table. Jether looked long and hard at the ashen faces before him. He laid the papers down, his hands trembling. 'Our records show that there are a hundred million of these hybrid "halflings" on the earth today.' He sat down heavily. 'The demon seed has infected the human race through this union.' He paused, overcome by emotion. 'I fear the contamination of man's DNA by the demon seed is . . . irrevocable.'

Xacheriel shook with a horror so terrible that he could hardly speak. 'I fear that will result in a complete mutation. The entire human race could become demonized!'

Methuselah, one of those at the table, buried his head in his hands. 'Mutation!'

Jether sighed deeply and placed his hand gently on

Methuselah's shoulder. A gasp of horror rippled around the table.

Xacheriel looked around at the appalled ancient faces. 'Our archivists' findings have so far revealed that the demon seed has penetrated every genealogical line. Every one. They are reviewing them one last time for any error. Without one uncontaminated bloodline, Yehovah's hand is forced. He will be left with no recourse save to destroy the entire human race.' Xacheriel slumped down heavily in his chair.

Jether spoke from his seat, his voice exceedingly quiet. 'The punishment for the transgressing of the Eternal Law is clear and irreversible. There is no doubt this is Lucifer's evil, his diabolical mind. But in this he and his dark apostle Charsoc are untouchable. In our punishment we can take only the ones who did his bidding. This he well knows.'

He clasped his hands together and looked around the council. 'Lucifer's generals, some of whom were once our close compatriots, are to be cast in eternal chains into the lowest regions of the netherworld – Tartarus.' His voice grew hoarse. 'The pits of gloom until the Day of Judgement.'

Hundreds of numberers and record keepers pored over the millions of records in the great Willow Library of Archives. Jether and Xacheriel paced up and down the aisles, past the countless towering shelves crammed with fastidiously preserved parchments, scrolls, and tomes.

Obadiah ran up to them, followed by a panting Methuselah.

'They are nearly finished with the second count, milord,' Obadiah reported. 'The final count will be ready by dusk.'

Methuselah wrung his hands. 'It is no use – there is not *one* uncontaminated generation. We have been through them meticulously.'

Jether looked up towards the enormous crystal chandeliers hanging from the vast frescoed ceilings. 'That this day would ever be upon us . . .' He wiped his forehead with a great white handkerchief. 'Methuselah, summon the full councils for the results of the final count.'

Methuselah hurried from the room, muttering to himself under his breath.

'This is Lucifer's evil genius,' Jether said grimly, still pacing. 'The outworking of his diabolical mind. He has planned meticulously that there should not be one family line left uncontaminated. If there is not one uncontaminated, Yehovah will be forced to destroy them all. He hopes to extinguish mankind forever – by Yehovah's own hand!'

Xacheriel pointed across the library. Methuselah shuffled through the massive mahogany doors followed by Paolomi, the chief numberer, and twenty-one Ancient Ones.

Jether led them past the never-ending corridors of archives and up a golden spiralling staircase to the uppermost floor of the great library, where an enormous polished jacinth table was surrounded by twenty-four jacinth thrones that stood beneath the open heavens. Solemnly all twenty-four elders took their seats, Jether at the head. He nodded to Methuselah, who stood, the final report in his hands.

'The numberers have scrupulously checked the records against those of our own. The final count was completed an hour ago.' Methuselah looked down at his papers. 'I regret to inform the council that the results are as follows. Paolomi, please read the findings.'

A tall angel rose, his gentle features grave. 'Milords, revered high council of Yehovah, the demonic seed has not been confined to a specific sector of *Homo sapiens*. We have cross-referenced hundreds of thousands of halflings infected with every genealogical line on earth. Our findings reveal that the reproductive history of every *Homo sapiens* line is contaminated.' Paolomi looked slowly around the table. 'Not one genetic generation remains pure.'

'There must be one!' Xacheriel's eyes flashed with passion.

'Surely *one?*' Jether pleaded.

'No, milord.' Paolomi bowed his head. 'I am sorry.'

Jether covered his face with his hands. 'A terrible evil has been perpetrated against mankind,' he muttered. Slowly he looked up. 'He has carefully crafted this.' He slumped in his chair, haggard. 'Truly, Xacheriel, this is a dreadful day.'

The council gathered in small groups, speaking in horrified whispers. One of Methuselah's record keepers ran to his side and handed him a sheaf of papers. They whispered intensively.

Methuselah, surprise on his face, shuffled over to Jether, who was staring straight ahead, his hand still covering his mouth in horror.

'Honourable Jether,' Methuselah whispered, 'this did not reach your desk.'

Jether looked up at him, his mind reeling, barely conscious of the upheaval around him and unable to bring himself to speak.

Methuselah stood fixed like stone. 'It took us longer than we would have liked to get the results.' He held out a paper, his wizened hands trembling.

Methuselah pushed the paper under Jether's nose. Jether half-heartedly took it from him and scanned the information. Then his mouth dropped open in wonderment. He rose to his feet and clasped Methuselah's stooped shoulders. 'You are sure?'

Methuselah nodded emphatically. 'The numberers have cross-referenced it four times.'

Jether thrust the paper to Xacheriel, suddenly exuberant. Xacheriel studied it intently through his monocle.

Jether held Methuselah at arm's length, then drew him

closer and kissed him fervently on both cheeks, his shoulders heaving with an unrestrained euphoric laughter. He snatched Methuselah's papers back from Xacheriel and held them high above his head in exultation. 'There *is* one! There is one!'

The entire assembly quieted. The Ancient Ones and Paolomi turned to stare at the exhilarated Jether, who slowly laid the papers down.

'There is one! A just and upright man, perfect in his generations.' Jether's voice was intense. 'One who worships Yehovah. One whose bloodline is not contaminated. He is our only hope for the continuation of the race of men. His name is . . .' Jether looked over the rapturous Xacheriel's shoulders.

'His name is *Noah*!'

CHAPTER TWENTY-SIX

The Ark

Xacheriel glanced at the huge stopwatch dangling from his neck. He turned to Jether. 'I'm late! The simulation ... the younglings will be impatient.'

Xacheriel pushed open the simulator door.

At least twenty youngling apprentices were gathered around a huge simulation of Earth's crust. A miniature barge-like ship sat in the centre of a mammoth tank of water.

At Xacheriel and Jether's entrance, the younglings bowed deeply. 'We await you, our revered curator of the universes and sciences.'

Xacheriel smiled broadly and moved to the centre of the activity.

'And milord Jether,' the younglings said, 'exalted steward of Yehovah's mysteries.'

Jether bowed and took his place seated in the simulator next to Xacheriel.

Xacheriel nodded. 'You may proceed, Tirzah.'

Tirzah's attention was on the miniature barge-like structure resting on the simulated Earth's crust. He pressed a remote control, and a light rain started to fall from above them onto the simulation. The intensity of the rain grew to a torrent.

Tirzah bowed to Xacheriel. 'We have christened it "the Ark", milord.'

'Humph!' Xacheriel sighed deeply.

The younglings tittered. Jether gave them one of his best dark looks, and they immediately quieted.

Jether and Xacheriel exchanged an amused private glance. Then Xacheriel frowned deeply, his bushy eyebrows almost meeting. 'Scientific data, Tirzah. Data, not baptisms.'

Jether's gaze was riveted on the 'ark', which was being tossed around violently. A youngling bowed and handed each of them a pair of infrared viewfinders. Xacheriel and Jether placed them over their eyes and foreheads. Instantaneously they were transported in the very epicentre of the simulated storm.

Tirzah's narration echoed in the simulator audio. 'When Earth's supporting pillars collapse, huge tidal waves will be generated in the surface and subterranean waters. The pillars will be crushed like powder into rock fragments that accelerate into space.'

Xacheriel and Jether reeled into the horrifyingly lifelike simulation of Earth's supporting pillars collapsing, generating huge tidal waves. The pillars collapsed with such violence that pieces of them accelerated into space as meteoroids.

Tirzah's monotone continued. 'Meanwhile the boiling black subterranean water – six hundred degrees – will rupture Earth's crust, creating giant cleavages. High-velocity fountains of black mud will jettison high above Earth. Oceans of water will explode from these fissures.'

Xacheriel and Jether rode the ark on the waters in simulation as it was beaten violently by the turbulent floodwaters and meteorite fallout – narrowly escaping being smashed to smithereens.

Finally, Xacheriel could take no more. He flung his

infrared viewfinders onto the model of Earth's crust in front of them, running his hand through his matted white hair. Jether took his off as well and held on to the wall, looking pale and struggling for breath.

'Tirzah . . . transfer it to the pulsar radar system immediately,' Xacheriel barked. 'Run the playback.'

Slowly the hologram of the ark rematerialized in front of them. The entire chamber watched, speechless, as the great ship rode the tsunami-like waves, battered but whole.

Xacheriel rubbed his forehead wearily and heaved a loud sigh. 'Open the door,' he instructed quietly. Slowly the ark's door opened. 'Scan for body readings.'

A laser pulsar calculated the body readings, which appeared as laser-green mathematical calculations in the air above them.

Xacheriel wrung his hands. 'As I feared . . . *every* human being and animal inside the ark – dead, smashed to a pulp!'

'With great respect, sire,' Tirzah beamed, 'they drowned *before* they were smashed!'

Jether shook his head in despair. 'An entire race – wiped out.'

Rakkon raised his hand eagerly. 'If I may speak, sire?'

Xacheriel rolled his eyes and lifted his hand wearily. 'Speak if you must, Rakkon.' He turned to Jether. 'He is a bright youngling, this one.'

'Surely it seems much simpler just to transport them here and save the new race.'

Xacheriel's ears turned beetroot red. He slammed the table. 'His brightness has diminished!' He glowered at Rakkon, who was now shaking like jelly. 'How many times must I spell it out? Their cellular component is matter – they would die on entry. We have to keep them alive in their own tailor-made atmosphere. There is no other way. We *must* find the solution.'

Xacheriel twirled his long moustache, then slammed his staff on the ground. 'Reconfigure the length-to-width ratio of six to one. Rakkon! That comes out to 137.16 metres by 22.86, with a height of . . .'

Rakkon wrote in the air like lightning.

Xacheriel paced up and down the simulator, muttering as one inspired. '13.716 metres . . . The total volume equates to 1,518,000 cubic feet – 20,000 tons. We must build a ship that is *impossible* to turn over!'

Tirzah spoke up. 'Permission to interject, milord?'

'Permission granted.'

Tirzah saluted. 'With the capacity at over twenty thousand tons, at three storeys, it's almost impossible!'

Rakkon jumped in front of Tirzah. 'And the leaking propensity, sire – we're dealing with an unenlightened race; the materials to work with are almost prehistoric . . . it leaks no matter what we put on it, at every pitch of the sea.'

Jether raised his head from his supplications. The younglings stared at him as one, subdued, silent. 'Younglings, younglings. Yehovah loves this man and his creation. He will not see them perish.' He rose to his feet. 'We *have* to find a way.'

Xacheriel was pacing again, his muttering accelerating. 'It leaks . . . leaks . . . at every pitch of the sea. Pitch of the sea . . . pitch . . .' He stopped in mid-stride. '*Pitch!* Rakkon, you *are* a genius!'

Jether frowned. 'You have something?'

Xacheriel slapped him vigorously on the back. 'Pitch, Jether! Pitch will make the ship waterproof – the gopher wood needs a lining to stop the leaks. What was I thinking of? Tirzah, Rakkon, get us pitch, and don't delay!'

The Holy Mountain was wreathed in silver mists and lightning that struck far above the rock face. The Holy Watchers guarded the sacred entrance to the throne room where the seven scorching columns of eternal white fire blazed.

Jether approached Michael and Gabriel from out of the flames. 'He would not destroy them,' he said softly.

'But their DNA is contaminated!' Gabriel exclaimed. 'It is defiled by demons.'

Jether nodded. 'He knows. If he does not destroy the demon seed, the race of man is lost to him forever. His decision is made, but still he grieves for this man he so loves and has lost.' Jether sighed deeply and turned to Michael. 'Go to him, Michael. He awaits you. He would issue his commands.'

CHAPTER TWENTY-SEVEN

Judgement

Michael and his dread generals approached Earth at great speed. They passed through the canopy of moisture and descended to the desert floor, riding like lightning. Michael tore across the desert on his magnificent white steed, his thousand angelic generals close behind him. They flew over the vast desert plains and mountains until they came to a full league from the forbidding black castle walls.

Michael lifted his visor. 'We must arrest all two hundred of his generals,' he said. 'I will take Zadkiel myself. May Yehovah guard our souls.' He saluted, shut his visor, and galloped ahead, his stallion's hooves thundering towards the tower keep.

They thundered over the moat's bridge and straight through the thousands of arrows fired by the human crossbowmen through the loopholes of the castle. Michael's legions smashed the portcullis and rode into the forecourt as the petrified guards threw their crossbows down in terror and ran for their lives.

Michael and his generals burst through the heavy wooden doors of the castle and surged into the huge banqueting room.

Seated at the head of the banqueting table, devouring a cow's leg, sat Gadreel, surrounded by his demonic underlings. He leered malevolently. 'If it isn't his Highness, pretty Prince Michael. Come to settle a score, have you?'

Michael's face was grim. He nodded to Raphael. 'You know what to do. I search for Zadkiel, supreme commander of His Excellency Lucifer's armies.'

Gadreel took another huge, slobbering bite of the cow's leg and wiped his mouth on his chain-mailed arm. 'My master, Abaddon, is occupied,' he growled. He looked towards the stairs. 'He copulates . . .' Gadreel leered at Michael. 'As for me . . . I am not so taken with the daughters of men. But *you*, my pretty . . .'

Michael raised his sword. His face was impassive.

Gadreel nodded to his angelic rabble and licked his lips suggestively at Michael. A dark, demonic fire filled their eyes as they stared at him. 'We have unfinished business, my prince.' Gadreel's face contorted into a vicious mask. He drew his metre-long broadsword, as did his hundred fallen angelic followers. Michael's warriors squared off against them.

With one deft move, Michael knocked Gadreel's sword from his hand and edged him against the stone wall, the Sword of Justice at his heart, emitting ruby lightning.

A raging fury filled Gadreel's face. 'Michael and his white sorceries!' he roared.

Michael turned to his generals. 'Shackle him,' he commanded.

Mayhem ensued as Gadreel's warriors threw tapered axes and swung their morning stars, clashing savagely with Michael's warriors. Broadswords and quarterstaffs clashed violently; axes and maces flew into shoulders, heads, and thighs. Eight of Michael's angelic warriors shackled the rabidly fighting Gadreel with heavy iron chains all across

191

his body and shackled his feet together in heavy irons. They rolled him into the centre of the room, face down.

'We seek only the generals,' Michael said.

'You seek for me, then.'

Michael looked up the ornate staircase to see Zadkiel, dressed only in his shift, staring down at him. Michael inhaled sharply. His eyes were pained from many memories – as were Zadkiel's.

Zadkiel bowed. His princely tones were gentle. 'His Excellency, the esteemed Prince Michael.'

Michael bowed. 'Zadkiel, supreme commander of Lucifer's armies.' He paused. 'I come only for the perpetrators.'

Zadkiel backed up the stairway, strangely perplexed. A beautiful fair-skinned woman – a daughter of man – walked towards Zadkiel swathed only in a cloth. Her body was covered with jewelled bangles and pierced with silver ornaments, her dazzling face adorned with cosmetics. Braided golden tresses hung to her thighs.

'Zadkiel . . .' She held out her delicate ringed hand to him.

Zadkiel stared back at her, as one entranced. 'Laleesha . . .' He smiled tenderly at her, gesturing to her to retire. She bowed her head and retraced her graceful steps.

Zadkiel stared back at Michael, his eyes assessing the situation. He stared down at the chained Gadreel, the dreadful comprehension dawning. He looked at Michael, horrified. 'I am not an animal like some of these.' He gestured to Gadreel. 'You of *all* know this, Michael.'

Michael looked down at the floor, refusing to meet Zadkiel's gaze. 'The punishment for transgressing the Eternal Law is clear and irrevocable. For cohabiting with forbidden flesh, you and your generals are to be to be cast in eternal chains into hell – the pit of gloom – until the Day of Judgement.'

Zadkiel blanched. 'Michael!' he pleaded. 'I beg you, no!'

Michael's chin set in a firm line. 'Zadkiel, mighty leader of Yehovah's Holy Watchers, partaker of the fellowship of Christ ... Lucifer has used you. You did his bidding, and your reward was the delectable pleasures of the flesh.' For a fleeting moment Michael lost his iron discipline, raw with the emotion and vulnerabilities of their age-old friendship. 'You violated the sacred mysteries of Yehovah – the *forbidden* knowledge ...' His voice broke, raw with anger and grief. 'At what price such treachery, Zadkiel?' His mouth trembled. 'Your eternal *soul*?'

Zadkiel's countenance filled with a deep bitterness. 'Then cast *him* in the pit. Your blood *brother* is the supreme master of treachery – he surely is the diabolical master of this scheme.'

Michael shook his head. 'In this matter Lucifer is untouchable. We can take only the ones who did his bidding. This he well knows.'

Zadkiel dropped to his knees, the full web of Lucifer's treachery suddenly apparent. 'He betrays his own generals?' he murmured, his voice unsteady.

Michael slung off his helmet and walked up the steps, for a fleeting moment no longer the warrior but the friend, his face a hand's-breadth away from Zadkiel's. 'Why did you not return with us when you had the opportunity?' He grasped Zadkiel's shoulders with his fierce strength. 'The Christ called for you by name.' His voice shook with passion. The darkness lifted momentarily from Zadkiel's eyes, and Michael caught a fleeting glimpse of the Zadkiel of old.

'Lucifer forced me to swear allegiance, Michael,' Zadkiel whispered. 'For eternity of eternities. My vow has taken hold of my very soul. My word of honour has become my curse.'

'Then break your vow!' Michael cried.

Zadkiel's eyes deadened. 'You of all should know the web of sorceries the black widow weaves.'

Michael's hands fell to his sides in despair.

Zadkiel turned to look at Laleesha, standing outside a doorway up the stairs. A terrible agony crossed his face. 'I am lost for all eternity,' he murmured. Gently he laid his broadsword down on the stairs and walked slowly, stair by stair, downward past Michael, to where Gadreel was shackled.

Michael turned. Hot tears pricked his eyes. 'He is full of grace – filled with compassion . . .', he pleaded.

Zadkiel stood at the bottom of the stairs. 'Redemption for mankind . . . but not for me.' He lifted his arms in surrender. 'Do your godly duty, Michael.'

Michael looked one last time at Zadkiel, then nodded to his generals. They chained Zadkiel and pushed him through the door as Laleesha sobbed.

CHAPTER TWENTY-EIGHT

Tartarus

Two hundred of Lucifer's generals stood chained and shackled on the unending plateau of smoking black onyx. The black stone was riddled with orange cracks from the blazing furnace that raged a thousand leagues below them.

Michael handed to Uriel the huge iron key to the Abyss. Uriel walked over to a huge circular lock that had been carved out of the granite. Reaching down, he placed the enormous key into the lock. Ever so slowly, it started to turn. A hundred angelic warriors grabbed the iron rivets of the door to the shaft of the Abyss, pitting their great strength against the cavernous door.

Billowing black smoke erupted from the shaft entrance of the blazing furnace, darkening the galaxies. The warriors were momentarily knocked off their feet by the blast of heat.

Gadreel stared, petrified, his entire body shaking uncontrollably, while Azazeal let out an ear-splitting scream of terror. Zadkiel stood, eyes lowered, and swallowed hard – courageous to the end.

Michael lifted the Sword of Justice high above his head.

'Thou art reserved in everlasting chains under darkness for the Judgement of the Great Day. Thou, Zadkiel, who art Abaddon, shalt be king over them. Enter into your abode – Tartarus, the molten core.'

The angelic guard pushed the shackled angels inside the shaft of the Abyss. Michael turned his face away.

Gradually, the smoke in the shaft of the Abyss thinned out. One by one, the hunched and shackled generals groped their way down the twisting shaft of Hades, with Zadkiel leading the way, terrified but contained. Downward, downward, and still downward, stumbling, burning in the pitch blackness. The walls of the caverns glowed red-hot with deadly coals that hissed whispering, vile obscenities.

Zadkiel came to a halt in front of a flowing river of molten fire and lava.

Sariel retched, stumbling to his knees. 'I *curse* Yehovah – I curse him!' His scream mingled as one with the hissing walls.

Gadreel fell prostrate, his eyes burning in their sockets. 'I curse the Christ – I curse his holy presence. I curse the one who brought us here.'

Zadkiel turned, his tongue blistering from the intense heat, his expression like stone. 'Then curse yourself, Gadreel. Curse yourself for rejecting the King of Glory, and curse yourself for embracing Satan – the King of Lies and the Damned. Curse Satan the Treacherous, and you curse the true perpetrator of our doom.' He turned, his still noble features set. 'But do not curse the Christ.'

Gadreel raised his huge torso from the dirt and smashed Zadkiel's head from behind. Zadkiel fell to the ground. Gadreel kicked him viciously to one side of the smoking tunnel.

'Who placed *you* king over us? I curse the Chrissssst . . .', he snarled as a huge blast from the furnace blew Gadreel, screaming, into the living, molten stream.

196

Azazeal and Sariel stood shaking uncontrollably, weeping
... terrorized. The semi-conscious Zadkiel clutched the hot
black earth in his fist. 'Michael ...'

Michael knelt. He was a lone, crumpled figure on the plains
of black onyx, his head resting against his broadsword. The
echoes of the fallen angelic generals' curses and screams
filtered upward through the ground as they fell burning
beyond Hades, beyond the menacing Abyss, to their final
destination: the cavernous subterranean pits of gloom carved
within the very lowest regions of Hades – the molten core
of Tartarus.

Michael's lips moved incoherently as he prayed, for he
well knew that they fell.

Lucifer studied the missive with the emblem of the Royal
House of Yehovah.

'So,' he said, raising his gaze to Charsoc triumphantly,
'Eternal Law prevailed. They left their first estate, cohabited
with the race of men, and he has banished them to Tartarus,
the molten core.'

He stared for a long while at Michael's golden seal in the
lower right-hand corner of the missive. Then, with a half-
smile glimmering on his mouth, he leisurely lit a black taper
and held it to the linen paper. He watched the flames as
they flickered across the seal, turning it into smouldering
ashes.

'It is precisely as you foretold, Your Excellency.'

Lucifer plucked a sweetmeat from an ornate platinum
bowl at his side. He caressed it between his fingertips.

'Zadkiel . . . Sariel . . . Azazeal . . .', he reflected. 'They were wavering in their allegiance. They and their regiments regretted their defection from the First Heaven. Their pangs of conscience had to be purged from our midst.' He popped the delicacy in his mouth and swallowed.

'They were traitors of the soul, Your Majesty,' Charsoc said.

'Insurgents, apostates,' Lucifer muttered. 'As for Gadreel,' he mused, 'he was fervent in his devotion to me. But he and his legions were unrestrained, unpredictable.' He picked up a second delicacy. 'They were expendable.'

He held out the sweetmeat to one of the six sleek hellhounds that lay coiled before his throne. 'Cerberus, my sweet.' Cerberus opened his mouth, revealing huge fangs. He devoured it in one swift bite, his eyes evil yellow slits.

'And you, Charsoc?' Lucifer stared at the thin bony face before him as he stroked Cerberus' glossy black head. 'Do you too miss the First Heaven? Do you not *yearn* as they did for Yehovah?'

Charsoc was quiet for a long moment. 'You can rest assured, Your Excellency,' he said quietly, 'that my soul's condition is unerringly as yours when it comes to all matters of Yehovah.'

Lucifer stared with hard eyes beyond Charsoc upward out of the black crystal dome. 'Then you *too* are conflicted in your soul, Charsoc!' Lucifer swept the bowl of sweetmeats on the floor with his sceptre. 'His hold on us, it seems, is *indissoluble*!'

Lucifer rose, a wild fire in his eyes. 'Even in the midst of hell.'

CHAPTER TWENTY-NINE

Two by Two

A re-created mammoth towered over Xacheriel. Next to it, Lamech was tottering up a ladder, studying the dimensions of the newly erected dinosaur. The portal of the natural sciences was jammed with thousands of Earth's prototypes. Along the walls were never-ending intricate diagrams of every species in a million galaxies.

Hundreds of younglings were bent over microscopes, studying DNA and blood types, while hundreds of others studiously gathered files of information and took copious notes.

Xacheriel was laboriously putting the finishing touches to a flying platypus. 'Kalleel, pass me the latest database!'

Kalleel staggered up to him, hidden beneath a vast pile of dog-eared papers that stretched from his knees past his corkscrewed ginger hair. Xacheriel clucked his tongue in impatience. He ignored the papers and whisked off the top a silver microchip the size of a pinhead. He held it up in the air, and immediately millions of gigabytes of information appeared.

Xacheriel sucked his pen. 'Lamech!'

Lamech looked down from atop the dinosaur.

'The ark blueprints . . . hard copy.'

Lamech teetered on the ladder and drew out a large roll of papers from under his apron.

Xacheriel tapped his staff on the floor impatiently. 'Come *on*, Lamech – we haven't got all day.'

Lamech wobbled desperately astride the dinosaur. Slowly, slowly, slowly it tilted. Xacheriel watched as if in agonizing pain, his eyes following every tilt until it came crashing down right at him, very nearly crushing him.

Xacheriel and his crown landed on the floor. He glowered darkly at the dazed but unhurt Lamech and grabbed the papers out of his hands impatiently. Dusting himself off, he laid out the blueprints of the ark over a table.

'Here you can see the ark is divided into three storeys,' he explained, 'each with varying compartments depending on the dimensions of the species.' He carefully smoothed out the papers. 'I have meticulously calculated the dimensions, keeping in mind that apart from the elephant and the . . .' He gave a dry look at the collapsed dinosaur and the long-suffering Lamech, who was trying to extricate himself from under it. '. . . and the dinosaur, the average animal will be approximately the size of a sheep, and that each species will be represented by its young.'

He turned to Dimnah, who was working away on a new design. Xacheriel raised his eyebrows and peered over Dimnah's shoulder at a complicated design for a kangaroo. Xacheriel frowned. 'How many times must I point this out, Dimnah? Miscalculations, miscalculations! Far too short!' He prodded at the kangaroo's paws. 'Completely out of alignment . . .'

Dimnah went beetroot red.

'That's the third time this week.' Xacheriel held him by the ear and dragged him to a door labelled 'Blunders – Prototypes.' They peered through the porthole. In the centre of the room were a kangaroo, a giraffe, and a panda. 'Long necks, short paws . . . and black-and-white bears. Blunders – all blunders!' Xacheriel heaved a great sigh. 'What would Yehovah say!' He turned to Kalleel. 'How many species are presently on your database?'

'Over a hundred and thirty thousand – out of a million species, milord. The ship will accommodate only fifty thousand.'

Peleg looked up from his microscope. 'It can accommodate double that, sire.'

Xacheriel waved him quiet. 'Yes, yes! At fifty thousand animals, the ark is still only thirty-seven per cent full – but we'll take no risks on review of the volume and pressure propensities. These are Yehovah's instructions.'

'But there are over a *million* of Yehovah's species, milord!'

'Kalleel, Kalleel,' Xacheriel groaned, raising his hands in despair. 'Think like a scientist!' He paced the portal, rattling off data. 'Of the total number of species, 838,000 are arthropods – lobsters, shrimps, barnacles; and marine creatures – 21,000 species of fish, 1,700 tunicates, 600 echinoderms, 107,000 molluscs, 10,000 coelenterates, and 5,000 species of sponges!' He retraced his steps. 'The amphibians will survive outside the ark, Kalleel, as will the majority of reptiles. In addition, some of the mammals are marine – the whales, seals, and porpoises. They will survive.' He rubbed his hands. 'Peleg!'

Peleg jumped to attention and saluted. 'Milord, we predict that the animals will undergo a type of dormancy – a hibernation. With their bodily functions reduced, the ark is equipped with fresh air and sanitation for a total of 371 days, sire.'

'Very good, Peleg. A male and female of all the selected species will reside in the lower vestibule of the ark – that way we will preserve the lineage of every creation. It's settled!

201

Review the databases, Kalleel – fifty thousand.' He tapped on the Blunders porthole and winked at Dimnah.

'Only if you have room!'

In a holy chamber not far away, the mood was serious.

Thousands of solemn angelic battalions were gathered on the Mount of the Congregation. Michael walked forward and knelt in front of the altar balustrades. Jether laid the Sword of State on the altar, then took it and placed it upon Michael's left shoulder.

'With this kingly sword do justice, forbid the growth of iniquity, maintain the things that are restored, punish and reform what is amiss, and confirm what is in good order. And doing these things, you may be glorious in virtue.'

Grimly Jether passed the golden Sword of State – which had been Lucifer's – into Michael's hands. 'Go and execute Yehovah's judgements.'

CHAPTER THIRTY

The Fountains of the Deep

Michael, in full battle dress, rode like the wind across the firmaments on his white steed, followed by a thousand great angelic warriors on horseback. He lifted the heavy golden Sword of State high above his head as he rode, shouting to his warriors, 'Loose the fountains of the deep!'

A massive, fierce lightning bolt illuminated the four corners of the sky, its brilliant orange fire striking the earth with unbelievable force, rupturing Earth's crust. The thousand dread warriors dispersed to the four corners of the firmament. The angelic riders pulled on huge chains.

Again the flaming lightning struck the four pillars on Earth's chamber floors. As in slow motion, they collapsed into rock fragments, generating huge tidal waves in the surface and subterranean waters, and accelerating into space as meteoroids. The boiling black subterranean waters ruptured Earth's crust, the raging waters beating the ark violently.

Michael and his warriors surrounded the ark like a shield as the great waves of muddy water jettisoned high above Earth, hurling up asteroids. The violent floodwaters unleashed their boiling frenzy upon all those on Earth – men, women, and the Nephilim desperate to escape its wrath.

Michael's angels rode the ark on the tops of the violent tidal waves, protecting Noah's family and the selected animal species. Continents crushed and thickened; mountains buckled. And finally, the ark smashed onto Mount Ararat, hidden beneath the raging waters.

A terrible silence fell over all of Earth and the firmament as the raging flood waters started to subside.

The angelic host waited on the ocean waves astride their huge stallions, silently watching the ark for signs of life. The great vessel had suffered tremendous external damage.

Jether and Xacheriel also watched, stony-faced, from the portal of the universes, intent on the door of the ark. Xacheriel put his head in his hands. 'The whole race . . .', he muttered. 'An entire race . . . wiped out.' Dry sobs racked his ancient frame. The body scanner pulsar showed no reading.

A sombre Jether placed his hand gently on Xacheriel's shoulder, restraining his own tears. He watched the ark silently.

Xacheriel raised his head, dazed. 'The calculations were meticulous,' he mumbled.

He turned to Jether, who stood at the portal, open-mouthed in astonishment as he stared at the vast, flaming rainbow that covered the firmament directly over the ark.

Xacheriel followed his gaze. Then he swung around to the body scanner. It was pulsing. The pulsing grew stronger. He started to chortle euphorically. 'Rakkon, get me the pulsar matter scans!'

And then Jether laughed – a loud, deep, joyous laugh that would not be stopped. 'Yehovah!'

And so the lineage of mankind was saved, and Lucifer's terrible evil was thwarted.

But gradually, as the aeons passed, men's hearts again grew cold as they fell to depravity and vice, to selfishness and greed.

And they once more forgot their Creator . . .

CHAPTER THIRTY-ONE

Babylon

J ether paced up and down the banks of the Tigris, his eagle blue eyes scanning the vast Babylonian horizon for signs of his one-time compatriot. His ornate crown was absent, and he wore simple white robes devoid of his usual jewels and fine stitching.

Far away in the distance, towering 230 feet high over the stark Babylonian plains, loomed the seven terraces of Nebuchadnezzar's Tower of Borsippa.

A distant thundering grew louder. Beyond the ziggurats a whirlwind arose from the north, bringing forth a vast cloud of fire glowing with blue and amber lightning. Flowing crimson robes materialized out of the flashing mists onto the far bank of the Tigris, followed by a head and the rest of his body.

Jether rolled his eyes in annoyance. 'Cheap tricks, Charsoc,' he observed tartly. 'Fit for a conjuror, not an ancient monarch – even a defected one.'

Charsoc smiled in gratification and turned blind eyes towards the voice. 'My honourable compatriot, Jether.' Charsoc's evil, wizened features were framed by his jet-black, straight hair and beard, which both reached to the dirt. He bowed deeply, his hair sweeping the ground. 'I regret that I have regressed to the lower boundaries of sorcery of late. Not quite as sophisticated as what we were used to.' He hesitated. 'But . . . rather agreeable, I might add.'

Charsoc levitated above the deep flowing waters of the Tigris, hovering and then landing gracefully opposite Jether on the bank.

Jether stood, his arms folded, his expression grim. 'You demanded my presence.'

Charsoc nodded. He stared in gratification at the Babylonian terrain. 'Babylon the Great. My master's pride.'

'She has laboured in sorceries and enchantments from her youth,' Jether muttered.

Charsoc smiled. 'I come on pressing matters as royal emissary.'

Jether closed his eyes and drew a deep breath. 'I saw this encounter many moons ago in my dreams.'

Charsoc nodded. 'You always were seer more than pragmatist, Jether.' He hesitated, enjoying Jether's discomfort. 'As for myself, I have always favoured the side of pragmatism.'

Jether stared at Charsoc grimly. 'And expediency.'

Charsoc smiled indulgently 'I have missed our repartee, ancient companion.'

Jether's lips tightened. He held his hand out towards Charsoc.

Charsoc nodded and drew out a golden pouch with his bony ringed fingers. He withdrew a missive sealed with Lucifer's royal seal and placed it in Jether's grasp. Jether tore it open, scanning the contents.

Finally he looked up. 'So, it is as my premonition bade me. He would lodge his claim against the race of men.'

Charsoc shrugged. 'They have deserted Yehovah. He demands judgement.'

Jether nodded wearily. 'It is written in Eternal Law. He is legally entitled to lodge a claim against mankind in the courts of heaven.'

Charsoc paced leisurely up the bank.

'You have disclosed the contents of the codices?' Jether asked.

Charsoc gestured to his sightless eyes. 'My master's rewards are more compelling than your overlords have been of late.'

'Transgression is reduced to ashes in his presence, Charsoc. This you well knew.'

'Yes, yes. I should really have been more careful. Well, really, I should have been burned to a crisp.'

'You are fully cognizant of all our undisclosed tenets, Charsoc. I take it that Lucifer is now well informed about them as well.'

'*Well* informed,' Charsoc said. 'We will ensure they are used to complete man's total eradication from our universe. He would enforce the penalty that every man's soul is his to be with him in hell and the grave and in Tartarus. And when his judgement comes, they will burn with him in the Lake of Fire.'

'And you, Charsoc?'

'That is all.' Charsoc lifted his bangled arm. 'I will take my leave.'

Jether indicated agreement and turned, the hot, dry south wind blowing his robes. 'Charsoc,' he whispered, staring out beyond the blue glazed bricks of the upper levels of the ziggurats glistening in the scorching Babylonian sun. 'You who were privy to so much, ruler of the ancient elders of the Ancient of Days, high steward of his sacred mysteries . . .' He turned and stared directly into Charsoc's face. 'Why did you betray us?'

Charsoc smiled thinly, and his pale blue eyes stared ahead

expressionless. 'I told you, Jether – I am a pragmatist. In simple terms, I wanted *more*.'

With that he vanished back into the mists of the Tigris.

Jether was seated at the enormous lapis lazuli table in the lower vestibule of the Great Elders' Hall, almost completely obscured from view. Only his crown was visible behind the numerous stacks of ancient tomes of Eternal Law that surrounded him.

'It is untenable!' he uttered in exasperation, closing yet another of the great jewelled tomes. Distractedly, he placed it next to the remaining volumes, then rose to his feet wearily and began pacing the cavernous room. He stared out of the wide crystal windows surrounding the great hall and gazed towards the Holy Mountain, then sighed deeply.

'What is it that ails you, old friend?'

Jether turned slowly from the vast crystal windows. An imperial figure stood in the upper vaults of the hallowed, ancient willow sanctum of the elders, looking down at him. 'Ah, Michael,' he sighed. 'It is this claim of Lucifer's.'

Michael walked down the grand willow stairs and came to stand beside the lapis lazuli table, where Lucifer's missive lay with the seal exposed. He frowned. 'You have not yet lodged the claim?'

Jether shook his head. 'I cannot.' His lips formed a thin line. 'Not until I have searched every jot and tittle of the tomes of Eternal Law.' He walked back to the table and sat heavily down in the midst of the tomes. 'Eternal Law,' he muttered, turning the pages. 'The race of men, conditions and ramifications, man's desertion of Yehovah, man's transgression of Eternal Law . . .' He turned another page and ran a gnarled finger across the ancient inscription. The angelic writings instantly took on a life of their own, the contents of the tome displaying themselves in the air as thousands of pulsing blue hieroglyphics.

The automated voice of the narration expounded: 'If a claim be lodged against the race of men that can be proven that the race of men has persistently and without penitence committed desertion and has transgressed Eternal Law, judgement will be due.'

Michael crossed his arms. 'There is no remittance?'

'No.' Jether shook his head. 'It is Yehovah's wish to mete out mercy, but the claimant has demanded judgment. And Yehovah is just, Michael. He cannot judge Lucifer and his fallen angelic host and not mete out the same judgement to man. Their transgressions are the same. Both were granted free will. Both have transgressed against Yehovah and Eternal Law as an act of their own volition.'

Michael noticed Gabriel watching silently from the stairway. 'Join us, brother.'

'He is omniscient, Michael,' Gabriel said as he walked towards them. 'Yehovah knew even before he created the race of men that they would desert him. He saw the great falling away of the race of men aeons back, before our universe was even created – and yet it pleased him to create them.'

'As it pleased him to create Lucifer,' Jether echoed. Jether opened a second tome and rifled unceremoniously through the pages. 'Conditions of the race of men to pay the penalty of judgement according to the tenets of Eternal Law – without the shedding of undefiled blood there is no remission of sins for the race of men.'

Michael inhaled sharply. 'So there could be a remission?'

'That's right!' Gabriel said. 'The tomes explicate precisely that a substitute *can* meet the claim – or pay the penalty or the ransom, call it what you will – allowing the race of men to go free.' He removed his blue velvet cloak and placed it over one of the ornate carved willow chairs, then sat down at Jether's right hand.

'Yes, that is true,' Jether said wearily, 'but under what conditions, my old pupil?' Jether rubbed his wrinkled forehead. 'Conditions that Lucifer has ensured man cannot possibly meet.'

Gabriel passed his palm over the tomes. A bluish electric beam arced from his palm through the pages of the codex.

The modulated voice narrated. 'Tenet 7728891977 of the Code of Eternal Law. If one undefiled from the race of men is willing to shed his or her lifeblood on behalf of the race of men and become a substitute for judgement, the said race of men – inclusive of past, present, and future generations – will be released from eternal judgement by the death of that one. This is binding Eternal Law.'

Gabriel spoke thoughtfully. 'If one undefiled could be found from the race of men to trade his life . . .'

'It is impossible for man to carry out the terms!' Jether said grimly. 'Absolutely impossible! The substitute must be *undefiled.*' He ran his palm down the tome. 'Definition of "undefiled" as pertaining to the race of men.'

The narration answered. 'The substitute's blood must be pure and untainted from the mutation of the Fall of Man.'

Jether leaned over and swiftly picked up Michael's cinquedea. He nicked Michael's arm, and the thin indigo fluid flowed out onto the table. 'Our angelic blood is undefiled,' Jether said. 'Untainted from the Fall. But we as the angelic do not qualify as a substitute. The law specifies that any substitute be from the race of men. *Every* generation of the blood of the race of men is defiled by the Fall. They do not qualify. They are all tainted from the start.'

Jether shook his head sadly. 'Lucifer is a veritable master

of the knowledge of the tomes of Eternal Law. He has painstakingly planned man's demise. He knew of this possibility in the law, and he has made sure there would be no substitute.'

Michael stood. 'So, the claim can be met, but there is no man to meet it.'

Jether nodded.

Michael's gaze was grim. 'He has damned the entire human race!'

Jether raised himself slowly to his feet. 'Summon the Grand Councils of Heaven. I must go to Yehovah.'

CHAPTER THIRTY-TWO

The Claim

Over ten thousand of the angelic host were seated in four vast circles around a tall, jacinth pulpit. In the inner circle sat the heavenly council, the twenty-four ancient monarchs, on their golden thrones. Lamaliel and Jether sat at opposite ends of the circle, while Michael and Gabriel were seated on two magnificent mother-of-pearl thrones set apart and slightly to the right of Jether's.

Obadiah and forty of Jether's youngling scribes knelt before the pulpit, quills in hand. The sound of excited conversations filled the auditorium.

Lamaliel walked to the pulpit, his white silk and gold cloak billowing. Jether wrote intensively, engrossed in studying the huge codices and archive papers.

Lamaliel picked up the great gold hammer and crashed it three times. The enormous roaring of the angelic company across the auditorium was immediately silenced, their attention fixed on Lamaliel.

'I bid you all welcome, full councils of Yehovah.' He turned to the inner circle and bowed. 'The Council of the Ancient Ones, stewards of Yehovah's sacred mysteries.'

The crowned elders rose and bowed in obeisance.

'The councils of the outer universes.'

A thousand in the next circle rose and bowed.

'The councils of justice, presided over by Chief Prince Gabriel, lord chief justice of the angelic Revelators.'

Gabriel and two thousand of the angelic company rose as one and bowed low.

'The warring councils, presided over by Chief Prince Michael, commander-in-chief of the armies of the First Heaven.'

Michael and ten thousand of his glorious warriors rose as one and bowed their heads.

Lamaliel turned to Jether, who sat at the far end of the table, now surveying the auditorium. He raised his eyebrows at Obadiah and the young scribes. Lamaliel nodded in understanding.

'And let us not forget our students, eager to show themselves well approved by the Ancient of Days – the younglings of heaven, the scribes!'

Obadiah and his group jumped to their feet in haste, all out of sync with one another, elbowing each other and bowing at irregular intervals.

'Scholars of the sciences and universes!'

Xacheriel's group jumped up, Rakkon and Tirzah waving their arms excitedly at the glowering Xacheriel, who laid his hand over his eyes to blot out the view. Jether watched, poker-faced apart from a cough into his handkerchief.

Lamaliel gestured to the groups to quiet them, then turned to Jether. 'My honoured colleague, Jether, please address the councils.'

Jether rose to his feet, his features now weighted with strain. 'The gravity of this assembly cannot be over-emphasized,' he stated, surveying the room. 'We have been summoned here today to review the fate of mankind.' Jether held up a missive sealed with Lucifer's black royal seal. 'A claim has been lodged in the courts of heaven against the race of men.'

He stood without speaking for a full minute, then opened the codex before him. 'It demands that they pay the highest penalty for their transgressions ... that they be destroyed.'

A ripple of horror circulated through the councils.

Jether waved them quiet. 'We have painstakingly searched the archives and studied the tenets. I can attest to this council that not a jot or tittle has been overlooked in our research. The facts remain. Yehovah, in his infinite mercy, allotted to mankind free will, establishing himself as their Father as well as Creator. Man has continually and through all the aeons fallen to depravity, therefore incurring judgement.' Jether picked up his papers. 'The claim is both valid and binding in the courts of heaven, according to Eternal Law. Man is guilty and must be sentenced.'

With heavy steps he returned to his throne. Gabriel clasped the old, veined hand. Michael leaned forward, and the three conferred in whispers as all around them the council erupted in noise and opinion.

A young record keeper jumped up. 'Destroy them, I say! I am sick to the heart of recording their lewd practices!'

A second record keeper sprang to his feet. He sifted through the huge pile of records. 'Greed ... envy ... fornication ... theft ... murder ... lies ... incest ... treason. They are depraved!'

More record keepers raised their voices from all sides of the auditorium. 'I keep the records here,' called one. 'The race of men grows more evil each passing day. Destroy them, I say!'

Michael stood up. The assembly quieted immediately, all eyes upon him. His voice was raised barely above a whisper. '"We, the hosts of heaven, do become liege servants of life and limb to the race of men, and in faith and truth we will bear unto you throughout eternity of eternities."' He looked over the angelic host. 'Remember well our vow to the race of men all those aeons past, compatriots. We, the angelic host, are stewards of the race of men – their protectors. I would remind you that there is a greater perpetrator of mankind's evil.' He sat back down heavily.

Gabriel stood. 'The one that Michael speaks of used to lead this very council – his eloquent debates used to ring through these halls. It is *he* who has sown the seeds of his own iniquity among the human race. And why? Let us not forget his own diabolical envy of mankind's position with Yehovah. His aim: to erase the human race from the universe and to break Yehovah's heart.'

A slow, solitary clapping resounded from the very back of the auditorium. Jether frowned, his ancient blue eyes alert. 'Well spoken, Gabriel . . .', the familiar imperial tones rang out. A huge uproar broke out towards the back of the auditorium as a tall, white-hooded figure strode down the aisle of the auditorium. Half the assembly rose to their feet in horror. The remainder sat, stunned. A dreadful silence fell.

Horrified, Michael rose, drawing his broadsword. Jether grasped Michael's wrist and frowned fiercely from under his bushy eyebrows. Lucifer watched them from across the chamber. Grimly, Michael replaced his sword in its sheath and sat back down.

Lucifer ceremoniously walked across the floor to the pulpit and stood before the assembly, brazen. 'Their crime is heinous,' he cried. 'It is unpardonable. The race of men must be destroyed!'

He flung his hood away from his face, revealing his scarred, ravaged features. The assembly sat in horror, appalled. Lucifer raised his gnarled hand into the shimmering living stream of atoms of Yehovah's light shafts blazing

216

through the crystal dome above him. The gnarled, yellowed nails morphed, becoming short and clear. Lucifer stared in marvel at his now perfect hand. A fleeting vulnerability, an ever-so-fleeting wonder, crossed his face. He turned to the blinding, pulsating light, shaking his head from side to side, bathing his deformed features frantically in it. Again he appeared Lucifer, the beautiful son of the morning.

'It is his former state,' Gabriel gasped. 'The angel of light!'

'He is on holy ground,' Michael said grimly. 'He suffers no ill effects from the purity of Yehovah's presence here as long as he is not in direct proximity.'

'Do not be deceived.' Jether's ancient blue eyes became steel. 'His iniquity is deep-rooted – he cannot maintain this form.'

Lucifer walked deliberately over to Jether and stood directly in front of him. Jether stared back, unwavering.

'Why, Jether, your most *avid* scholar is back.' Lucifer smiled sinisterly. 'To confirm your worst nightmare.'

Michael pushed out his chair and stood to his feet.

Without breaking his gaze, Jether placed his hand on Michael's arm. He shook his head. Gabriel turned his head away from Lucifer, suddenly intent on studying the codices.

Lucifer laughed triumphantly and turned to face the councils. 'In the archives of Perdition every generation of *Homo sapiens* is registered, with all its evil deeds. Their darkened intelligence, their degraded wills . . . their iniquity.'

There was an outburst of horror as his words sank in.

'The records are meticulous. Even my fastidious mentor Jether will find them indisputable.' He strode to the podium, his beautiful features starting to scar. 'They are a race of rebels! I, their rightful sovereign, put man on trial!' He made a sweeping motion with his hand, and thousands of records appeared across the chamber. 'I lodge my claim against mankind in the courts of heaven. He cannot banish me to the Lake of Fire and not banish man. I *demand* judgement!'

He lifted his rapidly gnarling hands to the heavens. 'The penalty *must* be paid. Every man's soul is mine – to be with me in hell and the grave and in Tartarus. And when my judgement comes, they will burn with me in the Lake of Fire!'

Lucifer stopped in mid-speech and turned his head. He stared intently at Gabriel; then an evil smile spread across his face. His gaze moved to Jether, who sat completely still, not a muscle on his face moving. Lucifer walked to where the brothers and Jether sat. He grabbed the codex from Gabriel's grasp and scanned it. Then he threw it aside and leaned his face near to Jether's.

'What are you up to, old man?' he hissed. '*Angelic* blood cannot be shed – it does not qualify as the substitute mentioned in that book. Our blood is astral. Only one *born* from the race of men can meet the legal demands and pay the penalty!' He turned to the hushed spectators, his maniacal laugh resounding through the auditorium. 'And man's blood is tainted, mutated from the Fall. Even the line of Noah. How easily it succumbed.' He swung back around to Jether. 'His scheme is flawed, old man. There is not one left pure. I claim my prize – the race of men must be destroyed!'

He stopped in mid-sentence. Sweat poured from his temples, and he seemed strangely weakened. His breathing became slow and laboured. The councils watched, transfixed, as his great strength ebbed from him. He leaned trembling against the podium, his head fallen over his chest, incapacitated.

'Christos,' Jether whispered.

A blinding light became visible at the back of the auditorium. Christos appeared and raised his hand, and instantly the Grand Councils froze in time. The council members on each side of the auditorium stood as wax figures staring straight ahead. Christos walked imperially down the grand sapphire steps of the chamber, drawing closer to where Michael, Gabriel, and Jether all knelt, paralysed. He stopped directly in front of Lucifer, who had collapsed on the podium.

'Lucifer.'

With intense effort, Lucifer raised his head inches from the podium. He was trembling as he stared into his countenance. Completely vulnerable.

'Christos . . .'

Gently Christos moved the raven locks that had fallen across Lucifer's face.

Lucifer's tormented eyes locked on the eyes of Christos. He clasped Christos' hand, his grasp so fierce that Christos flinched. A deep serenity crossed Lucifer's countenance, and a smile flickered at the corners of his mouth.

Christos looked upon him, deeply moved. 'Lucifer,' Christos said softly, 'it is dangerous for you to kick against the goad.'

Lucifer's eyelids closed heavily.

There was a long silence. 'When he destroys the race of men,' his voice was a whisper, '*then* I will repent.'

Christos vanished.

The Grand Councils broke from their paralysis. Lucifer stormed up the aisle. Several younglings stood to their feet in awe, hastily pulled back into their seats by their mentors. The great doors slammed as chaos broke out in the councils.

Michael stared angrily around the room. 'Would we give him licence to gain his end? We play into his hands. Surely not!' He hit the table with his palm. 'We *must* find a way.' He strode after Lucifer, his sword drawn.

Gabriel looked up from the tomes to Jether, who sat unmoving on his throne.

'I go to Yehovah,' Jether said at last. 'I will tell him we have failed. The race of men is lost to him forever.'

Michael tore across the golden meadows after Lucifer's swiftly disappearing black stallion. He had speculated that his brother could not have resisted one last dash across the eastern gardens that he had once so cherished. He had guessed well. He urged Ariale on, gaining on Lucifer with each second until he was almost neck and neck with his elder brother.

Lucifer turned, his hood flying in the gales, his disfigured face now fully visible under Eden's lilac horizon. Michael leaned across and pulled on Lucifer's reins with his great strength. The stallions whinnied as both magnificent steeds finally drew to an uneasy halt.

Michael and Lucifer remained mounted, staring at each other: Michael, raw with emotion, fierce; Lucifer, inscrutable. Both seemed dwarfed by the sheer majesty of the undulating rainbow horizons surrounding them.

Lucifer saluted and bowed his head in recognition to Michael. 'I greet you, my brother, Chief Prince Michael, full of wisdom and valour.' He put his hand up to his head, realizing that it was uncovered.

He winced. For a fleeting moment, Michael thought he appeared almost vulnerable. He remembered their last moments in this meadow, before evil had taken its full course, when he had clung, sobbing, to Michael, pleading with him to save his soul.

'I read your mind, Michael.' They stared at each other for a long moment. 'You would urge me to repent.'

Michael nodded. He closed his eyes and bowed his head, suddenly unable to trust himself to speak. The memories of their brotherhood swept over him like all-consuming, searing waves that sought to drown him in their ferocity.

Lucifer expelled a terrible, trembling sigh. 'I miss him, Michael.' His voice was barely above a whisper. A terrible suffering clouded his features as he stared up at the seven spires.

'You were his shining one,' Michael entreated. 'His confidant . . .'

'Evil's hold is far-reaching in me, my brother.' Lucifer swallowed hard. 'There is no way back.'

Michael raised his head; tears coursed down the noble cheeks. He wiped them away with the back of his hand, not caring. 'His mercies are endless.'

'There is no restitution for *me*,' Lucifer whispered. For a fleeting moment Michael could swear that Lucifer's eyes were wet. He gazed directly at Michael without guile, as when they were younglings. 'Even if I wanted it to be so.'

Michael was silent.

'You will tell our Father of our conversation?'

Michael gazed a long time at his brother's blistered, ruined features. He nodded almost imperceptibly.

'Thank you.'

'I pity you, Lucifer,' Michael whispered. His eyes filled with a terrible love and a terrible sorrow.

Lucifer looked back at him with a strange fire in his eyes and spoke a tongue that was neither angelic nor of man. And then he was gone.

CHAPTER THIRTY-THREE

The Holy Mountain of God

You were on the holy mountain of God;
You walked back and forth in the midst of fiery
stones.
You were perfect in your ways from the day you
were created,
Till iniquity was found in you.

Indigo lightning struck far above the rock face of the Holy Mountain. The sacred rubied entrance to the throne room was barely visible, wreathed in the silver glistening mists that rose and fell in Eden's zephyrs. Seven scorching columns of eternal white fire blazed fiercely and unrelentingly at the outer entrance of Yehovah's palace. An immense flaming rainbow was suspended directly over the mountain. Hues of every spectrum ebbed and flowed in intensity from violets and indigos through pinks and vermilions. Yehovah's eternal remembrance of the race of men.

Michael, his white steed held by Sachiel, paced incessantly up and down the gardens outside the entrance. Gabriel stood silent near him. Finally he spoke.

'They convene for many moons over the fate of man.'

Michael turned from his pacing, grief etched across his features. 'He is filled with a great and terrible regret. His heart is broken that so easily they have deserted him.'

His voice broke with sorrow. Gabriel clasped his arm gently. 'There are still those of the race of men who love him and seek after his presence.'

The colossal golden doors of the rubied entrance opened. Jether, exhausted, walked past the Watchers towards the brothers, his head covered by his grey mantle. 'Yehovah mourns,' he said softly. 'He cannot be comforted.' He looked at the brothers silently for a long moment, then bowed his head.

'He loves them beyond our comprehension.'

He looked at them, his features etched with grief. 'The penalty will be paid.'

Michael stared at Jether, uncomprehending. 'He will destroy man?'

'No,' Jether said, his eyes filled with agony. 'He will send himself.'

Michael rode bareback for a hundred leagues, his white stallion's hooves thundering across the fields of Eden, his blond hair flying. The tears dried on his strong, noble countenance. His soul was aflame with unanswered questions and raw with pain.

He came to a halt on the western side of the Holy Mountain, at the back of the entrance to the throne room, outside the western labyrinths of the seven spires. He dismounted and lowered his head as he entered the sacred caverns. His path was lit only by the flaming eternal torches high against the walls of the caverns, which were fuelled by the burning coals of the seven spirits of Yehovah.

There were seven hidden chambers in the mountain, each descending into the inner sanctum of the labyrinths. Michael knew that the mountain held some of the answers he desperately sought. Aeons had passed since he had last walked these paths with Jether. The memory was still as vivid as if it had been yesterday.

He had been just seven moons of age, a fledgling prince, clutching his mentor's muscled arm tightly, his eyes screwed shut at the same strange and terrible apprehension that nearly overwhelmed him now. And so they had passed the first flame, Wisdom, though he knew not to look or stop as he kept at Jether's steady pace.

Then they passed Discretion and Valour, but still they did not stop. They ascended to a higher chamber, and as they neared the fourth flaming eternal torch, the young Michael fell prostrate, as if dead, onto the stony chamber bed. And he had heard a voice, at once within and without, saying, 'Holy, holy, holy – worthy is the Ancient of Days.'

The youngling raised his chin awkwardly off the chamber floor. Jether's hand was upon his head, and a terrible burning sensation raced through his body. All at once he was upon his feet . . . he knew to look.

In front of him blew a stormy wind, and out of the wind burned a great cloud with a fire, and great lightning and flashings came out of the fire. Out of the fire came four living creatures – the mighty cherubim of Yehovah. The four-winged, four-faced creatures bowed in obeisance to the Ancient of Days. As they did, Michael could see the face of an eagle at the back of their heads. The eternal burning torch of Yehovah was in the midst of them, containing the burning coals moving to and fro among them. Out of the coals, lightning blazed. And beneath them were whirling wheels of living flame.

Then he saw Jether's face glow as burnished bronze, his

skin translucent with the glory of God. He walked into the midst of the whirling wheels of the cherubim. Michael saw a cherub stretch forth his hand and fill both of Jether's hands with the burning coals of fire. Jether came out of the midst of the cherubim, and as he spoke, it was as though his voice shook the chamber: 'Michael, partake of the stones of fire.'

It was a command. As though magnetized, the young prince started to walk, and as he walked, the cavern bed suddenly became a living, burning mass of gleaming sapphires, burnished as the summer sky. He found himself walking in the midst and up and down on the burning sapphire stones of fire.

'The fires of holiness,' said Jether. And as he spoke, he touched Michael's lips with the red-hot coals. Michael felt the burning white-hot sensation flood through his spirit, soul, and body. It was as though Yehovah himself had passed through him. He was flung to the ground.

'Consume!' Jether commanded.

Again the lightning bolts of holiness invaded him.

Michael shook with a trembling that would not stop. When he looked up, it seemed to him that many moons had passed. The living creatures and the whirling wheels were gone. Only the burning eternal flame on the chamber wall remained.

Jether's weathered face peered down at him as he tenderly lifted the young Michael's still trembling limbs from the floor. 'You did well, young prince.'

Michael gazed up at him, still feeling the red-hot fire coursing through his veins.

Jether smiled tenderly. 'You will not return until the appointed time.'

And Michael never had . . . until now.

He walked, head bowed, past the third eternal flame. But as he ascended higher into the chamber, a familiar dread seemed to fill his being. His ascent continued, climbing deep into the heart of the labyrinths. He stopped for breath.

His eyes were growing accustomed to the strange, unearthly light. He could vaguely make out eight or nine tall forms next to the fourth burning lamp: the Watchers, guardians of the flame. Tall and silent warriors, they stood with flaming broadswords. No word had ever been uttered from their mouths, for their mouths had been sealed with the very coals that they were guarding.

Michael stood next to the cavern wall, catching his breath. Beyond this point he had never dared venture. Nor had any archangel, for surely this was the hidden sanctum of the Ancient Ones. What did the labyrinths house? Sacred mysteries? Hidden treasures of his person?

The Watchers remained still. Michael saw them bow in recognition of his personage.

A voice from somewhere deep within the chamber echoed, 'Celestial prince of Yehovah's presence, commander of heaven's armies, full of holiness and valour.'

As one the Watchers raised their flaming swords to him in brief acknowledgement, then returned to their worship of Yehovah.

Michael continued through the darkness. As he passed the Watchers on the fifth level, a great and terrible fright took hold of him. Still he ascended . . . to the sixth eternal flame . . . past the very fear of Yehovah.

Then he saw them: the Watchers of the seventh flame.

The dread warriors' faces were as flint. The Watchers beheld him. As one, they lifted the weapons that barred his way through to the seventh chamber. Slowly, so slowly, he walked on through a huge iron grid.

Facing Michael was a strange and twisted crown. It was mesmerizing. He could hardly withdraw his eyes from it. In a manner that he did not understand, it held a strange and terrible beauty.

Michael reached out his hand to it . . . it ripped his flesh. He withdrew in agony. As he looked more intently at the crown, he realized that it was made up of huge, jagged thorns.

But he knew to move deeper into the cavern. As he did so, the Watchers drew back and disappeared. He was alone.

As his eyes became accustomed to the dark, he saw a large hill far in the distance. Facing him in the darkness was a group of beings that seemed not to be angels, for their bodies were not transparent.

'Man,' Michael whispered.

But as he watched more closely, he did not understand. For they were dressed as warriors in gold and crimson, but they were not of noble intent. They were jeering and laughing. He looked again and saw women; tears fell from their faces. Suddenly, he felt his attention drawn upward, and as he stared into the darkness, he saw the outline of a large, wooden cross.

All at once he was gripped by a great terror. A voice said, 'Come.'

Michael drew nearer until he stood directly under the base of the cross. A warm and sticky liquid poured down upon his hands. His garments went crimson with blood, and as he looked up, he could make out the outline of a form hanging from the cross. Directly above his head, a pair of feet were impaled on one enormous crude iron nail. The hole gouged through the man's sinews was a sight so terrible that Michael turned his face away.

A chilling scream rang out from the impaled figure: '*Eli, Eli, lama sabachthani!*' It resounded throughout the Holy Mountain as if the echo would never stop.

Michael put his hands over his ears to block out the awful, chilling desolation and flung himself onto the cold earth of the cavern as vision after vision of the sufferings passed before him.

He saw the crown of thorns being pushed into the man's head until the blood saturated his matted hair. He saw him scourged. And he saw, lying on the open hand of he who was seated on the throne, a scroll, closed and sealed with seven seals. And he heard an angelic voice crying, 'Who is worthy to open the scroll and break its seals?'

No one in heaven or in earth or under the earth was worthy to open the scroll. Then one of the twenty-four elders cried, 'See, the Lion of the tribe of Judah, the Root of David, has won. He can open up the seal.'

It was many hours, maybe even days, later that Michael lifted his head off the ground to see a Lamb standing before him, with seven horns and seven eyes.

The Lamb went and took the scroll from the right hand of he who sat on the throne. The twenty-four elders fell prostrate on the ground, and they sang, 'You are worthy to take the scroll and to break the seals that are on it, for you were slain, and with your blood you purchased men unto God from every tribe and language and people and nation, and you have made them a royal race and priests to our God, and they shall reign over the earth.'

He heard the voices of many angels on every side of the throne and of the living creatures and the elders, and they numbered ten thousand times ten thousand, and their voices thundered: 'Worthy is the Lamb, who was sacrificed, to receive all the power and glory.'

And every created thing cried out, 'To him who is seated

on the throne and to the Lamb be ascribed the blessing and the honour and the majesty and might and dominion forever through eternities of eternities!'

'Michael.' The voice called to him as the sound of many waters. 'Michael.'

Slowly Michael raised himself to his knees. In front of his face were two feet of burnished bronze. They were gouged and scarred, the wounds still fresh. Above them the hem of a white garment dripped crimson blood onto the chamber floor.

As the holiness and the glory of his presence coursed through Michael, he flung himself at his feet as if dead.

A third time the voice called tenderly, 'Michael.'

'Christos?'

Christos reached down to Michael and took his hand in his.

Michael saw the fresh, jagged wounds in his palms. As he rose to his feet, tears coursed down his cheeks. He could hardly speak for the terrible emotion that overcame him. 'The race of men – it will do terrible things to you.' Michael placed his hand on his broadsword, his heart filled with a dread fury. 'I will protect you. I swear it!'

The Christ smiled at him then. And in his smile were the mercies and compassion of a billion aeons. 'Nay, my fierce and noble Michael – stay your sword.' He placed his hand tenderly on Michael's. 'There is much I must suffer still at the hands of the race of men. Let this one thing be your comfort in the moons ahead: that these are the wounds of love.'

He held out his palm to Michael. Slowly Michael reached out his fingers and touched the jagged wounds.

Then he was falling. He fell and fell, as through a thousand worlds.

Whether he was awake or slept, he would never be sure,

but he awoke trembling and frozen on the ground, with a terrible dread. He sensed a figure standing over him, and he drew himself up, still shaking.

The figure stared down at him gently. 'The sacred mysteries, Michael.'

Jether reached out for Michael's hand. 'Come. It is time.'

CHAPTER THIRTY-FOUR

The Vaults

'The sacred vaults,' Michael said in wonder.

They stood in the seventh spire, before the stormy wind that burned with fire and great lightning and flashings. The mighty presences of the cherubim of Yehovah were visible through the iridescent light. Jether motioned to Michael to follow him.

Beyond the veils stood an enormous vault between the cherubim, covered almost entirely by their golden wings. As Jether drew nearer, his face began to burn with what appeared to be living flames. He fell prostrate, weakened by the cascading glory, his face lying against the transparent golden floor.

Michael watched silently from the entrance in awe as the cherubim's wings unfurled, revealing the enormous golden vault. Carved on the right side were strange angelic writings of which Michael had no understanding . . . except for the small, beautifully carved sign in the centre that he suddenly recognized: a cross.

Jether rose up, his face burning as the seraph's, aflame with the ecstasy of Yehovah's presence. With difficulty, he slowly opened the vault.

231

The fires of holiness forked like lightning and struck the cherubim and Jether, and Michael fell to his knees, his head bowed. The lightning coursed through Michael's limbs, his soul. He felt the presence of Yehovah surge through his being like an immense voltage.

Jether reached into the vault and brought out a small vial wrapped in a living, muslin-like substance. 'Yehovah creates a unique seed,' he whispered. 'Christos' pure, undefiled DNA.' He held the small golden vial high above him in ecstasy.

Michael stared at it, thunderstruck. Lightning emitted from its surface.

Jether nodded. 'Christos shall be born one of the race of men. The ransom *shall* be paid!'

CHAPTER THIRTY-FIVE

Ex Nihilo

'In man, conception is the result of the union of two germ cells: the egg from the mother and the seed from the father.'

Xacheriel's brows furrowed. He pointed to the hologram of living, pulsating DNA molecules, the chromosomes and scientific calculations. Gabriel, Michael, and Jether stood around Xacheriel as he spoke.

'In the race of men, these germ cells share equally in the inherited mutations of the sin nature – all from the Fall.' He swung around, exhilarated. 'But the Christos-man cannot receive any genetic inheritance through the host. He has to be free of *all* inherent sin damage.'

Gabriel's eyes grew large with understanding. 'Or he cannot meet the claim.'

Jether clapped his hands together. 'Exactly!'

Michael watched intently as Jether gestured upward. The crystal cupola directly over the small assembly opened, and a vast, brilliant chamber of light began to descend. They watched in awe, as they had done aeons previously when the first prototype of the race of men had been revealed in precisely the same chamber. The glass-covered chamber was now fully descended.

Xacheriel stared at the vial that stood in the very centre of the chamber, the source of the intense pulsating light. 'The Christ's seed, ex nihilo – a body that is fashioned neither of the seed of the man nor of the egg of the woman but by Yehovah himself.' He whispered. 'Not replicated. *Created.*'

Gabriel stared in wonder. 'He is the second Adam!'

'Like all of the race of men, he produces his own blood,' Xacheriel declared. 'When the Christ-child reaches maturity, his body will manufacture over thirty trillion red cells in his bone marrow, replenished at the rate of seventy-two million every minute, as measured by the race of men. Yet unlike men, *his* blood will be untainted by the Fall.'

'Undefiled,' Gabriel whispered.

Jether nodded. 'He meets the claim.'

He swept his hand across the chamber. A hologram of an adolescent girl appeared. Her copper-coloured skin was as smooth as porcelain, the perfect canvas for her high cheekbones, aquiline nose, and full crimson mouth. Her thick tawny locks flowed past her waist. The brothers watched, entranced, as she walked across her spartan chamber, her slender nut-brown limbs gliding easily over the stone floor with a grace far beyond her years. She leaned out of the window, her heart-shaped face resting on her palms, studying a tall young man with noble chiselled features who carved conscientiously at a piece of wood. She laughed spontaneously, her rich brown eyes glittering with merriment.

Gabriel moved closer. 'The host?'

Jether nodded. 'Her spirit is consecrated to Yehovah. She has not yet known a man. She will carry and give birth to him. She is young and healthy and strong. Her body will withstand well the rigours of childbirth. We dare take no risks.'

Jether moved to the far side of the portal, where the huge dome was open and he could see the orbiting Earth as it came into view. 'Christos prepares to join the race of men,' he said. 'As soon as he is prepared, his Spirit will enter the created seed and leave the First Heaven.'

Gabriel bowed his head.

'He is in his garden,' he whispered.

Jether clasped Gabriel's shoulder.

'I go to him.'

CHAPTER THIRTY-SIX

The Temptation

The twenty-four ancient kings knelt in a semicircle underneath the magnificent hanging blossoms of the Gardens of Fragrance. Their crowned heads were bowed, their mouths moving silently in supplications.

Christos stood before them in the centre of the ancient olive trees at the very edge of the Cliffs of Eden. His arms were raised towards the shafts of crimson light that radiated from the colossal rubied door embedded into the jacinth walls of the tower.

Christos drew his palm slowly over the horizon and stared in wonder at the image that appeared. A man around thirty years, as measured by the race of men, walked across the stark desert terrain. His long dark hair, lashed by the fierce desert sandstorm, flew across the strong, bronzed shoulders.

'He views the future,' Jether whispered to Lamaliel beside him. 'He sees himself as one of the race of men.' Jether broke off as he saw a second figure walking towards the earthly Christ. 'Lucifer!'

In the image Lucifer stopped twenty yards away from the earthly Christ. His dark hair was flying. He looked imperial, noble. They could be brothers. Now that Christos was one of the race of men, Lucifer stood three feet taller, his six wings spread behind him. In the distance, thousands of the fallen angelic host waited, menacing, covered in shadow.

Lucifer laughed maniacally. 'So this is what it's come down to. The great Yehovah – Christos – sovereign ruler of the universe, ensnared in matter. Yeshua. Jesus of Nazareth . . .'

Christos watched from the First Heaven. Silent.

'You have none of your powers now,' Lucifer said. 'You have to pass the tests as one of them. It is the condition of the ransom.'

Jesus continued to stare at him silently.

'That I would ever see such a day,' Lucifer spat. 'Almighty Creator denying your deity and taking on their inferior form. Lower than the angels!' His eyes narrowed. 'It insults me.'

Lucifer moved closer to Jesus. 'But maybe you are not truly *him*. I require proof!' He swung around. 'If you are the Son of God, then prove it – turn these stones into bread.'

Jesus stood completely still as Lucifer leaned down and touched the stones. He picked one up, and it turned to bread – steaming, freshly baked.

Jesus bowed his head, his famished body rebelling desperately.

Lucifer smiled, revelling in Jesus' torment. He held out the fragrant bread. 'Satiate your hunger. Matter requires sustenance to exist.' He sneered. 'Unlike the angelic.' He studied Jesus intently, then tore the bread and bit into it.

Jesus bowed his head.

Lamaliel watched with the others in the First Heaven. 'Lucifer revisits Eden in the future as the tempter,' he whispered to Jether.

'This is no Eden,' Jether said grimly. 'Christos will become one of the race of men. He is to be tempted under all the pressing conditions of the Fall.'

In the image before Christos they saw Lucifer move his hand across the skyline.

Immediately he and Jesus stood on the lofty pinnacle spire of the Temple of Jerusalem. Lucifer watched Jesus intently, drawing nearer to him. 'You suffer to be away from his presence, Christos,' he whispered. 'I sense it.'

A terrible grief crossed Jesus' face.

Lucifer knelt on one knee and bowed his head. 'Behold, O God our defender, and look upon the face of thy chief princes. For one day in thy courts' – a slow, cruel smile spread across his face as he raised his arms to the heavens – 'is better than a thousand elsewhere.'

As the earthly Jesus watched in silence, Lucifer displayed for him image after image of Lucifer and the archangels bowing before his throne. An agonized sob rose in Jesus' throat. He turned to Lucifer, suddenly vulnerable.

Lucifer was ready. 'I suffer as you do, Christos. Each and every dawn. I know what it is to be desolate – away from him.' He reached out his hand, which still bore his ring with the royal crest of the House of Yehovah.

Jesus stared in recognition at the royal seal. A violent yearning coursed through him.

The tempter continued, 'A carpenter's son from Nazareth cannot herald in a kingdom until they proclaim you their king. They do not understand your deity, Christos.' Lucifer caressed the ring. 'Descend, heaven-borne, into the midst of the priests, Christos. Jump from this pinnacle.' An evil smile played across Lucifer's mouth. 'Then they will know you are divine. Go on,' he hissed. '*Jump.*'

In the First Heaven Christos moved his palm across the horizon, and the panorama vanished. He stumbled onto his knees, his face raised to the throne room, tears coursing down his face.

'It is the agony of his soul,' Jether whispered. 'He sees himself separated from Yehovah.'

Steadily, Christos turned his head, and Jether could see his face. The look of harrowing suffering on the imperial countenance literally took his breath away.

Christos stood to his feet. Majestic. Resolute. His head held high. He turned to his twenty-four trusted elders and nodded. His voice was so soft it was barely audible.

'I am ready.'

Through all the millennia of all the universes, past and present, that day is engraved forever on my soul.

The day that he became one of the race of men.

The silence – oh, the heavy, unrelenting silence – overwhelmed the First Heaven. There was no sound, no movement. All was still.

And then I heard the sound.

As I approached the throne room, it became louder.

I found the cherubim and seraphim prostrate on the ground in obeisance. The four living creatures were in the midst of the throne and around the throne, the lion and the calf and the man and the eagle, their six wings covering their multitude of eyes. All of these were silent. The twenty-four ancient monarchs were fallen down prostrate on the sea of glass that glistened as crystal, their golden crowns cast before the throne – silent.

And yet there was a sound.

I stood in front of the seven burning lamps, the seven spirits of Yehovah that burned before the throne day and night.

I will never forget that sound. No amount of waking and sleeping throughout eternities, throughout the Second and the Third Heavens, will ever erase the imprint of it from my memory. It was neither angel nor man. It was neither cry nor scream. It was neither agony nor ecstasy. But at the same time ... it was all of these.

It was the sound of Yehovah weeping.

CHAPTER THIRTY-SEVEN

The Nova

Michael, the missive clutched in his hand, walked to the windows of his palace chambers and flung them open. Beyond the shimmering halo of Yehovah's bow and over the centre of the golden mountain, an enormous flaming star moved slowly across the lilac horizon of the First Heaven, down towards Earth's solar systems.

Jether walked into the chamber and silently watched Michael.

'What are these men to him that he is mindful of them?' Michael whispered. 'That he would send himself.'

Jether bowed his head, overcome with emotion. Michael held out the missive to Jether, whose eyes narrowed at the black seal of Perdition in the right-hand corner. Jether took it, studying its contents.

A great dread crossed Michael's face. 'You do not think he suspects?'

Jether folded the missive up carefully. Grim. 'Lucifer's evil genius will bring him close to the truth – closer than we might like. But no, he does not *know*.'

'We have a head start, then.'

The doors opened. Gabriel stood there, mature, majestic.

He bowed his head in reverence. 'His advent in the race of men is nigh.'

Jether gazed out at the star. 'Lucifer's magi will alert him. We must make haste.'

Lucifer reclined on the seat of Satan, an ornate platinum throne in the portico of his rubied palace, a white satin robe wrapped around him. He stared out through the enormous portico windows towards the newly erected gates of Hades. A sinister smile spread across his mangled features. He watched the infinite throngs that poured through the monstrous black iron gates, gates that towered hundreds of feet above the glowing red ground.

At each gate stood a gargantuan troll-like sentry with gleaming yellow eyes. Embedded at the top of each gate was a living black seraph. Across its head was inscribed in ornate script, *The Souls of Men*. Each demonic seraph metamorphosed into a dragon breathing luminescent flames, then into monstrous leviathans, and then into a man's face, which then transformed into the features of a demon.

Hundreds of thousands of grey-robed men and women, ashen-faced and ghoul-like, thronged through the gates of Hades in a never-ending mass. Clothed in grey mantles, they walked at a steady pace though the gates of Hades. Their features were pallid, their eyes dead and lifeless. Imperial-looking kings and princes of the earth, holding sceptres, walked as if bewitched. Queens followed with jewelled crowns upon their heads, alongside beggars and slaves.

They walked past the City of the Dead mindlessly, like zombies, as if in some deep stupor. They stared with morbid fascination as they passed the Valley of Catacombs with its thousands of massive sepulchres bearing profane inscriptions. Many of the crypts lay violated and desecrated, their occupants' shrouds and bones lying discarded among the sarcophagus stones and marsh bines. Derelict orangeries overflowed with bladderwrack and nightshade and the strange, menacing tentacles of bindweed – living, writhing, decaying hothouses.

A soft but insistent knocking rang on his chamber door. Lucifer's expression grew dark. 'Who disturbs my rest?'

The huge ruby-covered doors opened, and Araquiel stood trembling.

Lucifer glared darkly as Araquiel handed him a missive. Lucifer snatched it and tore it open impatiently. A thin silver mist rose from the missive. 'Charsoc and his dark sorceries,' he snapped. 'At this late hour?' Lucifer scanned the letter, his expression grave. Carefully he folded it closed. 'Bid him enter.'

Araquiel nodded and walked back through the doors. Lucifer rose from the throne and moved through the portico doors into his chamber. Hands behind his back, he paced the room impatiently.

Charsoc entered. Silver mists swirled around his head. His black albatross rested on his arm. 'Your Majesty.' He bowed deeply, then raised his blind face to Lucifer's. His eye sockets were two seared, gaping holes.

Lucifer stood, his back to Charsoc. 'Your missive speaks of a star.' He turned. 'A new and ... peculiar star.'

Charsoc swayed slightly, his voice changing to a deep monotone that rang with authority. 'One greater than yourself has entered the realm of men.'

Lucifer paled. 'What sour tidings do you bring?'

Charsoc flung silver mist into the air. A deafening roar shook the chamber, accompanied by an almost blinding nuclear light. The chamber shuddered as though with an earthquake. Charsoc's twisted body transformed into a white, wraith-like entity, and his voice took on a strange, serpent-like tone. He continued to sway in his trance. 'The nova heralds a newborn prince of the East, born to the race of men. One so powerful that he shall crush the serpent under his heel.'

Charsoc turned, his face literally burning in flames. He swept his hand across the chamber, and immediately a hologram filled the room. Lucifer stared, magnetized, as the Roman armies vanquishing Jerusalem became the Napoleonic wars and morphed into Hitler, screaming at a rally of tens of thousands of Nazi soldiers marching past. Then, as he watched, Chinese soldiers surrounded Jerusalem, bent on its destruction. But to their dismay hundreds of thousands of angelic warriors under Michael suddenly joined in fierce battle against hundreds of thousands of Lucifer's own dark angels – the legions of hell.

'In that day,' Charsoc proclaimed, his voice echoing through the chamber, 'the conqueror with his severe sword, great and strong, will punish Leviathan.'

The hologram materialized into Christos on a white stallion high in the sky above Megiddo, laser beams emanating from his mouth. Then it showed the armies gathered on the battleground, which was now littered with slain bodies and wrecked war machines.

'Leviathan,' Charsoc continued, 'that twisted serpent.'

Lucifer watched, frozen, as he himself appeared in the image. Then Michael and two colossal angelic warriors seized and chained him, while six massive angels cast him screaming into the Abyss.

'Thou shalt yet be brought down to hell, to the sides of the pit.'

Charsoc shielded his face with his arms. Suddenly the chamber was completely still. The roaring stopped, and Charsoc was flung to the ground.

Lucifer stood silent, trembling, leaning against the doorway, his crown awry on the raven hair. 'The Judgement . . .'

He walked over to the eastern balcony and flung the great doors wide open. The enormous flaming incandescent star was fixed in the night sky between the Second Heaven and Earth. He stared at the star for a long time.

'This newborn prince of the East, born to the race of men . . . how is he connected with Christos?' he hissed.

Charsoc stared sightless, trembling. 'I do not know, my lord.'

A tall, dark-haired angel with fire-ravaged features now stood in the doorway.

'Merodach!' shouted Lucifer. 'Summon the Darkened Councils to the crypt. We must conspire!'

Lucifer waved them away and turned back to the flaming star in the window.

Xacheriel and Jether stood on the edge of the Milky Way, in the portal, staring down at the enormous blazing star.

'The coordinates are sure?' Jether asked.

Xacheriel nodded slowly, deep in thought. 'The co-ordinates are sure, but the race of men's grasp of astronomical happenings is primitive.'

Jether stroked his long, sweeping beard. 'We have located an ancient priestly caste within the court of the kings of the Parthian Empire who revere Yehovah.' He drew his gaze away from the star and looked at Xacheriel. 'Magian astronomer priests, interpreters of dreams and celestial happenings. They watch each night from their astronomical observatories – the ziggurats – seeking for signs of the king that Daniel, their compatriot, wrote of. They study the star.'

Xacheriel bowed his head in reverence. 'May Yehovah grant them divine illumination.'

Jether picked up his train and walked towards the portal entrance. 'Lucifer's evil magi have alerted him.' He bowed to Xacheriel. 'Time is short.'

CHAPTER THIRTY-EIGHT

Mul Bar Bar

Gaspar, the youngest magus of the Chaldean order, stood on the highest observational post of the three ziggurats, at the furthest edge of the pyramid-like tower, gazing intently out at the inky-blue night sky.

'Melchior!' He stepped back. '*Melchior!*' he cried again impatiently. He rushed down the pyramid's steps towards where Melchior was seated in the lush ziggurat gardens. Melchior looked up from his astronomical charts and tables and frowned.

'The new star!' Gaspar exclaimed. 'It moves again!' He struggled to contain his excitement.

Melchior lifted his gaze to the heavens and immediately walked with a leonine grace swiftly up to the observatory. He studied the heavens attentively. 'It creates a conjunction,' he whispered in wonder. He turned back to Gaspar. 'We must inform His Excellency Lord Balthazar at once.'

Gaspar nodded, running full-tilt towards the main ziggurat, forgetting in his haste that he had been newly anointed a magus and such behaviour was unbecoming to one of his rank. He picked up his robe as he ran, his short, tanned legs kicking up the desert dust behind him, followed closely by the striding, regal Melchior.

Balthazar was well into his eighties. His black skin gleamed like ebony; his hair and beard were a brilliant silver beneath his turban. He paced beside twelve long wooden tables, where more than sixty scribes sat meticulously writing and inscribing astronomical data by candlelight.

The highest level of the tower was completely silent save for the unrelenting scratching of the scribes. Balthazar walked over to the far turret window and stared at the great flaming star on the horizon. His contemplation was interrupted by a loud knocking that came from the lower levels, then a thunderous thudding of footsteps up the old wooden spiral stairs.

Gaspar flung open the ancient tower door, panting. Melchior and Balista stood behind him, bowing in reverence. The sixty scribes bowed and immediately filed out of the chamber as the three astronomers knelt before Balthazar.

'We request an audience,' Gaspar blurted, 'Lord Balthazar, full of wisdom, revered rabmag of the line of the great magus Daniel.'

Balthazar nodded. The three magi rose from the floor.

'The wandering star Udi Idim aligns again with Mul Bar Bar, milord Balthazar,' Melchior said gravely.

Balthazar held out his hand. 'The numberings . . .'

Melchior passed him a thick ream of papers. Balthazar studied them intently, pacing as he sifted back and forth through them.

'They create a conjunction in the constellation of Pisces, the land of the Hebrews,' Melchior continued.

Balthazar rubbed his hand across his wrinkled forehead and moved over to the turret. Far out over the horizon was the flaming, brilliant star. 'Once each 804 years there would be a single conjunction of the wandering stars . . .', he muttered.

Seventeen-year-old Gaspar could not contain himself. 'But three times in a single year, milord – it is truly extraordinary!'

Melchior placed his hand on Gaspar's arm to restrain him.

But Balthazar smiled, his brown eyes filled with the same fervour. 'You speak truly, Gaspar. The wandering star Udi Idim designates the city of Jerusalem.' He stroked his beard. 'It aligns with Mul Bar Bar, the star denoting royalty to the descendants of our great and beloved magus Daniel, the Hebrew.' He turned to the other magi and pointed to the flaming star. 'But tonight – look!'

The magi followed his gaze.

'In the constellation of Aquila, the eagle, a new star blazes brighter than any in the sky. It foretells something extraordinary! It heralds a birth of great significance.'

Gaspar beamed. 'I would like to see this child, born with such signs in the heavens.'

Balista, Balthazar's aged Persian manservant, stepped forward. 'Let us make haste to the councils of Jerusalem, the Sanhedrin, milord Balthazar. They are well versed in the Hebrew writings. They will know of whom the stars speak.'

'Patience, my good friend,' Balthazar said. 'Yes, we will go to the land of the Hebrews. But first we must journey to Arêtes, King of Petra. His household are keepers of the relics of Solomon.'

Balthazar looked once more up at the flaming star. 'He keeps them until the day that they are to be presented to the king whose birth would be written in the heavens – the king that the magus Daniel prophesied would redeem the race of men.'

He lifted his hands towards the heavens in supplication. 'The Messiah!'

CHAPTER THIRTY-NINE

Darkened Councils

Lucifer sat in his throne room on the Seat of Kings, a huge gold and black rubied throne. Twenty-four fallen chief princes, rulers of the dark world, each wearing ornate black armour and a golden crown, sat in two circular formations around the throne.

They exuded the power and authority of great regents. Nine feet tall and of menacing aspect, they were Satan's most formidable generals.

Seated behind them were a hundred of Lucifer's sinister elders, the stooped Darkened Councils and magi. Their black hoods concealed their faces. In front of Lucifer's throne was a great assembly of thousands of rulers of the dark world.

Asmodeus, disfigured but still beautiful, stood and bowed his head in reverence. Then he turned to the assembly. 'You have been summoned, great princes of darkness and Darkened Councils, by the one and only true king of this world, Lucifer, crowned Satan.'

Lucifer waited for Charsoc to speak, who was seated with the magi behind the great princes of darkness.

Charsoc stood. 'Your Excellencies, great princes, Darkened Councils, and magi, the celestial bodies foretell . . .' He stared sightlessly ahead. 'A king is born among men – one whose kingdom would destroy our own.' He lifted up his staff. 'And hasten our judgement!'

A fleeting murmur of terror rippled throughout the assembly.

'We must act swiftly.'

Marduk, sinister head of the hooded Darkened Councils, stood. His voice was soft and cultured but filled with evil. 'I call upon Baraquijal, ruler of the dark court of astrologers.'

Baraquijal, prince of the court of astrologers, rose to his feet, his voluminous magenta and crimson robes flowing. He bowed deeply, then looked up at the council chamber.

Marduk circled him slowly. 'Baraquijal, explain to us the meaning of this star – the portent.'

'The appearance of the star is unprecedented,' Baraquijal proclaimed. 'Our seekers consistently number hundreds of supernovas – star deaths – but I have to bring to the attention of the council that never have we seen a star *born*. *Never*!'

He knitted his thick eyebrows. 'It signifies one born of a great royal lineage – a royal house of immense power. We are certain that the nova's final resting place will mark the location of this prince of the East.'

Lucifer stared straight ahead, grimly listening.

A member of the Darkened Councils stood up on the back of the chamber, his face hooded. 'The calculations of its rising?'

Baraquijal smoothed his robe. 'Its heliacal rising is in the eastern skies of the land of men, Your Excellency. In the kingdom of Media.'

A second member of the Darkened Councils stood. 'It rests there?'

'Our seekers report that it began moving this past hour, sire. Through Parthia towards the Persian and Babylonian kingdoms.'

Lucifer raised his sceptre. The room stilled in awe. All bowed. 'This king ... somehow he has a connection with Christos. I sense it. He *must* be stopped. You will seek it out, Marduk. Your archivists will study the Hebrew writings of our antagonist Daniel and his compatriots.'

Marduk bowed. 'Of course, Your Majesty. My seekers will report every variation of the star's course. We will track it meticulously through the Persian and Babylonian Empires, sire.'

One of the great princes stood, a fierce and terrible being. 'I, Belzoc, prince of the kingdom of Persia, lay at thy command the Dark Guard of the East – we will scour Persia for this newborn king. We will seek him in every palace, alcazar, castle; we will raid every highborn family ... and we will destroy him.'

A second great prince stood. 'I, Merodach, prince of the kingdom of Babylon, lay at thy command the Dark Legions of Babylonia.'

'I, prince of the kingdom of Greece, lay at thy command the Dark Grecian Battalion.'

The great princes of Assyria and Tyre stood and bowed as one:

'I, prince of Assyria . . .'

'I, prince of Tyre . . .'

The great princes of the earth stood, one by one, until all twenty-four in the room were standing. Their roar thundered out across the chamber in unison: 'Your word is our command. We will find him.'

Lucifer stood and strode forward, his sceptre held high. The satanic princes fell to their knees at his coming. He swept his arms over thousands of the Darkened Councils and sorcerors, each one eager to execute his every edict.

'Go, then!' Lucifer commanded. 'Seek for the newborn king. And when you find him, *destroy him*! Do not return empty-handed!'

CHAPTER FORTY

Reunion

Michael and Gabriel waited on Jupiter's molten surface, two blinding, dazzling figures standing at attention.

Gabriel turned to Michael, his gentle grey eyes grave. 'Two millennia, Michael. Has it been so long?'

'Brace yourself, dear brother,' Michael frowned, his noble features fierce. 'Sin ravages its champions. He will be much changed.'

'Maybe he will not come.'

Michael looked pensive. 'I smell his scent on the wind. The fragrance of pine and frankincense. Strange how that is unchanged.' He sighed. 'He draws near.'

Gabriel shivered. 'It is suddenly like ice, my brother.'

Michael drew the deep blue velvet cloak tightly around his shoulders, his chin resolute. 'The north wind heralds his appearance. The fallen elements are his ministers of destruction. He is here.'

Far off on the shadowed side of the molten planet a shadowed hooded figure materialized and swiftly drew near. The hooded figure nodded in acknowledgement. 'I greet His Excellency, the esteemed Prince Regent Michael.'

Michael bowed his head. 'I greet His Royal Highness, Prince Lucifer of the earthly and nether universe.'

There was a long silence as the two stared at one another.

Lucifer moved nearer. He lifted a gnarled hand, a large ruby set in gold on his ring finger, and pointed towards Gabriel. 'Gabriel.' His voice trembled. He threw back the hood, revealing the blistered and deformed features.

Gabriel stared, horrified, then stepped towards him, visibly distressed. Michael grasped his arm.

'Michael, you would stop our brother from embracing me?' Lucifer laughed bitterly. 'How callous.'

Michael stared at him, sober. Grim.

'What do you want with us, Lucifer?'

Lucifer drew his dagger and ran it down his thigh and smiled sweetly. 'Tut, tut, dear Michael. I see the aeons have done naught to develop your patience.'

He grasped Gabriel's shoulder and pressed his face to his ear passionately. Gabriel flinched. His gaze locked on the thin, cruel mouth, the sparse clumps of hair. He stared silently into the soulless sapphire eyes.

'My appearance offends you?' Lucifer smiled coldly, pressing Gabriel's chest against his own with his great strength. Flesh onto flesh. Michael put his hand on his sword. Lucifer laughed mirthlessly. 'Ten millennia away from his presence – the very elixir of life – ravages the body.'

Gabriel felt the heat of Lucifer's body trembling as it used to tremble in his worst rages. '*And* the soul.'

The yellowed and gnarled nails dug through Gabriel's gold braids into his sinewed neck. 'Gabriel, you will tell our Father of our visit?'

'Of course, Lucifer.'

Lucifer did not release his cruel grip. 'Also tell him that I *too* have heard of this pending Messiah.'

Gabriel flinched and drew himself back.

A fleeting smile played on Lucifer's lips. 'I shall be forced to destroy his hand, Michael.' He nodded mockingly in deference to him as he had done when they were young. 'I shall thwart our Father. But I do it because I love him.' An insane exhilaration lit the twisted features. 'I cannot bear to see him humiliate himself on behalf of a bunch of mewling, snivelling creatures who continually reject his very existence. He shall see that I was right.'

Michael moved himself directly in front of Gabriel and stared at Lucifer. 'Would you bring mankind to account before the time of the Judgement? You cannot. Or does some concealed regret lodged in the remnants of your soul still compel you towards all that was – all that used to be?'

Lucifer fixed Michael with his intense sapphire gaze. 'Yes, it is true that I would gaze upon my brothers' countenances.' His voice was very soft. For a fleeting moment his eyes held a trace of their previous haunting beauty. 'I miss our brotherhood, our fellowship, our camaraderie.' He was silent a long moment, then smiled malevolently. 'But nostalgia aside, I came to check on the progress of his Messiah – of which I see you know naught.'

He wrapped his hooded garb around him, and then turned back, a maniacal gleam in his eyes. 'Tell our Father that he shall have to reckon with me sooner than he deemed. He disquiets me. He is become most reticent. Relay to our Father that I am concerned for his well-being. He is overtaxed. He keeps too much to his chest. Could it be that his chief princes no longer minister to him with the adoration and attention as in aeons past when *I* was his chief attender?' A sinister smile glimmered on his lips. 'Or is there more dissension brewing in the heavenly courts?' His words were soft but unmistakable.

'Enough of your sedition, Lucifer!' Michael exclaimed.

'You know full well that what takes root so easily in fallen men's fallow minds has no resting place here. You inflict your torment onto that mass of earth you so despise – yet even there, there are still our champions who reject you and see through your evil schemes.'

'Ah, yes, there will come a time to target these "champions".' A thin malevolent smile crossed Lucifer's lips. 'But for now . . . this Messiah will do.'

Then he was gone, leaving nothing behind him but the soft fragrance of frankincense wafting on the icy north wind.

CHAPTER FORTY-ONE

Petra, 2017

Nick turned the last page of the angelic writings. For the hundredth time that morning he photographed the strange angelic hieroglyphics. He unscrewed the excitation filter from the quartz crystal lens of his camera and carefully replaced the gold-bound codex into the upper compartment of the jewelled casket.

'Waseem!' His tone was terse. Urgent. He removed the camera from its rostrum, thrusting it into Waseem's hands. 'Get this to Mansoor at the palace museum.'

Waseem nodded earnestly. 'Mansoor, the curator.' Nick explained painstakingly.

'Yes, Malik.'

'Take the motorbike,' Nick said.

Waseem took off, his lanky olive legs kicking up clouds of dust as he ran into the harsh daylight.

Nick followed, stumbling out of the Lower Temenos, weary and unshaven but elated. He shielded his bloodshot eyes from the blinding Jordanian sun, staring after Waseem, who was now showing off the camera smugly to a shorter Arab boy.

'*Yallah*! *Yallah*!' Nick shouted, gesticulating frantically.

Waseem grinned, a wide toothy grin. He jumped onto a bright red dirt bike and placed the camera carefully into the sidecar. He kicked the throttle, waved vigorously to Nick, then roared down the dust road towards the desert highway, following the signs that read *Amman*.

Nick fumbled for his cell phone and pushed the dial button. 'Mansoor, it's Nick. Waseem is on his way with my camera. Get the photographs developed as soon as he arrives.' He shaded his eyes with his hand, watching the red bike's trail of dust disappear over Wadi Araba's mountainous desert terrain. 'Increase the development time. I need a higher contrast black-and-white negative.'

Zahid rushed over to Nick's side, holding out a bottle of fresh water. Nick grabbed it with his free hand, pouring the icy liquid down his throat. He grasped his phone between his ear and his neck, rubbing the surplus water over his dirt-streaked face with his palms.

'It's greater than we could ever have imagined,' he said. 'Tell the princess that the royal household of Jordan holds the greatest discovery of modern civilization.' Nick gazed up at the towering hills of the rust-coloured sandstone that surrounded Petra. 'The mystery of the universe unveiled.' His face lit with a strange elation.

'The *origins* of evil.'

CHAPTER FORTY-TWO

St Michael's Mount, 1981

Marazion, Cornwall, England

The dark, imperial figure stood on a jagged outcrop beneath the towering granite slopes of St Michael's Mount. His indigo cloak billowed in the violent gales that blew up from the raging winter storm in the English Channel.

'Our Father . . .', Lucifer murmured, his soft, cultured tones barely audible. A bolt of lightning flashed, illuminating the soaring pyramidal mount crowned by its medieval castle.

'Who art in heaven . . .'

The heavens opened, and a driving, lashing rain hammered down.

Lucifer inhaled deeply, his face raised heavenward, bathing in the torrential downpour, and raised his hands in exhilaration to the darkening skies. Six monstrous black seraph wings rose behind him.

'My kingdom come,' he cried, his steel-blue eyes blazing with fervour.

The soaking strands of his matted locks thrashed against his face, masking the scarred imperial features.

'*His* will be done,' a soft voice echoed from behind him.

Lucifer smiled. A slow, satisfied smile.

'Michael . . .', he murmured, his back to his brother, 'you are late.'

Michael stood on the far side of the mount, his hand on his sword, silent. Lucifer pushed his long raven mane back from his face, turned, and studied his brother intently.

Michael wore the long white silk robes of his battalion's ceremonial regalia. The sapphires on his silver breastplate gleamed, and his flaxen locks were tied back in two platinum braids. The handsome, chiselled features were set.

Grim, pondered Lucifer. No, not grim – earnest. Earnest, noble Michael. *Nothing has changed*, he reflected. He laughed sardonically.

'You summoned me through the royal courts. What brings you here, brother?' Michael strode to and fro impatiently. Lucifer grinned his old magnificent smile, relishing Michael's frustration.

'I was passing by the area,' he said casually. He walked towards Michael, across the crests of the raging waves, in long, firm strides. 'I was *curious*, brother.' Lucifer drew his head close to Michael's. 'I would learn of the legends . . . of the white rock in the wood,' he whispered. Michael's clear green eyes locked on to Lucifer's inscrutable sapphire gaze. 'Legends of Michael the Archangel . . .'

Michael flinched as Lucifer's seductive dulcet tones penetrated deep into his soul. 'The stuff of fairy tales,' Lucifer continued.

'I traverse many lands.' Michael replied.

'Ah, but you reveal yourself to so *few*.' Lucifer slowly, lazily, circled him. 'They saw your apparition here in Cornwall, in the year 495.' He gestured at a lofty crag in the distance. 'You revealed yourself to a fisherman, a lone hermit . . . a *monk*?' Lucifer's eyes narrowed. 'Who was he, Michael? Was he one of us?' he hissed. 'The angelic, or one of the race of men? Is Yehovah *compelled* to pre-empt my every move?'

'You waste my time, Lucifer,' Michael said coldly. 'You summoned me with the royal seal, yet you speak of trivia.'

Lucifer observed him sceptically.

'More than trivia, I think, brother. No matter, I will assuage my curiosity another time.' Lucifer raised his hand to the skies. 'Let us get to business, Michael – our Father's business. And like him, I, too, would converse of messiahs.'

He surveyed the craggy shores of south-west Cornwall. 'And of this faded empire – this weakened lion ... this *England*.' He swung around. 'For she shall yet behold a king ... this year, maybe next ...'

He grinned mockingly at Michael, as when they used to sword-fight in aeons past, in worlds long departed. 'Perhaps tonight, Michael, a messiah is born in Marazion.'

'Speak plainly, Lucifer,' snapped Michael, losing patience. 'Enough of your parables.'

'Ah, but do I speak the truth, or merely a fabrication?' Lucifer needled. 'Relay to our Father that I, too, shall send a messiah.'

'Our Father is omniscient,' Michael replied. 'He knows your every conversation. Your every thought is preceded and beheld by him.'

'Ah, yes, but I stand by the legal process. I would have my thoughts on record in the royal courts in the codices of heaven. That is why you are here – so I meet the demands of *his* legal system.'

Michael indicated agreement. 'It shall be recorded as you request.'

'My strength ebbs from me ...' Lucifer scanned the heavens, strangely agitated. 'The Nazarene is near.'

An uncharacteristic dread crossed his marred countenance. 'You came alone?'

Michael nodded. 'Time runs down, brother,' he spoke softly, sorrow etched on his noble features.

Lucifer lifted his head, his breathing easing. 'He offers repentance with one hand, yet, with the other, seeks my demise.' Lucifer's eyes filled with loathing. 'Our Father is malicious.'

'As you would have it, Lucifer.' Michael looked at him, suddenly fierce. 'Your brazen iniquity affects your judgement.'

'As your shameless naivety does yours,' Lucifer sneered.

The two brothers glared at each other, severe, unyielding.

Finally Lucifer spoke. 'My messiah shall rise from these isles,' he whispered. 'A king of politics and of industry, courted by kings and queens – a greater orator than Churchill – rises upon these shores.' He stared out past the raging black waves to a lone star that glimmered through the rising mists. 'I think I shall give him brothers,' he declared. 'Like *us*, he shall have a family.'

His mood changed abruptly. 'They shall be three, even as you, Gabriel and I are three angelic brothers.' He gave Michael a mercurial smile. 'Three brothers of the race of men.'

An insane fire lit his gaze. 'And *like* us' – he bowed mockingly to Michael – 'one shall be an insurrectionist, a renegade.'

Michael bowed his head. 'You will lose, Lucifer,' he murmured, 'as you lost at Golgotha.'

'*Golgotha*!' Lucifer snarled, his countenance turning at once into a mask of hatred. He turned his back on Michael, looking out to the raging winter seas. His voice was hard. 'Tell Jether when he sees the White Rider in the heavens, my messiah will make his appearance in the race of men.'

And he vanished.

Michael turned as Gabriel strode out of the hanging

Cornish mists, up the rocks and towards him. Gabriel's platinum hair fell loose over his kingfisher blue vestments. His flawless features were finer than Michael's strongly defined ones ... gentler. But tonight his regal countenance was set.

'His messiah will be born tonight in Marazion,' Gabriel announced wearily. 'It is certain.' He stood on the rocks before Michael, the Sword of Justice hanging at his side. 'Lucifer's fallen angelic battalions already surround the area; our legions will do the same.'

Michael bowed his head. 'He will lose,' he said, 'at Megiddo.'

Gabriel nodded. 'Yes, Michael, he will lose – but at what cost to the race of men?' Together the brothers stood in silence, staring out beyond the dark swirling mists rising off the west Cornish coast, to the blazing star that now rose in the heavens over the small village of Marazion.

CHAPTER FORTY-THREE

Monastery of Archangels, 2021

Alexandria, Egypt

Two monks stood in the portal of St Michael the Archangel, the rotating telescope dome on the observatory of the Monastery of Archangels. Their features lay hidden by the grey cowled hoods of their Coptic monastic robes. They stared through the Coronado Solar Telescope directly into the Egyptian sun, transfixed by the unsettling apparition that hovered above the sweltering desert plain.

The older monk watched, mesmerized, as the spectre materialized into a sinister waxen form astride a magnificent white stallion. The form held a bow.

'The White Rider of the Apocalypse . . .', the younger whispered, fingering the cross at his chest. 'The first seal is broken.'

'The Son of Perdition comes forth to rule – one from the race of men.' The older monk looked grimly up from the telescope into the shimmering crimson skies of the Egyptian dawn. 'The Great Tribulation has begun.'

That dusk is still imprinted in my memory. The dusk when the sign of the White Rider of the Apocalypse hung in the Egyptian skies over the sweltering desert plains. The Son of Perdition coming forth to rule in the race of men. For the breaking of the First Great Seal was surely to herald the beginning of the devastations of the End of Days.

And as I stood with Jether, observing the waxen apparition, my mind raced back two thousand years earlier to a different dusk. And a different sign that had once blazed high in the eastern skies. A sign that was to terrorize the soul of my brother Lucifer, King of the Damned. For the chilling events of the coming moons were about to change eternity in the world of the race of men as we still knew it. And plunge the armies of the First Heaven and the Fallen into a cosmic battle that would reverberate throughout a hundred aeons.

Beyond Megiddo.

Beyond the termination of the world of the race of men.

Culminating in one final battle. Between my brothers. Michael and Lucifer.

A thousand years in the future.

At the White Gorge of Inferno, on the eastern shores of the Lake of Fire.

But it was here, aeons before, that our tale begins. For it was to be a different dusk.

CHAPTER FORTY-FOUR

Prince of Perdition

4 BC

Two Thousand and Twenty-Five Years Earlier

Lucifer flung open the colossal sapphire doors of his throne room and walked out onto the eastern portico of the Black Palace, overhanging the very edge of the bloodstone cliffs of Perdition. He raised his face to the skies as the twelve magenta moons of Perdition set in the pale amber horizon over the desolate smouldering lava wastes of hell. The enormous flaming star was still fixed in the night sky between the Second Heaven and Earth.

He gazed at the nova for a long time. Silent.

Miles below, in the shadowy crypts of the sinister Shaman-Kings, the slow, pulsating throb of hell's sinister war drums resounded throughout the lower penitentiaries of the damned.

A lingering smile spread across Lucifer's mangled features as he watched the steady grey-robed throng of ghoul-like men and women pour through two monstrous black iron gates that towered a thousand feet above the glowing red ground – the Gates of Hell.

267

Hundreds of jaundice-eyed, demonic gorgon seraphim nested on top of the immense black iron gateposts of hell's perimeter, their gigantic scaled brazen claws slashing at the posts, and red-hot flames issuing from their nostrils and ears. The gorgon's wings were of beaten gold, their wingspans measured a hundred feet, and across their scaled heads, inscribed in ornate script, was written *The Souls of Men*.

Lucifer pulled his violet velvet cape tightly around him. His gleaming raven hair, plaited in thick braids and inter-woven with diamonds, fell over his broad shoulders, blowing in the scorching tempests that blew from the stark onyx crags of Perdition. The diamond satanic crown of state rested on his head, and his glistening white silk robes trimmed with werewolf fur fell to the floor, half concealing his jewelled sandals. The once-exquisite countenance had been scarred almost beyond recognition in the torrid inferno at his banish-ment from the First Heaven. Yet still, in the rarest of moments, the haunting beauty of aeons past was strangely evident: the wide, marbled forehead, the high imperial cheek-bones, the passionate crimson mouth, the imperious sapphire eyes now shadowed deep in thought.

He held out a sweetmeat idly to his favourite hellhound, the pampered five-headed Cerberus, who licked his master's hand with his coarse tongues. Then Lucifer returned to his contemplations of the star.

Balberith, his chief attendant, stood in the doorway.

'Your satanic princes are returned from Earth, Your Excellency.' He bowed deeply.

Lucifer nodded and, tearing himself away from his star-gazing, strode through the doors towards the monstrous black onyx throne, the Seat of Satan. He sat directly beneath the black crystal vortex that soared overhead. Araquiel, his courtier, held out his sceptre on a velvet bolster. He took it. Directly behind the throne lay the Golden Gates of the Black

Necropolis which housed the great golden Ark of the Race of Men, manacled to the Black Sepulchre with monstrous iron chains. Lucifer's trophy.

Ahead of Lucifer towered the massive black iron gates of the throne room. His forbidding satanic guard, the Black Horde, stood at attention – a thousand of Lucifer's dread elite generals of his High Command. The corridors of Perdition reverberated with dark muttered tales of their bloody torturing and butcheries. The terror of the inmates of hell's penitentiaries. Their pale straw-coloured eyes stared pitilessly out from their scarred mangled faces. Their black braided hair hung well below their thighs. Alongside the fallen horde, a pack of snarling black yellow-eyed jaguars paced, chained to their depraved masters, their poisonous black fangs visible.

Dagon, commander of the Black Horde, stepped forward, helmet in hand, his black-gloved hands on his sword, and bowed. 'I announce His Majesty's satanic chief princes, the rulers of the dark world.'

The iron gates to his throne room opened, and two monstrous princes entered, followed by ten regents and their guards. The gates slammed shut, leaving the twelve regents alone before Lucifer and the Black Horde. They fell prostrate before the gates.

'I announce His Royal Highness, Prince Belzoc, champion of Perdition and satanic regent of the dark world from the kingdom of Persia,' Dagon declared.

The menacing Belzoc, satanic king of Persia, rose from his knees to his full nine feet, then strode across the gleaming lapis lazuli floor towards the throne. He was stopped twenty feet away by six of the Black Horde, who held up their broadswords.

The chief magus of the Darkened Council walked forward. 'You may address your emperor.'

Belzoc fell to one knee, then pushed his coarse mane of matted black hair away from his craggy face and raised his glinting red eyes to his emperors. 'I return from Persia, Your Majesty,' he rasped, glutinous yellow saliva dripping from his thin pale lips. 'My dark slaves of the race of men have executed your command. Every newborn prince and royal in the kingdom of Persia is slain.' His dark demonic tones echoed throughout the chamber.

Lucifer stared at him, grim and silent.

The chief magus spoke again: 'I announce His Royal Highness, Prince Merodach, regent of the kingdom of Babylonia.'

Merodach fell to one knee, trembling.

'Every royal house, every palace, castle and pavilion in the kingdom of Babylonia has been ransacked – all of royal lineage are slain.'

Lucifer stood, strode over to the east side of the chamber, and flung open the heavy velvet curtains.

'Yet still the nova burns flaming in the heavens,' he cried. 'He *lives*!' He spun around in fury.

Marduk, head of the Darkened Councils and Lucifer's chief of staff, entered the gates. Marduk slunk towards the throne and bowed, then raised his hooded face to Lucifer's.

'I bring news of the nova,' he wheezed, his sibilant hiss echoing through the throne room. He bowed again deeply. Only his jaundiced, straw-coloured eyes could be glimpsed under the fawn cassock hood. Lucifer waved his hand to the magi and his regents. 'Leave us.'

Immediately the twelve regents scattered to the outer court. Marduk moved closer to the throne and lifted his hood, his ravaged, sallow features now clearly visible.

'The star moves east, Your Majesty, to the Middle-Eastern regions of Planet Earth.' Lucifer stared out beyond the hunched Marduk, past the enormous sapphire doors, to where the star still hung, 'Our battalions have scoured Persia, Greece, Babylon, sire – he is not to be found.'

Lucifer slowly turned his gaze onto a tall sinister form who now stood at the gates' entrance.

Charsoc the Dark's iniquitous, wizened sallow countenance was now framed by a veil of jet-black, poker-straight hair and beard. Where his eyes had been, two seared, white, gaping eyeballs stared sinisterly out, minus both iris and pupils – an ever-present reminder of the day and the hour that Christos himself had visited the penitentiaries of the damned. His voluminous harlequin sorcerer's gown was of the finest taffeta and tasselled, tied in the middle with a thick vermilion satin sash. His bony, pale fingers were covered in gold rings set with sapphires, opals, and emeralds.

Charsoc vanished from the gates, then rematerialized directly before Lucifer's throne bowing deeply, his hair sweeping the floor.

'Your Excellency, great Prince . . .' Charsoc's voice was both sinister and cultured in tone. 'The nova heralds a newborn prince; this infant king to be born of the race of men is one of great royal lineage.' He caressed the fire opals on his thumb ring. 'A star of this magnitude signifies a royal house of immense power.' He moved his head closer to Lucifer's. 'One so powerful that his kingdom could destroy our own ' – an uncharacteristic dread fell across Charsoc's face, and he lowered his tone – 'and hasten the Judgement.'

A terrible silence descended on the throne room.

'Where is the infant king to be born?'

Lucifer's words hung in the chamber. He swung around to Marduk.

'What of the Black Murmurers?' Lucifer hissed.

Marduk raised his head, his voice tremulous. 'Sire, they have been traversing the borders of the land designated Israel in the land of men. The legions of your royal brothers, Chief

Princes Michael and Gabriel, surround the area; we cannot infiltrate.'

'Michael!' Lucifer snarled. 'This infant king will be born in that parched tract of dust. I sense it.'

He was silent a long moment, then turned to Charsoc, his eyes narrowed. 'The Warlock Kings of the West . . . they foretell this infant has a connection with Christos?'

Charsoc stared at him, trembling. Silent.

Lucifer pointed his sceptre at Marduk. 'You will seek it out, Marduk.'

He rose, resplendent in his robes. 'Yehovah continually vexes me through that spawning ground of prophets, patriarchs . . . and now rival kings. And now I shall vex *him*. Relay my royal edict.'

Lucifer raised his sceptre high. 'Dagon – dispatch the Black Horde. Divert my brother Michael to the west. Release the reconnaissance legion of the vulture shamans from their hell cages, to fly east.'

Lucifer strode back through the great jewelled doors of the eastern portico. He continued his staring out at the flaming pillar of fire that blazed in the black heavens, the nova that heralded his adversary – the infant king.

CHAPTER FORTY-FIVE

Aretas of Petra

The small party of magi journeyed on horseback for weeks across the treacherous, rocky terrain of the main Persian trade routes, following the Euphrates River, led by the strange flaming pillar of fire that hung high in the heavens. At the fringes of the Syrian desert, they met with an ancient caste of monks, who exchanged the magi's horses for ten camels.

The aged magus Balthazar led the caravan, his posture erect and regal, seated astride the leading camel. Behind him rode Gaspar, the youngest magus of the Chaldean order, next to the older, more sedate Melchior. Balthazar's manservant Balista and six magi rode behind, their camels weighed down with massive bags of fine spices, provisions, and astronomical instruments.

Their destination, Petra.

The city had housed the ancient relics of the Hebrew king, Solomon, for generations; the relics to be presented to the newborn king.

Days on end had melted into nights, and twilights into dusks as the magi pushed themselves to the limits of their endurance, beaten mercilessly by the scorching desert sun as they traversed the ferocious Syrian wilderness. Stopping for neither rest nor sleep, exhausted from the gruelling heat, magnetized forward by the furiously flaming nova, across the harsh and desolate wilderness, past Damascus, until the terrain transformed into a paradise of lush green valleys and babbling streams. Gaunt and weary, Balthazar lifted his hand.

'Ride ahead, Balista. Let the king's royal guard know that we are but a day's journey away. The relics of Solomon await us!' he cried, his voice hoarse from exhaustion, his eyes burning bright with exhilaration.

The caravan rounded the final mountain that dawn. There she lay, nestled in the remote, all but inaccessible valley in the mountains south of the Dead Sea: the mysterious ancient Nabataean city of Petra.

The city was surrounded by the towering rugged rose-coloured sandstone hills that rose from the desert plateau to protect the noble Arabian inhabitants from invaders. The party stared, enthralled, at the great chasm before them.

'The Shiq,' murmured Melchior in awe, 'the great cleft in the earth.'

One by one, led by Balthazar, the magi rode the long, narrow, winding route through the lofty cliffs until they rounded a bend. There, towering in front of them, was an immense thirteen-storey-high, ninety-foot-wide columned monument, chiselled from the pale rose sandstone cliff.

'Al Khazneh, the eighth wonder of our world,' Balthazar whispered in awe.

Then his head slumped onto his chest in sheer exhaustion and he collapsed forward, losing consciousness into blissful oblivion.

Balthazar, now bathed and manicured and with three full nights' rest behind him, was magnificently attired in his embroidered priestly robes. His black skin gleamed like ebony, and his silver hair and beard glistened after being meticulously trimmed and anointed with perfumed oils by one of the king's personal stewards. Why – he hadn't felt this young in most of his eighty-seven years.

He rode on horseback across the royal palace courtyard, keeping up with the handsome young king who rode ahead of him on his fine Arabian stallion, his crimson robes billowing, his steel-blue eyes clear and full of purpose.

Although only in his late thirties, the young monarch exuded a power and authority far beyond his years, one normally attributed to great and ancient rulers. Aretas IV, king of Petra and Southern Arabia, was pragmatic and decisive in temperament. His lean six-foot frame was burned brown by the harsh Arabian sun, his sinewy hands hardened from manual work. Long, dark-ribboned locks framed his strong, dark features and quicksilver smile.

Balthazar studied him. He was different from his father, Balthazar's old and trusted compatriot, the judicious old Nabataean king. The younger Aretas was a proud king, fiery and hot-blooded, on occasion overly imperious and leaning towards inflexibility. He would mature in time, as his father had before him; Balthazar was certain of it.

He followed Aretas and the royal guard down the colonnaded street, captivated by the beauty of the ornate royal tombs and lesser palaces. Aretas pointed proudly at his newly built amphitheatre, which could easily seat three thousand. They rode through the narrow, dusty streets bounded by the towering stone walls of Petra. The stench of rancid goats' milk mixed with incense and spices invaded their nostrils as they rounded the corner to the open-air lower markets. Hundreds of Chinese, Arab, Indian, and Roman tradesmen jostled across uneven pavements, haggling boisterously at hundreds of stalls over the price of incense, silks, and spices. Balthazar stared in wonder at the Paradisos, Petra's magnificent ornamental pool and gardens.

Ahead of them loomed the imposing triple-arched Temenos gateway, decorated with sculpted busts and ornately engraved inscriptions.

Aretas veered right and dismounted outside the imposing Temple of the Winged Lions. Balthazar gazed up at the exquisitely carved winged lions and griffins that decorated the limestone capitals of the colossal temple pillars. Aretas led the way up the temple's wide, gilded steps, striding up the nave, with Balthazar and the other magi behind him, until they reached the silver-clad pillars of the inner sanctuary. A huge magenta veil hung from gold rods above the darkened stone altar. Aretas, uncharacteristically solemn, dropped to one knee. Immediately, two high priestesses draped in gossamer white robes reverently opened the purple veil, then flung themselves prostrate on the marble floor, followed by the magi.

Aretas slowly rose, and the high priest drew open the gossamer inner veil. Facing them on the dark, damp stone altar was an ornate silver casket carved with cherubim and seraphim. Aretas turned to Balthazar and nodded. Slowly he lifted the great silver lid to reveal a golden cup, a small stone box and a golden rod. He stared in undisguised awe.

'Daniel's wonders,' said Balthazar.

'The cup of frankincense, the alabaster box of myrrh . . .' Aretas murmured.

'And the gold rod of Aaron.' Balthazar raised his head to

276

Aretas, his countenance radiant. 'The relics of Solomon's temple.'

'It has been over half a millennium since the Hebrew Daniel entrusted them to our royal house for safekeeping.' Aretas hit his golden staff twice on the ground.

The stewards rose immediately.

Balthazar turned to Aretas, tears welling in his eyes, overcome with emotion. 'The prophecies of great magus Daniel must be fulfilled. We must present the relics to the newborn king.'

Aretas nodded. The high priest clapped his hands, and immediately six priestly stewards reverently placed the casket onto their shoulders.

Aretas walked slowly back through the temple. He stood on the steps, staring out over the Nabataean city, deep in contemplation. 'My father's house looked eagerly to this day,' he murmured.

Balthazar nodded. 'Your father, my old and trusted compatriot.'

'Revered Balthazar, you know that I do not share his religious sentiment.' Aretas turned to Balthazar, an unusual vulnerability on his face. 'But for my father's name's sake, I would accompany you to Jerusalem.'

Balthazar nodded, moved by the offer.

'Who knows, old friend,' Aretas smiled, 'if this babe is the future king of the Jews, I could make an alliance with him and stop the eternal disputes over our borders.' Aretas stopped as his royal household chariot drew up outside the temple steps. Four royal maidservants alighted.

A toddler struggled vigorously out of her royal maidservant's arms, ran over to Aretas, and flung herself headlong into his arms. 'Papa, Papa! I go with you.'

Aretas' countenance immediately softened as he embraced the tiny girl, and then held her at arm's length, gently brushing the unruly dark locks that tumbled down her face. 'Jotapa! At all times you are a princess of the royal household of Aretas. You have been playing in the *dirt* again?'

Jotapa giggled. 'Jotapa build castle . . . for Papa, the king.'

Aretas threw back his head, laughing loud and long. 'I go to visit a young king, Jotapa. A king of the Hebrews.'

Tenderly he stroked his daughter's pretty heart-shaped face. 'If he is gracious and just' – Aretas looked adoringly at Jotapa – 'and handsome' – he sat her on his knee – 'very, *very* handsome, we could arrange a marriage, an alliance of the houses of Arabia and Judaea.'

Balthazar smiled and shook his head, gently laying his hand on the king's shoulder. 'My dear Aretas . . .' He gazed strangely into the distance. 'This is no earthly king we seek.'

'You speak as my father spoke. You are aware that I am not a religious man, Balthazar. Your deep sayings are best left for the evening feast, when I can digest them with jugs of wine!'

Aretas raised Jotapa from his lap high into the air and, amid her squeals of laughter, remounted his stallion and placed her in front of him, where she sang softly to herself. Balthazar rode at their side through the colonnaded streets until they reached the gleaming marble courtyard of the royal palace.

Gaspar and Melchior strode through the courtyard towards them. Gaspar bowed low. 'The star . . . the star, it moves, my lord Balthazar!'

Both Balthazar and Aretas looked up at the heavens. Balthazar dismounted, exultant. 'It moves towards the north-western regions, Your Majesty. It is there we will find the Messiah, our compatriot of whom Daniel spoke.'

Aretas dismounted and placed Jotapa firmly on the stone floor of the palace courtyard.

'We must make haste to the councils of Jerusalem, Melchior,' Balthazar instructed.

Aretas lifted his hand. 'My ambassadors are in contact lately with him they call Herod the Great, vassal king of Judaea.'

Melchior's face grew sombre. 'Herod the Edomite?' He frowned.

Balthazar's brows furrowed. 'The stories of his cruelty have circulated even to Persia, Aretas. He murders chief priests of the Sanhedrin. Even his wife and three sons . . .'

Aretas paced the courtyard, hands behind his back. 'You have heard, I am sure, from my father, that Herod's mother, Kufra, was a Nabataean princess . . . that Herod spent time in our midst as a boy.'

Balthazar nodded. 'This I know. I know also that when Herod was forced to flee Jerusalem, your father repulsed his request to find asylum in Petra.'

'Yes, there has been bad blood: Cleopatra . . . Syllaeus . . .'

'It is precarious at best. Be assured in this matter,' Balthazar stated grimly.

Aretas nodded. 'He is a cruel and ruthless tyrant, of that I am aware. Not to be trusted. But various political relations exist between our countries, and the disputes over our borders have intensified these last months. He presses to meet with me.'

He knelt down and caressed Jotapa's chin gently. 'Now learn a king's wisdom, my princess. The size and dignity of our caravan will at least bid him be hospitable until he searches out our real purpose. He will aid us in our search, with the intent of using us for his own.'

Gently he handed Jotapa to his royal steward, amid her protestations. He kissed her lovingly on both cheeks and waved them away.

Aretas stood upright and looked at Balthazar soberly. 'Rather, we will use him for ours!'

He clapped his hands and servants presented themselves immediately. 'Prepare the caskets of gold and spices for the king of Judaea.'

He turned to Balthazar and smiled. 'We shall receive a king's welcome in Jerusalem, old friend – and Herod the Great himself shall summon us!'

2021 Alexandria, Egypt

Nick De Vere pressed down on the accelerator of the rented silver 2009 sport Range Rover. He had arrived at Cairo airport this morning from Heathrow, exhausted, to find this, the only four-wheel-drive vehicle left in the car rental bays.

'Not bad for an old girl,' he murmured as he roared up the sprawling western desert highway at high speed towards Alexandria. It had been eight years since he last visited Alexandria, the 'Pearl of the Mediterranean'. Then the road had been desolate, traffic-free and truly barren but now great swathes of agricultural land, horse-breeding farms and palatial estates lined the roadside. Thirty kilometres outside Alexandria's city limits, just before the Desert Roads City Gate toll station, he made a sharp right turn, pushed the gear into four-wheel drive, and sped across the desert plains, leaving a huge cloud of dust behind him.

Nearly an hour later, far in the distance, the formidable fortification came into view. The ancient granite walls of the Monastery of Archangels, carved from the huge mountain behind the monastery fortress that had withstood centuries of Roman persecution against the Egyptian Christians, stood between ten and thirty-five metres tall and three metres thick. And now this was the final resting place of the greatest archaeological discovery of the twenty-first century: the secret annals of Lucifer.

Five weeks earlier, the priceless antiquity had been moved from the high-security archaeological vaults of the Royal palace museum in Amman, Jordan, to the monastery, immediately after the tenuous ceasefire pact following the bloody Pan-Arab–Russian–Israeli War. And here the antiquity would remain.

Nick's jaw clenched. It had been *his* discovery, three-and-a-half years previously, from his archaeological excavations at Petra. And the entire world was oblivious of the fact – and would remain so, thanks to the royal household of Jordan. And to his overriding need for the inordinate sum stashed in a Swiss Bank account in his name, in exchange for his silence. Nick sighed.

He slammed his hand on the steering wheel in frustration. Pulling to a stop directly outside the towering western gate, he found it deserted. He eased his tall, lanky frame out of the Range Rover and walked over to the gate.

Nick De Vere would be twenty-nine next month, the youngest of three brothers belonging to an inordinately wealthy banking dynasty, the De Vere family. He was handsome, almost pretty, with intelligent deep-set grey eyes above an aquiline nose and high cheekbones. His fine sun-bleached hair, cut long, grazed his dark grey T-shirt.

Life had recently dealt Nick De Vere two hard blows in succession. His trust fund had been frozen by his father, James De Vere, the evening before his fatal heart attack. And now Nick, too, was dying. Of Aids. He had been on the most advanced antiretroviral therapy for four years, but now his body was failing rapidly.

He swiped the blond fringe impatiently out of his eyes. Peering upwards, he could vaguely make out two Bedouin men playing backgammon, gesticulating and talking in rising voices, oblivious to his presence.

Nick got back into the Range Rover, slammed the door, and leaned on the horn. Instantly the two Bedouins scrambled to their feet and hurried to the gate, their long robes flying behind them. There was a loud scraping and groaning of wood as a huge lift contraption descended over the side of the monastery wall.

Nick looked in disbelief up at the swaying lift. The older Bedouin pointed down at him.

'You get in,' he said, giving Nick a wide, toothless smile.

'Open the gates!' Nick demanded.

'Gates no open – you get in.' The man pointed to the wooden contraption, then pointed upward to a door in the wall, thirty feet up.

Nick closed his eyes in disbelief, then banged on the car bonnet.

'My car?'

'Only foot . . . and helicopter,' the Bedouin shrugged. 'No motor,' he stated emphatically.

Nick slammed the car door, rolled his eyes and walked into the wooden lift, which started to swing wildly as the two Arab men hauled it up towards the small door by a system of pulleys.

'This way! This way!'

An elderly priest gestured for Nick to follow him through the fields, ripe with vegetables, pomegranates, and herbs. They walked past rows of date palms and olive trees, past an olive press, then through a second inner courtyard. Nick had the distinct feeling he was being watched . . . observed. As they continued past the monks' refectory towards an ancient watchtower, Nick slowed down, staring up towards the rotating solar telescope dome on the monastery observatory. The priest frowned, motioning him forward.

Nick obediently followed the hunched figure through a walled garden of sycamore trees onto a small stone path that twisted past a vast pond filled with exquisite pink lotus blossoms that rose above the murky waters. They stopped at a rusted metal gateway, the entrance to the sprawling ancient wing of the monastery.

Nick watched intently as the priest reverently made the sign of the cross, then swiftly entered a code in the sophisticated security system. The metal gates slowly opened. They made their way along numerous winding ancient corridors, permeated with the aroma of inks and leather mingled with myrrh, then through an enormous library occupied by hundreds of monks silently archiving data into state-of-the-art Apple Mac computer systems. Nick ducked as they continued through a low dank tunnel. Finally they reached what appeared to be a crypt door.

Two broad-shouldered soldiers holding submachine guns materialized, as if from nowhere, on either side of Nick. Their heads were clean-shaven, and he immediately recognized the digital pattern on their uniforms – Jordan's elite special operations command.

The old priest handed a document embossed with the Royal Hashemite seal to the taller soldier. 'He has been granted access to photograph the annals.' The old priest lowered his eyes to the floor, bowed, then scurried away.

Nick frowned. Suddenly he was shoved hard against the stone wall, his arms splayed out, and rigorously searched by the first soldier. The second grabbed his camera and unceremoniously dumped the contents of Nick's pockets and bag onto a tray, which he sent through a sophisticated-looking scanner.

He glared at the guard. Five seconds later, he was pushed roughly back towards the door. The first soldier gestured for him to remove his belongings from the tray. Seething, Nick bent down and stowed them back in his bag. He held his camera tightly.

The taller soldier gestured to Nick to follow him through the door. There he found himself in an enormous ante-chamber, surrounded by at least twelve separate smaller chambers containing the most magnificent collection of antiquities he had ever laid his eyes on. Egyptian, Etruscan, Persian, Assyrian, and Chaldean artefacts, Arabian mosaics and frescos, Greek and Russian icons, original works by Raphael, Leonardo da Vinci, Titian, Perugino. Priceless treasures.

But ahead of him was the largest chamber. Nick stepped inside, his attention caught by a diorite statue to his right. He frowned. It seemed strangely familiar. Now he remembered. Its photograph had been circulated throughout Europe on Interpol's red list of looted Iraqi antiquities. Fascinated, he moved nearer. Hundreds of volumes of manuscripts lay stacked from floor to ceiling. He caught sight of a stone tablet lying inside a glass case. He stared at the tablet, enthralled at the wedge-shaped depressions.

'The lost legacies of ancient Mesopotamia . . . the price-less collection of cylinder seals . . .' He stared at the tablet, mesmerized, feeling in his pocket for his camera. Slowly, carefully, he lined up the palm-size digital camera directly with the tablet. 'Unbelievable.'

Slim manicured fingers snatched the camera firmly from his grasp.

'No photographs here, Mr De Vere. You must abide by our conditions.'

Nick swung around to find himself staring down into a pair of flashing brown eyes. He bowed his head respectfully.

'Your Majesty . . .'

'We don't suffer fools gladly, Mr De Vere. Please make sure you respect our agreement, or I can assure you that all licences that we, the Jordanian people, have approved for your work shall immediately be revoked.'

Nick studied the princess before him. She seemed young . . . much younger than in any photograph he had ever seen of her – twenty-two, he guessed, definitely not more than twenty-four. She was petite and slim, fine-boned, her high cheekbones and regal features framed by gleaming black tresses that fell past her shoulders. She was understated, dressed only in a pair of faded jeans and white cotton T-shirt, the only sign of inordinate wealth the slim diamond Audemars Piguet watch on her left wrist.

She watched him surveying her, and a slight smile flickered across her mouth.

'The cuneiform tablets with the missing parts of the epic of Gilgamesh, the earliest written words, a bronze relief from 4000 BC – worth a hundred *Mona Lisas*,' the princess of Jordan uttered softly, as though reciting a sacred doxology.

'Our government returned to the State of Iraq thousands of stolen antiquities that had been smuggled into Jordan during the war in the early 2000s,' she continued. 'The sacred vase of Warka, the statue of Entemena, the remainder we bought back, for hundreds of millions of dollars, off the black market in Switzerland. They emerged everywhere: Tehrani bazaars, Paris, a US Airport.' She hesitated. 'We were patient. Most of the looted treasures eventually surfaced in London.'

She looked directly into Nick's piercing grey eyes.

'The world's largest centre for trade in Islamic art,' Nick murmured. 'Uncle Lawrence . . .'

The princess nodded.

'Lawrence St Cartier's network of contacts was extremely

useful to the royal house. We now own the largest and most important collection of illuminated manuscripts in the world, apart from the Vatican's.'

She continued walking. 'In 180 BC, the Nabataeans were bequeathed this monastery by an ancient caste of priests connected with the Royal Courts of Egypt. Egyptian governments throughout the centuries have held its historical heritage in high esteem and continue to honour its present treaty with the Hashemite Kingdom. The royal household of Jordan has kept its priceless treasures hidden from the prying eyes of the outside world, confined behind these walls, in these crypts. We are deeply indebted to your sister-in-law's uncle' – she hesitated – 'and, of course, to you.'

Safwat, her chief of security, walked towards the princess. He was lean and clean-cut.

'Your Majesty,' he spoke in a low voice in clipped Arabic tones. 'Your helicopter arrives in fifteen minutes.' She nodded in acknowledgement, then turned to Nick. 'Follow me.'

She walked briskly back into the antechamber and turned left down a narrow, dimly lit tunnel.

'Your English is impeccable, Your Highness,' Nick said. 'I read that you were educated at Oxford.'

'Ancient history and classical archaeology.'

Nick followed closely behind, keeping pace with her through the narrow winding corridors. He could distinguish the faint aroma of myrrh.

'An English education . . . like your father.'

'Ah,' the princess replied, 'but you, like us, are not British, either, Mr De Vere. Let me see . . .' Her English accent carried only the faintest Arabic inflection. 'You were born in Washington, DC, into the De Vere dynasty. Your father was named American Ambassador to the United Kingdom five years after you were born. You grew up in Great Britain – Regent's Park, to be precise. Educated at Gordonstoun, studied serious archaeology at Cambridge, Mensa IQ, gifted, your Achilles' heel – drugs and a playboy lifestyle. Black sheep of the family, trust fund frozen.

'Your eldest brother, Jason De Vere, US media tycoon extraordinaire, owns a third of the Western world's television and newspaper empires. Middle brother, Adrian De Vere, youngest prime minister of the United Kingdom and newly appointed President of the United States of Europe; Nobel Peace Prize nominee.

'In 2014 you were involved in an accident in which your eldest brother's daughter was permanently crippled. You were the driver; you were inebriated at the time. Jason De Vere has not talked to you from that day on.'

Nick glared in the direction of the princess's fast disappearing back.

'You contracted Aids four years ago. Adrian De Vere paid for the best treatments in Switzerland, London and the Mayo Clinic, but alas, in the past five months, your body has not responded favourably to any of the treatments.'

Nick fought to control the rage building inside him at this prying teenage royal. 'My private life is no concern of . . .'

'You are a *fool*, Nicholas De Vere,' she interrupted sharply. 'Since your brother's stellar political ascent, your entire family has been under every government's close surveillance: Interpol, Europol, the CIA, M16, Mossad, SAVAMA, the FSB, and the Jordanian secret service – *all* are watching you.'

She turned abruptly sharp right down into a small dank stairway. Nick followed.

'My brother, the Crown Prince, and I meet with your brother and the United Arab Nations next month in Damascus for the signing of the greatest peace accord in the twenty-first century. For the first time, we are all at the same table: China, North Korea, Europe, the Pan-Arab

Union, the United States, Russia, and Israel. There may finally be peace in our time.'

She turned towards him in the stairwell. 'We have granted your access to continue your study of the annals. However, Lawrence St Cartier asked me to return a favour – strictly business. You wished to see the cross that is spoken of in the annals?'

Nick drew a deep breath; all his anger instantaneously evaporated.

'The cross exists, then?'

Nick stepped towards the princess, a strange glitter in his eyes. 'Oh, yes, Nicholas De Vere, it exists.'

The princess walked briskly down the damp stone stairs. 'Legend has it that it possesses strange healing powers.' Nick's voice echoed after the disappearing princess. He clambered down the stairwell after her.

'Legends are very powerful in the minds of those who believe,' the princess countered.

'Legend has it that Aretas IV protected the Christ child in his flight from Egypt' – Nick's eyes shone with exhilaration – 'that he brought him here to this monastery, to an ancient caste of magi.' Nick stopped, sweat suddenly pouring down his brow. He grasped the stair rail to steady himself.

The princess turned back towards him from the lower stairs. She held his gaze.

He continued. 'That the boy Christ himself carved a cross when he was but a child and gave it as a gift to Aretas before returning from this monastery to Nazareth.'

'Cartier has briefed you well. It seems you know all our legends.'

They continued descending until they reached the lower crypts, then stopped outside a solid steel door, barely four feet high. Two thickset monks, standing hidden in the shadowed corner, moved towards Nick. A third older monk raised his hand. They instantly returned to the shadows.

'Thank you, Father Benedict. He is our guest.'

The monk bowed before the princess, entered a security code in the wall, then stepped back as the one-foot-thick steel door slid away, revealing an ancient wooden crypt door.

Nick ran his hand over the doorway in wonder. 'Cedar of Lebanon,' he murmured.

Father Benedict nodded. 'The ancient Fathers of the monastery imported it for the original monastery,' he said.

Nick eased his lanky six-foot frame through the doorway into the tiny mausoleum. There in the centre of the chamber, under thick protective glass, lay his discovery – the Secret Angelic Annals. He gazed at the strange blue light that still flickered faintly from its pages, mesmerized. Then with great effort dragged his gaze away from the annals.

In the far left-hand corner of the chamber, resting against deep-blue velvet under a glass dome, lay a small cross no larger than a DVD, perfectly carved from acacia wood.

Nick moved nearer, then frowned. 'It's been mended.' He examined it through the dome. '*Crudely* mended.'

The princess sighed. 'Two thousand years ago, King Aretas had considered that the Christ child would grow up a warrior, a colossus, and overturn Rome. But Aretas' warrior was not to be. After the Hebrew was crucified, it is said that in a moment of bitter passion and disillusionment, Aretas smashed the cross in a fit of rage.'

'There were wild, unsubstantiated tales that as Aretas lay dying, Christ appeared to him,' Nick said, staring at her curiously.

'We are a wonderfully dramatic nation, Mr De Vere.' The princess lowered her eyes. 'The recounters of Scheherazade's *Thousand Nights and a Night*. Our rich culture of poetry and prose has made our people the storytellers that we have been through the centuries.' She shrugged. 'That is why we have so many legends.'

The princess's voice broke off as her Prada sunglasses slipped from her grasp and fell to the stone floor. She knelt to pick them up just as Nick did the same. He grasped them in his palm and held them out to her, then stared, fascinated, at the small, plain silver cross that slipped out from beneath her T-shirt.

'Nonetheless, Princess, you believe,' he whispered.

She stared at him, silent, frozen in her kneeling position. 'My people respect and revere Christ as a teacher and a prophet, Mr De Vere. It is common knowledge, even among agnostics such as yourself,' she snapped. The princess quickly regained her composure, snatched the sunglasses, and stood.

Nick continued relentlessly. 'Yet your critics claim you choose to go a step further ... even as Aretas IV's daughter Jotapa.'

Safwat appeared out of the shadows in the doorway with Father Benedict.

'Your helicopter is here, Your Majesty.' Safwat's voice was soft but insistent. 'The Gulfstream refuels in Alexandria. We must leave for the palace in Aqaba before it is dusk, Princess.'

The princess nodded. 'You are in good hands, Nick De Vere.' She gestured to Father Benedict. 'But I must remind you: all digital film is to be delivered to Father Benedict before your departure – no images leave these grounds, or I *shall* revoke your licence. Even a De Vere brother has to bow to the rules of the Hashemite Kingdom.'

She turned, but he heard her soft voice from the shadows. 'She was my namesake – Jotapa.' And then she was gone.

Later

It was nearing dusk when Nick opened the door of the Range Rover. His face was flushed with exhilaration.

The hooded monks watched him from the Observatory of the Monastery of Archangels.

'He is very sick.'

'He is dying,' the elder monk whispered, 'and yet his greatest sickness is of his soul.'

'The identity of the Son of Perdition will be revealed to him?' the younger questioned.

'In not so many moons he will return. The revelations concerning his brother will begin.' The old monk turned from the observatory window. 'Then he will enter the dark night of his soul.'

The setting sun illuminated Jether's ancient noble features as he drew his hood back from his face. Weary.

'He has been chosen. May Yehovah grant him mercy.'

The younger monk watched as the Range Rover roared back across the desert plains. 'He has no faith.'

'And yet still he seeks for truth.'

Jether's tone was gentle, filled with wonder. 'Such is the marvel of the race of men, Gabriel.' He turned back to stare through the telescope at the white apparition in the Egyptian skies. 'Lucifer's messiah is here.'

Lucifer stood in the fading light of the twelve magenta moons of Perdition, playing his viol, his eyes closed in ecstasy.

The tall casement doors of his bedchamber were flung wide open and the exquisite melody echoed across the murky lava wastelands to the vaults of hell.

Lucifer's face was raised to the heavens. His raven hair, loosed from its diamond braids, fell gleaming over his bare shoulders, and a rare serenity rested on his countenance.

He swept the carved horn bow with long, passionate strokes over the strings of his viol, his mouth moving softly to the exquisite refrain, his long, slim fingers moving dexterously across the fingerboard.

A soft knock echoed through his bedchamber, and Balberith, his attendant, entered.

Lucifer opened his eyes, sensing the presence. 'I ordered that there be no disturbances,' he glared at Balberith, then lowered the viol from his chin.

Balberith bowed, holding out a missive embossed with the Necromancers' seal of the Warlock Kings of the West.

Lucifer tore it open with his free hand and scanned the letter, then carefully folded it closed, then nodded. Balberith walked back through the doors. Lucifer paced the room restlessly, viol still in hand.

A second courtier appeared, and unlocked the doors of the ornately carved music chamber housing Lucifer's vast collection of lyres, psalteries, dulcimers, fifes, flageolets, pan pipes, lutes, serpents, cornets, and gleaming golden shofars. Lucifer handed him the viol.

Balberith re-entered followed by Charsoc, dressed in his

flowing vermilion night robes and with a canary-yellow tasselled nightcap on his head. His black shaman vulture chick rested on his arm.

'Your Majesty . . .' He bowed deeply, a sinister smile on his blind face.

'You may speak,' Lucifer said, turning his back to Charsoc. Balberith laced Lucifer's satin night robes.

'Your Majesty, I have received word from the caste of Black Murmurers who traverse the Arabian kingdom of Petra. They report a caravan of magi arrived last dusk. The magi seek the newborn king.'

Lucifer looked over his shoulder at Charsoc, as Balberith pulled a heavy white fur gown over his shoulders, his expression inscrutable. 'Magi? What do *they* want with this king?'

'They are of the upper house of the Megistanes, Your Majesty – of an ancient priesthood. Their duties encompass the anointing of kings. They follow the star.'

'Kingmakers!'

'Your Majesty, there is one, a devout servant of ours, a king of earth – whose sorcerers consult with the Warlock Kings of the West. The magi would journey to him. They seek him out.'

'And this king who seeks our cause?' A faint smile glimmered on Lucifer's lips. He stopped under the hundred blazing perfumed frankincense tapers, inhaling deeply.

'His name is Herod.' Charsoc replied. 'He is greatly disturbed, Your Majesty. This new king threatens his power.'

Lucifer moved over to the enormous rubied windows. The nova had drawn much nearer to Earth. Lucifer watched its intensely burning light.

'Dispatch Darsoc, my sinister princeling – and my Grey Magi, to follow the magi. Instruct your Black Court Grand Wizards to accompany him. Charge the Warlock Kings to instruct Herod that, on arrival, these magi must make careful search for the child, and when they find him, they must bring him word. His excuse shall be that he might worship the child.' Lucifer turned from the windows.

'Then bring me word' – a slow, evil smile spread across his features – 'that I might worship the child also.'

CHAPTER FORTY-SIX

Brothers

Gabriel walked barefoot in silence, his feet sinking into the soft, glistening pearl sands on the celestial white beaches of the First Heaven that stretched for thousands of leagues in front of the splendid Palace of Archangels. His pale gold tresses were plaited with platinum and hung loose down his back over his shot-silk oyster-coloured frock coat. His ethereal features were flawless: the perfectly carved cheekbones; the regal countenance. His clear grey eyes were gentle yet piercing.

Gabriel gazed at the reflection of the twelve palest-blue moons that glistened on the First Heaven's horizon, watching the lilac hues shift to a deep majestic indigo. Towards the eastern horizon lay Eden, its magnificent, lush hanging gardens and amethyst waterfalls barely visible from the sea's edge. Shooting stars and lightnings arced over the foaming silver waves of the Crystal Sea as clusters of luminescent diamonds the size of pomegranates washed up onto the white sands, emitting a soft luminous light.

He stared up at the soaring gold-columned palace that towered high above the western wall. This was where he and his two elder brothers had dwelt in harmony and kinship before the darkening shadows of insurrection had fallen over the realm of the First Heaven – before Lucifer, seraph, great archangel, light-bearer, was banished.

Now only Michael's and Gabriel's grand wings of chambers were occupied. The majestic west wing of the son of the morning lay desolate, Lucifer's magnificent mother-of-pearl chambers deserted, their towering golden doors engraved with the emblem of the Royal House barred since the dusk of his banishment, in worlds long since departed.

Michael strode towards him down the gilded steps, his emerald cloak flying behind him.

'I am returned from Earth,' he announced, marching through rows of grand white columns, past the vast crystal orangeries of the eastern wing of the palace towards Gabriel across the pearl sands.

'It is good to see you, esteemed Gabriel.' Michael kissed him warmly on both cheeks, then removed his golden war gauntlets.

'As it is you, beloved brother.' Gabriel surveyed the tall, noble warrior. Michael's gleaming, flaxen hair was tied back with emeralds and gold in two thick braids that framed the noble features, his intelligent green eyes lost in thought.

He has grown much in wisdom of late, Gabriel reflected. *Since Lucifer's banishment*. Gone was any residue of the hot-headedness and intractability of his former years, and in its wake had grown a nobility and a graciousness that were unmistakable. This was his elder brother, Michael, his spirit clothed with honour, nobility, and valour, commander-in-chief of the First Heaven's armies – Yehovah's warrior.

Michael raised his head to the horizons and closed his eyes, a deep peace transforming his features. He breathed in the heady fragrance of myrrh that wafted across the shimmering beaches from the vast lush plains of great white poplars far beyond the eastern plains of Eden. He was silent a long moment, then followed Gabriel's gaze up towards Lucifer's chambers.

'Lucifer's magi have alerted him.' His voice was soft. 'It was just a matter of time.'

Gabriel nodded.

'We knew it would be so.' Gabriel walked to the very edge of the Crystal Sea, staring out at the indigo shooting stars that blazed overhead on the horizon.

'I can still see his raven hair blowing in the eastern breeze,' he murmured. 'It is strange – I remember Lucifer's every word as though they were ingrained in my soul.' He turned his face to Michael's. '"Each and every dawn,"' Gabriel whispered, '"we are tested as to whether we would serve our own will, our own desires, or would we serve Yehovah." That is what he told me at this exact spot. "Choose wisely each day, Gabriel," he told me' – Gabriel lowered his clear grey eyes – '"and you can never fail him. The greatest gift you can grant him is your free choice to serve him in obedience, which, in turn, is your true love."'

'Yehovah, by his choice, endowed the angelic race with free will,' said Michael. 'Lucifer chose his path, as we have chosen ours.'

'And as the race of men choose theirs,' Gabriel said thoughtfully. He continued his pacing along the luminous sands. A long silence fell. Finally Gabriel spoke again.

'Michael . . .' He raised his face up to the abandoned west wing, his eyes filled with intense sorrow. 'Do you think Lucifer has regret?'

'No,' a soft voice echoed.

Gabriel turned. Jether the Just, imperial angelic monarch and ruler of the twenty-four ancient kings of Yehovah, stood on the gilded steps above them, his silvered hair and beard blowing in the soft zephyrs off the sea. His wizened features were gentle, but underneath his bushy white eyebrows his pale, watery, grey-blue eyes glittered like an eagle's – intense, alert. Nothing escaped Jether's vigilant gaze. He well knew that the tender Gabriel had suffered much of late. The dreamings that night after night haunted Gabriel were the cost of the gift he bore as Yehovah's seer, the angelic Revelator. He smiled compassionately at Gabriel.

'If he has regret, Gabriel' – Jether walked towards them across the sands, the pearls covering his lime-green jewelled slippers as he walked – 'it is regret for himself, as he realizes the dire consequence of his choice . . . of his fall. But true regret . . .' Jether stared upwards north of the two trees of Eden, to the colossal golden ruby-encrusted door, ablaze with light, that was embedded into the jacinth walls of the tower – the entrance to the throne room.

'True regret is based on repentance – grieving for the sin, not the consequence of sin. The two are quite contradictory. Completely opposed.' Jether's pale blue eyes blazed with an uncharacteristic fervour. 'And they must *never* be confused.'

He gazed up towards the towering west wing, with its grand pearl balconies that now lay abandoned. Derelict.

'Perfect in beauty,' he whispered. 'Filled with wisdom – oh, how thou hast fallen, son of the morning.'

'What is this race of men to him that he is mindful of them?' Gabriel murmured. Jether placed his hand gently on Gabriel's shoulder.

'The High Council assembles. The presence of Yehovah's Chief Princes is requested.'

Michael bowed to Jether, 'It shall be so, revered Jether.' Jether smoothed his embroidered pale green satin robes. 'We gather on the Eastern Sands under the Great Willows. At dusk.'

Jether studied the brothers intently.

'The old world has gone,' he said softly. 'It can never be

revisited. This is a day of farewells.' And then he vanished, transported to the Tower of Winds.

Through all the aeons that had elapsed since Lucifer's banishment and our return from Perdition, there had never been a time that Michael and I had looked back to our previous world.

But somehow we both knew that this was to be a different day.

We stood – alone on the shimmering sands. In silence. Two brothers. Not Chief Princes. Not Warrior or Revelator. Just younger brothers. Remembering. All that had been. All that had transpired. Grieving.

For all that we sensed was yet to come, the memories of our triune brotherhood coursing uninvited through our souls like all-consuming, blistering waves. And I knew that it was in that very moment that we each said our final goodbyes.

For Jether was right. Our previous world could never be revisited.

The old world was gone.

Michael and I would never again look back . . .

For a new world lay before us.

A world whose fate now hung by a thread.

A world with whose destiny the First Heaven was to be irreversibly entwined.

The world of the race of men.

CHAPTER FORTY-SEVEN

The First Heaven

Jether paced with even strides through the winding corridors of the Tower of Winds in the First Heaven, his silken white hair and beard sweeping the sapphire floors as he walked. On his head rested a jacinth crown.

Obadiah, a youngling, was Jether's attendant. The youngling scurried behind, panting, hardly reaching up to Jether's waist. His stocky little legs almost in a trot to keep up, his tight orange curls flying, he vainly attempted to hold Jether's voluminous willow-green satin cloak off the polished sapphire floors. As they rounded a corner, Obadiah distractedly caught sight of Tirzah, another youngling, at target practice with what looked like an enormous iron cannonball.

The languishing Obadiah lost hold of the cloak just as Tirzah launched the iron ball, which arced high above their heads, plummeting down at high speed to land directly in the centre of Jether's train. Jether stopped precisely as the offending spheroid landed.

He sighed deeply and turned to glare at Tirzah.

'*Now* will you believe me that I have eyes in the back of my head, Obadiah?' He glowered darkly at the youngling, his white eyebrows knitting together. 'Take your tiffin!'

Obadiah scuttled away, Tirzah in tow. Jether chuckled softly to himself, then caught six tittering younglings hidden in the corridor, devouring their morning tea break of curds and junket. Catching sight of him, they dropped their tiffin, staring at him in awe. He scowled purposefully in their direction. They turned a furious beetroot red and scattered in four different directions. Jether hid a smile, then grasped his cloak with both hands and continued his striding. Grave.

High elder Xacheriel appeared from a small door in the wall. He fell in step with Jether, his great white eyebrows knitted together, striding the corridors in his violet experimentation galoshes. Carrying Xacheriel's train was the youngling Dimnah, short, dumpy, and freckled, shuddering violently from the blue arced electrical currents that were shocking him from Xacheriel's person.

Jether stopped, tapping Xacheriel on the shoulder. '*Humph*,' he coughed surreptitiously into his handkerchief.

Xacheriel frowned impatiently.

Jether pointed to the now convulsing Dimnah, blue electric arcs swirling in and out from his tight ginger curls down to his striped stockinged knees. Xacheriel looked down at his indigo rubber gloves and scowled.

'Rakkon! Jatir!' he bellowed.

A group of younglings all attired in rainbow-coloured galoshes and rubber gloves instantly appeared as if from a vapour.

'Disconnect the dullard Dimnah!'

With immense difficulty, the younglings managed to pry Dimnah free from Xacheriel's train.

'No galoshes!' muttered Xacheriel. He waved his hand towards the languishing Dimnah, now fallen to the floor in a dead swoon. 'A high-voltage experiment, and the dunderhead wears no galoshes!' Xacheriel sighed in exasperation, scrabbling beneath his oilskin in the voluminous pockets of his orange robes, and bringing out a small, sticky half-eaten cake with the consistency of an English doughnut with an indigo curd centre, which he thrust between the long-suffering Dimnah's lips.

'Brain food!' he declared, rubbing his large hands together, and continued his great tramping along the corridor.

Jether shook his head, his eyes twinkling with amusement, and followed.

'Lucifer and his cohorts are dangerously close to the truth, Jether,' Xacheriel declared darkly.

Jether looked up at him from under his eyebrows, without breaking stride. 'Lucifer's revelation of Yehovah's ways has waned these past aeons,' he replied. 'He and his evil magi seek after one born of a royal house of Earth – one of power and nobility.'

They walked out of the sapphire corridors across the lush lawns of the lower gardens of the Tower of Winds, through the lower chambers of the sixth spire, where they were met by two more younglings, holding the reins of two white-winged chargers.

Jether raised his eyebrows to Xacheriel as he placed his foot in the stirrup.

'We have a little time yet,' he said grimly.

Jether and Xacheriel mounted effortlessly and flew above the glistening diamonds paving the vast winding road through the massive pearl gates, two hundred feet high, across the crystal bridge, finally landing on the vast eastern pearl sands on the very edge of the Sea of Zamar.

Seated on jacinth thrones, under the open heavens on the eastern sands, were the high council of the eight ancient kings, Yehovah's high elders. Six ancient monarchs were already seated around a golden circular table, their heads bowed, each dressed in vibrantly coloured robes. Their lips

302

moved silently in supplication to the Ancient of Days. Michael sat on a carved silver throne.

Jether dismounted, and the six ancient monarchs and Michael rose as one and bowed reverently to his person. Jether nodded and took his seat at the throne at the head of the table, Xacheriel at his left. Jether bowed his head, his lips moving in supplication. He nodded to Michael.

'Lucifer is suspicious of these magi,' Michael said. 'My reconnaissance informs me that the sorcerers of the royal court of Herod of Judaea consult with the Warlock Kings of the West.'

Zebulon, an elder with a long white beard and a gentle demeanour, raised his head from his supplications. 'Yes, this is true, Michael, but Dracul and his Warlock Kings also consult continually with Melsoc of Persia and Babylon and with Babiel of the Medes.'

Methuselah raised his white-crowned head. 'Dracul keeps his options open. He speculates.' His words were calm and measured. 'All they are certain of is that the prince shall be born of the race of men, in the East.'

Maheel, a third ancient elder, raised his bowed head; his watery blue eyes were distant.

'You may speak, Maheel,' Jether said quietly.

'Our greatest danger comes when the star stands still again, this time over its resting place, Bethlehem.'

There came a thundering as Gabriel galloped across the sands on his white steed, escorted by ten Revelators. He drew to a halt under the great willows. Gabriel dismounted and strode towards them, speaking as he walked. 'Forgive my tardiness, my honoured elders, my revered brother Michael. I received urgent word from my Revelator scouts. Our greatest danger, I regret, is almost upon us. Lucifer dispatched Darsoc and the Grey Magi this very dawn to follow the magi. It will be only a matter of time before

Lucifer realizes that the newborn prince of the East, and Christos, are one and the same.'

All around the table lifted their heads; Michael and Gabriel exchanged a grave look. Lamaliel shook his head. 'His wrath will be unbridled.'

Issachar stroked his beard. 'His first action will be to investigate the constituents of Christos' blood.'

'We are well aware,' said Xacheriel, drumming his large fingers, rather too loudly, on the table next to Jether.

'Lucifer's evil genius is no match for the unfathomable wisdom of Yehovah,' said Jether, closing the Book of Eternal Law. He placed his wizened hand softly on top of Xacheriel's to restrain his pounding.

'He becomes blinded by his own preconceptions,' stated Issachar.

'His choice to consistently despise Yehovah's treaties struck with the race of men in aeons past could ultimately lead to his demise,' Gabriel said.

Jether nodded.

'His pride renders him more careless. He is contemptuous of the accords which will be to our advantage.'

Xacheriel stroked his bushy eyebrows. 'He will be more easily persuaded with his misgivings satisfied.'

Jether nodded. 'We must have faith.'

'Lucifer is become drawn to the Eastern regions,' Michael rose. 'He dispatched Dagon and his Black Horde deliberately to divert me to the West. I sent forty legions after Dagon to dispel my brother's unease – eighty of my legions remain hung well back in the First Heaven. They await my return to the East.'

'My Revelator legions are mobilized,' Gabriel added. 'The Proclaimers and scouts left for the Eastern horizons at dawn. They await your command, brother.'

Jether stood up slowly from the table, as did the seven

elders. Jether clasped Michael's arm, and they followed Gabriel across the pearl sands to the marble-columned pergola, up the gilded steps to the lush tropical gardens where the archangel brothers' thrones stood beside the Waterfalls of Nectar. The blue gales blew violently. Jether stared out past the Sea of Zamar at the winged stallions galloping across the pearl beaches. Far above the stallions an enormous white eagle with golden talons soared towards them.

The eagle landed gracefully on the sands next to Jether, who unclasped a missive with the seal of Yehovah from its diamond collar. He read silently.

'Yehovah summons me,' he murmured, then turned to gaze up at the shimmering indigos and lilacs of the rainbow overarching the crystal palace. To the north of the two massive trees in the hanging gardens, above the labyrinths, a colossal ruby-encrusted door, ablaze with light, was embedded in the tower's jacinth walls – the entrance to Yehovah's throne room. There were few, so few, who had ever gazed upon the beauty of Yehovah's countenance. Jether, faithful steward of Yehovah's mysteries, was one.

Jether closed his eyes. 'The codices of the White Judgement,' he whispered. 'They are to be opened.'

Michael stepped back, stunned.

'The codices of fire,' Gabriel echoed.

Jether nodded. 'The Day of the Seventh Stone approaches.'

He mounted the great eagle, sitting astride the golden saddle and stroking its soft white neck feathers. The eagle looked up at Jether, its piercing brown eyes gentle, awaiting his command.

'Faithful Vespar, I would journey to the labyrinths of the seventh spire,' he said, his eyes strangely misted.

'Michael – make haste to the eastern heavens. Gabriel – meet me in the seventh spire of the labyrinths. Let us never forget, my angelic princes, that we fight on behalf of Yehovah for the greatest prize in the universe.'

His voice shook with passion as Vespar ascended into the skies. 'For the redemption of the race of men from their tyrant king, Lucifer!'

CHAPTER FORTY-EIGHT

Herod

A huge group of the councils of Jerusalem, including the seventy-one members of the Jewish supreme council, the Sanhedrin, and all Herod's scribes and his own magi, were gathered in the palace's inner court. Herod sat on his elaborate golden throne in the inner court of his palace. He was dressed in the most ostentatious purple finery, his crown awry on top of his thick, ill-fitting ginger wig. He limped heavily over to the nearest window to stare balefully at the pillar of fire that blazed in the night sky.

'The star burns brighter with every hour!' His face was florid with rage. 'You knew I had a rival, yet you did not *warn* me?' He slammed his sceptre down on an ornate vase, smashing it to the floor. 'There is a king of the Jews; your Hebrew writings are clear on it.'

He rose from the throne and swung around to the chief priest, who was shivering with terror. 'They are clear, aren't they?'

'The writings are clear, sire,' the chief priest stammered.

Herod flung open the Torah scrolls. 'Bring him nearer, that he might know his subject more intimately.'

Herod's guards grabbed the chief priest by the arms and

thrust him in front of Herod. Herod pushed the Torah in front of the chief priest's face.

'Where is this king of the Jews to be born?'

Petrified, the priest fumbled through the scrolls until he found the Book of Micah. Trembling, he stopped. Herod snatched the scroll away from him and scanned it avidly, his fleshy jowls shaking as he read.

'Where, *where* does it say "king of the Jews"?' He pushed his face right up to the high priest. 'Show me.'

'In Bethlehem of Judaea, for thus it is written by the prophet Micah: "But you, Bethlehem, in the land of Judah, are not the least among the rulers of Judah; for out of you will come a ruler who will shepherd my people, Israel."'

'Is this ME?' Herod screamed, red in the face. 'Is it Herod the Great they prophesy? Is it Herod? Or is there . . .' He spun around. 'ANOTHER?' he hissed, his two chins shaking.

The chief priest gulped. Suddenly finding courage, in a holy fervour he blurted, 'There is another.' His words were soft but unmistakable. 'The Messiah, the ruler of Israel – his kingdom shall see no end.'

Herod rose, apoplectic, from the throne and smashed the sceptre against the chief priest's chest. The priest rolled down the marble stairs, blood flowing from his head onto the marble floor. The council stood terrorized, silent.

Herod lifted up his voluminous robes. 'GET OUT OF HERE! GET OUT!' screamed Herod. 'OUT!'

The council scattered like geese, out of the throne room, two of them dragging the semi-conscious priest behind them. Herod's advisers clustered around his throne, trembling and whispering feverishly.

'Stop your infernal mumbling,' Herod snarled. 'What is it that you whisper of now?'

His chief adviser stepped forward. 'We speak of the

caravan, Your Majesty, that draws nigh to Jerusalem from the East.'

A second counsellor bowed. 'The caravan is of exceeding wealth and pomp, Your Majesty. It is the talk of all Jerusalem.'

Herod sat back heavily on his throne. 'Yes, yes, my magi informed me. They are Parthians – interferers ... king-makers! They fell kings from thrones at their whim!'

He bit his fist, his eyes gleaming with insanity. Sweat poured from his furrowed brow below his crown. 'It is a plot. The Parthians take me for a usurper – they would murder me ... dethrone me. And put this ... this infantile king of the Jews ...'

'Nay, Your Majesty. This caravan belongs to a king, Aretas, sovereign ruler of Arabia.'

'Aretas! The king of Petra – why, he is no philosopher, no magus's accomplice.' Herod relaxed visibly. He exhaled deeply and readjusted his wig.

'He is a pragmatic man, one who has seen bloodshed.' Herod's eyes glittered. 'Does he come in peace or war?' He bunched his robe in his fist, trembling. 'War!' he whimpered. 'He seeks revenge. He comes to murder me and annex Judaea to the Nabataeans!' A thread of spittle hung suspended from his chin. He was seized by paroxysm, coughing up blood into his handkerchief.

His chief attendant held out a sealed missive. Herod snatched it and tore it open, eyes wild, scanning the contents.

'He would honour me and solve our border disputes.' He wiped his brow with a silk handkerchief. 'He seeks peace.' He exhaled heavily in relief and held out his trembling hand to his cupbearer, who immediately placed an ornate goblet of wine in it.

'This upstart king could well threaten Aretas, also.' He sipped from his cup delicately. 'Get word to his ambassadors

309

that my palace awaits him. He shall indeed be my welcome guest.'

Herod caressed the goblet thoughtfully. 'The royal houses of Petra and Judaea would do well to make alliance. Together we shall destroy this upstart king!'

Herod turned to a tall, sinister figure to the right of his throne. 'Mephisto, relay to me the Necromancers' counsel.'

Mephisto chanted, and slowly the thirteen Warlock Kings of the West materialized next to him, unseen by Herod. Dracul, their ruler, spoke, echoed by Mephisto, almost as an alter ego, speaking with him in a strange, unearthly unison. 'Let them make careful search for the child and report back, that you may find him and destroy the newborn king.'

Gabriel thundered bareback on his stallion, through the lush rainforests, across the vast bulrush meadows of the eastern plains of Eden in the First Heaven, his platinum hair flying. He came to a halt leagues beneath the holy mountain, near the base of the throne room's rubied entrance, outside the western labyrinths of the seven spires. He dismounted and entered the underground entrance to the sacred caverns. Seven hidden chambers in the mountain each ascended into the inner sanctum of the labyrinths. Gabriel walked, head bowed, his path lit only by the flaming eternal torches high against the cavern walls.

As he ascended higher into the chamber, an unaccountable dread clutched his heart. His ascent continued, deep into the heart of the labyrinths, until he reached the sixth burning lamp.

Nine tall silent warriors stood with flaming broadswords. The Watchers, guardians of the hidden sanctum of Yehovah. They raised their flaming swords to Gabriel, bowing in acknowledgement.

Gabriel continued through the dim passage, ascending until he saw them: Yehovah's dread warriors, the Watchers of the seventh flame.

The Watchers beheld him, and as one they lifted their flaming swords, which had barred his way to the seventh chamber. Ever so slowly, Gabriel walked on through the huge iron grid, magnetized towards a blazing light on his left. The Watchers drew back and disappeared. He moved deeper into the cavern. In front of him blew a stormy wind, and out of the wind burned a great indigo cloud with great lightning and flashings coming from out of the inferno.

Gabriel stared ahead in wonder. There before him stood Jether, in the very midst of the burning flames, his arms raised, his staff, the staff of the white winds, held high. His hair and beard flew in the tempests that rose from the indigo cloud. Blue lightnings blazed from the staff. His face glowed as burnished bronze, his skin burning translucent. Dimly visible in the midst of the coals of fire lay seven enormous gold-bound lapis lazuli codices, their pages blazing with a fierce blue fire – the codices of the White Judgement. Gabriel watched as two majestic flaming cherubim became visble through the flames. The first lifted the top codex from the midst of the burning coals. He stretched forth his hand and passed the sacred tome to Jether.

Jether clasped it, holding it high. 'The Codex of the First Judgement!' he cried. 'The secret counsels of Yehovah are unveiled!'

Herod nodded and slowly opened the voluminous red velvet curtains. Before him stood King Aretas, Balthazar, Caspar, Melchior and a hundred magi, with coffers of gold and precious stones. Herod bowed deeply to King Aretas, who bowed as well. Herod looked at the overflowing caskets, simpering like a child. He sat down on his throne, motioning to Aretas to sit opposite him on a smaller, ornately gilded throne.

'Your royal name has travelled often across the desert plains to me, great Sheikh Aretas of Petra and Arabia, Aretas the noble, the warrior, protector of his people.'

'Your royal name is one of fame and renown throughout the eastern plains, O Herod of Idumea, Herod the Great, feared by all.' Aretas bowed again.

A smile of pleasure spread across Herod's slack-jowled face. 'You come to Jerusalem not only to seek peace, Aretas. You seek a king other than myself. Of this I am convinced.'

Aretas stared deeply into the old king's eyes. He was debauched and evil, but he was no fool – even near death, a formidable enemy. This Aretas knew. 'I seek to pay my respects to Herod the Great, but yes, you are correct in your assumptions. There is another that I seek, O Herod.'

Balthazar stepped forward and bowed deeply. 'Your Majesty, we seek the one who has been born king of the Jews. We saw his star in the East and have come to worship him.'

Herod's eyes narrowed. He clutched Aretas' arm and drew him away from the magi. 'You are a brilliant man, Aretas' – Herod lowered his voice – 'to have realized the threat of a new king who would ravage our kingdoms, and to have allied yourself with the very magi who can locate his presence.'

312

Herod turned back to the magi and smiled agreeably. 'My chief priests tell me that the newborn king is to be found in Bethlehem. Go, make careful search for the child. And when you find him, report to me, that I, too, may go and pay my homage to him. My armies are at your disposal, as is my hospitality.'

He clapped his hands. 'Our minor disputes – the Dead Sea Valley, Syllaeus – are all behind us. Melech, show my royal guests to their quarters.'

CHAPTER FORTY-NINE

Christos

The princeling Darsoc stood at the head of the Grey Magi, his cultured, sinister demon sorcerers. Ruthless and cunning beyond compare, the Grey Magi were Lucifer's finest informants, serving as his senior intelligence corps. Archivists, philosophers, intellectuals. They stood, a hundred strong, their white hoods pulled down over their faces, shadowed in the darkness.

'Shepherds! Pah!' Alastor, Grand Wizard of the Black Courts, snarled to Darsoc. 'This is no king's dwelling!' He turned his black charger around impatiently. 'You and your magi waste my time!'

Darsoc stood, not a muscle moving, every sense alert. Alastor threw back his silver turbaned head, his squat blood-red cat eyes gleaming with disdain.

'A fool's errand!' he spat. '*We* intend to return to the Black Courts in possession of the facts!'

'Then ride, Alastor.' Darsoc's words were spun like silk laced with venom. 'You would not want to disappoint your unforgiving master, Grand Magus Charsoc, and forfeit your jewels ... and advancement.' A small evil smile played on Darsoc's lips. 'Or your head.'

Alastor turned his black charger to face his company of Black Court Wizards. 'Turn back, there is nothing here – we ride to Persia!' he cried, thundering away on his monstrous fire-breathing stallion, his blazing staff held high.

Darsoc threw back his hood. His pale, fine features exuded a strange luminosity. Only on closer scrutiny was it noticeable how his once perfect skin was now marred and how his beautiful grey eyes glinted a dark evil. The gusts blew his long strands of hair across his white cloak.

'I smell the scent of the Revelators on the winds,' he hissed. He held up a grey gloved finger to his pale lips.

A tremendous wind blew overhead, accompanied by the sound of a monstrous beating of wings. Instantly the sky was filled with thousands upon thousands of giant white eagles, their wingspans a hundred feet, their collars and talons of molten gold.

'The scouts of the White Knighthood.' A malicious smile spread across Darsoc's face as he watched Alastor and his company of Charsoc's Black Court Wizards ascending into the black skies in the direction of the east. 'Michael is here.' he murmured, a gleam in his cruel eyes. 'We wait.'

King Aretas, Balthazar, Gaspar, and Melchior led the great caravan, seated on white Arabian steeds. Balista and Ayeshe, Aretas' manservant, followed close behind. Balthazar gazed up at the star, now stationary, fixed directly above a summit that lay in the distance, then pulled on the reins of his horse, gesturing to the party to do likewise. He dismounted, his heart pounding, swiftly leading the way up the terraced hills of Bethlehem guided only by the solitary lamp that swung from the centre of a rope hung across the entrance of a lone inn ahead of them. He stopped outside the low structure, built of rough stones. It consisted of an enclosure where a small herd of cattle was huddled together, tied up for the night. Above the enclosure were six small stone rooms. Balthazar walked slowly past each low chamber, studying the inhabitants closely, then turned to Aretas and Melchior and shook his head. Frowning, he walked further out to a crude stone grotto attached to the inn as a stable. Four small dogs, their ribs sticking through their mangy coats, yapped at him relentlessly, nipping at his feet. He covered his face with his robe as the pungent stench of waste from cows, mules, and camels hit his nostrils, stopping outside the filthy area where the mules and horses were tethered. Hesitantly, he peered inside, then turned, gesturing to the party to follow him. Aretas frowned. Balthazar nodded. Aretas shrugged in assent as Gaspar and Melchior followed Balthazar further inside the stable. There among the hay and straw spread for the food and rest of the cattle, sitting cross-legged on a mat in the far corner of the threadbare room, sat a young girl, scarcely more than a child. Her thick waist-length tawny locks framed her fine olive features with its high cheekbones, aquiline nose, and soft rosebud mouth. She stared at the guests, exhausted, but her brown eyes were exultant. Her gaze turned to the babe in her arms. As one, the magi fell prostrate. She placed the infant gently back down in the manger, then walked across the straw floor towards Balthazar.

Aretas watched silently from the doorway, staring at the empty stable, the wooden manger the only furniture in the room. Balthazar fell to his knees, tears falling down his wizened ebony cheeks. 'All these years . . . these aeons, we have faithfully guarded these,' he whispered, 'kept them safe for the Jewish Messiah prophesied by the great Hebrew Daniel.' He bowed his head, trembling.

A pale Gaspar gently laid the gifts at Mary's feet. 'The cup of frankincense; the box of myrrh . . .'

Melchior stepped forward. 'The gold rod of Aaron. With these we pay homage to the Messiah.' He knelt, his head bowed.

Mary lifted her head, brushing the long dark tresses of hair away from her enchanting face. 'We humbly receive your gifts,' she replied.

'We thank you.' Joseph quietly watched from behind the manger.

Balthazar raised his hands. 'That I would live to see this day.' He lifted his head and turned to Aretas, who still stood pale, and silent by the door. 'Aretas, come.' Balthazar's eyes shone. 'It is he whom our forbear Daniel longed for.'

Joseph held out his hand to Aretas, who shook his head. 'I am not a religious man . . .', he stated firmly.

Balthazar grasped his arm firmly and guided him over to the sleeping babe, no longer wrapped in the snug swaddling bands of his early days. Aretas stood back, his hands held before him. Mary smiled tenderly and held out her hand to Aretas.

Again he shook his head impatiently. 'Forgive me . . . I do not believe as these . . .'

Mary continued to smile at him, her gaze locked to his. She took his brown, hardened hand gently in her small olive one.

'Tell them I do not believe.' Aretas looked pleadingly to Balthazar.

Mary looked compassionately at him with her liquid brown eyes as if he were dull of understanding, and placed his hand over the babe's.

Aretas fell backward as if jolted by a violent, shocking force. Balthazar, Mary, and Joseph stared, astounded, while

Aretas' entire body shuddered as in the throes of a violent fit. His breathing became short and shallow and he flung his head from side to side, raising his hands to his face before crumpling to the floor.

Balthazar stared down at him in horror. 'Forgive me . . .' He raised his face to Joseph's. 'We must assist His Majesty at once – we will remove him from your midst.'

Joseph frowned. 'He is in no state to be moved, sire.'

Mary nodded in agreement, her eyes filled with consternation. She placed her hand on Balthazar's. 'There is a space at the back, with the innkeeper. Let us take him there till he is stronger.'

Balthazar nodded and turned to Gaspar, who stood trembling. 'I will stay with King Aretas. Look after our caravan.'

Gaspar nodded, dumbstruck, and exchanged a bewildered glance with Melchior.

Balthazar turned to gaze at the infant once more, then grasped the king's hand in his; his fingers were still shaking violently. But it was when Balthazar looked into Aretas' face that his blood ran cold, for the young king was staring straight ahead, his eyes wide open. He had been struck completely blind.

CHAPTER FIFTY

The Revelation

Lucifer sat bathing his legs in the balmy amber and gold pools that shimmered under the pale, gloomy moons of the west horizon, sipping pomegranate elixir from his golden goblet. He turned to Marduk on his left. 'These kingmakers, the magi – what did they find?' He plucked a blue fruit from the silvered vines that flourished in his nocturnal orangeries, slicing it deftly with a small sharp blade.

Marduk nodded to the palace sorcerers, who stood petrified behind the ornamental pools. 'The nova was moving, Your Majesty,' the chief magus replied. 'They left Herod's palace at dawn. They were to report back to Herod, sire, as you ordered.'

Lucifer sat silently, waiting. He placed a sliver of the fruit on his tongue and swallowed.

'We received rumours they did not return, Your Majesty,' the chief magus stammered.

Lucifer stared, his mind reeling. Marduk drew his face close to Lucifer's.

'They left by a different route.'

Lucifer handed his cup to his cupbearer, his expression inscrutable, and rose as Balberith dried him with a gold cloth. He strode through the western terraces, Balberith following, through the orangeries back into the throne room, dressed only in his white silk loincloth, then snatched his satin robe from Balberith's grasp and flung it over his shoulders, enraged. 'Rumours!' he roared, waving the sorcerers away. They scuttled down the marbled chamber, past the Luciferian guard and out through the throne room gates. 'Rumours!' he bellowed.

Alastor moved to the Black Gates, consulting in deep whisperings with Marduk. Meanwhile Lucifer paced up and down before his throne, hands behind his back, staring at his reflection in the polished black floor. Marduk hurried back up the nave of the throne room, strangely perturbed.

'Charsoc's Black Court Wizards are returned, Your Majesty.'

Lucifer did not look up from his pacing. 'Grant them audience,' he commanded.

Immediately the gates opened to reveal Alastor's corpulent black-cloaked figure. Behind him hovered his company of silver-turbaned wizards, their black staffs issuing orange fire.

Lucifer stood facing his northern balconies, his back to them. 'Where is the newborn king?'

Alastor walked slowly up the nave of the throne room towards Lucifer, the only sound in the throne room his narrow crimson pointed shoes that squeaked with every awkward step. Charsoc materialized at the Black Gates. Silent. Observing.

Alastor stopped halfway up the nave. 'We found no king, Your Majesty.'

Lucifer turned, his face contorted with fury, then flung open the massive golden doors of the north wing. The nova had drawn nearer, far nearer to Earth and blazed furiously.

'The nova yet burns.' He clenched his fists in fury. 'WHERE is the infant king that is born in the East?'

Darsoc and his Grey Magi entered the throne room. The Grey Magi stood, a hundred strong. Breathtaking. Their strange beauty, bewitching. Tall and pale, their waist-length platinum hair fell smooth as glass over their billowing white velvet cloaks fastened with delicate silver clasps intertwined with live asps. Darsoc slid silently over the lapis floors towards Alastor and the throne.

Alastor stopped in front of Lucifer. 'We found no king of noble birth, sire, but only a peasant babe wrapped in swaddling clothes, before whom shepherds worshipped.'

Marduk scowled impatiently. 'Shepherds! You waste His Excellency's time.' Lucifer grasped Marduk's arm to still him, his nails digging deep into Marduk's flesh. Marduk frowned, perplexed, but obeyed.

Alastor turned his head back to the approaching Darsoc, then dropped to his knees, 'No – my Lord.' An evil sneer spread across his flabby features. He raised his shadowed eyes to Lucifer's. 'It is *Darsoc* who wastes your time with shepherds,' he rasped. 'We, the Grand Wizards of the Black Courts, were prudent. *We* turned back to Persia.'

Charsoc slowly caressed the silver serpent on his staff, observing Alastor intently, deep in contemplation.

Lucifer walked over to the huge open doors, staring out a long while at the nova.

'Darsoc – my wicked prince.'

'My Lord.' Darsoc bowed deeply to Lucifer, then knelt beside Alastor.

'Tell me about these shepherds.' Lucifer's voice was solicitous, soothing, his back to Darsoc.

Darsoc lifted his shadowed eyes. 'Alastor deemed it a distraction, Your Excellency ... a mere diversion,' he answered, his voice listless but cultured.

Lucifer turned and stared at him, his face inscrutable. 'But *you*, my loyal and cunning slave?'

'There came a great commotion in the Second Heavens. A vast company of the heavenly knighthood descended.'

'Their purpose?' Charsoc strode up the nave directly towards the throne.

'They were scouts.' Darsoc's voice was measured. 'Of the White Knighthood of the Holy Mountain, sire.'

Alastor shifted his cumbersome frame, suddenly uneasy, looking from Charsoc to Lucifer.

'Of your brother Chief Prince Michael's battalion, sire.'

'Michael dispatched his scouts and proclaimers for a peasant babe?' Lucifer frowned and pushed his hair back from his eyes, momentarily confused.

'Pale fool!' spat Alastor. 'You waste His Excellency's time!'

Darsoc moved his platinum head close to Alastor's silver-turbaned one, then pressed his pale grey lips against Alastor's fleshy ear. 'I think not,' he hissed. He removed his silver gauntlets and signed deftly to a tall, pale form, shrouded in a white velvet cloak who instantly materialized next to him.

'I am one of the Grey Magi designated Jequon.' Jequon spoke in a low silken voice. 'Chief archivist of the Grey Magi.'

'And what did your archivists document, Jequon?' Lucifer enquired softly, his back to Alastor.

Jequon stared down at his long, pale trembling hands, then looked back at Lucifer's back. 'My archivists documented the pronouncements of the White Knighthood.' Sweat broke out on his temple.

'Relay the declaration, Jequon.' Charsoc commanded. 'It may distress my sovereign emperor.'

Jequon bowed again to Lucifer. Charsoc rested his hand ominously on the hilt of his glinting necromancer blade. 'Relay it. Word for word.'

Jequon took a deep breath. 'That . . . that this day a child

322

is born – this day in the town of David . . .' Jequon looked up at Lucifer, his courage deserting him. 'A saviour who is . . .' Not a muscle of Lucifer's face moved. 'Who is . . . Christ . . .'

Lucifer swung around in astonishment to face Charsoc. The blood drained from Charsoc's face.

'*Chris . . . tos*,' Lucifer hissed, appalled. A terrible horror contorted his features.

'The Lord,' Jequon gasped, his eyes never leaving Lucifer's. A strange smile played on Darsoc's pale lips as he watched Charsoc walk unsteadily towards Alastor, his whole body trembling.

Alastor stared in shock from Lucifer to Charsoc. 'An error, my lord.' He stood to his feet, his chins trembling.

'An error,' Charsoc murmured.

With one savage thrust, Charsoc impaled Alastor on his necromancer blade. Alastor stood choking on his own blue blood, retching.

Then with one sudden, brutal thrust, Charsoc sliced straight through Alastor's neck. Alastor's head landed on the floor with a thud. 'Errors are never tolerable,' Charsoc muttered. His blade slipped out from his hand and clattered onto the empty floor.

'Errors are *never* tolerable!' Like lightning, Lucifer swung around to Charsoc, his own sword raised directly above Charsoc's neck. 'Your magi have failed me, Charsoc!' Charsoc's entire body shook uncontrollably, sweat poured from his temple.

'This nova . . . this king . . .' Lucifer grasped Charsoc's long hair savagely in his fist and wrenched him so close that Charsoc could feel Lucifer's hot breath burning against his cheeks. 'This king is none other than *Christos*! His blood – is it undefiled?' Lucifer gave another cruel wrench on Charsoc's hair. 'You know, as I, the tenets of Eternal Law.'

Charsoc stared at Lucifer, horror-struck, his mind reeling. 'If his blood is undefiled, he will exchange his soul for the souls of men and wrest my kingdom from me!' Lucifer roared.

Lucifer stood, silent for a full minute, then flung Charsoc savagely from his grasp. He stumbled to the floor beside the unfortunate Alastor. Alastor's head vanished. Then his body followed, disappearing straight to the Abyss.

Lucifer flung his broadsword down, then strode to the window and threw open the curtains, raging blasphemies at the star still overhead in the Second Heaven. 'Yehovah's genius! He sent himself! Tricked by my own preconceptions, as he knew I would be!'

He pushed past Charsoc to where Darsoc stood, trembling.

'His Messiah will have no palace, no royal robes. His Messiah is born of dust and clay! Tell me, Darsoc, the destination of the infant king,' he hissed, his face only inches away from Darsoc's own.

'I followed . . . I followed your royal orders, sire,' Darsoc uttered in growing dread. 'My Black Murmurers followed the magi back through the desert towards Persia.'

'The infant is with the magi?' Lucifer circled him.

Darsoc held out an unsealed missive, his pale fingers shaking uncontrollably. Lucifer snatched the missive, then crumpled it in his hand, his face contorted with sheer hatred.

'The child has *vanished*!' he snarled.

Lucifer leaned heavily against the pillar, running his fingers through his raven locks, muttering to himself in an evil, peculiar angelic tongue as one demented.

'My brothers deceive me,' he muttered. He turned to Charsoc, still trembling on the floor. 'Investigate the circumstance of the infant's birth. Find out what Jether is up to. Do not dare fail me again, Charsoc!'

324

He wrapped his robe tightly around himself, then he turned to Marduk. 'Stir up the demonic hordes that torment that imbecile Herod day and night. Infect his dreams that he may have it in his heart to kill all males under two years old. The swaddling prince shall not escape my wrath. Summon Belzoc!' he cried. 'Great prince of Persia, Prince Michael is his! Prepare our war chariots! Amass all regents to make war against my brothers. Astaroth!' he screamed, 'Alert all powers, principalities and rulers of the darkness of this world . . . the great satanic princes . . . Nakan and his Necromancer Kings, the Thrones of Folcador, the Warlocks of Ishtar . . . Call them to assemble on the great plains of Perdition. And *find* my brother Michael. Where Michael is, *there* will be the child Christos, also!'

Lucifer hissed, 'Then we strike!'

CHAPTER FIFTY-ONE

The Seventh Stone

Jether sat on his jacinth throne in the seventh chamber, deep in the underground crypts of the labyrinths, poring over the great blue codex. Gabriel stood across from him, studying him intently . . . waiting.

'The codex unveils Yehovah's plan, his secret counsel prepared aeons before the advent of the race of men,' Jether said, closing his eyes in reverence.

'Yehovah prepares a place for the infant king in Egypt, in Alexandria. There is one king of Arabia; his name is Aretas. He has been chosen to bear his name. He will aid the infant in his flight.'

'Lucifer has not seen the codices?' Gabriel asked.

'Lucifer was long captivated by the codices of fire. They have lain in the labyrinths for aeons before his origin,' Jether said. 'His soul yearned to gaze upon their pages, but no, he has not looked upon their contents.'

'And what of Charsoc?' Gabriel questioned. 'He was privy to the sacred mysteries. Keeper of the sixth stone.'

'Charsoc . . .' Jether's expression grew hard. 'He well knows of their existence. The sixth chamber of knowledge was his abode but the chamber of the seventh flame was sealed from him.'

'So the sacred mystery of the Messiah is safe from their polluted sorceries.' Jether closed the book; its golden inclusions of pyrites shimmered like little stars out of the codex's deep blue lapis casing. He looked up at Gabriel.

'I go to retrieve the seventh stone.'

Gabriel stared at Jether, incredulous. 'Six stones resided here within the labyrinths,' he whispered. 'One went missing ... from the sixth chamber ... at Charsoc's defection.' Gabriel stared at Jether intently. 'No angelic being has ever laid eyes on the seventh stone.'

'The seventh stone, the stone of fire, possesses all the combined power of the six. It lies beyond the ordinances of heaven.' Jether's eyes grew dim with wonder. 'It lies beyond the treasuries of winds and hail, beyond the seven seas of wisdom. In the very cradle of the universe.'

Jether carefully picked up the codex and deposited it into a large crevice in the cavern wall into the great silver casket of the sacred writs. 'It will protect the infant while he walks as one of the race of men, until its seal is lifted when he will face the ultimate test ... against Lucifer himself.'

Jether placed his cloak around his shoulders and clasped it with shaking fingers. 'We have no time to waste. The child *must* be sealed with the seventh stone. At present he is vulnerable. Unprotected. You, Gabriel, make haste to Joseph. Instruct him of Yehovah's plan to take the infant to Egypt. Aretas is Yehovah's instrument to lead them to the monastery at Alexandria.'

'I will leave at once for the land of the race of men,' Gabriel said.

Jether nodded. 'I dispatch Vespar, my warrior eagle, with a message for Michael to leave the eastern horizons. He must journey at once to the caravan. He is the infant's only protection from Lucifer's evil scheming until I seal the child at Alexandria with the seventh stone of fire.' Jether removed a small ampulla filled with myrrh and cassia oils from his robes. Gabriel knelt before him.

'Time is against us.' Jether anointed Gabriel's temple, then laid his hands gently on his head in a blessing of consecration.

'Avoid the eastern corridors,' he whispered. 'The Black Murmurers traverse them incessantly. I prepare for my journey.'

Balthazar had paced the small square room all night in his supplications, pleading to the God of Daniel to help Aretas, his king and his friend. He bathed Aretas' fevered head with the rags that Mary had given him, soaked in myrrh from the caravan's store, in the hope it would bring him back to his right mind.

He paced the room for hours, praying, pleading. Yet the ancient Balthazar sensed that Aretas was being weighed in the hands of the Omniscient. He would wait.

It had been past midnight before Aretas' hands stopped trembling, and nearing dawn when Balthazar could first make out his first incoherent ramblings and Aretas opened his eyes again. And it was daylight before he rose from the pallet on the floor and took his first unsteady steps.

But when he finally took Balthazar's hand in his, his hand was steady, his eyes were clear, and his face exuded a peace that Balthazar had never before seen in the proud, headstrong young king.

Aretas tried to speak, but no words would come, only tears – tears that Aretas could not stop. Tears of a king's past bloodsheds; tears of a king's thousand murders; tears of a king's thousand debaucheries and treasons . . . and the tears of a man's thousand regrets. And so it was that he wept on the ancient astronomer's arm, so that Balthazar's robes were soaked from Aretas' weeping.

And then, suddenly, he grew calm.

'The babe is in great danger. We must protect Daniel's Messiah and the holy family.' He looked around him. Ayeshe, his ageing faithful steward, stood outside the door. 'Ayeshe, prepare my royal guard!' He stood up, his voice clear and strong. 'My royal ancestors were bequeathed a monastery in Alexandria by an ancient caste of magi of the Royal House of Egypt. It will be a safe house for the infant king. We ride to Egypt!'

High up on the eastern elevation of the Black Palace, the sharp steel of broadswords glinted as Lucifer and his chief of armies, Lord Astaroth, grand duke of hell, thrust and parried as they did each dawn, an integral part of Lucifer's rigorous physical regime about which he was fanatical almost to the point of narcissism. This dawn, however, he seemed strangely distracted. Astaroth's broadsword hit Lucifer's chest a ferocious blow, and Lucifer doubled over in agony. The strapping Astaroth laughed triumphantly and turned his back. Like lightning, Lucifer brought Astaroth gasping to the ground, his hands twisted beneath his torso in agony.

Lucifer raised his fencing mask, a smile of satisfaction on his face. 'That is why I am King of Hell' – he threw his broadsword down on the lava floor and took a cloth from Araquiel to dry his face – 'and you, Astaroth, are but a duke . . . albeit grand . . .'

The scarred but still handsome colossus shook his blond mane, still dazed. Lucifer looked fleetingly down at the fallen warrior. At times, Astaroth's bearing was eerily reminiscent of Michael. From the back, he could be Michael's double. In worlds long departed, Astaroth had been commander of Michael's finest legions, his most trusted general, Michael's closest compatriot. Lucifer's expression darkened at the thought of his brother. And now, Astaroth was Lucifer's champion, commander-in-chief of Perdition's armies. Did Astaroth have regret? Lucifer wiped his face with a silk cloth. He would never be sure.

'Prime your legions,' he growled. 'We ride tomorrow at dawn.' Astaroth bowed in reverence, striding to the far portico, then mounted his black winged stallion and rode the skies in the direction of his vast battalions' war chariots gathering on the vast plains of Perdition.

'Your Excellency.'

Lucifer turned. 'I still smart from your folly, Charsoc.' His mouth tightened.

'I redeem myself, Your Majesty. Our demonic scholars and sorcerer sages have examined the circumstances of the infant's birth. My archivists confirm their findings.'

Charsoc moved towards Lucifer.

'The infant was indeed born of a woman of the race of men. The birth was witnessed. The Black Murmurers have verified their findings. He was born one of the race of men, like any other in a town named Bethlehem. His mother is a Hebrew girl. A youth. The father – one named Joseph. The possibility, however, exists that a created egg could have been implanted by Yehovah in the host.'

'Christos incarnate.' Lucifer rubbed his chin, deep in thought. 'No possibility is to be excluded. What of the egg's conception?'

'As is the way of the race of men, the infant's conception is the result of two germ cells: the egg from the mother, the seed from the father. In the race of men, these share equally in the inherited mutations of the sin nature – all deriving from the Fall. The egg *still* has to be fertilized by seed from the father, Joseph, to enable its conception and replication.' Charsoc smiled triumphantly. 'It is the way of *all* of the race of men.'

'I am well versed in the biogenetic engineering of the race of men.' Lucifer paced back and forth. 'Every drop of blood the child produces is as a result of the introduction of the male sperm. The foetal and maternal blood do not come into actual contact, separated by the double layer of chorionic epithelium.'

He turned his face to Charsoc's, an unnatural gleam in his eyes. 'What if they have an *alternative* plan – a plan to deliberately bypass the male seed?' Lucifer's expression grew dark. 'And *prevent* the inherited mutations.'

'A substitute seed?' Charsoc frowned.

'A seed that is *not* of the race of men.' Lucifer stood staring out beyond Perdition's magenta horizons. 'One that is *incorruptible*.'

Charsoc turned to Lucifer, thunderstruck. Lucifer nodded.

'Yehovah,' Lucifer declared.

'Sire!' Charsoc gasped. 'It is strictly forbidden – prohibited by the tenets of Eternal Law issuing from Yehovah himself. You know first-hand – your generals who left their first estate by having intercourse with the daughters of men. Their punishment for their transgressing of the Eternal Law was to be to be cast in eternal chains into the lowest regions of the netherworld – Tartarus.'

'I am well aware. The pits of gloom until the Day of Judgement,' Lucifer murmured. 'So – if Yehovah fertilizes the created egg, he would be culpable of cohabiting with the race of men, just as the fallen host banished to Tartarus.'

Lucifer walked to the far side of the eastern wing housing Perdition's royal aviaries, pacing restlessly up and down before hundreds of colossal gilded cages that housed his sinister scavenger scouts.

'My brothers will have their schemes, their well-formulated conspiracies, but when it comes to the issue of Yehovah – he is bound to his own Eternal Law. He cannot transgress it,' he muttered, 'even to save the race of men.'

He unclasped an aviary door and gently clasped in his gloved hands a hissing vulture scavenger chick wearing a diamond collar. He caressed its black feathers soothingly, his sapphire eyes shadowed in thought.

'Against my deeper instinct, I find myself persuaded,' he spoke softly to himself. 'Yehovah will have no part in the conception of the Christos seed.' He spun around. 'No!' He strode over to a hell-cage filled with screeching pale blue-eyed writhing bat-like creatures and grasped one by its long slimy rat tail. 'There will be no incorruptible seed, Charsoc!' he declared. The scavenger chick screeched deafeningly, opening its cruel curved beak, its red fangs visible. Lucifer dangled the shrieking bat creature face down. The chick crushed its head with its ferocious fangs and swallowed it with one bite.

'Good boy, Cagrino.' Lucifer stroked the chick's head. 'The Christos-infant had to have received its genetic inheritance through the father's seed,' Lucifer murmured. 'He partook of the inherent sin damage present in Joseph's seed and blood, therefore the Christos infant's blood is defiled.' Lucifer frowned. 'Only one with undefiled blood, free from inherent sin damage, can exchange his soul for the souls of the race of men and release them from my rule.'

He placed Cagrino gently on a velvet cushion back into the gilded cage and clasped the door, deep in contemplation.

'Yet he comes to destroy my kingdom. I sense it.'

Lucifer walked over to the eastern terrace and stood surveying his armies. Hell's immense and terrible militia were assembling on the smouldering volcanic wastelands of hell. 'Why is he here on my planet?' he whispered. 'We must destroy him before he grows in strength.'

'There is a *way*, Excellency.' Charsoc held up a missive with the First Heaven's seal. 'The vulture shamans took a Revelator eagle "into custody".' Charsoc waited. 'It was Vespar.'

Lucifer's eyes narrowed. 'Vespar . . .', he echoed. He turned, immediately alert.

'He carried this missive from Jether the Just . . .' Charsoc hesitated, a sinister smile on his face. 'It was addressed to your brother, Prince Michael, sire.' Lucifer strode over to Charsoc and snatched the letter from his grasp, Charsoc watched intently as his liege lord examined the note.

'Jether meets Michael and the infant king near Alexandria, with the great seal – the seventh stone,' Lucifer murmured, a strange exhilaration in his gaze. He stared out towards the horizon, his back to Charsoc. *Remembering.*

'The seventh stone's power is indomitable. It holds in itself the combined powers of all six stones of the labyrinths. Once the infant is sealed with the stone of fire, we, the Fallen, are powerless against him. Our only opportunity is . . .'

Charsoc moved towards Lucifer, clasping his arm with his bony fingers. 'The breach in time, sire, before the infant reaches the monastery and Jether. His greatest vulnerability.'

Lucifer stared at him with an unnatural glint in his eye. 'He comes to destroy my kingdom. Instead I shall destroy him. You have surpassed yourself, Charsoc.' Lucifer held out his hand with the great damson ruby of Satan. Charsoc knelt before him and kissed his ring. 'You are pardoned.'

'Thank you, my lord . . . my king.' Charsoc bowed deeply.

'The disciples of hell assemble!' Lucifer cried. 'Instruct

Astaroth to marshal them for war without delay to the land the race of men call Egypt. We slay the infant king!'

The fierce, relentless desert winds blasted across the caravan. It was nearing dusk, and the party had been travelling through Egypt for what seemed an eternity. Dozens of camels, laden with frankincense, gold, and treasures of the East, headed the enormous caravan across the vast desert plains, their progress impeded by raging sandstorms. Ten elegantly caparisoned white Arab stallions paced in the caravan's centre. Mary clutched the swaddled baby tightly to her breast, her features almost hidden by her hood, her eyes resolute. A sudden chill blew over the caravan and the sky grew dark as an immense shuddering began. Mary covered the babe and held him tightly to her.

'Jether! Jether!' The pressing cry filtered from the colossal balconies of the Royal Amber Chamber that hung high above Jether's private monastic cloister quarters in the Tower of Winds, down to where Maheel and Issachar were assisting Jether in his varied preparations for his journey to the cradle of the universe.

Obadiah carried an empty silver amulet over to Jether, who threaded it deftly on a long silver chain.

'Jether! Jether!'

Looking up, Jether and Maheel watched Xacheriel making his precarious way down the wide polished-amber spiral steps of the Royal Chamber. He clung distractedly to his embroidered purple and golden taffeta toga as he descended, his curled satin slippers sliding dangerously on the steps.

Dimnah clung desperately to his arm, hindering rather than aiding his progress.

Xacheriel misstepped and they both tumbled in a precarious heap of purple and gold into Jether's private libraries, landing in an undignified sprawl on the gleaming amber floor.

'Drat and bumble!' Xacheriel mumbled, scrabbling for his monocle, now buried under mounds of newly bound annals. He glowered at the trembling Dimnah as though it were all the youngling's fault.

Jether shook his head. He placed the silver amulet around his neck and closed the clasp, then strode over to the languishing pair, followed closely by Maheel. He stared down at Xacheriel's enormous feet, which were crammed into a pair of tight cerulean satin slippers obviously several sizes too small. One of Xacheriel's rare leanings to vanity.

'You didn't, by any sheer chance,' Jether addressed Xacheriel, 'place any of your newly concocted time-travelling lubrication grease under your ceremonial slippers, did you?'

Xacheriel glared indignantly up at him. 'I was conducting a voltage experiment in the hologram chambers.' He scowled sheepishly. 'My – my latest time-travelling experiment – and I wandered over into the Red Zone by mistake,' he declared dramatically. 'A temporary *lapse* of my instruments. The grease aided my hasty departure.'

Maheel shook his gentle white head. 'You know we have cautioned you again and again not to travel on those co-ordinates.' He frowned in concern. 'It is dangerous, my dear Xacheriel. Hazardous at best. Charsoc's spies frequent that time lock, and they are most ruthless with their methods of torture.'

'Yes, yes.' Xacheriel gave a dismissive wave.

'The demon werewolves frequent the time corridors in the Red Zone,' Jether said darkly and deliberately. Xacheriel paled momentarily, much to Jether's relief. Dimnah's mouth dropped open, enthralled.

Jether decided to press the point while he had the advantage. 'As do the flesh-eating Necromancer Kings.' Jether glowered. Xacheriel's hands trembled visibly. 'One of the myriad advantages of not being constituted of matter.' He consoled himself, then yanked his enormous scarlet spotted handkerchief from his inner pocket and wiped the sweat that suddenly poured from his brow. Dimnah's mouth hung wide open in awe. Issachar strode up behind Jether.

'You needed me?' Jether asked Xacheriel. 'I leave to retrieve the stone of fire.'

Xacheriel frowned, then smacked his temple violently with his large hand. 'Yes . . . Yes . . . of course!' Xacheriel strode round in circles, ordering his thoughts.

'It is a *terrible* tale, revered Jether,' he declared ominously.

Issachar yawned loudly and deliberately. Jether glared at him from under his eyebrows.

'A *terrible tale*.' Xacheriel's big hands shook. 'One that affects your journeyings,' he whispered.

Jether frowned, placing his hand gently on Xacheriel's shoulder. 'Calm yourself, Xacheriel, old friend. Breathe deeply.'

Xacheriel inhaled, his great chest heaving. 'On my way back past the Red Zone, in the Second Heaven, I encountered the Revelator scouts, Gabriel's first rank of Eagles.'

Jether waited patiently, knowing he would eventually get to the point.

'They had in their custody one nasty-looking and -smelling customer. Vulture-like organism – mangy feathers.'

'A vulture shaman – one of Charsoc's scouts.'

Jether nodded.

Dimnah's mouth gaped so wide that Jether reached over and physically closed it with his hand.

'Dimnah!' Xacheriel barked.

'Anyway, the nasty-looking feathered life form had *this* – he called it his "trophy".' Xacheriel scrabbled in his voluminous pockets, eventually fishing out a great silver-and-diamond collar bearing the seal of the eagle Revelators. He passed it to Jether, dabbing gingerly at his eyes with his handkerchief.

'Vespar,' Jether uttered, stunned.

Xacheriel clasped Jether's old fingers awkwardly in his own.

'I am sorry to be the bearer of miserable news, old friend.'

Jether extricated his trembling fingers from Xacheriel's iron grasp, then swiftly turned over Vespar's collar. The scarlet insignia that signalled a missive was in flight was still in place. Jether stared past Xacheriel, his features frozen in horror. For he knew with a terrible certainty that if Michael had received the missive, he would promptly have replaced the scarlet insignia with a gold one from the royal house to signify his receipt of the communique. It was the simplest rule of the corridors, adhered to by one and all of the First Heaven's legions.

'The insignia is in place.' Jether's voice was barely audible. 'Vespar did not reach Michael with my missive. Consequently, Michael did not receive my instruction to leave the East and escort the child to Alexandria.'

Jether held on to the balustrade for support, his hands trembling. 'The infant travels as we speak. Unprotected.'

He turned to the elders, his face white as a sheet. They stared at him, appalled.

'Far worse. If Lucifer discovers the missive, he knows I meet the infant king near Alexandria with the seventh stone. He will be mobilizing hell's armies even as we speak.'

Jether hurried up the amber stairs, the elders following

close behind. 'Send Sachiel to Michael. He must leave for Egypt without delay.'

He turned to the elders on the stairway.

'We no longer have the element of surprise. Prime Raphael and our armies for assault. We leave at dusk.'

CHAPTER FIFTY-TWO

The Hordes of Hell

Hell's immense and terrible armies mobilized on the smouldering volcanic wastelands of hell. Folcador, hell's fearsome archduke and Lucifer's finest general, a ferocious demon with the face of an angel and the wings of a griffin, rode fierce and proud in his black war chariot, leading a hundred legions of the fallen. Astaroth, grand duke of hell, rode the skies, his war chariot pulled by the fierce white ice dragons of Siberia. His barbaric generals – Pruslas, Barbatos, and Rashaverak – marched below, the menacing Black Horde marching behind.

Forneus, the great and scheming marquis of hell, rode the skies on a monstrous, coiled leviathan, followed by twenty-nine legions of silver-tongued winged serpent demons.

The vast companies of Dark Grey Magi on their headless three-humped camels rode alongside the dread warlocks of Ishtar on the backs of werewolves and dragons. Overhead in hell's crimson, murky skies flew the demon Witches of Babylon on leviathans, and Hera and the Banshees of Valkyrie on their flying giant serpents. Marching to the rear was the great, macabre company of Necromancer Kings, leading their armies of living skeletons.

Astaroth, barbaric prince of Persia and Lucifer's commander-in-chief, led twenty thousand of hell's legions, riding their black war chariots pulled by hell's formidable dark-winged stallions.

Lucifer stood, menacing and proud, in his monstrous black war chariot, its silver wheels sprung with jagged war blades. The crimson flame on hell's infernal flag flew proudly.

The sinister Shaman Kings stepped forward; behind them marched the vast company of hooded Shaman Drummers.

'Armies of hell, I salute you!' Lucifer cried. The slow, menacing throb of war drums pulsed beneath his voice. 'Slaughter the usurper king before he is sealed!'

A terrible, bloodcurdling roar went up from the armies of hell as the rulers of the dark world thundered towards Egypt's skies.

One by one, fine hairline cracks started to appear on the great idols of Egypt in the Great Temple. The shuddering built to a crescendo with an overpowering roar as, one by one, the imposing golden images crashed to the ground. Temple priests ran for their lives as the idols continued to fall until not one remained standing.

Mary bowed her head and stared down at the sleeping babe. She shivered. Thousands of silent sinister-looking vultures had descended towards them this past hour, circling the caravan, casting strange dark shadows across the desert.

Aretas frowned. 'We must make haste,' he said. 'There is danger in the wind.'

He flicked the reins and galloped to the head of the caravan, strangely troubled.

Raphael, resplendent in his full ceremonial battle armour, rode past the front line of the armies of the First Heaven in his platinum war chariot, pulled by twenty winged stallions. He stood tall, imperial, the valiant general of Yehovah's armies on the Mount of the North in the First Heaven.

To the left marched Gabriel, attired in his ceremonial war regalia, followed by his vast company of the Revelators, his swift and agile archers, in their suits of gleaming silver armour. Their great bronze crossbows reached from the ground past their heads, at the ready.

Overhead flew a million of the Revelator 'scouts', occupying the length and breadth of the skies – the First Heaven's huge white-feathered warrior eagles, with their beaks and talons of gold, their wingspans over one hundred feet. The archangel princes led Michael's battalions. Juhdiel the Daring led a thousand legions. Uriel the Fearless rode ahead in his enormous silver chariot, leading four hundred legions of the First Heaven's finest swordsmen, followed by his multitude of warrior princes. Jether and his twenty-three royal compatriots, the angelic monarchs, were mounted on their royal white chargers, standing in a semicircle, their lances raised.

Gabriel drew the Sword of State from its jewelled sheath and raised it high above his head. 'We fight for Yehovah, that truth and justice may prevail!' he cried.

'We protect the infant king!'

The deafening roar from the First Heaven's armies resounded through the First Heaven. Jether rode over to where Raphael and Gabriel stood surveying heaven's armies. He clasped Raphael's arm.

'My spies inform me that Lucifer sends Belzoc, prince of Persia, ahead to slaughter Michael before he reaches the infant.' Jether lowered his eyes. 'Hell's depraved champion would settle an old score.'

'He defeated Belzoc once over the Hebrew Daniel,' Raphael declared. 'With Yehovah's strength, he shall defeat him again.'

Jether frowned. 'One clean thrust of the Sword of State, and Belzoc is banished to the Abyss to await the Judgement. Your aeons as Lucifer's commander-in-chief will serve you well against their malevolent strategies.'

Raphael spoke with a hard fierceness. 'Once Belzoc is slain, speed is Michael's advantage. Lucifer will be close behind. They are evenly matched.'

'You have your fastest warriors?'

Raphael nodded. 'My swiftest legions are my escort.' Raphael pulled down his golden visor. 'The Messiah's kingdom come!'

His twenty winged stallions and war chariot thundered into the lilac skies, followed by a hundred thousand of his legions' war chariots.

Jether stared after them, strangely troubled. He turned to Gabriel and placed his hand upon his shoulder. 'You are prepared for Nakan and his necromancer sorceries?'

Gabriel gestured to the amulet around his neck. 'Well prepared, revered Jether, our arrows dipped in the sacred ointment from the labyrinth's sixth spire.'

'The entire destiny of the race of men rests on the outcome.' Jether looked silently into Gabriel's eyes. They clasped hands, and Jether embraced him.

'Yehovah be with you, noble Gabriel. Press any advantage against Lucifer. Tell Michael to bring the child safely to me. I shall be waiting.'

Jether placed his hand on Gabriel's shoulder. 'I go beyond the treasuries of the hail, Gabriel,' he whispered, 'to the wake of the universes – to retrieve the seventh stone. I await you at Alexandria.'

'Your Majesty, Your Majesty!' Ayeshe galloped up alongside Aretas at the front of the caravan, his stallion whinnying in terror. Ayeshe tugged at his arm with his scrawny brown fingers. 'The noise, sire – it frightens the camels!'

Aretas nodded; the royal servants exchanged looks of trepidation. 'Stay in my place, Ayeshe.'

Aretas pulled on his stallion's reins and galloped to the back of the caravan. He turned his Arab steed around and scanned the vast expanse of desert. He could hear the great thundering of horses' hooves far behind him, but the desert was empty. Flat. A plateau stretching to infinity. And then the hair on the back of his neck crawled as he watched the desert sand a full league behind being kicked up, as if by the hooves and shadows of a great army on horseback, drawing down on the caravan.

The string of horses and camels started to move faster, and the Arab steeds whinnied with fear.

A second great thundering was now coming towards them from the opposite side of the desert. The white steeds of the caravan now panicked visibly as the camel riders struggled to keep their beasts under control. Joseph and Ayeshe, chilled with fear, watched the desert plains, as the two waves of invisible moving sand converged towards the caravan. Aretas galloped over to where Joseph rode with Mary and the babe.

'Some strange magic is afoot,' he cried. 'Surround the infant king!'

Immediately Aretas' royal guard surrounded Mary and the sleeping infant. 'Full speed – make haste!'

Aretas rode next to Mary, keeping a grim eye on the infant. Jesus slept peacefully.

Belzoc and his ferocious hordes closed fast, riding from the west, gaining ground on the now galloping caravan. But suddenly a small white throng appeared ahead of them on the eastern horizon, Michael and his lone company of warriors advancing towards the caravan from the east.

Michael stood tall in his flaming chariot pulled by twenty winged seraph stallions, racing along a full league above the stark desert plains, leading a hundred angelic warriors astride their white steeds.

Belzoc pulled the reins brutally, bringing his vicious black steeds up short on the desert plain, and turned hell's monstrous black chariot to meet the oncoming Michael head-on. They faced each other on the sweltering sand, less than a length apart.

'Belzoc, prince of Persia,' Michael cried, 'prepare to war!'

Belzoc stared in relish at the empty sands yawning leagues behind Michael, then turned to the hundreds of thousands of his black-armoured Persian angelic legions behind him.

'Michael, chief prince of Israel . . . Your armies are late!' Belzoc spat, giving Michael a menacing grin, then swung his six-foot black blade savagely in the air. 'Prepare to die!' Immediately his savage hordes let out a bloodthirsty roaring, stampeding towards Michael's angelic warriors. Thousands of the savage hordes of darkness rained blows on the ferociously fighting warriors of the First Heaven, broadsword against broadsword.

Michael's and Belzoc's chariots thundered across the sand towards the caravan, their flaming wheels grinding against each other as they raced neck and neck.

'Your swordsmanship has grown soft, Michael, since our last skirmish over the Hebrew Daniel!' Belzoc shouted derisively. He pushed his filthy braided hair away from his face. Caked with dirt, it hung down past his brawny thighs.

'You have never forgiven me for defeating you in front of your armies, Belzoc!' Michael cried. Sparks and rivets flew from the princes' chariot wheels, the stallions straining to breaking point as, all around them, the violent battle played out.

'This time you shall pay with your life, chief prince of the royal house of Yehovah. I shall exhibit your head on the gates of Hades.' Belzoc spat on the ground, wiping his mouth with a grimy arm.

'By the setting of eleven moons, you shall be banished to the penitentiary in Tartarus!' Michael yelled, never taking his eyes off his enemy. He followed Belzoc's gaze far in the distance, to Mary and the sleeping infant.

Michael stood still, all senses alert, his gaze fixed on Belzoc. Belzoc moved suddenly and, with his immense strength, jumped across from his chariot onto Michael's, ploughing his sword through the air at Michael's neck. Michael neatly evaded the stroke and slammed his sword down across Belzoc's chest, catching him off guard and knocking him, winded, to the floor of Michael's chariot. Enraged, the demon prince thrust savagely at Michael. Belzoc thrust. Michael thrust back. Belzoc rose to his feet, leering. The ring of steel on steel resounded across the desert, as the chariot veered furiously ahead.

'I shall feed Christos' tender flesh to the wild dogs that roam these mountains,' Belzoc smirked. He thrust his sword through Michael's thigh, then drew it out savagely as hundreds of small curved barbs tore Michael's flesh to shreds.

Michael fell to the chariot floor, collapsing to his knees in pain.

'My latest addition – rips to the very bone,' Belzoc leered lecherously. 'I shall tear Christos limb from limb.' Sweat

345

poured from Michael. Incensed, he attempted to stand but collapsed, overwhelmed by the excruciating pain.

Belzoc shoved him to the floor, towering over him triumphantly. 'This day – you go to the Abyss, Michael!'

He raised his broadsword over Michael's neck, then turned his head to follow Michael's gaze over to Raphael's war chariots thundering towards them, now visible on the horizon. In that instant, Michael grasped Belzoc's tangled black mane hanging at his thighs and wound it in his fist in an iron grasp, savagely wrenching Belzoc's head down onto the chariot floor with his great strength, then swung his sword across and through Belzoc's neck in one clean thrust, severing his head from his body. Thick black blood spurted up in twin fountains.

'Till the Great Judgement!' Michael kicked the body off his chariot onto the sand. Belzoc's head vanished. Then his body followed, disappearing straight to the Abyss.

'The Messiah's kingdom come,' Michael cried, saluting grimly at Raphael overhead.

Jether hovered at the cusp of the ordinances of the heavens and the treasuries of the hail, the scorching luminous white waves of the seventh sea of wisdom churning beneath him, at the very edge of the wake of the universes, his silver robes billowing in the tempests, his long white hair and beard flying in the rushing hail blizzards. His face was burning in ecstasy. His veined hand clasped a burning azure sapphire the size of a duck's egg. In its epicentre burned a fierce crimson flame – the seventh stone of fire.

Jether reached into the folds of his robes and produced a silver amulet. He opened the case, placed the stone of fire within, and closed the clasp, then placed it around his neck on a silver chain. And mounting his white-winged charger, he rode the colossal flashing thunderbolts of hail towards Alexandria.

Michael turned his monstrous chariot around to follow the disappearing caravan that held the infant king, then looked back to the west. Stampeding straight towards Michael on their headless winged chargers rode the legions of the sinister Necromancer Warlock Kings of the East, followed by their vast armies of living skeletons. These were the foulest, most depraved and feared of all Lucifer's armies, their sorceries vile and potent. This he well knew. And he was trapped in their pathway.

He glimpsed Gabriel out of the corner of his eye, racing towards him from the left through the skies, with a hundred legions of archers. The only way to destroy a Necromancer King's power was with a silvered arrow drenched in sacred ointment from the censer on the white altar of the labyrinth's sixth spire, sent straight through the heart. This Michael also knew.

'We shall eat you alive, Prince Michael!' cried Nakan, iniquitous Warlock King of the East, as his headless charger raced alongside Michael's thundering chariot. Michael felt a sharp pain and clutched his wrist. A tiny silver barb had penetrated the skin. He stared at it in dread: Necromancer poison. 'First, I shall peel the skin from your torso,' Nakan hissed, his foul oiled tones reverberating strangely in Michael's head as his demon magic began to take effect. Michael grasped for the poisoned barb, flailing at it clumsily. 'Then I shall sip your thick, glutinous blue blood from my goblet.'

Nakan held a golden goblet high in his left hand. Sweat

poured from Michael's temple down his cheeks, his eyelids grew heavy . . . far too heavy. Nakan smiled a slow evil smile. 'Once your eyelids close, Michael, my pretty,' he hissed, 'you have only five seconds before the Abyss.'

There was a sudden dull thud. Nakan stared down at his chest in disbelief; a second later, his head turned to green vapour before Michael's eyes. A thousand more arrows found their marks among the horrified Necromancer company.

Gabriel thundered through the skies towards the chariot, his gaze locked on the fast weakening Michael, now collapsed, his head flung down on the chariot floor. Gabriel's huge seraph wings billowed behind him as he rose through the skies and landed directly in Michael's chariot. He wrenched Michael's head from the chariot floor, just as Michael's eyelids closed heavily.

Gabriel grasped for the tiny steel barb in Michael's wrist and pulled it from his flesh, deliberately forcing Michael's eyelids open with his free hand. Instantly, the effects of Nakan's demon magic started to drain from Michael's limbs. Gabriel exhaled in relief, gently pushing the thick blond hair matted with sweat away from Michael's temple. The recovering Michael grinned sheepishly and saluted feebly from the chariot floor. 'Close shave!' he mouthed, then he stared frowning beyond Gabriel.

Gabriel turned to follow Michael's gaze. Rakkon, Jatir, and Obadiah, led by an exhilarated Xacheriel on his flying white charger, were launching hundreds of flying iron cannonballs towards Hera and the flying demon witches. Directly behind the younglings a pack of drooling demon werewolves headed straight for the dramatically gesticulating Xacheriel. Xacheriel, blissfully unaware of the impending danger, was lambasting Jatir on his erroneous coordinate calculations. Gabriel saluted to Michael, then thundered back into the skies towards the ancient elder. Michael staggered to his feet, clasping the stallion's reins. He glanced back to see the vast company of the Black Horde led by Dagon thundering on the horizon towards Raphael and Uriel's battalions. He swiftly loosed his lead charger from the chariot and jumped astride its back, then thundered across the desert after the disappearing caravan.

Then Michael's blood ran cold, for he sensed a terrible evil, a malevolent presence. He turned.

There, only three lengths behind, stampeding towards him astride his monstrous winged stallion, his broadsword lifted high, his six black seraph wings extended, raced the king of hell himself. Lucifer . . . escorted by the thirteen Warlock Kings of the West.

CHAPTER FIFTY-THREE

Alexandria

The caravan travelled across the sweltering desert plains, the ancient granite walls of the Monastery of Archangels becoming visible far in the distance on the horizon. The walls were thirty-five metres tall and three metres thick, carved from the huge mountain behind the monastery fortress.

Mary gazed up towards the formidable stone monastery, then looked questioningly across at Aretas, who smiled gently. 'The Monastery of Archangels,' he said. 'He will be safe there.'

Michael and Lucifer raced bareback on their stallions, thundering neck and neck across the desert. Overhead flew the thirteen Warlock Kings of the West, astride their monstrous dark-winged leviathans racing towards the Monastery of Archangels.

'I shall yet see you to the Abyss, Michael, my brother.' Lucifer drove his rapier savagely into Michael's wounded thigh tearing the wound freshly open. Michael clasped at his leg in agony, incensed, the blood spurting over his palm gushing down his thigh.

'But I have come for a greater prize than Michael. I come for the supreme trophy,' Lucifer spat. Michael grasped for his bayonet with his free hand.

'Your supreme trophy awaits you, brother.' Michael thrust the bayonet brutally straight towards Lucifer's right shoulder. 'In the Lake of Fire!' Michael cried. The bayonet found its mark, ripping Lucifer's flesh savagely. Lucifer erupted with an agonized roar. He glared at Michael venomously, then raised his javelin with his left hand. With one last desperate thrust, he savagely ripped Michael's leg from thigh to knee, sending him hurtling violently onto the desert sands.

A sadistic smile of triumph spread across Lucifer's face as he thundered past his maimed brother, catching up to the Warlock Kings. Michael pulled himself to his knees, blood pouring onto the sand, then staggered in agony to his feet and remounted his stallion. In the distance, he could see the caravan already drawing up outside the monastery gates.

The caravan drew up outside the formidable black iron gates of the Monastery of Archangels. At the crest of the gateway, a sign was engraved in gold Nabataean script. The towering gates slowly swung open revealing ten priests of the ancient caste of the Archangels, dressed in simple cassocks who stood at the entrance. The great caravan began its entry through the towering iron gates.

Jether turned to face the desert.

Lucifer and his stallion were thundering towards Jether over the desert sands. Above him, the thirteen dread Warlock Kings of the West raced through the skies, their long black capes billowing, their pale green parchment-like skin and hooked noses visible underneath their crimson hoods, as they rode their monstrous scaled dark-winged leviathans. Searing crimson flames erupted from the monsters' enormous jaws as their powerful black-webbed seraphim wings beat the air in a frenzy.

Jether strode over to Mary, her attention riveted on the babe nestled in her arms. He lifted the infant from Mary, never taking his eyes off Lucifer and the approaching Warlock Kings. Removing the silver amulet from under his robe, he unclasped it, revealing the seventh stone. Deliberately, he raised it high in the direction of the oncoming leviathans.

Fierce crimson lightnings forked from the stone towards the mammoth winged monsters, striking their flaming yellow eyes. The pack of leviathans screamed in unison, a blood-chilling, eerie, high-pitched screaming. Seething black smoke spewed from their nostrils, then one by one, the creatures plummeted like lead to the ground, hurling the Warlock Kings violently onto the desert sands.

'No-o-o-o!' Lucifer roared, lashing his stallion savagely with his razored cat-o'-nine-tails, drawing blood. The stallion extended its black wings, soaring into the skies over the great palms on the road to the monastery, directly towards Jether.

Jether removed the stone of fire from the amulet, his eyes, hard as iron, never leaving Lucifer. The blue stone glistened, the crimson flickering fire at its centre blazing fiercely through the sapphire.

'The seal!' Lucifer screamed, thrusting his barbed spurs deep into his stallion's flanks.

Jether made a strange mark of a cross on the baby's forehead with the blue stone of fire and, instantly, a blazing incandescent lightning radiated from the sapphire onto the infant's forehead. The fire of Yehovah's presence. Aretas and the monks fell prostrate.

Then monstrous, iridescent flames a league high leapt up, encircling the monastery walls, erupting in a ferocious firestorm that exploded through the desert skies, engulfing the armies of hell and flinging Lucifer from his airborne steed down onto the desert floor. Michael flew through the skies, watching in wonder from his stallion, his savage wounds healing swiftly in the consuming fire.

Lucifer lay, gasping and winded, trembling in terror, shielding his eyes from the torrid conflagration of light, his skin blistering in the unrelenting, scorching inferno. The Warlock Kings' frenzied screaming mingled with the demented cries of Lucifer's ravaged fallen armies, echoing through the Egyptian skies.

With a mighty shudder, the gates closed.

Michael wrote at an old wooden desk in the monastery chamber. He was clothed in a simple white robe; his golden armour hung next to the cloister window. To his right lay an open missive bearing the black seal of Perdition. On it Michael wrote, 'Yes, he is safe. Fled to Egypt, hidden safely in her bosom. Growing in stature and favour, both with Yehovah and with man.'

He stared out through the window onto the roof of the monastery, where the boy played under Mary's watchful eye. Michael dipped the pen in the inkwell.

'He wears the seal. You cannot touch him, Lucifer – not until Christos places himself into your hands.'

From the portico of the Black Palace, Lucifer gazed out at the Earth far in the distance. He crumpled Michael's missive in his fist.

'No matter, Michael,' he breathed, his eyes gleaming with venom. 'I will wait.'

And so Christos became one of the race of men.

Sealed by the seventh stone, protected from Lucifer's unbridled wrath and Herod's murderous schemings, he spent his days and nights sheltered under Egyptian skies in the Monastery of Archangels in Alexandria. And Michael and I and Jether, chief of the twenty-four heavenly elders, ministered to him.

The Great King of Heaven.

The story continues in The First Judgement, now also available where good books are sold.

354